THE COOKING CLASS IN
San Sebastián

KAREN TRIPSON

The Grady Press

Seattle, Washington

Chapter 1

Laurence was unable to focus on anything because he was sharing the stage tonight with Eva Russo, a mind reader whose smile made him weak-kneed. It was embarrassing. He hoped she wouldn't be able to tell by looking in his eyes how his heart and knees were betraying him.

The food contest tonight at the art gallery should be easy and provide several opportunities for a moment alone with her to invite her to dinner. The format of the contest was simple. Ten local chefs make dishes showcasing Russo Imports, the sponsor's products from Italy. As the food judge he tastes each entry and makes some comments for himself and at the end of the evening he announces the top three dishes. The wine judge does the same with the wine paired with each dish. Prizes and applause are given to the top chefs. He gets a paycheck. Goodnight. Except tonight, he wanted everyone to be a winner with no ill will in the room. Maybe he would call his employer Drew, while his clothes were washing and suggest the awards be expanded to include everyone with maybe one grand prize. The award-creating software program in Drew's office could spit out remarkably official looking certificates that said anything you wanted them to say. It would only take a little extra time to make something for each chef to hang on the wall of recognition in his restaurant that would last forever and create good will for the event in everyone's memory. He wanted the evening to be as perfect as it could be.

In the last six months he had seen her four times, twice at the food events she had attended at Drew's gallery to decide if she wanted to hold her event there. Laurence had helped Drew show her around and talk about what they offered sponsors of fundraisers. When she decided to hire the gallery he had attended two meetings about her event. He'd thought she was special the first time he saw her across the gallery space talking with his colleagues. Her posture was regal with her head crowned by white hair that swept back away from her face in short soft waves. She wasn't very tall but her hair made her seem taller than she was. She wore a bright colored dress that showed her body had nice curves, not plump but not too thin. She was the center of attention and appeared to be completely comfortable with the admiration of the group. He'd approached her as if it was a normal activity for him to be social and looking for an introduction to the prettiest woman in the room. She watched him approach and he thought that she knew from long experience exactly what would happen. Good-looking women knew the effect they had on men of any age. His handshake lingered on after the introduction. They smiled at each other and listened to whatever conversation continued after his interruption.

Her eyes were dark brown in a perfectly balanced face with high cheekbones that was not too long or too short and with a thin nose that was the perfect length. Anyone who looked at her would notice how attractive she was but he knew it was the symmetry of her features that was so pleasing.

Standing next to her he felt like he had been anointed some new status and reveled in the feeling of being part of her circle. She had accepted him serenely, nodding, appropriately impressed after Drew had announced his name and role on the event team, giving and getting a sly grin from everyone on the often used phrase, "Laurence is the Walter Cronkite of food judges, if he says it, then it is true." You had to be a certain age to get the Cronkite reference and she got it. That had been a heady moment only because she was there and believed Drew. Laurence had been the beneficiary of this introduction before and usually smiled modestly and thanked Drew for high praise, probably undeserved. That day he only shook his head as though it was a bit too much, but probably deserved.

That had been the wonderful beginning of knowing her and he had savored the memory many times of their conversation about making pasta in Italy with artisanal ingredients. They shared a reverence for hand-milled flours. She knew a lot about flours. She sold a huge variety of extruded and sheeted pastas made from different flours that for centuries had been attached to a specific sauce. Apparently Italians from every region had their own idea of what went with what and they weren't changing now. Laurence so seldom ran into anyone that was knowledgeable or passionate on the topic. They had both been excited to find a kindred spirit. Drew had even kidded him about her afterward asking what it was they were talking about that seemed so exciting, a book, a play, a movie? Drew laughed out loud upon leaning the subject was flour. The second time she visited the gallery she greeted him like an old friend she was happy to see and tried to engage him in a conversation about olive oils. Unfortunately, he did not have a deep knowledge of any aspect of the process of creating top quality oil. He gave her examples of his favorite uses for oil in cakes and breads and how the result differed with poor quality oils and butter. Her face didn't light up as much as it had during the flour conversation. He promised her he would do some research to learn more about the process. She had smiled at him and seemed pleased he would do that to be able to talk with her about it. Making her smile became a goal.

Eva Russo was the star of the show tonight. The charity beneficiary seemed irrelevant in comparison. They had no say in any of the preparations but the director of the charity would give a speech of thanks for the money raised on

3

his behalf. As the president of Russo Imports, Eva would give a speech and pass out the awards. At the meeting a week ago there had been no conversation about him standing next to her during the award presentations, although he usually stood at the side of the sponsor. He and she had discussed some changes to the scorecard to better suit her products. He nodded and seemed to be carefully following the discussion, but he wasn't. He was contemplating her earlobes, another small perfect feature that contributed to the whole ensemble.

Whatever she wanted was fine with him. Julia would take care of the changes. Eva and Drew talked about mailing lists, marketing and promotion. Julia, acting as the events team digital marketing manager, one of the many hats she wore at the gallery, took notes and asked questions about following up with social media data and online ad metrics.

Laurence sat and enjoyed being in Eva's presence. She brought a special feeling to the room. She elevated the conversation to bigger words and fewer acronyms. She always asked him a question about something, which verified to him that he was an important participant. At the end of the meeting when the conversation had turned to real estate and restaurants, Eva had asked him where he lived. That was personal! When he said lower Queen Anne, she said, "I live on Queen Anne too, on West Highland. I'm going there now, would you like a ride home?" She had remembered that he didn't drive anymore and rode the bus. He could drive, he had a license but he had given up his car when he moved to Queen Anne six years ago to begin his new life in a small apartment as a widower.

No one he was working with tonight had any idea that last week after the meeting, not only had she given him a ride in her Audi to her apartment just a few blocks from his apartment, he had been her guest sitting on a balcony overlooking the city of Seattle from Kerry Park, drinking a glass of Barolo, possibly the finest red wine he'd ever tasted. His knowledge of Italian wines was not deep and he was learning that hers was extensive from all her travels there. They had laughed and talked about eating and drinking wine like old companions. He felt a strange energy inside himself bubbling around and making him speak effortlessly. It was probably the wine making him loquacious. He could hardly recognize himself in the body on the balcony. She had also told him a little about her husband Antonio's death five years earlier after a long bout with dementia and he had then shared a brief version of Ingrid's slow death six years ago. They sat quietly for a few minutes in a silent confirmation that they were both alone and had been so for a while. They had both experienced a similar ordeal.

He suddenly decided he should be a gentleman and leave before it became awkward and said, "Thank you for the ride, a delightful visit and the fine wine. I thoroughly enjoyed myself but must be getting home."

They stood up together and walked to the front door of the apartment. He took her right hand and kissed it in the old fashioned way that said silently, *you are special.* With him still holding her hand she looked up at him, right into his eyes as though she had just thought of it and said, "Would you like to stay?"

Oh, her frankness and her dark eyes looking directly into his mind took his breath away and made him feel faint. He put his arms around her and held her close to him, more to steady himself from the shock of the invitation than to reciprocate affection. It had not occurred to him even once since he'd met her that she might want to get into bed with him. She excited him, no question, but he had talked to so few women since Ingrid died it was a novelty to be interacting socially like this. He didn't think people his age had sex like younger people do. He felt sure he was past being able to do that even if an attractive, vivacious woman asked him like she just had. Her head fit nicely under his chin. The thought of lying side by side was very appealing, the comfort of another body in the dark with him. She must have felt him considering the invitation and a muscle in his neck tensed up, which made her pull back and look up at him smiling and said, "I'll give you a rain check."

He nodded maintaining eye contact while struggling for a response. "That's very kind of you. I look forward to seeing you again soon." He meant that he was grateful not to have to say it or explain why he couldn't possibly stay and she had understood it. Did she really know that? She opened the door and stood back to let him pass through. To thank her for her invitation he gave her a brief farewell kiss on the lips and said, "You are such a smart woman. I must be careful around you to think concisely since you don't miss a thing." She smiled at him receiving the compliment and closed the door.

Laurence had relived that farewell several hundred times since that night. He anticipated, hoped, planned and plotted his possible interactions with her tonight, before and after the awards ceremony. He wanted to make it clear that he was happy to see her and planned to spend more time with her. Maybe she would become a friend. Maybe there would be romance. Maybe his sex life wasn't over. It was unbelievable that all this was happening to him when he was so old, although he wasn't feeling old right now.

Tonight he would ask her to go out to dinner with him and if she said yes, he could think more about the astonishing concept of having sex with her. She had approached him. That was a powerful point on the plus side. He had many positive memories of sex with Ingrid as teenagers, as married people and as middle-aged people. Sex had been a dependable strength in his marriage, a comfort to each other as a couple. Sex was the free thing Mother Nature provided for pleasure and solace. They had enjoyed each others bodies right up until she started cancer treatments.

After that he could only offer the warmth of his body next to hers to remind her she wasn't alone.

Technically he was an expert on the subject of sex with more than 60 years of experience. That history was on the plus side too. On the negative side loomed the fact he hadn't done it in years, maybe ten years, but on the plus side it didn't mean he'd forgotten how. He understood the physics, knew a substantial amount about how to begin, and knew variations on process to choose from for the middle part. With collaboration and a bit of luck everyone should finish agreeably. He was interested. That was key on the plus side. Eva made him feel like it was a good idea to attempt an old fashioned seduction with dinner, compliments, poetry and then get the clothes off. Once the clothes were off, it got much easier. The thought of being naked with her made him feel energetic.

To get this day back on schedule he needed to immediately start on the laundry he had planned to do earlier before this daydreaming slowed him down. He wanted the scent of the damp cotton fabric transforming under the hot iron to envelope him and then smell and feel the freshly pressed shirt on his skin. It was as pleasurable to him as the smell of yeast proofing before kneading the dough created a new smell. That was the pleasant sequence that preceded one of the finest aromas, bread baking in an oven. Thanks to his nose ironing and making bread were always a pleasure.

While he was ironing he thought again about how thin the facade of these fundraising events seemed. He couldn't believe people spent big money eating and drinking in the name of a cause. The rosy glow of charitable consuming eluded him completely. If a person cared about a cause and had the money to give, they should send it directly to the charity. Skipping all the expenses of putting on a big event would put a lot more money in their coffers. He would, however, keep his opinions to himself and enjoy cashing his check. It also seemed silly to pay him to do what he did — tasting food — but he was glad it wasn't free. The money he was paid by Drew made it business, not personal, pleasure or charity. He liked the money. It made a difference to his lifestyle, a little freedom after several years of living solely on social security. It was also very flattering to be 76 years old with a job, even a part time job, which came with respect for his cooking abilities that he had never dreamed in his life could be a moneymaker. He had been an aerospace engineer for 40 years who cooked dinner most nights and enjoyed baking bread and making pasta on the weekend. He had baked Scandinavian pastries for charity every year since he was a teenager, learning as his mother's helper and keeping up the good work later at Ingrid's insistence. He didn't love making those pastries. It was a skill he had, something not everyone could do and should be put to good use according to his mother and Ingrid. His mother got full credit for inspiring him as a child in engineering by showing him the steps to making delicate pastries. Cooking was a hobby for him, like woodworking. The tasks were as pleasurable as engineering tasks were with logical steps and procedures. Baking had been his springboard into cooking all sorts of things and reading the classic cookbooks. Cooking encompassed a vast body of knowledge that he could never exhaust no matter how long he lived. It was worthy of pursuing like science and engineering.

Tonight he was going to combine his confidence in baking and engineering to launch a successful invitation to dinner to Eva Russo, which would make her smile and say yes. She might even offer him a ride home.

Chapter 2

It was early afternoon when Drew unlocked the door to his art gallery. The space gave him a thrill every time he opened the door. It was his. He had made it and it was brilliant in concept and execution. As an exhibition space it offered the drama of size and high ceilings. Lots of wall space with no windows was perfect for hanging art. The end of the bigger room acted as a stage for performance art and made the space feel intimate with 50 chairs. He was proud of filling those chairs for unique artists, eager to perform but not yet able to draw a bigger crowd. A few of them never would as their message was directed to such a discriminating audience. Hosting experimental performance art was a natural expansion of his talent for discovering new artists. Renting the space for fundraisers or private parties wasn't that interesting, but it paid well so he spent time cultivating this third leg of his revenue. So far the business model was working well.

The Great Recession had inspired him to innovate. Most of his peers around town were envious of his daring and his success and that he'd saved his money from previous success to afford the expansion. There were a few who loathed him for his business acumen, making disparaging remarks about his art selection deteriorating as his space expanded. He knew they were jealous — and wrong.

He paid no attention to Julia's desk by the door, which was always cleared at the end of the day. He proceeded through the smaller room to the behind the scenes area hidden from the public and entered by a door in the paneling that was not noticeable. He turned on the lights in the small kitchen area and in his spacious office with a leather couch, a round meeting table with five chairs, his desk and a credenza that hid office supplies inside and displayed his collection of art books on top. Art covered the walls. It was mostly his art, favorite paintings from his student days and early in his career when he still painted and thought of himself as an artist. Advertising his early ambitions made a good impression on other artists and patrons. Artists knew he would be sympathetic, as he too had struggled before accepting his talent wasn't strong enough. Patrons felt confidence in his ability to spot quality art from his experience in trying to create it. Both artists and patrons admired him for his honesty about how he'd come to be a gallery owner. He hoped that feeling translated to them that he was just as honest about everything else. That of course was difficult sometimes. Many situations required enlightened exaggeration and innuendo to set up the right atmosphere for the buy or sell. A good salesman knew how to put the art and the customer in the most flattering light. His duty was to the art, to find it, to place it, to preserve it.

His office welcomed him silently and he responded in kind, hung up his suit jacket and made a pot of coffee. Julia would be here soon and they would talk about the day. He loved the quietness of the opening of his shrine to art and commerce. The stress of making money was always in the background but the opening sequence was like the second meditation of the day clearing his mind for the work ahead. Later it would be a busy place with crowds of people and the noise of business.

His desk was clean except for the computer, which he turned on and got out a pad of paper from the top drawer to begin his list for the day with his favorite pen. He played the telephone messages and made notes about calls to return and details to follow up on.

He heard Julia's key in the door and her high heels coming across the gallery floor. Julia was his precious, only fulltime employee, assistant manager of the gallery and art student who brought him joy everyday. Her physical beauty and energy pleased him. She was a delight to watch in motion. He called her his business partner, which she wasn't as she had no money invested in the gallery, but they discussed most everything about the business. He trusted her. He kept little from her. She worked hard at the gallery and did a good job with all he asked her to do, plus contributed youthful items he didn't want to learn to do such as handling social media. She had taken over managing the gallery web site and distributing the monthly email newsletter he wrote. The software and tools for all those things were much better than they had been when he'd realized the gallery must have a web site. She designed the advertising for gallery exhibits for online and print media. He encouraged her about her painting, which was improving with his help. No question, she was talented, she just needed more time to paint and mature. When she became famous, so would he for discovering her. When the art discussion became ardent there was also occasional sex with her on this couch or at her apartment where she painted on Sundays and Mondays when the gallery was closed. Intimacy inspired by being such kindred spirits in art seemed appropriate. He paid little attention to her boyfriends that came around the gallery to pick her up after work. She was the same way with his women visitors and sporadic live-in girlfriends. They made an excellent team dedicated to art. There was no better business to be in as far as they were concerned. It was important. People need art and the gallery was the essential link between the artists and the people. They felt lucky to be chosen by art to provide the services it required and slightly superior to many other occupations, maybe more than slightly.

She put a bran muffin and a banana down on his desk.

"Oh, Julia, I appreciate you worrying more about my health than I do, but I hate eating in the morning. This is not new."

She said, "I know. You're not up on the current science of nutrition. It's essential for your body's performance to eat a variety of things to give you energy all day long." She smiled at him and said, "Who knows if we'll have a chance to eat tonight at the event."

She poured coffee for herself and sat down on the couch with her own pad and pen. She said, "What's on your list?"

"The Russo event tonight is in good shape. Charles will be here to manage the set up process for the restaurants. William and Laurence will be in later and can help out if needed. I plan to spend time tonight with Eva's son, Antonio, whom we haven't met yet. I want to make sure he has future events here. I think annually would be good for his public relations, don't you?"

She nodded in agreement. "We can also mention in our thank you to the director of the charity, that we want to discuss at his convenience the possibility of more events with different sponsors."

"Yes, let's do that tomorrow. Of course, I will say something to him tonight as well after the awards. I had a message from Laurence when I got in that he wants a certificate of excellence printed out for each of the contestants tonight to take home in addition to a few for the most outstanding dishes. He wants everyone to get a prize tonight for goodwill in the event. That seems fine to me. You don't mind doing it do you?"

Julia said, "Not at all. It's such a sweet, small event that it's nice for everyone to get something. It won't take long to print them. Shall I frame them?"

"I think an envelope will be OK for the certificates. They may want to frame them to match what they already have hanging in the restaurant. They may want to spend more on the frame than I do." He smiled at her. "I'll call Eva and tell her about the certificates. I'm thinking of taking her out for dinner as a token of our appreciation for having the event here. Do you have a better idea?"

Julia said, "No. Mrs. Russo seems like someone who already has everything. I can't imagine what gift we would buy her."

"I will ask her tonight then," Drew said. "Now for the bad news. Justin has cancelled on us for the January-February slot. I was on the phone for hours with him last night. I couldn't talk him out of it. He's having some sort of crisis of confidence. He's thinking of throwing out all he has and starting over on a new tact."

She grimaced and said, "Oh, that's awful news. Do you have any ideas about replacing him?"

Drew shook his head and looked concerned. "I will make phone calls this afternoon to find out who has been prolific recently, but I'm not optimistic. We have been relying on the gallery artists under contract for so long we will look like a garage sale if we bring everybody out to hang again. I can't bear it. Justin was going to be the fresh, exciting air we need for more crowds and new customers. I think we have to come up with something unique and fast or else plan on a two month vacation."

"Yikes! I couldn't go anywhere for two months."

Drew said, "You mean go without a paycheck?"

Julia said, "Exactly."

Drew said, "I feel the same way. Let's be alert to new ideas tonight and plan to brainstorm tomorrow while the cleaners are here. We need something revolutionary to create some buzz about our business. I think we're stale and on the verge of being yesterday's news. I'm worried."

After Julia left the office Drew tapped his pen on the pad of paper. He'd tried being sympathetic, supportive and then hard hearted and all business with Justin. Dealing with the artists was part of his job he was good at. He loved them, encouraged them and when necessary he could usually cajole them to do what he wanted them to do. He failed last night. His strategy now was to let Justin stew alone for a day or two and then try again with the leverage of last chance to change his mind before Drew signed up two other local artists to share the exhibit. Justin wouldn't know that neither one had enough art ready to make a two month show.

He'd studied his list of artists under contract and artists who had shown with him without a contract. Nobody on the lists had enough art to fill the gallery space. He had sorted the lists backward and forward looking for a pattern he could follow to a group show but couldn't see one that would create some excitement. He'd have to find more artists and create a different type of show. A dynamic theme was what he needed. Tonight's audience would be a well-heeled group. He would talk to as many people as possible looking for trends. Surely he would hear something tonight that would spark an idea. Three and half months was a tight schedule to create and stage a special exhibit, but two months of being closed would be harsh on his savings account which was somewhat healthy now.

The Great Recession hurt everyone in Seattle but his strategy in moving into this space so he could host special events and performance art was keeping him afloat when selling art was difficult. Calling a few theater directors and agents might be the fastest way to fill a few dates on the calendar. That's what he would do today. He wrote down three names to call and then added a fourth item, a restaurant for Eva. The dinner with her would be a special treat for him, probably as much as it would be for her. Eva Russo was a pleasure to deal with in every way. She was smart about making money. He admired how she handled herself. She was a class act with intelligence and beauty. He thought of her as a mentor. If she were younger he might pursue her. She had to be 60 years old, way too old for him at 55. He hoped her event tonight would be imitated by the paying guests, the restaurateurs, and the charity itself that must have a list on file of candidates to sponsor events. Eva kept the scale of the event small and quality oriented with 10 good restaurants and 50 premium-paying guests. He should choose one of those restaurants participating tonight for his dinner with Eva! It would be even better business to make a reservation with one of the winners tomorrow.

The gallery space was brightly lit and bustling with activity when Drew saw Laurence arrive and immediately take a bus pan full of tent cards and sample packages out of Julia's hands to help her out. The tasting tables for each restaurant already had red linens, chafing dishes and kitchen crews finishing the setup. Thank God for Laurence. He always seemed like a bulwark for the gallery. Laurence could and would do anything that needed doing. He was so competent. Julia with her long blonde hair swinging side to side headed back to the office for more. Laurence began placing the cards with the name of the product and the samples next to the restaurant menu displayed in a Lucite stand on each table. He also knew what to do without being told, the hallmark of a good employee. When Laurence approached the table near Drew, he asked Drew's opinion about the new certificates.

"Excellent idea," Drew said, "I called Eva to let her know and she thought it was a great idea too. I gave you credit of course."

Laurence said, "Thank you." And thought, *Plus, plus for my date campaign tonight.* They both watched Julia return quickly moving through the space, her petite young body well defined in a one-piece clinging outfit of many colors. She was demurely covered from wrist to ankle but this provocative fashion item left nothing to the imagination. It was a form of modern art impossible before the creation of Spandex. High-heeled black boots didn't slow her down at all. She embodied youth, style and enthusiasm. Laurence and Drew exchanged a look and both thought, *Oh, to be 25 and have the world going your way.*

Laurence said, "She reminds me of you, Drew, always smartly dressed and never looking stressed."

"Thanks, I turned a few heads, but I never looked that good." He shook his head and walked away.

Laurence chuckled at him. Drew was being funny. Drew looked like art too, handsome and stylish in every element of his slimness, short white haircut and partial beard and expertly fitted black suit. His hair stylist and tailor were dear old friends and artists in their own right. Laurence had felt like an anachronism when he first started working in the gallery as a food judge a year ago but soon realized he was a prop as much as they were. Each member of the team looked the part they were playing. Drew was the arbiter of good art. Julia was the youthful excitement of the art world. Her costumes became art in motion. It was hard to take his eyes off her when she moved and he noticed he was not alone in this.

Laurence knew his role was *gravitas*. He provided credibility. From the double starch in his shirt to the old school tie and navy blazer, he looked unimpeachable. He would never tell anyone that Drew bought this outfit for him at Nordstrom to be his uniform at all gallery occasions. Laurence thought of it as his parliamentary robe. Luckily he had his own full head of white hair and a short beard, both professionally trimmed, and needed no wig to complete the costume. He supposed that being over six feet tall and thin with good posture and a little residual swagger from being a proud Boeing engineer made him somewhat as attractive as Charles and William were.

His palate and knowing how to make pasta got him in the gallery door. He'd done well as a judge at the first pasta contest Drew hired him for and at another contest the next month. Between the First Thursday Art Walk events, performance art events and sponsored fundraising events, there seemed to be something he could do to help out at least once a month and sometimes more. If a food judge wasn't needed, he'd acted as a host/ticket taker at the door and several times had prepared hors d'oeuvres to cater small private viewing parties for friends of the artists.

When he completed distributing the samples he went back to the office where Charles, the event team food and beverage manager, was in conversation with William, the wine judge. Laurence liked Charles and William. They had deep knowledge about wine, which he did not. He enjoyed working with them. They always had a few laughs and he always learned something new. Charles was young and good-looking with dark hair and restaurant management experience. He aimed for a top job in the wine industry by attending a sommelier program and working as a wine salesman for his day job. He knew how to get the room set up to look good and move the crowd efficiently. He took charge of the support staff from the restaurants as though they worked for him. Charles was the person to ask for a decision. Drew wasn't interested in dealing with anything about food and beverage. Charles was engaged with William about how he would work with so many duplicate wines on the tables tonight. He felt it was his fault he hadn't managed the restaurants' selections.

William shrugged. "It makes my job easier. Don't worry about it. We will turn it into a positive, a new prize for the most versatile wine. All the restaurateurs want a recommendation for a house wine so food friendly that it goes with everything—only you hotshots want it all specific." He was ribbing Charles who felt strongly at this point in his life about specific wine recommendations. "The distributor of the wine that wins that prize tonight will have a new marketing message in the morning."

"Hey, Laurence, let's conspire about how we're going to stroll tonight." William was giving him a wily smile. He was a few years younger than Laurence but he had been in business a long time as a wine salesman, wine distributor and now retired as a wine drinker and wine judge for hire. He worked as often as he wanted to. He was the wine expert, knowledge and charm in a bow tie. He was shorter and rounder than Laurence and had less hair but a pleasant face that wore a smile more often than not. Although tonight he had on a black suit, the official art gallery uniform, Laurence thought he looked like a college professor with wire rimmed glasses who would wear seersucker suits in summer with a yellow bow tie.

"William, I want you to give me a short course in Italian wine. I have never had the time to study it and I want you to tell me where to begin," Laurence said.

"Who are you trying to impress?" said William.

"Me? I have a life of the mind only. I just like to know things. I drank some Barolo recently and thought to myself, why have I been deprived of this all my life?"

William said, "The short answer is money. Chianti is reasonably priced, Barolo is not."

"Ah, of course, that wretched locked gate to the good things. I'm sure you know tricks that would let me enter the Italian gate at an affordable price," Laurence said.

"Come with me," said William. They began to walk around reviewing the tables in order and noting who would be ready first so they could get a head start tasting before the crowd began. Laurence tried to listen to William's description of the wine on each table and make a few notes for himself. He was happy for the duplicate wines as it made fewer bottles for him to learn tonight as part of his new education program. Italian food didn't have to be paired with Italian wine, but the trend tonight was half Italian wine made in Italy and half Italian grapes grown in Washington for the state's interpretation of Italian wine. Sangiovese, the grape of Chianti, was making a strong showing.

William said, "Watch for Nebbiolo, the noble grape of Barolo. Very little is grown here but we might see it. That's why people have wine cellars. They want to keep the Barolo safe for generations. You should look for Barbera and Dolcetto, also made from Nebbiolo, because those regions make drinkable young wines that may be reasonably priced since they don't need much aging."

While listening to him, Laurence kept an eye on the door watching for Eva. He finally saw her walk in wearing a sky blue silk dress that shimmered in the spotlights. She was majestic. He flinched and his knees responded to her presence by trembling. Drew materialized out of nowhere to welcome her and the man she was with. Drew must have been watching the door like Laurence had been. Who was the man? Laurence hoped William hadn't noticed him flinch. He watched Eva scan the room. Was she looking for him? He hoped so. He kept still but looked directly at her and soon she saw him. He smiled and nodded a greeting to her. She returned it and then began paying attention to Drew and the man. Oh well, it was too much to hope for that she would be alone. It was much more logical that she would have an entourage from her company. He hadn't thought that far ahead. Dumb, dumb, dumb. Who was the man? Middle-aged by his receding dark hairline with gray temples and olive skin, not handsome but polished, well dressed, probably European, or hello, Italian. Maybe he was a vendor of hers. That would make sense. Drew was leading them toward Laurence and William.

Laurence looked down at his clipboard and gave William a low toned, "Heads up, here comes the boss."

William put down the wine bottle he was looking at and turned around to greet them.

"You gentlemen know Eva. Let me introduce you to her son, the new president of Russo Imports, Antonio Russo. This is William, our wine judge and Laurence, our food judge."

The handshake was quick and cold as was the glance into the eyes, rather than meaningful eye contact as is considered polite. Antonio Russo was poker faced and soon looking around the room ignoring the conversation of the group he was in. He reminded Laurence of the quality control officers at Boeing always looking for something to criticize. Eva was quick to grab William's hand and then Laurence's with a warm squeeze and a smile at both of them. He squeezed back. Laurence felt warm all over his body from the touch of her hand. She was glad to see him, although she had said *them*, and knew the evening was going to be a great success for everybody. Drew agreed with her and asked if she and Antonio had any questions, or how about a glass of wine?

"Nothing for me, thank you. I'd like to review the product placement." Antonio said and looked at Drew.

"I'd love a glass of wine," Eva said, "I don't need to see the placement."

Drew took Antonio's elbow and said, "Come with me. My esteemed judges will provide Eva with wine and entertainment while we're away."

"Our pleasure entirely." William took Eva's elbow and guided her in the opposite direction. Laurence followed on her other side but he did not touch her elbow. That gesture seemed a bit too much at the moment with the wine charm taking charge. What a relief Drew had taken the stone face away with him. Laurence had been sure that job was coming his way. Here we go, he thought, as though stepping onto a moving sidewalk where the room seemed distorted and it was moving too fast.

Chapter 3

The paying crowd started to roll in the door while William and Laurence were chatting with Eva and sipping a locally grown Nebbiolo William had found on a restaurant table. Laurence had been hoping to get a few minutes alone with her and now it was starting to feel hopeless. He really needed to get a head start on the tasting or be stuck in a slow moving crowd. William, who could go on forever on his topic, was doing so. Finally, Laurence looked at his watch to get his attention and said, "I hate to interrupt your fascinating monologue but we need to get started. It won't look fair if we have the sponsor at our side."

Eva laughed at him. "I think I win tonight, no matter what, so who cares if I'm escorted by the handsome judges."

"Don't call him handsome in front of me!" said William. "I always think those dark eyes of yours are looking at me, not at this old baker."

"It's marvelous to be traveling with wine and bread experts." She smiled at both of them. "I know you have work to do, so go ahead and leave me here. I will find someone else to talk with. In fact, I should go look for my son and try to keep him from antagonizing the contestants or the staff. Don't forget that each of the contestants is a valuable customer of mine I worked hard to secure and a very talented chef."

"Eva, I want to show you the new certificates for the chefs after we've completed our rounds." Laurence tried to put meaning behind each word so she would know he meant, *You and I must talk alone later.*

"All right. In Drew's office?"

"Perfect." He was relieved she had understood and confirmed. She wanted to talk to him privately. Reluctantly he nodded farewell to her and turned to William.

Clipboards in hand Laurence and William started with a bite of food, a swirling glass and a sip of wine and one more small taste of the food before putting the plate down and picking up their pens to write a few notes. They had agreed to not using the dump buckets tonight unless the wine was bad. No reason to be serious or sober for a light-hearted event like this one where everyone was going to get a prize and recognition. By the end of their rounds they would truly be jolly good fellows. What a great job this was! It looked like he would get to talk with Eva again. It was essential he got a moment alone so he could make the dinner date. Obviously his plan to ride home tonight with her was not happening, so on to plan B.

When Laurence and William had completed the circuit the gallery space was quite full of people and the noise level was high. Laurence was happy to take a break in the office where it was quiet. No one else was there. William settled into Drew's big leather chair behind the desk and Laurence sat down at the table with his back to the door to confer about their first choices for best wines and dishes. They made a list of the names for Julia to print out on winning certificates. William wrote out the language he wanted for the prize winning most versatile wine.

"Well, old man, I think we did quite a good job tonight of assigning praise where it was due and glossing over the less successful attempts," said William.

Laurence said, "My opening remarks for the crowd will be, 'when a talented chef uses a great product, the result can only be delicious. I have never experienced such a consistently high level of dishes. No ordinary categories can be applied here. It is truly a pleasure to be the judge here tonight and I congratulate you all on exceptional creations using the wonderful Russo products.' How does that sound?"

William said, "More B.S. than usual from you, but appropriate. Hello, Eva. Your timing is excellent. Laurence has just pronounced every chef here tonight outstanding."

Laurence turned around in his chair to see her standing in the doorway. He stood up and offered her the chair next to his. He was so happy that she had been watching to see them go into the office. She wanted to talk to him.

She sat down and said, "I agree with you. There's a good feeling in the room too, as though everyone is having fun."

"Hello, Drew. Please join us," said William. "We're thinking of toasting to a very successful event and now that you're here we could open a bottle of your private stash. What do you think?"

Drew remained in the doorway and surveyed the bright faces and then sat on the edge of the couch arm. "Eva, what do you think? Are you pleased?"

She nodded. "Very."

"Good, I'm glad. However, Antonio's not sure yet."

"Don't mind Tony Jr., he's never effusive even when he is pleased. I'm telling you that I'm pleased. That's all that counts. He may be the new president, but this is my event."

Drew said, "All right then. I detect a rosy glow and the evening isn't over yet, gentlemen. Let's save the celebrating for later. Why don't you two go mingle with the customers and let me talk with Eva for a minute." Drew wanted her to himself to hear again how pleased she was and to ask her out to dinner at one of the winning restaurants that hadn't been announced yet. William and Laurence looked like they were having too much fun. They needed to get back to work charming the guests.

Laurence felt sick not to get a chance to talk to Eva alone. Now he'd have to come up with another way to distract her in the crowd. Maybe after the award presentations he would get an opportunity. He scanned the crowd looking for familiar faces that would be easy to talk to.

Several tables away Amy and Kevin were sipping wine and chatting. He was always glad to see them at the gallery. He met Drew at a party at their house, which made it seem like he was a friend and gave him extra status with Drew to be friends with customers. Laurence had never given Drew any of the very few details of his acquaintance with them.

Kevin nodded a greeting. Amy said with a smile, no hug, kiss or handshake, "Hello, Laurence, good to see you. Hello, William."

Laurence appreciated people that didn't need all that social touching.

"Laurence how was the show tonight for you?" Amy asked.

"What's hard is picking the best. What did you like?"

"Well," she looked at Kevin, "I think the wild mushroom ragout and the venison bolognese were our two favorites."

"I noticed them both also," Laurence said as he saw Drew approaching. He wondered where Eva had gone after her private chat with Drew and what they had to talk about that was done so quickly.

"Hi, Drew." Amy turned her cheek toward him for an air kiss.

"Thanks for coming out tonight. We are always glad to see you here. What else are you up to for fun?" Drew looked at Kevin and hoped for a miracle, a small nugget from a successful guy that he could massage into a moneymaker for the gallery.

"We're taking a *pintxos* cooking class in San Sebastián," Amy said before her husband could answer.

"We're off to the Basque Country tomorrow for three weeks of indulging and not worrying about anything like cholesterol or tax incentives," said Kevin.

A solid gold nugget! thought Drew. He felt a buzz running through his body. "Ah, the magic of the Basque Country. How did you choose it?"

"We were there thirty years ago and thought we'd celebrate a milestone by visiting again. It's almost the pinnacle of the food world these days. I think more Michelin stars per capita than anywhere else in the world," said Kevin.

"Well, well, happy 30th anniversary." Drew recalled seeing full color double page spreads of the Bay of Biscay and lists of Michelin starred restaurants. The Guggenheim Museum Bilbao designed by Frank Geary exhibited the newest masterpieces of modern art and attracted record crowds. Yes! A destination idea that would entertain his best clients and draw in art collectors he wanted to meet. He would look into Basque art as soon as this event was over.

"Thanks. Whoever thought we'd be this old or married this long?" said Amy. "This class is my reward."

"What is it you're learning?" said Drew.

"*Tapas* to the rest of Spain, *pintxos* in the Basque Country. It's a small plate or a small bite of food and extremely popular way to hang out with friends. You go to a *pintxo* bar to eat and drink. Sounds like fun, right? Anyway San Sebastián is one of my favorite places. We're excited too about visiting Bilbao and seeing the Guggenheim museum," said Amy.

Drew looked alert and focused his blue eyes on Amy, "When you get back, let's all get together and hear about your trip and your cooking class. The fellows and I are going to think about what we could do with a Basque theme. Are you going to the best restaurant in the world?"

"No. I am not keen on the long tasting menu experience full of smoke and foam and mysterious things on the plate. Drew, are you talking about doing a food event or an art event?" Amy asked.

"I don't know yet. It's a new idea as of thirty seconds ago but I'm eager to learn more about it. The Guggenheim and the modernist cuisine are getting great press in the travel magazine I read. I marvel at the price of the experience." He needed more customers who enjoyed spending $500 on lunch after spending the morning looking at art. It was worth reading this magazine at his hair stylist to ogle the lifestyles of the affluent who could be art buyers. He didn't really enjoy traveling that much.

"OK, I'll be in touch. I think a *pintxos* tasting here at the gallery would be very fun! I bet there's art close by in Nevada and Idaho where the American Basques are. This is a great idea for an event that could be art and cuisine together," Amy said.

"Thanks, Amy for the tip." Drew felt his energy level increase. His theme had arrived! And it was delivered by a beautiful demographic he was fond of. He beamed at her to make sure she knew he thought her idea was terrific.

"Are there still sheepherders roaming the hills?" William seemed ready to jump into this new juicy topic, but was stopped by Drew introducing Eva to Amy and Kevin.

Everyone turned their attention toward Eva. Laurence was keenly aware of not only the men, but Amy too, staring at Eva before she caught herself and made a flattering remark about the wild mushroom dish. So, even women were captivated by her presence. Eva received the compliments from the crowd graciously. Before anyone could interject another comment, Drew took Eva away to introduce her to someone else. Eva looked back over her shoulder at Laurence and slightly shrugged in a way that suggested to him she meant, "Sorry, there's nothing I can do about it."

Amy looked at Laurence and said, "Wow, Eva is impressive isn't she?"

"Yes, she is," said Laurence still following her departure and wondering how many more chances he might get to be alone with her for a few minutes. What was this crazy Basque idea Drew was talking about? He felt like he'd missed something in the conversation that everyone else knew about.

"Yes, indeed," said William looking at his glass.

"Yes, I'll say that too," said Kevin looking at Amy.

"What do you say?" Amy asked Kevin.

"What they said."

Laurence thought the director of the charity spoke too long about the goals of his organization and what the funds raised tonight would be used for. The director finally introduced Eva whose speech was short and friendly. She thanked everyone for coming and being enthusiastic about her products and the chefs for such creative dishes and the great pairings with the wine. Then she introduced her son, Antonio, who was the new president of the company as she was giving up the day-to-day work but would remain on the board. The son wasn't so charming but he was brief and that was Laurence's cue to move to the podium with the envelopes for the winners. Eva stepped forward to stand beside him. Laurence was glad he had practiced his remarks about the quality of the products and dishes. Standing next to

Eva could have rattled his typical composure. He handed Eva the envelopes and she called out the names to come forward for special recognition. Laurence stepped back so William could take his place beside Eva with flattering remarks and a short stack of envelopes.

After the final applause died down and the crowd started moving toward the door Laurence stood to the side halfway between the front door and the podium watching Eva say good night to people while her son waited for her, speaking to no one. She was so close, surely she would say goodnight to him. She finally looked at him and turned toward him. He helped by approaching her and took both her hands in his.

She looked down at his hands holding hers and up into his eyes and said, "Thank you for the wonderful job you did tonight."

He kept holding her hands. "Would you like to have dinner with me this week?"

"I would like that. Maybe on Wednesday?"

"I'll call you on Tuesday to confirm the time and place." He loved that she didn't hesitate or give an excuse of having to look at her calendar. She was interested in him!

She turned away to join her son who was looking impatient. They both said goodnight to Drew and left. Laurence watched her disappear outside the door with a clear vision of her looking up into his eyes making her very positive response to his invitation. He was elated. He thought Drew looked pleased with the event as he continued making farewells at the door. Laurence went to look for Charles to see how he could help clean up.

Open wine bottle remnants from the restaurants were on the meeting table in Drew's office. William was pointing out the best choices to everyone and handing out clean wine glasses from a box. Drew watched the crew come in, pour a glass and take a seat. He didn't say much until everyone was seated.

"Job well done tonight. The sponsors, the vendors, the beneficiaries and the guests are happy," Drew began. "The situation here that is not happy is that Justin, our January-February exhibit artist, has cancelled his show. I need everybody to spend some time in the next two days doing extreme research on an element of Basque art and cuisine to see if we can come up with enough for a show that has the legs to run 60 days. William, I want you and Charles to develop the concept of a wine tasting event. Laurence, I want you to look into the *pintxos* business that Amy is interested in and get a grip on what it is and what about the new cuisine that gets so much press. Julia and I will tackle agents and exhibitors in the U.S. and Europe to try to understand what the art market is and try to find an existing show that could be shipped here."

Drew looked at each one of his crew and could see they were already thinking about the assignment. Charles had the least free time and he waited to see if Charles would bow out right now.

Charles shook his head and said, "Drew, I think a Basque wine tasting is a great idea. It's fresh and perfect with *pintxos*. But there's no point in calling the few distributors who deal in it until we know how big and what sort of event we're pouring for. There's not enough time to ship an order from Europe."

William said, "I will make a few calls tomorrow to people I know. I'll just ask, 'what if we needed 10 cases or 50 cases of Basque wine, can you do it?' I think they will know the answer off the top of their head."

"Thank you, William for doing that tomorrow. That's helpful," said Drew, "Laurence, what do you think?"

"Only one question right now. Have we ever featured a cooking demonstration with an expert?"

Drew said, "No, never. But that might be a good idea to attract a new audience, and a logical tie in to wine tasting."

William said, "The local Basque restaurant, The Harvest Vine, might be a good candidate for a show like that. They could bring wine they already own and sell it."

William was displaying his best 'we can do this' face, which made Drew feel hopeful this was a concept that could be developed without too much trouble. What a relief. It paid to have good people around who knew what they were talking about. Drew nodded his head yes! That's why he liked these old guys. They understood the urgency. They had the right attitude to come up with whatever it takes to make things happen. They were problem solvers. Now, what could he find to hang on the wall to sell to go with this wine tasting and demonstration?

Chapter 4

On Wednesday morning Laurence sang in the shower, "Don't you know she's just my style, everything about her drives me wild..." Amazing how an old ditty from the 1960s could suddenly pop into his head when he hadn't thought of it for about 40 years. His research on Basque cuisine for Drew was done and delivered. He had studied the map of the Atlantic coast of Spain and France and the key cities and famous villages of the coast and in the Pyrenees Mountains. He'd checked out a number of cookbooks from the library and was able to explain the cuisine to Drew who did not cook. The *pintxos* idea seemed perfect for the gallery. Although there were some sophisticated examples it was mostly simple and could be assembled from jars and cans of olives, seafood and roasted peppers. The specialty products were available locally and online. The old cuisine featured simple ingredients slowly nurtured into complex sauces. The new cuisine was intricate with industrial ways to spin plain thread into gold with surprising flavors. It required elaborate tools and immediate service after assembling so it would not be good for the gallery. Caterers they used in the past said no problem to a *pintxos* party. The local Basque restaurant, The Harvest Vine, would be happy to do a demonstration. He'd read a wonderful short history of the culture and felt the concept had lots of possibilities. The Basques were a fascinating bunch that appeared to have been around forever. Amy's cooking class in San Sebastián was bound to be a good experience for her and he hoped for the gallery too.

The research project had stimulated him. He felt like a new man, young, full of energy and optimism for the future, or more certainly, for this day and this night. Eva was his alone tonight with nobody else to distract her or interfere with his plans. The prospect of no interruptions to their conversation was exciting. He imagined staring into her eyes as she revealed her heart at the restaurant. Afterward he envisioned a romantic walk back to her apartment on West Highland Drive where he hoped to continue to romance her mind and then her body. Before he saw her tonight he would chose a poem that would help his mission. He thought of the famous poets of love, beginning with the Brownings and Lord Byron, quoting a few lines to himself. He tried Neruda and Mary Oliver. Then he was swept by a tsunami of insecurity realizing he was infatuated with her, but she hardly knew him and he really didn't know her well. He had no idea of her favorite books or music. He was doomed to failure tonight. He would look foolish with his desire out of control and showing all over his face. She would despise him if he looked at her with the moon in his eyes. What was appealing about that? She would never be interested in him if he revealed how besotted he already was. To calm his fears he turned to his bookshelf to pick out a favorite title to study. He finally found one by an unknown poet that talked about her beauty clothed and unclothed. How perfect was that to find something flattering and suggestive. She would smile about this poem.

> My love in her attire doth show her wit,
> It doth so well become her:
> For every season she hath dressings, fit,
> For winter, spring, and summer.
> No beauty she doth miss,
> When all her robes are on:
> But Beauty's self she is,
> When all her robes are gone.

After picking the poem he considered a few favorite opening gambits in bed. The first time was bound to be a bit awkward. Everyone would be a little nervous and apprehensive about how they looked without a carefully chosen costume. He wanted to surprise her and throw her off whatever her regular game was. The novelty he planned should distract her from her fears and turn her focus on them. She was so bright he felt sure this strategy would capture her attention. They needed time to warm up their engines and find their own speed.

She wanted to go out to dinner with him. She had said so on the phone yesterday in a way that had made him think she was happy to be invited and looking forward to it. She liked the idea of the little French restaurant on Queen Anne Avenue North and walking there with him. She would come down to the street, she said, when he rang her bell. He had made a reservation for 7:30 p.m. He hoped that wasn't too early or too late. Laurence had no idea what time was popular these days, but he had read several reviews of the restaurant and they were consistently favorable. How marvelous it was to have the money to do this without thinking much about it, to just dial the number and ask for a reservation for two like he did it all the time. The voice at the restaurant thanked him and he thought, Thank you, Drew.

At 7 p.m. he locked his apartment and headed up Queen Anne Avenue North, walked a few blocks to West Highland Drive where he crossed the street and walked two blocks more to her building. What a coincidence to live so near each other for several years and to become friends now. A courtship conducted on foot on city streets was practical urban style, particularly for seniors. He wondered if she had an Orca card for the bus or if she always drove her car. He felt his heart rate increase when he pressed the combination for her apartment. That feeling came again of the moving sidewalk going too fast, but he must jump on.

Through the speaker he heard her say, "I'll be right down." She appeared a few minutes later in a bright pink sleeveless dress with a floral silk shawl draped around her elbows and flat pink shoes. He took a deep breath and admired her from head to toe. "You look terrific."

She smiled at his appreciation. "Thank you. You're kind to invite me."

The sidewalk was electric beneath his feet and the ten blocks to the restaurant didn't seem long enough. Laurence wanted the walk, with her on his left side, to go on and on. Businesses were open. The windows were dressed. Other people walked by them in both directions and didn't seem to notice them. He occasionally caught a glimpse of their reflection in glass as he looked at her face to respond to something she said and could hardly recognize himself in the dark blazer with the pretty woman in rose pink on his arm. Two white haired people strolling toward a French dinner. They looked good. They didn't look old. They looked healthy with good posture and prosperous. He sighed at the vision in the glass and his good fortune to be in the picture. What a wonderful evening this was.

He loved looking at her framed on the banquette in the restaurant. Her necklace sparkled. Had she planned that? She ordered fish and a glass of Prosecco. He ordered duck and a Côte du Rhône. They toasted to the evening and sat relaxed, sipping and comparing notes on the wines.

"I've never had a chance to ask you what you like to read," he said.

Eva didn't answer right away. She didn't look surprised, just thoughtful. "I guess mostly nonfiction. I love history and biographies. I do read some fiction on airplanes. What about you?"

Laurence said, "I'm eclectic. I read three or four books a week."

"Three or four a week! That's astonishing. How do you do that?"

He said, "I'm retired and read is what I do for my hobby, my sport and entertainment."

"What are all these books about?"

"I have topics I'm interested in, aerospace engineering, science, technology, hacking, cooking, etcetera. My reading program is more like continuing education. Mondays I study cooking. Tuesdays I study aerospace. I do each one at a different branch of the library so I'm out on the town every day going to a different neighborhood. Does that sound ridiculous to you?" She seemed to be listening to every word and impressed with the information. What a delight to have her for an audience.

"Oh, no, not at all. I am awed by it. I never thought about reading during the day. It's the last thing I do before I go to sleep."

"Now that you're not the president any more, what are you thinking of doing during the day?"

"I've been thinking mostly of not doing business and not worrying and just enjoying myself, all things I've never done. Does that sound ridiculous?"

"Not at all."

Laurence thought the duck was quite good when he could stop looking at Eva and work with his silverware. The chef had been paying attention to get it medium rare on the inside and crispy on the outside. Thinly sliced with a drizzle of prune and Armagnac sauce it was a worthy choice for a special dinner out. She liked the King Salmon preparation with a squash tartlet. They were both eating very slowly. He loved listening to her talk. What she had to say about everything seemed articulate, interesting, surprising. All her conversation pointed to an extremely sophisticated, smart businessperson. Laurence couldn't think of any other women he'd ever met in his life at her level of accomplishment. She was not a successful middle management bureaucrat. She truly was presidential with vision and leadership. He'd known some intelligent women at Boeing but not one possessed all the trappings of success she wore so easily. She was very comfortable with herself. What did she see in him? His life at Boeing seemed too complicated to explain to a non-engineer. He didn't feel like sharing his mostly uneventful married life. It might sound like a boring life to Eva, and it seemed disloyal to Ingrid. What they had both liked about their long life together was that it was quiet and loving. He couldn't think of any amusing anecdotes about the gallery. With no travels to compare he doubted she would be interested in him after this dinner. He decided to just focus on listening to her and not talk about himself.

He learned that her work had consumed her for many years and she was ready to let it go and let Antonio Jr. be consumed by it. He was almost 50 and eager to be totally in charge and do it his way. She had nurtured her children, the customers, and the vendors and felt like they were all equipped to go forward without her attention. She was particularly tired of flying to Italy and working day and night for weeks on end. Flying wasn't fun or exciting anymore. It left her exhausted. She planned to indulge herself in every way possible that she hadn't had time to do in the last 40 years. She wanted to putter around her apartment, the city, maybe the state. She wanted to take a class to learn something new. She wanted to go to a spa. It seemed she'd hardly seen an art exhibit or been to a park in years.

When the plates had been cleared but before the server returned he said, "Would you like to order dessert?"

"No thanks. I think I'll save the calories for another glass of wine. What about you?"

"I'm with you. Do you need to see the wine list again?"

"Would you like to have it on my terrace?" She looked directly into his eyes and his mind.

"That would be nice." *Definitely, I would. Thank you for asking so simply,* he thought. *She does like me.* Laurence asked out loud for the check. Balancing his inner and outer conversation was going smoothly. He didn't think he'd made a mistake. But how would he know? Being alone with her in a restaurant was better than he imagined. He was excited about the prospect of being even more alone with her at her apartment.

Strolling back to her place in the now dark night, well lit with streetlights and commerce, she was on his right side with that electric sidewalk under his feet. Whenever she looked up at him and smiled he felt like he was lighting up too. The evening was going well. All his worries seemed silly now. Her invitation to the terrace must mean that she was thinking about having sex with him.

Inside her apartment he followed her across the big living room into the kitchen, which he hadn't seen on his previous visit. Any other time, stainless steel high-end appliances could have distracted him for a closer look but he was determined now to be physically close. It was important that he make the overture to seduce her. She shouldn't have to ask him again. That would be a point against him.

She paused in front of an under-the-counter wine cooler next to the refrigerator but instead of opening it to select a bottle, she turned to him and said, "Do you have any special requests?"

He shook his head no.

She said, "How about Champagne?"

"Are we celebrating something?"

"I just like it. I don't need to be celebrating anything to drink Champagne, but if you want, how about celebrating you taking me out for a nice dinner and a walk? I loved both."

"I like your style, Barolo and Champagne." He stood back a step against the counter while she got a bottle out and expertly popped the cork in few seconds. *Well done*, he thought. He didn't think he could have done it that quickly.

Eva filled two flutes and handed him one. They both sipped. She put a metal clamp on the Champagne bottle and put it back in the cooler. She said, "Where would you like to sit?"

"I'm enjoying standing. It's easier to see you. Am I crowding you?"

"Not at all. I quite like kitchen parties." She moved to stand next to him and lean against the counter and against him.

"This is quite a kitchen. Sometime you can tell me about your appliances. All I want to know now is more about you and what you like. Tell me something else." He watched her consider this request. She seemed amused.

"I like being with you, without the usual crowd, even though I'm fond of Drew and the rest of them," she said.

"I'm not missing those guys at all right now. I enjoyed the restaurant but this is even better. Maybe we could cook together sometime."

She nodded. "Sure, that would be good. You want to make pasta for me?"

"I've never prepared it for an expert," he said.

"I know a great deal about manufacturing pasta but I'm not an expert at anything in a home kitchen," she admitted. I'm not a good cook. I have never made pasta from scratch."

"You tried to tell me that before when I was here, but I didn't believe you. I thought you were being funny," said Laurence. "I laughed about it."

"It's true. I try to keep quiet about it. No one but my kids know how bad a cook I am." Eva giggled. "It wouldn't be good for business if that got out."

Her kids were a topic Laurence wanted to avoid. He wanted to keep this conversation focused on her — and him, no one else. She seemed relaxed and happy. Hopefully she would like his next idea he'd been saving for the appropriate moment, which seemed to be now.

"I envy the anonymous poet who could describe what it feels like to be here with you. It goes something like this..." When he finished with "When all her robes are gone," he raised his flute to her.

"You recite poetry! That's a first, and what a lovely message."

She looked genuinely stunned and pleased, which made him happy. *Good choice on the verse*, he told himself.

"You inspire me." He leaned over to give her a kiss on her lips.

She turned to stand in front of him leaning into his chest, and looked up at him. "I'll do my best to keep the good work coming out of you," Eva said. "Do you write poetry too?"

"No, I wish I could. I love reading it. The efficiency of a few words accomplishing complicated feelings is so appealing. It's like the elegance of short coding versus long coding. The programs may both produce the correct result but all the extra lines create a space for problems."

"That's computer coding you're talking about?" She looked earnest and waited for him to affirm before continuing, "I never knew coding could be elegant. I am going to learn so much from you."

Her words thrilled him. "Are we going to spend much time together?" He put his arms around her with his face very close to hers. When she said, "I hope so," he kissed her. She responded to him with equal intensity and put her arms around his waist. She leaned into him for another kiss.

He held her back from him to watch her face. "I would like to do more of that. Would you?" She nodded yes. "Your beautiful dress is in the way," he said.

"I'll take it off. Shall I take it off right now?" she said.

"Let me help you."

He followed her across the living room into the dark bedroom. She turned on a lamp on the bedside table. He sat down on the king-size bed. She stood in front of him and put her hands on his shoulders and gave him a kiss.

Laurence took one of her hands and held it over his heart. "Are you feeling brave?"

"Yes," she said.

"I have a good track record at this activity but I may be rusty."

Eva smiled and kissed him again and then turned around to present the zipper. "You're doing great. We haven't been here ten minutes and I'm taking my clothes off. You'll know in a minute how beautiful I am."

"All right. Here we go." He unzipped the dress with a flourish and she stepped out of it and threw it over the chair by the desk. Eva watched him remove his coat and tie and throw them over the dress. She unbuttoned his shirt. Soon all the clothes were on the chair and they surveyed each other in the soft light of the lamp.

He said, "I have been imagining this moment and you are as fabulous as I thought you would be 'when all your robes were gone'." He put his arms around her and held her close to him. "It feels wonderful without the dress."

"You look and feel wonderful yourself," she said suddenly sounding a little shy instead of worldly. She felt his arms and shoulders. "Where did you get all those muscles you've been hiding?"

He flexed his biceps for her showing off. "I have a fitness routine. You've got to be ready to run if you live in the city."

"Do you want me to chase you around the apartment?" She looked serious for just a second and then smiled.

"Not tonight. Maybe in the morning."

She folded the bedspread and the top sheet halfway back. She got in between the sheets and moved over to the other side of the bed. She lay on her side watching him as he got in beside her and then she pulled the sheet over him. He propped himself up on one elbow and with his other hand pushed her hair back and caressed her face.

He said, "I've given this a little thought for a sort of slow, get acquainted approach. I'm in the mood to start top down as opposed to bottom up. Does that appeal to you for our first time together?"

She looked a bit alarmed. "What's the top?"

"Your head."

"What's the bottom?"

"Your toes."

"Oh my, this is new to me. Show me how it goes. And then it's my turn?"

"Yes, that's the idea." She had gone for it just like he thought she would. He began by kissing the top of her head and working his way gently around her ears and face and neck and shoulders.

He hadn't gone too far when she said, "This approach is working well. You engineers are full of surprises."

He continued kissing inside her elbow. "I'm glad you like it."

Eva said, "You have my complete attention."

Laurence woke up in the middle of the night with his chest pressed against Eva's back, her head under his chin and his arm around her. He didn't want to move for fear of waking her. He wanted to savor the moment. He could almost weep it felt so good to be embracing someone. Not just anyone, but this incredible woman. He was glad he was lying down so all these emotions didn't knock him down. What an evening it had been with the sparkle of the windows along the sidewalk, the city lights, her necklace and her eyes. The exploration of her body had been exciting for both of them, a good way to begin knowing each other intimately, slowly, gently and generously. When he had made her extremely happy, she began kissing the top of his head kneeling over him. The anticipation of the next kiss as she made her way down his body was exquisite. He didn't feel rusty at all. He felt terrific.

Chapter 5

In the morning, daylight came through the slightly open bedroom door, interrupting his sleep. He didn't hear any of the traffic noise that generally woke him up. Eva must have high quality windows to block the outside sounds. First he wanted to replay the memory of her telling him several times how much he had pleased her. His own pleasure seemed secondary but it had been a thrill to be in action again after so many years and feeling like a much younger man while it lasted. He promised himself he wouldn't push his luck by trying a repeat performance today.

He felt her stir and before she could turn over and move away from him he kissed her ear and whispered, "You are magnificent in every way."

"So are you." She rolled over to kiss him and put her arms around him holding him close. "Imagine me at my age learning new tricks. I wouldn't have thought it possible. You have no idea how impressed I am with your body — and your brain."

"I feel the same way about you." He lay back on the pillow with both arms around her thinking none of his fantasies included this waking up scene with so much warmth and affection. It was almost as heady as the sexual intensity had been last night.

Eva said, "Now that I've got you here and you make me feel so good everywhere, I don't know if I want to get out of bed at all. We could make a day of it right here."

"Please don't get your hopes up that I can be as virile today as I was last night. That could have been a fluke. You make me feel like a 20-year old or a 40-year old, but I'm not. I am thinking we should save bottoms up for another time, but there is no reason I can't show you something else you might like."

Later with her head on his shoulder, she said to him, "I should offer you breakfast now and call to have some food delivered. Are you starving?"

"Hungry but not starving. How about you?"

"How about fresh bread and butter with coffee in bed?"

Laurence said, "That sounds fine. I hate to see you get dressed though."

She got up and walked across to the closet where a robe hung on the inside of the door next to the chair with his clothes piled over the pink dress.

"You look just as divine by daylight as you looked by starlight."

She blew him a kiss and laughed as she left the room. "It's always the woman parading around naked while the man is in bed covered up to his chin."

Laurence plumped up the big feather pillows behind his head so he could sit up and survey the room. He hadn't paid much attention to it last night except for the chair. It was a large room with a worn Persian carpet over a hardwood floor and gold velvet drapes covering a large window. He admired a small desk with a waxed finish, the perfect size for correspondence. Italian country furniture, he guessed, that looked sturdy enough to last generations and probably already had. It was made of a golden wood, fir or spruce, with simple curved legs and carved embellishments around the edge with two shallow drawers side by side for paper and pens. The top of the desk was bare except for a small lamp with a black shade. There was an almost matching tall chest of drawers with a few Italian ceramics on top. He hadn't seen any clutter or photographs anywhere in this home. Eva had nice things. All the furniture was comfortable. He hoped he was being a gentleman staying in luxury linens while she was in the kitchen. Maybe he should have said he would get up. It was hard to know what to do in this extraordinary situation. He was truly out of his experience zone and felt a little giddy. He tried to remember when he had slept overnight with a woman he didn't know that well. Never. Ingrid had been his lover for so many years since they had been teenagers, he could hardly remember the other girls he'd sex with. They'd all been too young to have their own place. Long before he and Ingrid slept together in a bed all night, he knew her very well. They were experts at sex outdoors, in the car, in the alley and in bathrooms at parties. He remembered they both thought it was funny when they got married and started sleeping in a bed and waking up together. She was long limbed and lithe then. He tried to hold on to that youthful vision and not succumb to the last version of her when he had become the caretaker of that body that weighed even less than she had at 17. He shook his head to block the memories and think about the amazing woman who would be back in a minute with coffee for him. He needed to focus on her.

Eva returned carrying a tray with a newspaper, coffee cups and an insulated pot and a plate with small baguettes and butter. She put it down in the middle of the bed on top of the sheets beside him, opened the drapes and got back in bed on the other side.

He poured coffee for them both and said, "Thank you. I'm sure it's no better at the Ritz this morning."

"I like room service," she said. "It's such a civil way to start the day."

When they had finished the newspaper and the coffee and eaten all the bread, which he agreed with her was

---

excellent with the extraordinary Irish butter, he put the tray on the floor beside him. He put his arm around her and took her hand in his. "This has been so great. I feel like it's time for me to go home now so you can take care of your business."

"No!" She was adamant.

"You don't have things you need to do?" he asked.

"No," she said.

"OK. My schedule, as you know, exists but is flexible. What would you like to do?"

"If we must give up this bed, which I am in no hurry to do, why don't we go for a walk, say to the Betty Bowen view spot or Kinnear Park?" she asked.

"All right. I must go home first to shower and put on clean clothes."

"No. Please, take a shower here. There are all sorts of grooming supplies in the bathroom, including a box of new toothbrushes. Your clothes aren't dirty."

He kissed the top of her head. "Well, all right, if you insist. You definitely know what you want, don't you?"

"And how to get it." She looked so serious. "Do you want to go home?"

"Not particularly. I just don't want to overstay my welcome. I'd like to be invited back."

"I promise you will be invited back. I'll tell you when I feel like I need some privacy," she said.

"All right then, if I can do the same, that's the deal."

They strolled down West Highland Drive toward Elliott Bay. At the Betty Bowen viewpoint they sat on a bench for awhile admiring the water, the ferries and the silos of Washington wheat destined to fill container boats headed for Asia. Laurence could hardly speak because of the foreign feeling of being part of a couple. Eva seemed relaxed like nothing was unusual to her. How could that be?

At Kinnear Park they strolled once around the loop trail and sat on another bench overlooking the bay. They decided to walk the long way home up 10th Avenue West to West McGraw where they stopped for coffee at the Macrina Bakery, a café for eating in or taking out freshly baked goods for breakfast and lunch. Sitting inside with the café doors completely folded back open to the sidewalk, they shared a tall iced coffee and a hazelnut bar.

Eva said, "I love this but I never order it. I'm splurging because this is such an extraordinary day and I'm getting so much exercise." She smiled at him clearly delighted with the day and the sweet.

He wanted to go home now but made up for that deceit by saying, "If you love it, I will make you some that are better."

"Really? Is this a specialty of yours?"

"No, but I have a good recipe and have baked them a few times. My crumb is different. I toast the nuts more and I think that enhances the result."

"I would love that. What else do you like to cook?"

"If experience counts, my specialty might be roast chicken. I can cook anything though. Would you like me to make you something?" He meant sometime in the future. The coffee had not perked him up but he could feel her energy rising.

"I'd love for you to make me a roast chicken. We could stop at Ken's Market on the way home and get one, unless you'd rather buy it somewhere else."

"Do you mean today, right now?" She indicated yes with a big smile. "Are you sure this isn't a good time for me to go home?" She shook her head no. "OK, if you're sure, Ken's is good with me."

With one free-range chicken, Yukon potatoes and organic carrots in a bag, they walked together on West McGraw toward Queen Anne Avenue North. He pointed out Amy and Kevin's house as they walked by.

"Are they good friends of yours?"

"No, just acquaintances. She rides my bus and works on Mondays at the downtown library. She invited me to her house once for dinner to celebrate what she learned at a cooking class in Kuala Lumpur. This week she is taking a cooking class in San Sebastián. I bet she will have a party for that too. Did I tell you that her house is where I met Drew?"

"No. I never heard that story. Do you have many library friends?"

"No. I see the same people all the time but I don't know their names. I don't talk to anyone. I really don't have any friends at all."

Eva looked at him, "Tell me, how did you get to this stage in your life with no friends?"

"Very easy. I never had many to begin with. Ingrid and I were always in our own world and never did too much with other people. Saturday nights in the bars we'd see people we knew and hang out together, but we seldom had anybody over to our house. When our parents were alive we did things with them. I parted ways with my Boeing friends over union politics. Others died or moved away. The first five years Ingrid was gone I hardly spoke to a soul. This last year I have talked to people at Drew's once or twice a month and I am enjoying it. I am not an anti-social geek." He looked at her to see if she understood.

"I never thought you were the least bit odd. You are a good listener, which is a rare skill."

"And I am fascinated with you," he said and smiled at her, pleased with her delight. It was almost as good a reaction as the poetry had received. He was astonished by this whole experience with her since 7:30 last night.

While the chicken was in the oven they sat on the balcony. After they ate what she told him was the best chicken she had ever had, they watched the sun set and the city lights come on and decided to go to bed early. He could not believe he was in this bed two nights in a row, unselfconsciously enjoying himself and her. They were getting to know each other without any inhibitions. It was incredible to him how easy it was to be with Eva.

The next morning after the breakfast tray was empty he said, "It feels very special to be part of your world and your mind, but…"

"But? No buts allowed here."

"I must go home and get clean clothes now. I have a thing about clean clothes every day."

She looked astonished and then laughed. "OK, I'll go with you."

"No, I don't think I'm ready for you to see my place."

She laughed. "That's hysterical considering what we've been showing around here."

"You have a lovely home with nice things. I live a simple bachelor's life. It's no frills. I'm afraid you will be horrified."

She said, "Now I am eager to get over there right away. I can't wait to see your monk's cell. Let's don't even shower here. Let's shower at your place!"

"No, no, no. You cannot shower at my place. Please don't insist on this. You shower here."

Walking the five blocks to his building went too quickly for Laurence to gather his feelings about this revelation. He didn't like how she had insisted and got her way. He'd never shown anyone this apartment. He couldn't think of a thing to say. Words of warning seemed inappropriate. Oh, his lobby looked old and shabby compared to hers. This was a terrible idea.

She panted after the second flight of stairs and said, "I understand now how fit you are. Taking the elevator has become a habit with me. I should take the stairs too."

"You'll be looking a long time to find the elevator here."

With trepidation he opened the door and let her enter first. She stopped to survey the studio plus sleeping alcove. He looked around to see if everything was in its place. Of course it was. That's how he kept it.

"It's so clean! I had no idea a man would have hardwood floors with no dust anywhere. Your furniture is gorgeous. You're right, your style is minimalist, but that's manly. Tell me where the furniture came from."

Laurence sighed in relief and sat down at the kitchen table. "Please, sit down. May I offer you a glass of water?"

"No, I don't need anything at the moment. It's marvelous to be inside your space. It's seeing another facet of your mind. And I love the bookcase. I'd love to look at your books too, do you mind?"

"No, please do. A long time ago, I made it."

"You made the bookcase?"

"The bookcase and all the furniture."

"All this furniture?"

"Yes. It's well made. I'm proud of it."

"I can't tell you how impressed I am. You are truly a talented person, an artist." She rubbed the grain of the kitchen table and admired the legs.

"Thank you. My father was a wood worker, if that's what you call someone who worked in the shingle factory in Ballard. He taught me. He was one of the only guys at

—
51

the factory with all his fingers. That's how good he was. He had a few tools at home and I bought more as I wanted to make more things. It was good hobby when I was young and we needed things. Ingrid and I designed them together."

She reached across the table to take his hand in hers. "Thank you so much for letting me in. I realize now it was a big step for you. I feel a little overwhelmed with yet another of your skills. You are so modest about yourself."

He squeezed her hand. "It's nerve-wracking to be revealing my private world. I haven't ever told my history before. Ingrid knew it all from teenage years. I haven't talked about my parents or being a young man to anyone ever. There's no reason for anyone at work to know these things. Do you feel odd telling me about your history?"

She said, "No, I know how to tell my story to various audiences to provide what's needed to make the connection or the sale. Italians have to get to know you before doing any business. I've never had much privacy and I've seldom been alone. I'm more accustomed to the crowd knowing most everything about me and my family thinking I am not anything special but a mom who's behind the times and technology."

"That is so shortsighted of your kids."

"Don't be annoyed with them. They can't help being kids. It's humbling being a parent," she said. "How did you end up with no kids with such a long happy marriage?"

"It wasn't a lack of sex. I've always been interested in that grand physics experiment. It just wasn't in my genes to be a father. We made our peace with it and didn't mourn the life we didn't have."

Eva didn't make any response so he didn't know if his stoicism offended her or just sounded cold. He hadn't thought about his infertility in a long time. The way he remembered it was that it seemed sad at first, but he and

Ingrid shrugged and knew their life together would still be meaningful without children. Knowing how fiercely people felt about their children as a centerpiece in their lives he struggled to come up with a bridge over that canyon with Eva. He said, "You have such a rich fabric of people around you. I feel so solitary with nothing to offer that's similar in any way."

"You have a rich mind. I am enjoying being alone with you and having your attention. Learning about you is a great experience for me. The physics thing between us that seems so easy is a revelation to me. I was married too young to someone who was too old for me. I knew nothing and assumed he knew it all. Sex always seemed overrated to me until I had some good experiences. My marriage was strong because Tony and I worked well together, and the business and our kids were successes we shared."

She looked so intently at him as she said this. It was so personal, and she revealed this painful information so honestly. Now Laurence couldn't think of anything to reply. He didn't want or need to know anything else about her marriage.

When he was ready for the day she suggested he pack a suitcase to take to her house.

"It's a modern world where a man brings his suitcase on a date," he said.

"I am thinking of this as a vacation now! The date was a few days ago."

"You really want me to bring a suitcase with clean clothes to your house as though we're going on vacation?" She seemed enthusiastic about it. He wasn't sure this was a good idea. He was afraid they were going too fast on this path of getting to know each other. He wanted to slow things down. He didn't want her to leave without him, but packing a suitcase seemed like agreeing to days and days of being in her apartment. That was a big leap for him who had been alone for so long and seldom been on vacation anyway. "I would have to bring some books."

Eva said, "You're not going to start reading and ignore me are you?"

"Well, I need to read every day. I can't go away without my books."

She said with humor, "You are a funny old man with your clean clothes and books and flip phone."

"I like my dumb phone. You have no idea how few pay phones are left in this city. Besides, it's a job requirement of Drew's, although he doesn't call often."

At the Olympic Sculpture Park they admired the Richard Serra piece from all angles and sat on one of the red metal benches overlooking Elliott Bay. For some reason he could not understand, he was suddenly telling her his fears. He confessed he had felt too old for romance and was very surprised by where they were today, together, and how effortless it all seemed, this 72-hour date they were having.

Eva dismissed his fears, "You are not old! You are so healthy and fit. You amaze me with your ability to romance me."

"If you knew how old I was you might not be so certain. I'm 76."

"Oh my. I had no idea. I thought you were 70, the same as I am." She looked at him to see how that news settled.

He carefully studied her face and realized he was taking too long in his response and said, "The years have been kind to you."

Eva hesitated before saying, "That's good. I try not to worry about the inevitable sagging. My theory is that when you start falling down and breaking bones, that's when you know you are old. Have you ever fallen?"

"Nope," he said.

"Well that's proof you aren't old yet. I'd like to be as fit as you are. Why don't we take tai chi classes together? Balance, strength and agility all in one lesson."

"I'm not much on group activities. I have my own exercise program. Do you take this class now?" he said.

"No. I've never had time to, but I always wanted to."

He could see in her face how earnest she was. "I'm impressed with how easily you have relaxed with me these last few days after 40 years of working. You can even walk around without a cell phone in your hand. You haven't called the office once."

"I left the phone at home. You are a marvelous distraction. I couldn't possibly think about work while I have you paying attention to me. You have no idea how special that is."

"Well, I told you what I was apprehensive about. Were you apprehensive about me?"

"No. I had studied you at the gallery. I thought you were intelligent and a gentleman. You seemed to be interested in me. Offering you a ride home seemed a bit forward but you didn't ask me out any of the times I saw you, so I thought how else was I going to be alone with you to see what might happen? I got what I wanted. You are kind and funny and a pleasure to be with in every way," she said.

He shook his head. "I thought you were just being nice because you wanted me to like your products. I had no idea you were expecting me to ask you out. I never would have thought of it. I haven't asked anyone for a date since before I got married."

Eva said, "I have to be aggressive at my age. I want a man in my life now. I want to have someone to share the day and the evening with. I have been looking here and in Italy since my husband died, maybe even since he no longer recognized who I was. Lots of men seem interested in me, but after spending time with them, I find they are not really interested in me. They only want the appearance of being with me, and probably my money. With a few exceptions most of them were lousy in bed or had already given up trying. I would give up the idea of a sex life if someone were good company and kind. I could live with a less worldly man if he offered me warmth and affection. You have no idea how outstanding you are to have the mind and the body thing."

She was delivering a lot of information to process and he felt overwhelmed again, how to respond to her frank admissions. She was looking for a man and had found *him*. Was that what she was saying? He couldn't quite believe he understood her properly. Why would she tell him that after only a few days together? "I'm not surprised you have candidates around the world. I'm surprised I'm one of them."

She said, "No one I know comes close to you. You have all the great qualities."

This was an intense conversation. She was being so honest he couldn't stop himself from asking, "Weren't you insulted when I declined your first advance?"

"No, I thought I'd made an excellent choice, an extraordinary man who was taking me seriously. What did you think?"

He said, "I was stunned you wanted me. I had no idea that's what you had in mind. I thought my sex life was over years ago. You are making me feel things I haven't felt in years and maybe things I've never felt before. I'm running out of words to describe my feelings."

Eva exhaled slowly but didn't say anything else. He thought her very courageous to have told him she had been looking for a companion and to have admitted that her quest had been disappointing. It was too much information but he admired her even more than a few minutes ago and knew why she was being quiet now. There was nothing else to say for a while. They needed to adjust to the new altitude they were traveling at after these revelations. It felt surreal to be sitting next to another human being who was speaking from the heart — and about him! He couldn't believe how directly she told him she wanted him to be her companion. Did he want a companion or to be a companion? That seemed like a huge leap after knowing someone for a few days. He wished he had some response but all he could think was that he liked being with her. He didn't want to go home alone just yet. Maybe tomorrow he would go back to his apartment and try to think about all this. After sitting for a while looking at the bay, Laurence finally found some words to say. "I've been thinking about that French bleu cheese in your refrigerator. Why don't I make you a cheese soufflé for dinner?"

"Oh, my God," she said, "You don't want to leave me on this bench and never see me again? You want to make me a cheese soufflé for dinner? You are the most amazing man." Her eyes were very moist. He looked away to give her privacy.

Chapter 6

Since Eva's event Drew had spent long days online looking at art museums and galleries in the Basque Country, particularly along the Atlantic coast destinations in Spain and France that had been popular summer resorts for more than a century. From the gallery websites he could see the patterns of art that people would buy on vacation. Paintings in oil and watercolor of bucolic fields and vineyards invited shoppers to stop and admire the natural beauty. Sheep, cows, oxen and geese were popular. So were boats of all sorts, new and old, in harbors or at sea. The cities and villages seemed to be all rustic stone. The many paintings of houses seemed to be mostly white three stories featuring red wood trim and shutters. The coastal cities promoted attractive beaches and landscaping. Who wouldn't enjoy a watercolor of the sand and harbor of San Sebastián, Biarritz or Saint Jean du Luz after a week of lounging in the cafés along the promenade? No question this part of the world was photogenic, but would people buy the art if they hadn't been on vacation there?

The photos of the inside and outside of the Guggenheim Museum Bilbao made him and Julia giddy. No matter how much he hated flying he might have to make a trip to see this icon of architecture and the art in it. Julia thought she'd like to go see it too. Maybe they would go together sometime when they had made a lot of money on an exhibit and felt like devoting a week's vacation to seeing great art. The museum's presence in Bilbao inspired more avant-garde works in the nearby galleries than they had seen elsewhere. The work was sophisticated and dramatic in many mediums. Drew and Julia would love a chance to sell this art. Abstract ironwork was prevalent and summoned a vision of a powerful, muscled artist pounding huge pieces of hot steel with force. This art required brute strength and was definitely not from some of the coddled urban artists they knew who worked indoors in all seasons.

Many of the websites offered a choice of languages, but only a few of the galleries had someone available with good English when he called them. That was a snag he hadn't considered. So much for English being the international business language. As a young man he had studied French and spoken it fairly well, but his middle-aged mind didn't remember as much as he needed to conduct business. His idea of shipping a show across the Atlantic quickly faded over the expense of shipping, even if he could assemble an exhibit, as no one knew of a collection ready to travel.

Laurence called with a positive report on the *pintxos* food angle of the potential exhibition as well as caterers and a restaurant to do demonstrations. No matter whatever else happened, a Basque food experience to sell could be created for the gallery. Drew thanked him for all the details and when he hung up the phone he sat for a minute congratulating himself on hiring Laurence. The old engineer earned his money every time.

William too had responded without as much detail as Laurence but with confidence that some Basque wine could be sourced and substantial quantities of wine from neighboring regions would be easy to come by. There could be a wine tasting with food and a cooking demonstration that would also include wine and food bites. Do that twice and now four of the eight nights needing entertainment over two months were slotted. Hah! Four more ideas to go!

A few days after his stated drop-dead date to make a decision, after talking it through with Julia from every angle, with hope and despair, Drew decided to commit to the project. It was the biggest leap he'd ever taken. Not knowing exactly what and how much art there would be to show defied logic but his instinct about what he'd seen so far insisted he say yes. To recreate the singers and dancers in costumes he'd seen online without being certain he could hire performers for the right price was a little crazy but why not try? The food and wine aspects didn't faze him. He had experts to take care of that. The alternative of the closed sign on the door was worse than his anxiety about the art. That closed sign would be like the advance notice he was going out of business and he couldn't bear that. He was *not* going out of business. He was smart and flexible and changing with the times. He and his gallery would survive. This was merely a recession even though the newspaper liked to call it the *Great Recession*. He had lived through other recessions.

Drew decided he had to give up on Europe and focus on regional artists closer to Seattle to simplify shipping and communications. He began looking for Basque artists through the agent and gallery network he knew without any luck. If they were out there, they weren't marketing themselves as Basques.

Another disappointment was the Basque Cultural Centers in Boise, Idaho, and Reno, Nevada. They attracted lots of visitors, and the gift shops sold Basque themed art but an artist of Basque heritage didn't necessarily create the art. Much of this art was not sophisticated enough or at a price point that made sense for his gallery. He couldn't make money and keep the doors open with what he saw there. Seattle wasn't Boise and his customers weren't tourists. But it did give him the idea of creating a few souvenirs to sell. He'd never done that before. Why not offer some $20 mementos for those not wanting to plunk down 2 or ten grand for original art?

The galleries near the Basque centers offered contemporary art of interest to him but he didn't find a gallery specializing in Basque artists. What he began to feel was that the contemporary artist didn't see a marketing advantage in advertising being a fifth generation Basque. Their artwork was not inspired by the heritage. His hunting and pecking was yielding small returns and causing him some sleepless nights. He began regretting pursuing this crazy idea. At least this failure would be a quiet one very few people would know about.

One of the gallery owners suggested he try the western universities offering Basque Studies as a degree program. The existence of the cultural centers and the academic degree programs in Basque Studies showed a passion for preservation and education that resonated with Drew. The culture of the Basques in the Old World apparently was worth saving. He began to be more impressed by the character of these people with each new block of information.

The art professors turned out to be the best resource of names to pursue. One of the professors was of Basque heritage and wanted to be considered and was sending him photos of his work. He finally had his first few artist names to begin researching and contacting.

Each of these artists referred from the professors was surprised — and ecstatic — to be contacted but none of them had a large enough body of work to make a solo or small group show, although he might take two or three works from the best artists. It was going to have to be a big group show, which Drew doubted had been done before. That was exhilarating and terrifying. Almost two weeks had gone by and that's all he and Julia had to show for their time. *Aaagh!* Drew screamed in his head.

Drew said, "We need to get out of here and have some fresh air to breathe."

Julia said, "Want to have dinner at my house? You could take a look at what I've done lately while I cook."

He said, "Do you mean while you dial for a pizza to be delivered?"

She grinned and nodded yes.

At Julia's apartment Drew sorted through the canvases in progress and put a stack on the floor next to a large antique chaise, which was the only furniture in the room other than a side table and an easel. He sat down and picked up the top one up to study the brushwork up close. It was a half done portrait of him. She had followed his advice to always make the subject look better than they do in real life. He quite liked it and it certainly reminded him of himself about 20 years ago even though this was a new portrait. From the kitchen Julia brought him a long stemmed glass and a bottle of gin from the freezer. She poured it almost to the rim.

"No vermouth?" he said.

"I'm not a bartender."

He took a sip and said, "It's nice to have a chilled glass. Cheers. What are you having?" he said eyeing her full glass of something greenish.

"Kombucha, you know my fermented beverage. It is so good for you! Want to try it?"

"Absolutely not for the 10th or 20th time. It looks different to me every time you have it."

"That's because you can flavor it with any other juice or fruit. This has melon in it. You should try it just once."

"No, thank you. Gin is medicinal too, made from berries and perfect for me."

While he looked at the next canvas, a cityscape of the view from the window next to the easel she went into her bedroom. Drew loved the ambiance of the *atelier* of the young. The open space freed his mind to new thoughts. Who needed furniture, costumes and props anyway? It was over rated. Julia didn't need to dress her subjects. They arrived in their own costumes. He loved the canvases stacked three deep leaning against the wall as unlimited entertainment. Julia's wide interests were expressed in fabric and wallpaper swatches, magazine pages and found objects pinned and nailed to the old wall. The wood floor was worn and scuffed and bare except for a big drop cloth under the easel. When she returned she was wearing a floor length Chinese silk robe with dragon motif tied at the waist.

"Comfort and style. When is your roommate coming home?" he said.

"I don't know. I can call her later and find out if you like," she said.

They sat together and talked about a half dozen different projects in progress. They were mainly abstracts and he was impressed with what she was experimenting with. One of them he found particularly moving. "Are you going for bleak?"

She said, "Yes."

"I suggest you try building up the lower edge tones for a harsher base note to anchor it and add drama. What's inspiring you about bleakness?"

"The Recession is what I call it."

"All me, huh? You should start a new one called the Alternate Universe Where the Basque Artists Are Hiding. Who knew they would be so hard to find?"

"Well, I never would have guessed that calling museums would be a bust. All those artists we would love to sell, if only the museums knew who was Basque. Not enough relevant tags in the database seems so lame," Julia said shaking her head.

"How many of the Basque clubs have gotten back to you now?" said Drew.

"None of them yet. I'm not giving up on them until they call to say they couldn't find anybody," said Julia. "It's not their day job, and I don't want to appear desperate by calling them again this week. That never helps. You got to be cool when you want people to do stuff for you for free."

"What would help is if I'd never started this crazy search hunting for artists. I'm thinking of calling a halt to it," he said.

"Drew, it's discouraging for sure, but we will find them, and we can't quit now. The options we keep discussing are worse than quitting."

"Remind me how bad they are," he said.

"There's the closed sign on the door in January and February, which will make all the regular artists think we've left town in the middle of the night. There's cleaning out the storage rooms and having a motley garage sale, which will make all the regular customers think we're planning to leave town. Do you want me to go on?" said Julia.

"No. Let's don't ever mention any of those ideas again. What else could we do on a Thursday and Friday night that would be fun and different and be something about Basque art?" Drew said.

"How about an author, a poet, a dancer, a photographer, a movie maker? How about a Basque film? Do they have any famous films?" Julia asked.

"Yes! *For Whom the Bell Tolls*, the Hemingway story of the Spanish Civil War, a classic in black and white. I loved that movie of romance and danger in the 1930s! That is such a good idea. Gary Cooper and Ingrid Bergman were great. I bet there are art films too. We can get my old buddy at the Seattle International Film Festival to help by looking into Basque directors and themes to find something available to rent for a small audience, meaning not too expensive. Do we have movie buffs in our patron lists, or would this be a new group for us? What could we charge for a movie? If we have two movie nights we only need three more ideas for entertainment." Drew was excited now.

When the pizza arrived he lined the canvases they had been discussing back against the wall to look at while they ate. They sat with the pizza box between them eating and not talking, still thinking about the paintings. Drew felt very relaxed. It was so comfortable to be here in this well-known space with this dear person absorbed in what they both loved best. When they finished eating he put his arm around her and kissed the top of her head. "Julia, you're really doing well in every way. You should be pleased with your work. I'm going home now."

"You don't want to stay a little longer?" she said.

"No, I'm tired."

She stood up in front of him and opened her robe to reveal her naked body. Her navel was right in front of his face. He kissed it. She leaned down toward him and he kissed both breasts and pressed his head against her body. "I'll stay."

Chapter 7

Laurence lay stretched out dozing on the Italian leather couch in Eva's living room with a book on his chest. The couch was so big it turned a corner and had an ottoman at each end. He did not even come close to taking up all the space. The comfort and the feel of the leather reeked of money spent on good wood, a craftsman and fine leather. He couldn't imagine how much something like this design statement might cost, but he was certainly enjoying being the recipient of the artist's intent. Propping his head on the armrest, he tried to read while Eva got ready for the day. The blue sky and the cool breeze through the open French doors distracted him. Another unusually sunny fall day and here he was reading in luxury like he owned it. Over a few days he had slowly relaxed into her world and no longer felt like a stranger or self-conscious about being here. He wouldn't have minded spending the day right here on the couch.

"What a thrill it gives me to see you reading! You are so relaxed." Eva sat down beside him. He put his book on the floor and gently pulled her over to lie alongside him with his arms around her and her head on his shoulder.

"I was thinking of spending the day right here," he said.

"Why not?"

"Would you lie here with me?" he said.

"Would you read to me?"

He reached down for the book and held it out in front of the two of them and began, "Calculating the curvature of the new wing uses a different algorithm..."

"Oh, dear." She laughed, "Is that really fascinating to you? I might die of boredom before you finish the paragraph."

"Yes, the implications are profound, truly beautiful! But we can't have you dying over it. I wish I had some Robert Browning. Then I could explain the attraction of the wing properly to you as he says, 'If you get simple beauty and nothing else...' How about a little classic Basque instruction instead?" He picked up a cookbook from the stack and showed her a picture of peppers simmering in a copper caldron at a gastronomic society kitchen.

"The sauce looks good. Are you in charge of the food for this Basque exhibit?"

"Probably not as Charles has so much more experience than I do at running the food, but I'm researching. I want to know as much as possible before Amy gets back so we can have a good discussion about her cooking class, the cuisine and what we might do at the gallery. I need to get more books at the library. How'd you like to go today?"

"To a library? That would be different for me. I haven't been in years," Eva said.

"Do you have an Orca card?"

"Definitely not. I barely know what it is."

"There you go, new things for you to do. First, a bus ride, then I'll show you the big library and we'll get you your own card. If you're going to be with me and frequent libraries, you'll need one. You can ride on my Orca today and see if you'd like to have one too. Since we're downtown, why don't we start at the Frye Art Museum and see the new exhibit? Then we can walk down the hill to the library."

—
67

"Nothing gets a man off the couch like a trip to the library!" She laughed. "I wouldn't have believed it. You're a funny old man. What's wrong with the Queen Anne library we could walk to in ten minutes?"

"No adventure in that." He looked at his watch, "It's twelve minutes until the next bus. Let's go.

"How do you know?"

"I've been riding the bus for years. I know all the schedules."

"Without looking it up?"

"I'm a numbers guy, remember? And they don't change often."

Riding down the hill in his regular seat on the bus with Eva at his side put a fresh look on the old storefronts and bus stops. He could feel the novelty through her as they watched the bus come and climbed the steps. She watched carefully as the driver made the adjustment for two riders before Laurence tapped the Orca card tap and it chimed. He could tell she had never done this before. The bus driver looked at him, raising his eyebrows but didn't say a word about his companion. Riders he saw routinely also looked a bit curiously at him as though they weren't sure what was different about him, but of course said nothing.

They got off the bus at 9th Avenue by Virginia Mason Hospital and walked along shaded streets to the Frye. They spent a half hour almost alone touring an exhibit by a current artist in multi media format and another half hour in the founding collection of European paintings that belonged to Mr. and Mrs. Frye.

Sitting in the café afterward sipping green tea Eva looked at him, smiling, "Thank you so much for showing me this very sweet art experience. I am so used to Italian art exhibits being mega sized and colossal with thousands of years of history. The size of the Frye is refreshing and the art seems so new."

"It's very Seattle, don't you think?"

"Yes, in the best way."

As they walked down Madison Street toward the library, Eva asked Laurence why Drew thought so highly of Amy's opinion.

"Her demographics are good. She comes to First Thursday and special events we have. She brings friends. Drew figures she can go on vacation anywhere in the world she wants and if she chose the Basque Country, other people who enjoy art and cuisine will be interested too."

"The Basque Country is very charming. Have you been?" Eva said.

"No, I've just read about it. As you know by now, I am not a traveler. I'm happy to read about places. I don't need to go see for myself. The Basque history is fascinating to me, and the food looks terrific. I'm going to start cooking from these books and I'll make you a *pantxineta*, a classic Basque party dessert that is revered. I want to try all the seafood stews too. We must find some salt cod to experiment with."

Laurence was enjoying himself with Eva's elbow in his hand showing her one of his favorite spots in the city, the Seattle Central Branch, his Monday place to study. She seemed genuinely interested in each area he pointed out to her. She marveled at the size of the collection. They selected a few to check out and a few to look at while seated at a table overlooking 5th Avenue.

"It's really something. I'm so glad you showed me," she whispered.

He smiled at her, hoping he didn't look besotted, merely pleased. "Why don't we go down to the Market and pick a fish to have for dinner?"

She said, "I want to cook for you tonight. You need a day off."

The Pike Market was bustling as always. Eva wanted to look at every fish at each fish stand before deciding on a branzino, a small Mediterranean fish she was fond of.

Laurence nodded at her, keeping to himself the questionable wisdom of buying a fish that had traveled 6,000 miles to be eaten. Italians, even Italian-Americans, have their own way of doing things. If this fish was farmed nearby, that fact wasn't well known and he wasn't going to bring that up.

"I will stuff the fish and make a nice salad."

He carried the library books in his book bag, and she carried the plastic bag with the fish, shallots, mushrooms and potatoes. The shopping and the upcoming meal animated Eva in a way he hadn't seen before. She tied a chef's apron around her waist, talking while looking for the right baking pan and seasonings. He could hardly take his eyes off her. No longer the cerebral queen of commerce, she was in mom mode, providing food for her family. She talked faster and moved faster than usual, rapidly and carelessly chopping shallots with no regard for uniform sizes or proper knife technique. She soaked the mushrooms in water and didn't let the pan get hot before pouring in a huge amount of olive oil. He didn't say a word, just watched in amazement at these and other odd ways of assembling the dish. Now he knew it was true she didn't know how to cook, but she made him feel special, catered to, by performing the ritual. He was sure she would ruin this poor fish so far from home, but she cooked it for him with great pride and he was appreciative.

Eva said, "This was such a great day. I loved seeing new art. I love your library. This is what I thought retirement would be like, exploring and enjoying myself. Thank you for being the tour guide today."

"You're welcome." Eyeing the cutting board he said, "You're going to stuff the fish with all that?"

"Some inside and some scattered on top for different texture."

He could imagine the dried out leather texture of over-cooked porcini mushrooms on top of the fish to contrast with the moist mushrooms inside the dry fish but said, "Shall I wash the lettuces?"

"Sure. You know where the colander is? Of course you do."

Over the dinner, which he assured her was unusual to him and delicious, she looked at him several times and then said nothing.

Laurence said, "Please tell me what you're deliberating about. I'm ready for it, whatever it is." He sipped his wine and waited.

"Your *pantxineta* idea got me thinking about having a party just so you could make it. I need to have my kids over for Sunday dinner at some point soon. I usually do that every month or two to appear to be a loving mother but not a needy one. How'd you like to meet them?"

Laurence grimaced, "So soon? Is the vacation over? I'm not ready for that."

"What? To meet them or end the vacation?" Eva looked concerned.

"Both. I like it like this, just how we are. I don't want anyone else around."

"It would just be for a few hours. They come around 4 o'clock and leave by 7. It's a school night." She was almost pleading.

He said nothing. Didn't she get it that when she let them in the vacation bubble would burst? He wanted to hold onto the feeling as long as possible.

"Do you want me to go back to my apartment?" Laurence's tone made it a threat. He wasn't loud but he was fierce.

"No!" Eva was loud and exasperated.

"But I can't be here if your kids are here. What would they think?" Laurence softened his tone to stop her from responding at high volume.

"They aren't going to know you're sleeping here. But what if they did? I'm 70 years old and can do whatever I want." She lowered her voice, but it had not lost any intensity.

"Kids don't want their mother to have sex with anyone, not even their fathers," he said, sounding weary of the conversation.

"Well, they will have to get used to it sooner or later that I have a new life, and that's a good thing. Having an unhappy mother is bad for them."

Laurence was relieved at the lower, less angry tone to her logic but not willing to give up his resentment at the interruption of his life by these kids of hers. "They'll probably want an FBI search on me or something like that."

"I think Google suffices these days," she said.

Eva's disdain stung him so he tried to change the course of the argument by summing up the issues so they could be discussed. "I'm sorry I am not enthusiastic about your party. I just don't feel like I'm ready for the inquisition. The first thing they will ask you is how long you've known me. What can you say but, well, he moved in a week ago but I've known him for a few months?"

"How do you know what my kids will think or feel?" Eva was still annoyed with him.

"Eva, they are human beings even if they are your extraordinary offspring. Books and plays are written on this subject. It never goes easily. They love their mother and feel protective of you. You are strong alone, but the minute a new man appears, you're suddenly vulnerable to robbery and worse."

"Oh dear. I didn't realize this was going to be Pandora's box," she said.

He wasn't going to let her get away with that pretense. "Yes, you did. You were hesitant to bring it up. I could see that. I knew it would be something bad."

"Well, I wish you weren't afraid to meet them. They're good kids. Maybe Antonio is difficult but not the rest of them."

"How many kids do you have?" he said remembering he hadn't asked much at all about them and now was paying the price for not being interested. To not even know how many kids was an appalling lack of manners.

"Four."

"Oh my God. I had no idea. That's a lot of kids," he said.

"Compared to none it is. Compared to six or eight it's not."

"This is not a conversation about family planning or lack of it. This is about me not being ready to embrace four strangers plus spouses and children and them being rightfully curious about who the hell I am." He tried to keep his voice even, but he was feeling exasperated with her.

"Laurence, what do you think is so wrong about you that my kids are going to be upset? You're a highly educated gentleman who conducts himself as a scholar. You can talk to anyone about anything and fit in anywhere."

That was her attempt at changing the course of the conversation and he refused to fall for the compliment. *Let's keep it honest,* he thought. "They are going to see me as an eccentric gold digger."

"Now money is in it! Please let's not make an issue of that."

"So says the woman who has some. I have none. That's a big difference," he said.

"I don't care if you don't have any money. I like you just the way you are. You're perfect for me."

Laurence shook his head, "That is a nice sentiment. I'm glad you feel that way, but I'm sure your children will feel differently about this disparity."

"Here we are having our first argument. I am sorry about that. Let's agree to think about it and let more time go by. It's not like I need to have them next week. Sometime you have to meet them."

Eva was done with the conversation, but he couldn't let it die. "I have one more personal question related to this topic, please."

"All right. What?"

"I notice the phone doesn't ring here. Don't your kids call you?"

"The ringer is turned off so we wouldn't be disturbed by junk calls. The kids know I'm on vacation."

He looked at her and shook his head in disbelief. "You planned this vacation enough to let them know not to call you?"

"I wanted to make a clean break from the normal routine and the office. I thought it was a good idea to be unavailable so they could work things out without even thinking about consulting with me." She was speaking very lowly and calmly, backpedalling like a professional politician.

"When did you tell them?"

"The day you took me out for dinner."

She said it so softly he could barely hear her. "You are a strategic planner! I am so glad I cooperated with your plan," he said caustically. "How long are we on vacation?" He was outraged now.

"A few weeks," she said quietly and looking down at her plate.

"You were that certain I was besotted with you?"

"No, but I was hopeful," she said.

"What was plan B if this funny old man couldn't deliver or you didn't like it?"

"I planned to go to the San Juans by myself. We could still go if you want."

Laurence felt whiplash from that last comment. What cheek to try to jump out of the argument by offering a gift so big it was insulting. He said nothing, trying to filter all the data and trying not to feel lied to, conned or manipulated. He believed her heart was in the right place, but he was mad as hell about the duplicity with her kids and him.

Eva took his hand in hers. "Please don't be angry at me. It sounds worse than it is. I just wanted some options to distance myself from the business and have a chance to explore things with you. If not with you, then to take some time to myself. I think we're doing well here. It feels right between us."

He waited almost a minute to get his emotion and voice in check. She waited patiently, saying nothing. "You are a scary smart woman. I understand what you are saying. I am enjoying being here with you, but you have to understand how stupid I'm feeling right now. It seemed odd to have a phone that didn't ring, no appointments for days, but I was happy it was quiet so I didn't question it. You're playing all of us, me and your kids, like a board game and it's not right while giving lip service as if you were being honest with me. I won't ignore my instincts again. When it doesn't look or sound right I will ask you what's going on.

You may get away with that with your kids, but not me. I like the straight, hard, cold facts every time."

"I wouldn't lie to you about anything important. Try to understand it would have been inappropriate for me to mention to you the vacation time I had put on the calendar. That would have put undue pressure on you and me. I had to let it unfold however it would and see what happened. You very well could have gone home the first day thinking I was too much too soon. That was my first fear." Eva held his gaze throughout this plea.

"You could have been disappointed with me. That was my fear," he said.

"I haven't felt that way even once. Not now either." Eva was pleading again with her voice and her eyes.

He paused again to compose himself and his response. "OK, enough of this conversation. We're all right. I don't want to go home. I'll get over feeling not quite as smart as I think I am. But I want you to be honest with me all the time, not just when you think it's important. I'll try to think positively about all these children of yours that I am not yet ready to meet, even Antonio who can be difficult as you keep saying. What's wrong with Antonio?"

Her voice lightened at the change of subject. "I don't know. His glass is half empty. He's always skeptical and easily angry. I kept hoping he would grow out of it, but he hasn't. I have blamed myself, but the others are so like me, easy to get along with. I really try not to worry about it anymore. I have spent too much time worrying about Antonio."

"OK. Scratch Antonio, that's one less thing to worry about. Let's go sit in the living room. I think I'd like to know more about the vacation in the San Juans you're not taking because of me being here."

They resettled themselves on the couch. "Well, Lummi Island was my first idea. The Willows Inn gets such a good

—
76

write-up for the gardens and the restaurant tasting menu. But it books so far in advance we'd need to happen on someone's last-minute cancellation. I can phone them to see what's available. The value alternative is the Bellwether Hotel in Bellingham with all the benefits of the San Juans without waiting for the ferry to and from. Plus, the room at the Bellwether is a much nicer room with a view for a similar price. Whatever we pick, it's my treat all the way. You must promise to not argue with me about that."

"I am a value type of guy. I promise I'll let you wine me and dine me with a view in the nicest room. Do I have to bring my suit?"

Chapter 8

In the morning they walked over to Laurence's place to repack his suitcase for a trip to Bellingham for a few days. It felt strange to him to go to the underground garage and load their luggage in the trunk of Eva's Audi. Laurence was apprehensive about this trip. He had seldom been on vacation. He preferred relaxing at home. The extravagance of it made him nervous. But she had insisted it was her treat. She was normally frugal, so she said, but this was a special occasion and worth every penny. He thought to himself that everybody has their little economies; some people wash aluminum foil and reuse it repeatedly. Some people save money by booking the owner's suite with their AAA card discount.

The mid-morning traffic on I-5 North was not too congested. Laurence felt strange in the passenger seat, hurtling past the highway commerce interspersed with bits of undeveloped forest. This was one more thing he hadn't done in a long time, go for a drive in a car, and being driven was even more unusual. After Ingrid died he'd sold the house and the car and moved to the apartment on Queen Anne where he had a bus stop across the street and could walk to shopping and culture. It was traumatic to sell and leave the Sunset Park area in Ballard, but he also felt he needed something new to learn to distract him from his exhaustion of caring for her and the future of empty days with nothing to do now that his caretaking job was finished. After a few weeks he hadn't particularly missed either. The house had been Ingrid's parents' house and was too big for one person, plus he needed the money for medical bills and a cushion for his Social Security check. There was no easy or free parking on Queen Anne. Learning Queen Anne had helped him make the transition. The steep avenue became an aerobic program. His journeys to the libraries became his continuing education program. After a few years he felt at home, and the only thing he missed were the Ballard bars he couldn't afford to drink in anymore. It all worked out. Now he was going on vacation with a rich widow who seemed as besotted with him as he was with her. *When life throws you a curve ball you have to try to catch it as best you can*, he counseled himself. *Be calm and pay attention to her. Be appreciative that all these highly unusual things are happening to you.* He pulled his seat belt a bit tighter.

Eva was a confident driver, moving defensively with the traffic flow but a bit fast for his comfort. He couldn't exactly tell how fast she was going as the speedometer was recessed and obscured to him by all the details of the dashboard. There were a lot of lights on that dashboard enhancing the driver's feeling of guiding a powerful machine. It seemed fancy compared to his Volvo, which had been old when he sold it.

"You get many speeding tickets?" he said.

"Not too many. Am I making you nervous?" She turned to look at him with her eyebrows raised.

"No, you're a good driver. There's the usual number of idiots on the road. No change there."

"When were you last in Bellingham?" she said.

"I don't remember. I knew a few old pubs and parks from the late 1970s when some friends ran or rowed in the Ski to Sea Race. I doubt I'll recognize anything but the parks. It will be nice to explore. How about you?"

"It'll be new for both of us. Years ago, once or twice we rented a vacation cabin near Chuckanut Drive. I took the kids hiking around Mount Baker. Whatcom County is on my list to get to know better in my new life. I chose it because of the great reviews of the Bellwether and the Willows Inn, but there's much more to it with the university culture."

Laurence said, "I don't have any experience at it, but I don't think I'm a fan of the long tasting menu. Three hours of eating and drinking is too much for me. This old body doesn't need it. I think it's tough on the palate as well. The chef has got to work too hard to make the courses at the end stand out."

"Have you noticed much change in your palate over the years?"

"I think it is reduced, but it's still better than average. Don't tell anyone, but no matter what Drew says, I am not a professionally trained taster. I'm a good amateur. My taste memory is my strong suit. I seldom forget a flavor whereas I struggle for words sometimes."

"I haven't noticed you struggle for words." Eva said and looked concerned.

"Well, I do. Do you?" he said.

"Yes," she said.

"I haven't noticed it even once," he said.

"Great. Another indication we're not old yet. Look! There's the first view of the Skagit Valley. I love this valley."

They drove into La Conner, and both noted right away how upscale the main shopping and dining street was and how many art galleries were open. The sidewalks were full of tourists.

"Why don't we look for a back road into Whatcom County from Skagit County? I bet we can start from here," Eva said.

"Do you have a map?" he asked.

"Of course." Eva pressed a button on her console and a digital map appeared that soon centered in on La Conner. "Isn't that something? I love GPS when you need it."

"I didn't realize you had all that science and service in this car," he said.

"I seldom turn it on. I find it annoying around town. Right now it is excellent."

Eva pulled over into a public parking lot near the visitor's center. "This is so great for me to show you something about technology! You start by pushing this button and it knows where you are, and then you enter the destination or a part of it. You can scroll down. It suggests possible destinations to select. Isn't that wonderful that so you don't have to type it all in?"

He looked at her and shook his head smiling, "I love being your pupil. How did you learn it?"

"My kids, of course. They know how to operate everything. They don't even have to learn it. They look at it and know how to do it. It's incredible."

The simulated voice of a British man began with "turn left in ten feet" and off they drove toward a country road far from the main highway. Eva was in the high spirits of a road trip that was taking its first detour. Laurence tried to feel her excitement for the adventure instead of his apprehension about doing something so new. The farmland stretched around them as far as they could see. It seemed to be their private road for the day. Eva drove slower than she had on the highway with no competitors for premium lane space to egg her on. They talked about the crops and the farming economy of the area, which was improving due to new farms being formed by migrant labor who were becoming landowners. The community was working together in a harmonious way, which was so unusual and refreshing. Flat agricultural land soon became curving coastal forest and mountains as the shady Chuckanut

Drive revealed the blue Puget Sound water. The GPS man had no trouble finding Bellingham or the Bellwether Inn.

The front doorman and the desk clerk greeted them warmly as though they had been waiting for them to arrive. Eva gave him a credit card and filled out the registration form. The clerk handed the key to the bellboy and said, "Please take Mr. and Mrs. Russo to the owner's suite."

Laurence looked startled for a moment and then smiled and took her elbow to follow the young man with the brass luggage cart who tried to chat with them all the way to the door about their drive and vacation. With a flourish he opened the door and let them enter first. They stood in the center of a large room with a king-size bed and a sitting area complete with a couch and a loveseat and surveyed the 270-degree view of the water and the marina.

Eva turned to the bellboy and said, "This will do nicely. Would you get us some ice please?"

When he left the room with the ice bucket Laurence bowed formally. "Madame President, I am glad you're satisfied with your accommodations. What are you going to do with the ice?"

"Employees like to earn their tips. I always ask for ice. In this case, I have Champagne to chill." She opened her handbag to get the tip ready.

He smiled and shook his head, "Traveling with a president is quite an experience. I have so much to learn. I never knew about the ice." He approached the balcony for a better view, "Shall I open the balcony door?"

Eva said, "The young man will do it when he gets back with the ice. Let's just admire the view until he gets everything arranged."

When the young man had performed all his welcoming tasks with the luggage, the ice, the television and window shades and had collected his tip, they were alone holding hands on the balcony. Eva said, "Do you like it?"

"Of course. More importantly, do you?"

"Yes, it meets my expectations from the photos on the web page. Internet photos can be so deceiving. The service is as it should be, excellent. You are handsome and charming, so I can't ask for anything else." She leaned into his body and put her head on his shoulder.

"So, what happens next on your fantasy vacation?" he said.

"We put the Champagne on to chill, go for a walk around the marina path and have lunch. How does that work for you?"

"Very well. What about after lunch?"

"A nap? Champagne? Champagne and a nap? It's flexible."

"I'm feeling very flexible. Let's go for a walk and see our new neighborhood."

They fell into a pattern of having coffee in the room before walking miles in the morning exploring the city and a different park every day, sometimes two. There were so many parks to choose from. They ate lunch out and came back for a nap and reading in the afternoon. Around 5:30 they went down to the terrace of the Lighthouse Bar and Grill in the hotel and ordered happy hour wine with small plates of oysters, shrimp and wild salmon or fruit and cheese. Afterward they did the marina walk 1.3 miles to Zuanich Park. To be outside most of the day surrounded by the Northwest colors of sea and the sky was exhilarating. They slept very well at night.

Laurence caressed a hipbone early in the morning and said, "Eva, according to my scientific measurements, I do believe you are losing weight on this vacation. This bone is evidence."

"That's always good news but hard to believe given the great food we've been eating every day."

"I think I'm getting used to eating out. Dangerous habit," he said.

"I'm not ready to go home yet, but I'm beginning to want to go a little farther down the road. What do you think?"

"Nobody but my bus driver will be wondering where I am."

"Why don't I go look online and see what we can find?"

"I'm getting very used to your presidential way of doing things. I'll just lie here and give you an occasional weather report. The sunrise is partly cloudy right now."

Eva got up and found her iPad on the desk where it had been for days used only for park and restaurant research and got back in bed.

"Please don't look at your email," Laurence said.

"I'll look for the cottage first."

"One look at email and I predict we'll be headed back to Seattle today instead of going on down the road."

"No. There isn't anything that would make me go back when we could go forward," Eva said.

"Business, your kids, births, deaths, divorces, all could make you change your mind."

"No, my mind is made up. I want to go forward. Don't you?"

He nodded in agreement. Eva started reading out loud descriptions of rentals available that day that had a view. "How about Lopez Island?" she said.

"You'll have to wait for that pesky ferry from Anacortes."

"This one sounds really good, and it has a terrace with a hot tub with a view of the sound. I like the way this one looks though, perfect for lounging in front of the fire and a short walk to the village. Look at the view from the kitchen window! That's the view for you."

"Your boy-toy here will get up and go anyplace you want. But I want you to know that I think I am experiencing sloth. Not really feeling like I need to or want to move at all. Isn't that sloth?" he said.

"No. You are merely feeling contented, and it's a revelation."

"Lopez is very quiet. Are you sure you won't miss the city lights and restaurants?" he said.

Eva said, "Not if you're cooking for me. We're all relaxed now after being here a few days and it will be easy to do even less than what we've been doing."

"I don't think I could get more relaxed, but you are my vacation expert."

Eva said, "What about groceries? Should we shop here? The island selection might be minimal and more expensive."

"Or better quality there. Look up farm stands and a name with a horse in it on Lopez and see if you can find their address or phone number," he said.

Do you think we can make a 12:30 ferry?" she said.

"Sure. It won't take *you* an hour to drive to Anacortes. We have plenty of time. There's no hurry. We can stop at the Co-Op on Forest Street on our way out of town for the wine and coffee. I don't think the farm will have that. Before we leave, do a search for a granary. If anyone is making flour on the island, I'd like to try it."

Chapter 9

Networking was the core of doing business in the art world. Drew routinely asked every artist he talked to what they had seen recently that was noteworthy and followed up by learning about it. Any friend who recommended an artist to Drew would alert the artist to reach out to Drew immediately or be expecting his call.

As often as they could bear to do it, artists ran marketing programs by calling or sending requests to galleries to have their work examined. Typically the artist would have studied the galleries to see what stylistic fit there might be with previous exhibitions, mentioned as part of the pitch. Drew and Julia went together and individually to all sorts of art fairs and events where artists were showing looking for fresh talent. They attended art school exhibitions and took notes on graduates who seemed promising. When they felt the time was right for the artist, they reintroduced themselves and set up a studio visit and a gallery visit to get to know each other better. For the Basque show they began by splitting the gallery's list of artists and calling them to see if they knew any Basque artists. That strategy yielded little.

Julia turned out to be the gold miner of artists. The Basque clubs started calling her back. It took more time than she would have thought for the local person to check around and get back to her, but just about every club had an artist or two. Even the clubs that didn't have an artist called back, which showed extra courtesy. She then began calling the lists of artists to ask for information about them, including websites, photos, places they had exhibited. She learned from the first name she called and each one after that the artist thought it was a crank call, a practical joke or an attempt at identity theft. They asked her how did she get their number? No one believed a gallery in Seattle was contacting them to consider their art for a Basque exhibition. Why Basque? Why them?

Julia and Drew were surprised and flabbergasted at this reaction. It was hard to believe these artists were unaware of the gallery's long-term reputation. They realized they needed to deal quickly with this skeptical reaction and figure out how to best present the gallery's ambition with the show and gain the artist's trust. They decided that trying to do business far away from Seattle required a special invitation that provided a history of the gallery as a successful business offering the artist a rare opportunity to find a new audience and make money. Hopefully that would be enough to make them comfortable enough to talk more. Drew and Julia created a lively invitation that announced the unique group show of American Basque artists who would be the commercial focus of a cultural display for entertainment and education. A brief history of the gallery and artists represented referred the receiver back to their website for more details. On the flip side was a small form to return that said the artist invited would like to learn more and agreed to the concept of a group consignment show with a 50/50 split on all works sold.

Armed with the invitation and a concise sales pitch for the gallery, Julia called each artist name given by the clubs and asked if they would like to receive an invitation to a group show and got a mailing address. When she received the interest card back, she and Drew called them for more information about their work and asked what other Basque artists they knew who might like to receive an invitation. She and Drew began methodically working through the master folder of names and information, looking at their work and creating a second folder of the most promising looking artists for Drew to drill down further. The artists needed to know how sincere he was in reaching out to them to become familiar with their work and how powerful his ties in the Seattle community were to expose them to a large audience and sell their work. He wanted to talk with each one about their vision and learn more about them, their sales history, what pieces they would be able to send for the exhibit and what price they expected to receive. For a few young ones who hadn't worked with a gallery before, he had to explain the business end of the gallery's share and the salesman's commission. The whole process had to be done carefully and sensitively to develop trust. And because he was viewing the art online, it was also important that there be no misunderstandings when he actually received the art and it was worth more or less than had been discussed on the telephone. The artist must understand Drew would set the final price and they had to agree to all the requirements to show their piece in the exhibit.

The clubs on the East Coast yielded artists doing contemporary work. Classically trained in Europe and located in the New York area because it was an international art center, these artists had little in common philosophically or stylistically with the western artists. Drew and Julia deliberated about creating a new category for these East Coasters that would identify them as a group and might be a selling point. These artists were veterans of the galley business and were pragmatic enough to quickly say to him after hearing about the exhibit, "If you think you can sell it, I'll ship it."

Now that he had artists to talk to and think about Drew began to feel this Basque business had the potential to be a distinctive success for him and the gallery. What could be better for his reputation than to create a one-of-a-kind exhibition? The very nature of it might attract even more people who had never been there before and get them excited. He frequently strategized how to get the food freaks and the performance lovers to come see art while they ate and drank wine. The third group he spied on the horizon included the travelers, the culture seekers, and the students of history. He'd never had a chance at attracting them, but if they had the money to travel, they could be buyers. Where would these travelers hear about his show? He needed to create publicity to be published not only in the Basque communities but in the urban art news of the surrounding states to announce this show. What a sensational failure it would be if nobody came to see it. Then he probably would have to close his doors out of shame.

As he sorted the photo images sent in by the artists, the main categories slowly formed as western landscapes, ranching and farming, heritage and abstract art. Fish were the stars of the animal world over cows, horses and dogs until sheep nudged them aside when he discovered that Sun Valley, Idaho, sponsored a popular festival every October called the Trailing of the Sheep with a parade, sheep dog trials and "paint outs" of the local shepherds and an opportunity to sell paintings of sheep to the thousands who attended every year. Drew thought the winning art was surprisingly good and he and Julia acquired some more artists' names. An abundance of sheep was somehow fitting for a Basque show, as shepherding was the only job Basques could get in America (or elsewhere) around the turn of the century. The job required no language skills. The Sun Valley crowd distinctly appealed to Drew and Julia because of the high quality galleries doing business there. They would prepare some special reach out to the galleries there hoping to encourage a visit to Seattle to see the show, just as they had with the galleries around the Basque cultural centers.

Drew managed his mood swings with meditation in the morning and a martini at night. He reminded himself several times a day that taking a risk like this was good for his character. Life had been safe of late and it was bad for a man not to be challenging his abilities. The current show in the gallery was decorative with Northwest naturals, landscapes in watercolors and oil by three local artists. Not exciting art but popular with interior designers and women who owned nice houses. He made sure to put a show like this on every year or so to support the local artists and the buyers. These were regular customers that he kept meticulous notes on, as he did all customers. He knew what they bought and where they hung it and any preferences for colors and subjects. With all big purchases he volunteered to hang the picture personally so it would be shown in its best light. It was very useful to see the house to take more notes of styles and colors and the potential for future sales. He and Julia enjoyed the distraction from the Basque work to talk with these hunters with fabric swatches and hear about their color schemes and room dimensions. They were earnest in the quest for the perfect piece to go above a mantle, make a bedroom special or create a focal point in a dining room. If nothing worked for them in the current show, he told them he would keep his eye out and give them a call if he saw something right for them. Flirting with all of them improved his mood. They loved that feeling of having a handsome professional watching out for them. Of course they would stay in touch and visit again soon. It was calming to have daily visitors, mostly women, stop in to take a look at what he had for sale. This was how business got done. Slowly inventory was being sold and the gallery would look fine until the new show began. It had to be staged for the opening on the First Thursday Art Walk in January. The deadline was firm.

Julia began working up ideas for the advertisement that would promote the Basque exhibit. She liked a shepherd in a beret his dog at his side, standing before an easel painting his flock in the mountains. Drew's favorite so far was inspired by the Old World travel poster styles with a male dancer in a Basque white and red costume poised in mid air with his toes pointed. If everyone kept working hard, all would be well. Drew believed that most of the time. He was living more easily with the moments when doubt hovered over him. He waited for them to pass.

Looking for art reviews in regional newspapers he found the most astonishing photographs of aspen trees taken in remote locations throughout the west with their trunks decoratively carved by sheepherders. Drew and Julia poured over all the photos and the articles about them. These carvings were the diaries of the lonely sheepherders. Photographers and academics were fascinated with deciphering the carvings and documenting the words, symbols and graphics. Basque provinces and names were thought to be the heritage of the carver. In some cases it seemed one person left a message for the universe, which was answered by another person. As the trees aged, the etchings in them became more pronounced. Ultimately they would be lost forever when the tree died and decomposed. Drew thought these carvings were poetic and piercing, the desire of the human being to express himself. He contacted several photographers who had made studies of the trees and decided he would show two photos, carved and uncarved, by a Basque artist who specialized in aspens. Trees became a new category. Drew and Julia experienced the joy of discovery, that rare uplifting event that would keep them in the art business forever. It was easy to make a deal with this professional photographer who was thrilled to be selling originals and not prints that were available online at reduced prices. It was a great day in the art gallery business.

"Why don't we close early and go out for a drink?" Drew said.

"Sure," Julia said. "I don't have any plans until midnight. What are you in the mood for?"

"Let's go to Pioneer Square and do some window shopping."

They strolled around Occidental Park and 1st Avenue South discussing what was displayed in the windows of their competitors. Maybe it was because of securing the arborglyphs, but they weren't jealous of anything they saw. Sitting in an old bar having a cocktail, they saw some of the competition. Drew waved at them. One owner came over to chat and hear what was new with Drew and his muse. Julia said nothing but struck a pose for him and Drew launched into the amusing highlights of the hunt to bring in 30 artists never shown before in Seattle. He quite enjoyed this first time describing the Basque show to a peer.

"You're crazier than I thought, Drew. Why make such work for yourself?" the man said.

"It's the challenge that sucks me in. I can't resist. It's going to be amazing or abysmal. I'll hope you'll come by and have a look when we open," Drew said, grinning. "What's new with you?"

The answer should have been "Not much" since Drew had just seen what was in his window, but instead it was spun to be exciting and attracting crowds.

"That's sounds great," Drew said. "We'll have to come by and have a look soon."

When they were alone again, he said, "We should get out more often. That was like a free radio advertisement for our show. I bet he tells ten people before tomorrow's over."

"I love how you can tell the story now for laughs. Big improvement, Drew. Where shall we go next?" said Julia.

"You want to go to my place where the parking and the drinks are free?" he said.

"Sure."

After parking the car in the underground garage of Drew's building near the Market they stopped in a Thai restaurant and ordered some food to take out. Julia loved the green papaya salad. Drew ordered the Isaan steak salad with lemongrass. Julia immediately made herself at home in the apartment taking off her high heels, and they sat down at the small table to eat.

"I don't have any of your favorite beverage. What would you like?" Drew said.

"How about water with a splash of vinegar?" she said.

Drew shook his head, "Another abominable combination. I'll get the vinegar out. You make it yourself so it will be perfect. What are you thinking about for this evening?" he said.

"Whatever you want to do is fine with me. I'm happy to hang here with you if you want company. If you don't, I will go after dinner. Like I said, I might go out later. There are some people meeting at a bar in Ballard for music. They will call me when they get there, and I'll decide if I want to go or not. It might be fun but I may feel like doing something else then."

"No commitments in advance?" Drew said.

"Why would you do that? You don't know what you'll feel like until it's time."

"No one cares that you can't make up your mind until the last minute?" Drew said.

"Of course not." She looked at him as though she couldn't understand why he would ask that.

He considered the ways young people dealt with each other and wondered how they ever did anything if no one made plans in advance. He wasn't sure what he felt like doing this evening now that he thought about it. There were books in progress he was enjoying reading and an article on art trends he was writing that he should complete. He was enjoying Julia's company and wanted her to stay. Lately he'd been alone with his anxiety about the Basque show. Making a dinner date to inflict his worries on someone wouldn't be fun for them. Not talking about his troubles would be hard for him. Julia was easy to be with day or night. She understood the issues and didn't mind discussing them again. She didn't talk too much and was articulate when she did talk. He usually felt he knew what was on her mind. Although he hadn't been invited, driving to Ballard at midnight didn't seem that appealing to him.

"Do you think I would enjoy the music?" he said as though he might be interested.

"It's techno. Do you like that?"

"Hum a few bars for me," he said.

Julia jumped up and started dancing like a robot while she hummed some discordant high and low squeaks.

He laughed and said, "Not tonight, maybe another time."

When they were finished eating she moved over to the leather couch arranging her feet underneath her for the best view of the wall holding several good pieces of modern art. Drew sat opposite her in a leather chair and put his feet up on the ottoman. If there had been any daylight left, he could have seen Elliott Bay out the window behind Julia's head. They sat silently. He was enjoying thinking of his interaction with the competitors earlier and the comfort of being at home with his art. He was proud of his collection and how he had staged it in this apartment. He had spent quite a bit of time on it, and it was pleasing to him. The style was minimalist with each element carefully chosen for a peaceful haven in which he could relax and contemplate. Julia looked serene and he could tell she was thinking about the art she was looking at. She got something more out of it every time she studied it. He felt the same way. Good art is worth the investment for years of pleasure.

Julia broke the silence saying, "How'd you like to watch a movie on Netflix?"

"You need to take a break from art?"

"Yes. You know it's fun for me because I don't have a television."

Drew said, "You pick something. I'll make us a fresh round of cold water. Do you want more vinegar in it?

"Skip the vinegar. How about *Lost in Translation*?"

"Again?" he said.

"Yes, I love it."

"OK," he said.

The television was on a low chest of drawers in the bedroom close enough to the bed to create a good viewing experience. Drew kicked off his shoes. They settled in propped up with pillows on top of the bedspread against the upholstered headboard each with a glass of water on the bedside tables and the lights on dim. He liked the film about the famous actor, played by Bill Murray, far from home and family in every way, making an advertisement in Japan and the lovely young girl, Scarlet Johansen, whose husband had abandoned her in a Tokyo hotel while he worked elsewhere with a vivacious associate. They were both jet lagged, lonely and trying to cope with their personal situations that weren't going well.

Julia seemed to identify with the young heroine although she'd never been married or abandoned that he knew of. He thought Julia enjoyed her solitude as much as he did. She was free to paint on her days off without negotiating with anyone, which was important to her. She had friends, a social life and a sex life but was not too seriously attached to anyone, which she also thought was important. Her art was her first priority, and she guarded her freedom to pursue it. Nothing got in the way of her painting except maybe shopping for shoes. Drew could certainly identify with that. He zealously guarded his freedom. He didn't have to put too much effort into his social life because people, mostly women, came by the gallery to visit with him and ended up spending the evening out to dinner or having sex here. If he wanted company, it was easy to call someone to join him for dinner. Maybe he wasn't managing his life that differently from Julia's crowd. His last live-in relationship had ended disastrously like all the others with tears and screaming. She had wanted more than he had to give. He had learned to be more sensitive and honest and a better listener but ultimately they all wanted a deep devotion that wasn't available from him. They thought they wanted honesty until they heard it and then learned it wasn't what they wanted to hear.

He woke up at 2 a.m. Julia was gone. The lights and the television were turned off. She was always thoughtful that way. He got undressed and went back to sleep happy he was not in a bar in Ballard dancing like a robot. He wondered if he had seen any of the movie.

Chapter 10

Waiting in line for the ferry, the view of the evergreen forests, snow-capped mountains and smooth blue water under partly cloudy skies was worthy of a postcard. Lots of birds were fishing. People abandoned their cars to walk down to the water's edge. Children were whooping it up, skipping stones on the water. Laurence watched the ferry approaching in the distance and then blocking the view of the mountains when it arrived at the dock. Everyone got back into the cars. He looked around carefully at everything he could see, ending with Eva sitting next to him already on the alert to drive forward when instructed by the ferry staff. She turned to look at him with her eyes wide with pleasure or anticipation. She was so competent at everything she did. No wasted movements. He loved watching her drive the car or study a menu. He decided what he was feeling was exceedingly lucky. He committed the feeling to memory promising himself to remember exactly the color of the sky, the temperature of the air coming through the open window, how many birds and her profile facing forward.

They walked around the upper open deck of the ferry during the hour-long ride to Lopez, feeling the San Juan air permeating skin, lungs and hair. The air in Bellingham had seemed so fresh and cool. This air was even more so. They agreed it was a great idea to give up the palace on the marina and come out here. They would ride more ferries in the future. Maybe they would ride to Bainbridge Island and back because that was so easily done from Pier 52 in Seattle about every thirty minutes. Making plans for the future also gave him a strange sensation. It seemed easy to be talking with her about doing things in the future such as a ferry ride for lunch. But conceptually it gave him a pause. What exactly was going on here? Two old people were having fun for the first time in years. Now that he was getting used to being — and having — a constant companion — and the expense not making him nervous, he could almost feel the vacation was well deserved, for both of them. *Deserve* was a slippery concept. He had worked hard all his life. He had suffered loneliness and despair after the trauma of Ingrid's death. Frolicking with Eva was fun, and he was enjoying it. *Stop feeling guilty about taking pleasure in this unexpected circumstance,* he told himself several times a day. Who knows how long this will last?

The road as they left the ferry displayed wide waiting lanes for cars queuing for the return ferry to the mainland but little commerce, and it became even more rural as they followed the directions to the farm. From the last bend onto a dirt and grass road they could see a big barn and a smaller adjacent building, both looking sturdy but old with the wood weathered pale grey. A hand-painted wooden sign hung outside the building announcing the name of the farm in a quaint country script and logo. There were no other vehicles or people about. They went inside the wide open entryway and saw a row of standing freezers each labeled with a piece of standard white paper taped to the door: "pork," "lamb," "poultry." Another wall was lined with double bins of all sorts of vegetables and a U-shaped row of double bins to make more efficient use of the space. A refrigerator with a clear glass door displayed lettuces, herbs and greens in plastic bags. A small open counter space at the end held a scale, a small metal box, pencils and a small paper receipt book. On the wall above was a big chalkboard with the products and prices.

Eva was dumbstruck, surveying the scene carefully. "This is phenomenal. I don't know when I last saw a rural farmer trust the customer to make change. Let me get the shopping bags out of the trunk."

He laughed at her as he put one pound packages of frozen meat in the cloth bag, boneless leg of lamb, ground lamb, pork sausage and bacon. She was writing very neatly on the small receipt pad. He said, "You are showing your business skills. One arugula, one butter lettuce, one kale, basil, rosemary and oregano. Add four tomatoes, two onions, two garlics. Do you want Yukon or sweet potatoes? How about some eggplant?"

She carefully weighed everything that needed weighing and noted the math clearly in the column. They arranged one bag with the green vegetables on top of the frozen meat to keep them cool on the rest of the ride. One more bag held the root vegetables and tomatoes on top.

"It's not enough money. We should give them extra for the shopping experience," Eva said after she had put $40 in the metal box, which was full of dollars and coins. She didn't take any change out. "We will be eating like kings for days. We should stop here on our way home and load up for winter!"

Back on the country road Eva said, "How do you know about this place?"

"Amy told me about it. She drives out here once a year with a girlfriend when it's butchering time to buy lamb, which is supposed to be the best of the best."

The cottage garden had no roses but it didn't lack for blooming plants and an open view west toward San Juan Island. Situated on a bluff above the road, the views from the white stone terrace were open to the north too with the village of Lopez in easy walking distance. Laurence went right to work on the sandwich by defrosting the bacon for a minute in the microwave while he found a cast iron skillet. Eva went out on the terrace to admire the view again and unfurl the striped umbrella. She sat down at the wrought iron table with four chairs and breathed deeply. He could see her shoulders rising and falling rhythmically from the kitchen window and knew what she was doing. She was feeling grateful and so was he. He was happy to be along for the ride and to be with her wherever it was.

While the bacon cooked in the skillet he toasted the bread and layered it with lettuce, tomato slices and hot pieces of bacon directly from the skillet. Who needed mayonnaise when there was bacon fat to flavor the bread? He touched his finger to one of the hot slices and tasted it.

"You're going to love this bacon. It has the most pork meat flavor but the least seasoning I've ever had in my life. It's naturally sweet, not salty or smoky." He put the plates down on the table for four where she was waiting.

She took a bite of the sandwich. "This might be the best BLT sandwich I ever had."

"The tomatoes are up to your standard?"

"As a tomato connoisseur from the Mediterranean to the Pacific Northwest, I pronounce them right up there with my most memorable. You can taste the sun and the local soil, nice acidity, not too sweet. Italian farmers might quibble with me, but terroir is terroir. It's also perfectly ripe for eating."

Laurence said, "I had planned to make a little fresh sauce with them for the eggplant and ground meat, but it will be hard to cook them at all. Maybe I'll just squeeze them and dice the flesh and gently toss it up with hot meat."

"You never stop thinking about the best way to handle the goods, do you?"

"No. Why should I?" he said.

"You're right. Don't stop thinking about it."

The next morning, they explored the village wine shop, bakery, bookstore, markets, thrift shop, galleries and gift shops. They sat outside the bakery with coffee and shared one of the famous cinnamon buns. They didn't really need anything, but it was fun to look in the windows and absorb the flavor of Lopez at a retail level. It was all low key and agreeable as were the merchants they spoke with. They inquired about the location of the granary they had researched but couldn't get a specific address. Laurence wrote down the directions. He was excited about baking bread. On a shelf of delicacies they discovered a can of sweet powdered pimenton, an important Basque spice, and a jar of roasted sweet red peppers so he could begin trying some Basque recipes.

Inspired by one of the Basque cookbooks he'd been reading, Laurence made a rub with the fresh rosemary and garlic for the leg of lamb that would marinate overnight. He made a piperade sauce to go with it that the Basques loved serving with many things by pureeing a few roasted peppers seasoned with a teaspoon of pimienton. The new flavor profile pleased him. He baked lightly seasoned eggplant slices in the oven to concentrate the flavor, coarsely chopped them and added them to the hot ground lamb he had sautéed with garlic. Served in a small soup bowl with chopped parsley on top it was a perfect light lunch. The Basques probably would have served it with rice, but it was good all on its own. Eva was delighted with it and said it reminded her of her vacation in Biarritz. He liked what he was learning from reading the Basque cookbooks. The pimienton offered a quick way to create Basque flavoring. It was good to be cooking again.

Eva curled up on one of the white couches in front of the fireplace.

"May I bring you your book?" Laurence said.

"Thank you. You are working way too hard to have cooked the lunch and bring the book!"

"It's totally my pleasure." Laurence went in to the bedroom to retrieve the books from the nightstands and settled into the couch. "After becoming accustomed to giant couches, it's going to be difficult to sit in those hard library chairs designed to keep you awake." He regretted saying it the moment it was out of his mouth.

Eva rubbed his feet. "When I have such a comfortable couch, even bigger than this one, why sit in a hard chair?"

"A man needs a reading room of his own. You wouldn't want me to take up space in your living room every day. I'm not that decorative."

"Yes, I would. You give my living room a high style lived-in look, very desirable. The furniture manufacturers try to achieve it in advertisements with a small fluffy dog sleeping or a half-naked young woman. I'll submit a photo of you sleeping with a book on your chest to be considered for the next ad campaign. I bet you would sell more couches than the dog or the woman."

"I'm flattered you see an aesthetic in an old dude relaxing."

"Beyond aesthetics, it would be a status symbol to have a good looking, white-haired man permanently ensconced on my Italian leather."

"Oh, I don't know what to say about that. That's very high thinking — and high praise." Laurence couldn't see her face from where he was and wasn't exactly sure if they were having fun or if she was casually leading up to a serious conversation he didn't want to have. He was so immersed in the moment he was unable to think about the future and certainly did not want to bring it up in conversation.

"Am I frightening you?" Eva asked.

"Yes."

"I'm sorry to intrude into the vacation bubble you want so badly to maintain. I can't help it. I'm enjoying myself immensely, and I do think about what will happen when the vacation is over. It's impossible *not* to think about it," Eva said.

"Please, be reasonable," Laurence said. "You and I are a new combination. It's only been about two weeks since I took you out to dinner. It's delightful. It's extraordinary. But I feel it would be premature to discuss making plans for the future."

"Neither one of us has unlimited time, so why not make the most of it?"

Laurence couldn't think of anything to say and was worried he was insulting her with silence. Then she stood up and before she could get away he reached out with his left hand to grab her hand as it passed close to his and gently pulled her down to sit beside him. He kissed her hand, one of his habits that he hoped spoke volumes when he couldn't find the right words. "I too am immensely enjoying being with you. I don't have to be in a rose-covered cottage overlooking the sea to have that feeling. I have it walking on the avenue or riding the bus or cooking in your kitchen. Don't you know that?"

"Sometimes."

"I'm sorry I'm not communicating enough to make you feel that way all the time," he said.

"Time should be on our side here. We're both experienced enough to know what we feel and think," she said.

"Time is definitely *not* our side. I could die tomorrow and it wouldn't surprise anybody," Laurence said.

"You're delusional about your age."

"It's a miracle to me at my age that I am carrying on like a teenager with you. How long can that go on?" He was emphatic.

"Let's don't waste any precious time we could have together by being cautious or stubborn," Eva said.

—

"You are so certain of yourself, so confident that your first instinct is the path to choose. You're a natural leader. I am not. I was trained to be cautious, examine every angle and to be stubborn if I didn't believe the data supported the plan. We can't change that about ourselves."

Eva stood up and removed her hand from his. "You are making me mad and making me sad because you do not acknowledge what I am saying even though I am saying it as clearly as I can." She stood up and walked to stand in front of the fireplace with her back to him.

Laurence felt beaten but knew he needed to stay in the game, so he sat up for a stronger presentation and hoped being upright would help him gather his wits to consider carefully what he might offer her that would be true, not false just to buy peace. Peace too cheaply bought seldom lasted. What might possibly buy him some time? "What would make you feel that I do understand what you're saying?"

"What would be the right amount of time to wait for you to be sure what you are feeling now is true?" she asked without emotion and looked at him, waiting for his response.

He exhaled deeply and shook his head. "That's very difficult. You are asking me for absolutes when it's impossible to define them. Please, take this conversation back to where it belongs, to the part where sometimes you don't think I care enough about you. That's something I can do better right away, no waiting." Laurence stood up and walked over to her in front of the fireplace and put his hands on her shoulders and looked into her eyes. "You are an amazing woman who thrills me every day just by being near me. Even though we've only been together a short while, I can't imagine being without you now."

"See? That's how I feel. I don't want to be without you, and I want you to feel that way too."

"I do."

"So why not talk about the future and what we might do together?"

He shook his head. "I'm so involved in the minute-to-minute feeling I can't envision tomorrow, much less next week or month or year. All these feelings are momentous for me. I've tried to describe to you how I feel like I've been sleepwalking. I've been isolated for years with no contact with anyone. Now I'm overwhelmed by the emotions I feel all day and night surging inside me every which way. Please, come and sit down with me."

"Are you feeling dizzy?" she said.

"Yes."

"The conversation is making you dizzy?" Eva asked.

"The emotions and the effort to articulate," Laurence said.

They sat back down on the couch facing the fireplace and held hands.

"Do you have heart trouble?" Eva said.

"No, not the bad kind. I have the good kind."

"You don't mean cholesterol do you? What kind of heart trouble is good?" she said.

"The hopelessly in love with you kind," said Laurence.

"Oh, it's so nice to hear you say that. I love you too, so much." She put her head on his shoulder.

He had no idea what to say now. He hoped he had said all he needed to by declaring himself, out loud, to be in love with her and even surprised himself with it.

After a few minutes went by she said, "OK, I'll take that as assurance, almost a commitment from you, and try to restrain myself from wanting to plan the future today in such a way that we'll always be together, no matter what."

"Thank you," he said and was truly grateful she didn't pursue it any further.

In the evening they were happy to get in bed early to read and enjoy the intimacy of sharing the dark together in each other's arms. During the day they took long walks and drives around the island to see the viewpoints. They had a visit with the man who owned the granary and milled the flour the ancient way. Laurence bought several pounds to experiment with, starting right away by making a loaf of bread. They both thought the bread was excellent. While they ate it, they discussed coming back for another visit to Lopez. The cottage was rented to someone else the next day. They decided to go back to the city rather than move on to another place. They couldn't resist stopping at the farm stand to buy more of everything on their way to catch the late afternoon ferry back to the mainland.

"Farewell, Lopez. It's been wonderful." Eva waved at the island from the top deck of the ferry. They sat on a bench to watch it diminish in the view all the way to Anacortes. They were happy to sit quietly and hold hands soaking up the last moments of the San Juan experience.

Chapter 11

It was almost 9 p.m. when they reached the door of Eva's apartment laden down with bags of produce and luggage. When Eva opened the door she gasped, "The lights are on! I didn't leave the lights on!"

"I turned them on, Mother." Eva's son Antonio appeared from the kitchen. "Where have you been?"

"What are you doing in my house?" She put down her packages down on the couch.

"I came to see if you were dead. I've left you 20 messages on the phone and email and you haven't responded to any of them. Where have you been?"

"Did you forget I went on vacation for two weeks?" She was annoyed.

"I didn't think you were really going anywhere. But it's been two weeks and that's why I came to check. Who's this with you?"

"Antonio, this is outrageous. If you came home from vacation and found me in your house you would have a fit." Eva voice was getting louder.

"There would be no reason for you to be in my house," he said.

"Exactly! So you understand how I feel right now."

"Mother, I didn't think you would be mad about me being concerned."

Laurence tried to recede into the wall by the front door. He felt awful for her to be involved in this ugly this scene and miserable for himself as a witness.

"Antonio, you didn't think at all. If you had thought about it, you would have come to the conclusion that when I got back from vacation I would return your call."

"So, who are *you*?" Antonio turned his attention on Laurence who had been standing still while Eva and Antonio had moved closer together in the center of the living room as the volume of their voices got louder. She sounded so angry Laurence was speechless. He was considering putting his things down so he could shake hands but before he could, Eva turned to look at Laurence.

"This is my friend Laurence Hansen." Then she turned back to her son. "We are tired from traveling. I am sure you understand that after a long day. I will phone you in the morning."

"Where have you been?"

"You're not listening to me. Please, say goodnight. I will phone you in the morning to discuss all these things." Eva approached to touch his elbow to escort him to the door.

He angrily shook his elbow away before she could and moved farther from her. "Now you are outrageous — you showing me to the door because I was concerned."

She looked at Antonio with such cold eyes Laurence was stunned. "You and I are done here."

Laurence stood still, holding a big bag of vegetables and a suitcase. He couldn't believe his eyes that this drama was going on with the front door open and so loud he expected the neighbors to come out of their doors to see what was happening.

Antonio met his mother's stare with one of his own and Laurence could see the wheels turning in Antonio's brain as he made the decision to drop the conversation.

Eva grabbed the doorknob holding the door wide open and motioning for Antonio to come through. "Good night, Antonio."

He shot Laurence a hostile glance and walked angrily though the door without saying another word. Eva closed the door quietly and locked the dead bolt.

"I am so sorry that happened. What an awful welcome home." She took the bag of groceries from his arm and put it on the coffee table. He put down the suitcase. She took both his hands in hers. "I apologize for Antonio's horrible behavior. He means well but he doesn't think. I could kill him for spoiling our return. Please try to not worry about it."

"Wow. That was quite a lot of emotion on everybody's part. Are you going to be OK?"

"Of course. I'll be over it in a minute and he will have forgotten about it by the time he gets down to his car."

"You're incredible. I don't think I'll even be over it by morning."

"Nonsense. Let's open some wine and put the groceries away and make a snack. It's really nothing."

"You fooled me. It looked and sounded ugly from where I was standing."

"Laurence, trust me when I tell you, I know how to handle my son. His mind wanders. He's sometimes inappropriate. I have to be clear and consistent with him. That's what works."

"How did he get in?"

"He has a key for emergencies. The building management might need to get in for some reason. They would call him if there was a problem and couldn't reach me."

"Are you sure you wouldn't like a little time to yourself?"

"I'm positive. He can be so annoying, but I'm not mad anymore." She took the bag of groceries into the kitchen.

"Well, if you're sure." He continued standing not far from the door.

Eva came back out to him and put her hands on his shoulders. "Hey, it's OK, it's over. Let's move on. Why don't you bring the bag of frozen meat into the kitchen and put it away?" She gave him a quick kiss and picked up her suitcase she had left by the door and took it into the bedroom.

He looked around the living room, which looked vaguely familiar as though he had visited long ago. He had never seen anything like that exchange between mother and son. The tone of voice and volume were unnerving. She was devastating in her delivery of annoyance and anger. He couldn't believe the son hadn't backed down right away, but no, he was going at it with equal strength of emotion. Evidently they were accustomed to dealing with each other this way. He hoped he would never find himself on the other end of that sharpened steel voice. If this type of interaction were common, it would take some getting used to. He'd known some families where screaming was common and sometimes violence occurred, but not at his house. He saw no need for screaming at any time. His family was always quiet, even in anger. That was civilized to him. One could argue and discuss without raising your voice. He shook his head and picked up the bag with the frozen meat and went into the kitchen.

When Laurence woke up the next morning, he still felt tired, and resolved to go home today alone. He put his arm around her and kissed her ear. "Eva, my love, I have business to attend to today. Why don't we get together late in the afternoon, go for a walk and I'll make you something nice for dinner?"

She didn't answer right away, so he kissed her again. "Ravioli with porcini?"

She didn't turn over but took his hand and pressed it gently to her chest. "It was a lovely vacation. I'll always treasure it, no matter what happens. Would you like some coffee?"

"Of course I would. Please don't say, 'no matter what happens.'" He actually had been thinking of not having coffee, but knew that would be a profound blunder.

While she made the coffee he put on yesterday's clothes and looked around the closet and the room for anything of his to put in his vacation suitcase to take home. He planned to do laundry among other things. It was time for him to be alone in his house and feel the quiet around him.

Eva had little to say over coffee, and when he finished his he said, "So what time shall we meet?"

"Let me phone you later."

The farewell embrace at the door was warm but quick. He looked in her eyes and could see the moisture forming. "I love you. I'll see you soon." He kissed her and hesitated for some response from her but she only nodded her head yes and opened the door for him and his suitcase.

Laurence had a bad feeling as he walked down the corridor to the elevator. He knew she hated to see him leave, but it didn't mean what she thought it did. He would be back later today. He wasn't done with her, not over that alarming scene last night with the son, but he needed some time alone. She would have to get used to that. Almost two weeks of all day and all night was a lot of companionship. It had been wonderful, even exhilarating, being with her, but he felt desperate to be by himself inside his own four walls. He wanted to be quiet and not focused on her every word and movement. He needed privacy from her always alert and sensitive mind. The last two weeks had been tumultuous with emotion, and he was exhausted. The only way he could rest was to be alone.

Chapter 12

Laurence caught up with his mail, laundry and dust on the first day back from the San Juans. The routines were calming and the sense of accomplishment was satisfying. It was good to be alone. Late in the afternoon, he called Drew to inquire about what plans were made for the First Thursday event. Drew said not enough to need Laurence's help. That was disappointing. After considering several ways to announce his relationship with Eva, he went with the simplest, "You may be interested to know I have just returned from an unexpected vacation in the San Juans with Eva Russo."

Drew said, "What? You and Eva Russo have been on vacation together? I'm fascinated. Tell me about it."

"Yep, she was planning to go to celebrate her retirement and invited me along."

"You are a lucky man indeed. How did that come about my friend, if you don't mind me asking?"

Laurence hadn't been prepared for Drew's enthusiasm for details. Given the gallery business relationship with the Russos, he felt Drew should be aware of his personal relationship but he didn't feel like sharing many details. "Well, I took her out to dinner after her event, and one thing led to another and that's occupied the last few weeks," said Laurence.

"I took her out to dinner too, and absolutely nothing happened."

"Did you want something to happen?" Laurence sounded skeptical.

"You're right. I didn't. She's lovely but a bit old for me, so I'm happy for you to be romancing a beautiful widow. Is romancing the operative word?" asked Drew.

"Yes, that would be accurate," said Laurence.

"You must be impressed. Are you?"

"Yes. No one is more impressed than I am to be in this situation at my age. We are both amazed by it." Laurence hoped that was all he needed to say that meant the two of them were pleased to be together.

"Congratulations! You're an inspiration to me about aging."

Drew pressed for details, but Laurence refused, as the situation was too new, and he had no idea where it was going. The truth was he did not want to talk about sex or love with Drew or anybody but Eva. Laurence was able to easily distract him from that topic by asking for the latest developments of the Basque event and how he could focus his research now to help. It was very important that he stay on Drew's mind and in his plans. The money and the feeling of belonging to a team effort were equally valuable to him.

Drew was happy to bring him up to date on how hard he and Julia had been working looking for Basque artists. "It's been bleak here, my friend, since we saw you last." Drew recounted the volume of the phone calls and how after too many discouraging days, the number of potential artists was finally growing. As each one was found, they were providing more leads into the artist community. There were still many unknowns, particularly where the performers were coming from that Drew wanted but they (Julia and Drew) were beginning to feel optimistic about the project. The biggest surprise so far was how many animals were involved, namely sheep, cattle and fish.

Laurence and Drew again discussed the strategy on approaching Amy when she got back. Drew had his calendar marked with her return date. He planned to send her a "welcome home" email inviting her to come down to the gallery on Friday to tell him and Laurence about her trip and cooking class in San Sebastián. Laurence would follow up at the library the following Monday to get an overview of her impressions so he could do more research if necessary before the meeting at the gallery. They had talked about the merits of going out to lunch or ordering in. Drew liked the informality and intimacy of eating in his office. The downside was appearing cheap. He was cheap, but appearances were terribly important to Drew. Laurence voted for eating in as it appeared more friendly.

They agreed that what Laurence had learned so far about the culture and well-known ingredients and dishes was valuable, but they needed Amy's response to it all to inspire more specific direction how food and wine would be linked to American Basque art. Drew wanted her to buy into the event, possibly have a role in planning and the execution. He would love to get her behind the podium to give a presentation of some sort. Perhaps she could do a cooking demonstration, showing how to prepare something from her cooking class in San Sebastián? Or maybe she could assist the chef from the Basque restaurant.

Perhaps Amy's husband would be a sponsor of the event? Who else might be a sponsor? That was a question Laurence couldn't help with as he didn't know many people, much less knowing anyone with money to sponsor. He told Drew he would look into the producers and importers of the Basque products for sponsorship ideas. Maybe the wholesaler who called on the local shops would like to do a demonstration or get involved with the restaurant demonstration.

As usual, Drew was thinking big. He described a dazzling multimedia event. Laurence admired this ability to envision a complete circus when there was only a small stage to work on. Laurence planned to go back to the library for more research.

When Drew hung up the phone he walked out to Julia's desk and sat down in the visitor's chair. "You will never guess what has happened to Laurence."

Julia looked at him quizzically, "I hope nothing bad."

"No, not bad. Amazing. Absolutely amazing."

"Won the lottery?"

"No, but close, maybe better. He has been on vacation for two weeks with Eva Russo in the San Juans and had a very nice time." Drew looked at her and grinned.

Julia looked uncertain that she understood what was so amazing about that. "They're both old and alone. Why not go on vacation?"

Drew shook his head at her and said, "Eva and Laurence are now your role models for having sex until you are very old."

She looked stunned. "Sex? They have sex together? I didn't think old people had sex."

"Now you understand how amazing this is," said Drew. "I've heard rumors but now we know for sure. This makes my day, maybe my week, to think about me romancing in my 70s."

"How old will your girlfriend be then?" Julia said seriously with no humor or irony.

"Stop! You're ruining my fantasy. I shouldn't have told you. I should have called William. He would get how amazing this is."

"Sorry. It must be a guy thing. I'm glad Eva and Laurence are hanging out together. They are both cool."

Drew stood up and said, "OK, I'm going back to work." Sometimes Julia's age kept her from getting the point.

That was a small flaw in having a 25-year-old for a business partner. She was so excellent is so many other ways. Maybe he should offer her a ride home tonight to look at her canvases. He felt like celebrating the progress of the Basque event and Laurence's good fortune by having some fun himself.

When he switched off his cell phone, Laurence lay down on his couch to reflect on why he felt he was conniving sometimes when dealing with Drew. There was nothing illegal in what Drew did. It was the unabashed expectation that people should help him that stunned Laurence at first and continued to do so. If they didn't offer help right away, then Drew began the mental process of figuring out how to get people to help. He didn't try to hide it from Laurence or any of his employees. He wanted them all involved in what he thought of as successful thinking and planning for a profitable result. There was entitlement in this attitude that Laurence couldn't fathom the origin of.

Amy as an object of Drew's process also had a cringe factor to it. Laurence liked her and thought she was a decent human being. He didn't want her to be deceived or mistreated in any way. His plan was to be absolutely up front and honest about his and Drew's interest in the event. If she didn't go for it naturally, he wasn't going to be part of trying to convince her. If she needed convincing, that would be Drew's job. And he also hoped he didn't have to try to sell her husband on anything. Drew thought everyone could be sold something. Laurence disagreed with him on that. Amy's husband Kevin was shrewd in every sense of the word. Kevin probably had a weakness when it came to her but unlikely enough to be manipulated if there were money involved. The little bit Laurence had been around him, he knew Kevin kept his eye on everything in the room. Laurence wanted to keep this event planning with Amy open and friendly.

When Eva hadn't phoned him by five that afternoon he dialed her cell and her landline and left the same message on both, "Call me about getting together." But she didn't. He tried to shrug his shoulders and think the best. She was involved in something and would phone him when she returned. His instinct was that this silence was retaliation for him leaving today. He didn't like that concept. It was somehow beneath her character, but he couldn't talk himself out of that assessment. Going back to his apartment for an hour or a day had to happen sometime. The vacation was over and they both had to deal with the reality of it. Why was she having a hard time with that?

At 7 p.m. he dialed Eva's numbers again and left a new message. "I miss you and hope you miss me too. I'm hungry now and plan to go out for something quick. Call me."

Other than coffee and cereal, his cupboard was bare. Expecting to cook and sleep at Eva's, he hadn't thought of going to the grocery store. Now he wasn't sure what he ought to do about shopping. The Metropolitan Market on the avenue at lower Queen Anne had a large prepared food department. Why not just go there and eat something at the store? The food would be better and less expensive than going to a restaurant. Sitting at the tables with a window viewing the bus stop outside would feel like being in a desolate Edward Hopper painting of a late night café but the food would be hot.

The sidewalk was busy with people going to bars and restaurants. The grocery store was busy too with people like himself looking for something to eat immediately or cook quickly. Laurence studied all the dishes on the steam table and decided the beef stew looked better than the meatloaf. Seated in the brightly lit table area, he did feel like a sad sack from a late night diner scene. There was no ambiance whatsoever. Mediocre food and unappealing dining companions succinctly characterized life without Eva. He hoped she was OK, no unexpected family troubles

118

or illness. Maybe she'd gone to visit one of her kids and stayed to dinner. Why didn't she call him? The possible answers for that could give him indigestion. No, he must remain positive. This was no reason to think the worst. Everything would be fine. He was almost sure of it. No, actually, he wasn't sure at all. The incident with the son was still worrisome to him. They might have forgotten about it, but he hadn't. He dreaded dealing with her kids in general. He had to meet them, get to know them, see them and show up at all the social functions that families do. That was in his future if they stayed together. Life without her required no imagination beyond looking around this dismal dining area of a grocery store.

Walking up the hill home he noticed his heart rate increasing with each step. The two-week vacation from exercising had taken its toll on him. He must get back on that program tomorrow. Entering the dark apartment, he felt yet another pang of missing Eva. He was alone in a bad way now, not the good way of earlier today. Even though they quietly passed hours together, reading, walking, relaxing with the view, her presence was powerful. Her body warmed the entire bed and him down to his bones. He was never cold when she was beside him. He marveled at how quickly he had adapted to sleeping with her after years of sleeping alone and he slept well. It felt natural to embrace her when she was asleep or awake. She told him she felt the same way about the comfort of his body day and night.

He took the cell phone with no messages on it out of his pocket and put it in the charger on his bedside table. Early to bed would help him with his day tomorrow as well as exercising and being at the library when it opened to drill down through the open data bases for compelling gems on the Basque people. Drew had his heart set on colorful costumes, music and beautiful young girls dancing. Laurence hoped his research would support Drew's vision.

Laurence was turning the pages but not sure if he was reading or not. He couldn't remember the last sentence. He gave up and turned out the light. He wondered where she was and what she was doing. He imagined her laughing over a candlelit dinner table in a fancy restaurant. She was amusing the crowd with tales of travels in Italy and wooing vendors to do her bidding. She was back in her milieu, far away from him and the simple life they had been leading. They had needed no outside influence or personality to amplify being together into something more than it was. No television or newspaper entertained, distracted or interrupted. They didn't want anybody else around. They felt perfect and content with each other. It had seemed idyllic at the time, and now in the dark of his austere apartment in an old building on Queen Anne Avenue North where the traffic noise never stopped, the vacation days in Bellingham and on Lopez Island seemed a fantasy, a romantic fantasy. It was unbelievable to him that he was having sex again, not like he was 20 years old or 40 years old, but pleasurable. What was different from being young was that he did everything more slowly. Youth was always in such a hurry to get to the finish point. He liked this new slower pace. Passion was still in him, and so was generosity. She told him he was the best lover of her life. He believed her whenever she said it. Of course, he had found it motivating. Being as smart as she was she probably knew exactly what effect it would have on him.

They had talked a little bit about their married lives. They thought it was meaningful they'd both been married only once and for a long time. She had told him that the strong suit in her marriage had been working together and growing the business. Although she never said anything derogatory about her husband, from the few stories he heard, Antonio Sr. seemed lacking in warmth. Maybe the first son was a cold fish like the husband had been, but Eva never compared them. Eva seldom asked about Ingrid.

When he had related some incident of relevance, she said how lucky Ingrid had been to have him for so many years. He agreed with that and told her he felt extremely lucky to be with her now. Tonight he felt his age, cold to the bone, a little creaky and very lonely. Where was she and why hadn't she called him back?

When the early morning traffic woke him, Laurence felt tired but began dutifully with his stretching exercises and then pushups. Each one felt like the first he'd ever done in his life and that he couldn't do another one. He made coffee and tried to read a few pages of his physics book that had failed him last night. It was no better this morning, so it would go back to the library unfinished. He was eager to get out of the apartment and into fresh air. After he climbed several flights of stairs inside his building to complete his workout, he decided to walk part way downtown and stop somewhere for breakfast.

He resisted the impulse to dial her number again. Two messages on each phone were more than enough to remind her of his interest and affection. He had said he missed her. Her last words to him were, "Let me phone you later." No, that wasn't right. She had said that before they had coffee. His last words were, "I love you. I'll see you soon." She hadn't said any last words. He thought she was going to cry, but she didn't, at least not in front of him. That had been 24 hours ago. What was going on that it seemed so long ago? Had she cried? Should he have turned around instead of getting on the elevator? Would he be here alone today if he had done that?

He shook his head as he headed down the avenue. The old man of science was becoming a blathering idiot. They had been apart for one day. There was no reason to think she didn't love him anymore. Time away from each other was important for perspective and to keep things fresh. She would have interesting stories to tell him tonight about her dinner companions, whoever they were. He would describe his latest research and his melodramatic dinner in a painting in a grocery store. It would be funny the way he would tell it. She would laugh at him. Everything would be fine.

Chapter 13

Downtown on a library computer on the fifth floor, elbow to elbow with several hundred other people, Laurence tried to work efficiently to maximize his allotted 90 minutes. He was experienced at data research and image searches. He captured some good images to email to himself and Drew. He made a list of books to check out he could examine more carefully. He was after visuals that told a story. They might be able to blow these up poster size or bigger to display, particularly if no Basque people could be found to do real life dancing or demonstrations. Dancing on a video monitor was also possible. Drew would find somebody. He was not beyond employing actors from the art school. Students and unemployed graduates were happy to do almost anything creative for resume credit, no money necessary. Laurence's best captures were a series of an ancient fisherman in a black beret and boats from another era. The man's face portrayed the difficulty of the job, the visceral photographs grabbing Laurence's gut. The Basques had always been great seamen hunting whale and cod fish. They were admired as shipbuilders. It was said no 15th century Spanish or Italian explorer would travel without a Basque navigator and sailors. Some historians felt they had discovered the New World long before Columbus. This aspect of the culture might succinctly be told in photographic displays as well as in including traditional Basque recipes for *marmitako,* a classic fisherman's stew of tuna, potatoes, tomatoes and sweet and hot peppers and *bacalao,* stew with salt cod, onions, eggs, potatoes, peppers, raisins and capers.

The search results made him feel very confident they could make a compelling presentation. They wouldn't need Amy necessarily. The material was powerful. Oh, Eva. Where are you, and why aren't you calling me? The cell phone in his pocket was still. She said she would call later. Maybe she had meant today all along, not yesterday.

Late in the afternoon the cell phone finally proved it was fully charged, vibrating and softly squealing. He flipped it open so fast he fumbled and dropped it on the floor.

It was Drew. "Good job, old man! I love the photo of the fellow with the beret. With any luck we'll find some paintings too. I made more connections today and with what you sent me, I agree we have a solid concept. There is a lot of work to be done, but it has the promise of being a crowd pleaser. I think we might ring in the New Year with a Basque Blockbuster."

"Good to hear you're optimistic," said Laurence.

"Yes, it's a pleasant change to me too." Drew hung without saying goodbye or what the next step was.

Laurence shook his head. Drew's moods moved at extraordinary speed. He noticed the time on the flip phone before he closed it and put it back on the coffee table. It was now 36 hours since he had seen Eva. He was starting to understand why her son came to investigate after leaving 20 messages. He was determined he would not call her again. She had to call him back.

What to do about dinner again was the next question. He hadn't eaten since breakfast and couldn't decide if he should make the assumption he was a bachelor again and go shopping at the grocery store or find something to eat out on the avenue. There were probably a dozen restaurants north and an equal number south of his apartment. He didn't really know the menus of any of them. Frugal habits kept him from going out to a restaurant or calling for a home delivery. "Well, old man," he counseled himself, "go shopping and cook your dinner like a smart person would. Stop feeling sorry for yourself."

On the way down the hill to the big supermarket, he considered his shopping list as a plan for the next few days. He would assume dining alone and make something that would be enough for two or three meals. A few pieces of fresh fruit to go with breakfast would be nice. If anything changed, he could share it with Eva, or it wouldn't be much of a loss. If he were to spend his new days, just like the old days, researching or reading, it would be good to have some food in the house. What was more depressing than an empty refrigerator? A few things were, but at least this was something he could change.

At the fish counter he surveyed all the choices while the fishmonger helped people who could make quick decisions. He spurned all the marinated, ready to go in the oven choices as too salty or too sweet even though he had never tried them. Laurence finally selected a white moist-looking true cod filet and a half-pound of shrimp that would make two nice portions of a Basque seafood stew. He would make a quick sauce with sautéed shallots and garlic and add vegetable stock and pureed tomatoes. After it had simmered a bit with his new favorite Basque pimienton seasoning and chopped potatoes, he would gently poach the fish cut up in small pieces and shrimp to make a fisherman's stew just like he'd been reading about. Simple but fabulous, a little salt and pepper would be all it needed, maybe a splash of vinegar or the wine Eva always had. He would miss drinking her wine. Maybe he would treat himself to a bottle of wine for cooking and medicinal purposes.

The fresh produce was next to the seafood counter, so with the fish in his basket he retraced his steps, added three Bartlett pears, new potatoes, and grabbed two shallots and a head of garlic. On his way back to the front of the store, he had to pass through the wine department again cleverly positioned between the prepared food and fresh produce. *They sure made it easy to find the wine,* Laurence thought. He debated about a humble Zinfandel or a Rioja and went with the Spanish wine for the extra fruit and warmth in his glass and in the stew for his dinner. Feeling almost cheerful about how this was going to work out, he got in line to pay. He had time to admire the unusually well-dressed crowds on the sidewalk passing by the front of the grocery store on Mercer Street. There must be a play on at one of the theaters in the Seattle Center.

As he rounded the corner of Mercer Street to walk up First Avenue North, he saw Eva in her pink dress, coming his way with two young women, one on each side. No question, they were her daughters, the main difference being their dark hair. He could see what a stunner she had been at thirty something. He stopped to watch her approach wondering when she would notice him. They were all dressed up. They must be going to the theater or out to eat, or both.

She saw him when she was about 20 feet away. A small start of her head indicated surprise and a small grimace of her mouth as though swallowing must mean she was unhappy to see him and then a straightforward smile right into his eyes. What did all that mean? He nodded at her but didn't smile. She stopped in front of him, and the women looked at her and then at him to see what was happening.

"Laurence, how nice to see you. Let me introduce my daughters, Sophia and Angelica."

They smiled at him and shook his free hand without a grocery bag and said nice to meet you and then seemed uncertain about the next step. Ever the smooth actor, Eva filled the space naturally.

"We're on our way to see a play at the Rep Theatre. Laurence is a friend of mine from the gallery where we had the event recently."

"We're sorry we couldn't come. We heard it was a good event. Tony told us all about it," said one of the daughters.

Laurence nodded at the speaker. "Maybe another time. We frequently have special events like your mother's."

"Oh, I didn't know that," said the other one.

The daughters, who could have been twins, although Eva had never mentioned that — in fact she hadn't had too much to say about them at all — were checking him out as young people do. When had it become OK to blatantly inspect another person? He wondered what else Tony had told them and if Tony was the sort of person who got on his phone the minute he was in his car to report an incident of interest to them all. To reward their attention to him at this moment, Laurence smiled at both of them in his gravitas mode.

"You are both very beautiful, just like your mother. It was my pleasure to meet you." He gave the three a little bow and stepped out the way so they could pass.

"Oh, thank you," both young women said simultaneously.

Eva looked up into his eyes and with her eyebrows raised appeared amused. "Girls, we need to get going. Good night, Laurence. We'll talk soon." The three of them walked on arm in arm.

He walked on too, trying to breathe slowly and shallowly to quiet himself and his heart beating loudly in his chest. He didn't want to betray any emotion in case they turned around to watch him go or say anything else. He had planned to walk home those few blocks with one long, steep block with his groceries, but now thought he'd like to ride the bus. He sat down on the bench at the bus stop to rest and think it through.

Well, he thought he'd done well at the charming old man routine. He'd imagined he'd had his gravitas suit on to match their outfits. They were the same height as their mother so had to look up at him and into his blues eyes, just like she did. As first impressions go, it was probably just fine.

He thought he'd done well to gather himself in the moments before she noticed him. She had no warning but never seemed to need any, her mind worked so quickly.

What the hell did "we'll talk soon" mean? This innocuous phrase usually meant NOT. It had the same phony ring as "we'll be in touch" or "let's do lunch". It never meant "I'll phone you tomorrow" with certainty. He couldn't come up with another translation. The more he thought about it, he felt she had dismissed him. That's what she had done. She had relieved him from his role as lover and soul mate. So, they were done. She hadn't called him, and she wasn't going to call him. He sighed heavily enough to startle the person sitting next to him on the bench. He whispered, "Sorry."

When he got home, he opened the wine first and poured a glass, toasting himself on his genius for buying it. Then he started mechanically making his Basque seafood stew, feeling like an old man alone at sea in harsh weather and no consolation other than his humble meal to warm him. It tasted pretty good for a sauce that hadn't simmered very long. He was happy about the wine and the way it buoyed him up after suffering the sad news of his new life alone after Eva. What he'd done today was pretty much the forecast for the future, doing library research and reading with occasional evenings with Drew and the gallery team for company. He cleaned up the kitchen and went to bed. He wanted to take advantage of the wine buzz for swift sleep.

The cell phone vibrating and purring on the bedside table woke him up from a deep sleep. He picked it up in the dark without looking at the caller ID and said. "What?"

"I'm downstairs. Can you buzz me in?"

"What?"

"I said I'm downstairs. Can you buzz me in?"

It was Eva's voice and he wasn't sure if he was dreaming or not, but just in case, he got out of bed with the phone still in his hand and found and pressed the buzzer for the front door. He didn't think he'd ever buzzed anyone in before. "OK," he said and heard the buzzer sound through his phone and her phone. As she started up the first flight of stairs he looked around the room for a clue what he should do next. It was too dark to see anything and he was naked. He decided to do nothing but stand behind the slightly open door to let her in.

There she was still in her theater dress, he could see by the hall light as she came into the dark room. He closed the door behind her and locked it. She threw her arms around his neck and pressed herself against him. After a moment's hesitation, he embraced her back.

"Laurence, I missed you so much I didn't want to phone you. I wanted to tell you in person. I pushed the buzzer downstairs but you didn't answer. It must be broken."

He couldn't think of anything to say so he waited to see what else she might say.

"I told my daughters after the play when we went out for a drink that I'd been on vacation with a man. Once they absorbed that information and quit giggling I told them the man was you. So the cat's out of the bag so to speak and they are excited for us."

"Oh, jeez, I'd better put my pants on and sit down," he said.

"Oh, no, don't do that. Let me take my dress off. Maybe you should turn your phone off," Eva said.

Laurence looked down at the cell phone with a green light still counting the seconds of the ongoing call. He snapped it shut. "Now it's really dark in here. Shall I turn on a light?"

"No. Get back in bed and I'll join you. We can talk in the dark."

"I'm warning you this bed is smaller than yours," he said.

"It will be perfect, but you have to lead me to it. I can't see a thing."

He led her to his sleeping alcove and got back in between the sheets. He could hear her taking off her shoes and putting down her bag.

"Do you need help with the zipper?"

"That's what I love about you. You're always thinking about the other person."

She sat on the edge of the bed, and he unzipped the dress. She threw it over the chair and crawled in beside him and put her head on his shoulder. He put his arms around her confirming her presence. He was not dreaming.

"I am so glad to be here with you. I hated being without you last night. Are you glad I'm here?" she said.

"Eva, as soon as I get over being surprised, I'll be glad. I'm a little slower than you are at transitions."

"Oh, are you mad at me about last night?" she said.

"Mad and sad, as you say."

"Well, I felt bad not phoning you back, but I just felt like I had to try to take a break, as you say. If I had phoned you before or after I got home from dinner with my sons, I wouldn't have been able to stay away."

"I thought you were retaliating for me wanting time to myself."

"I hate to admit it, but that is true. You are so honest it makes me seem small," she said.

"What did you mean tonight by *we'll talk soon?*"

"Just this. That I would see you later tonight," she said.

"I did not get that at all. I thought you meant never again." He heard the finality of that statement in his voice.

"Oh, no. I smiled and looked right at you to see if you got it."

"Eva, I didn't get it."

"I thought I was reassuring you that we would talk tonight," she said.

"This old engineer has so much to learn about love and mental telepathy. You always seem to read my mind, but I can't read yours. I thought you were saying good-bye forever."

"Oh, Laurence, that's so sad you thought that. I do try to speak clearly so you don't have to try to read my mind. I can't read your mind, but I can read your eyes. You are expressive in ways you don't realize. Listening to you talk to my daughters on the street practically made me swoon."

"They are astonishingly like you. I knew immediately who they were. Are they twins?"

"More like Irish twins, about a year apart. Your compliment was widely commented on by everyone. Of course, they thought you were handsome and charming. When they learned you were my vacation friend, they were giddy with imagination. I don't think they had ever considered their mom might be a sex goddess."

"You certainly are that."

"Only when I'm with you." She caressed him. "Do you have a headache?"

"No, I don't have a headache. I'm exhausted. I find being in love with you very strenuous. I want to know how you enjoyed your time away from me."

Eva said, "Not as much fun last night as tonight. My sons are so serious about everything. My daughters aren't. Sleeping without you was miserable. How was your break?"

"Mostly miserable, but I did get some good research."

"You worked on the Basque thing?" Eva said.

"Yes. Drew thinks, at least some of the time that we're onto something good, maybe a blockbuster. Did you tell your sons about us?"

"Not really. They aren't into details like girls are. Nice vacation, good. When asked, I said I went with a friend. When asked, I said no one you know. We moved on to business and grandchildren."

Laurence said, "Has Tony recovered as you predicted?"

"Yes. Have you?" she said.

"Not really. When will I bake them a *pantxineta*?" he said.

"Soon."

"Oh, boy. Please, let's get some sleep," he said.

Chapter 14

Laurence woke up feeling like he'd had a good night's sleep and that today was a fresh start. He lay on his back quietly enjoying listening to Eva breathe and the reassuring feeling that the world was spinning properly with her by his side. She was back. She loved him. She never wanted to be without him again. He believed her. He vowed to himself he would not hold this episode against her or keep it handy in his mind to create doubt or resentment. That would be forgiving her. He really didn't want to dwell on the experience or the emotions. It was too painful to revisit. He wanted to think forward now. Planning their days and nights together seemed like a good idea, but he wanted to keep his apartment. He needed a place of his own to retreat to and be alone. The vacation was over.

He noticed a change in her breathing and rolled over on his side to put his arm around her and kissed her ear. "Good morning, how are you?"

Eva snuggled against him and murmured, "As long as I can feel you, I'm great."

"OK. We're in no hurry to get this monumental day started."

"What's monumental today?"

"I think this is your first real day of being retired. Time to consider what sort of schedule you should try. What do you want to do or accomplish?"

"Oh, I don't know. I might not be ready to embrace scheduling and goals. I'm just glad to be here with you.

Surely you will make me coffee and we'll read. Later on we can think about what we might have for lunch or dinner. Isn't that enough?"

"Sergeant Hansen here to jumpstart your day. We begin by flexing our feet, then rotating our ankles. You work your way up your body, each joint and muscle group separately."

"It's much too early for exercise." She stretched her back and turned over to face him.

"I have a routine that I abandoned while vacationing with you. I need to get back to it. You don't want a flabby old man for a boyfriend."

"You flabby? Never!" she said.

"I will be if I don't exercise."

"How is me flexing my foot going to help you?" Now she was teasing him.

"I stretch before I get up. I thought you might enjoy it too. It makes you feel good."

"Before coffee?" She was incredulous.

"Yes."

"Oh, I don't know about doing things before coffee. That seems extreme." Eva pulled the covers back up to her chin to protest any movement that hinted of getting up.

"The point is to wake your body to be ready for the day. To begin, just lie flat on your back, fully elongated. Point your toes, flex your feet and repeat."

Eva shook her head. "The things I do for love."

Laurence worked though his stretching routine with her. "See how good that feels everywhere?"

She laughed. "Oh, yes I feel so amazing now, we should stay in bed and exercise more parts."

"No. Now we do push-ups."

"No, sorry, never in my life have I done a push-up." Eva was adamant.

"It is the most efficient form of exercise. It tones your whole body and is aerobic. I promise you I have studied this."

"I bet you have, but that doesn't mean I can do it," she said, looking amused at him.

"Watch here." He stood up and stretched a bit more and then got down on the floor and started counting. "One, two, three, four..."

She leaned over the side of the bed, looking and laughing. "I couldn't possibly do that, but oh my, your whole back side does look toned. I see what you mean about the muscle groups, all the way down to your feet. No wonder your trousers hang so nicely."

He relaxed to lie down on the floor and rested after ten push-ups and looked at her smiling at him. "Guess what happens next?"

She was giggling. "I get underneath you for the full benefit?"

"Ten more and then you do it."

She laughed so hard she had to roll onto her back. "Impossible!"

He began counting out the next ten and she had to lean back over and look to see if he was really doing them. He not only was doing push-ups, he was looking up at her to see if she was watching.

"Now, you," he said.

"No, no, no. I don't want to do it. I can't do it."

"Come here on the floor, like this."

"I can't believe I'm doing this." She got out of bed and then considered how she was going to get on her knees and ended up more in a yoga style prayer position. "I'm getting that beached whale feeling. Does this make me look fat?" She laughed so hard she collapsed flat forward while still on her knees.

"You're doing great. Now, put your hands here. Now stretch out your legs. Raise yourself up. Now, on your toes. That's the position! Now lower your chest almost to the floor."

Eva collapsed flat to the floor, laughing. "It's even harder than it looks. I can't do this."

"Of course you can. I'll help you." He stood with his feet on either side of her hips and clasped her waist in both hands. He picked up the center of her and guided the raising and lowering while counting to five. "Maybe five is the right number for the first day."

Pink with exertion Eva said, "I'm sure five is perfect."

He lay down beside her on his stomach and put his arm around her. "That was so good for the first time."

"No wonder you keep your floors so clean. Do you really do this every day?"

"After breakfast, we'll climb some stairs," he said.

"So this is retirement. I never thought of naked calisthenics," she said, shaking her head. "What do you think your neighbors will think about a naked lady in the stairwell?"

"Some of them would like it. I guess we'll have to postpone that until we find something appropriate for you to wear."

Over cereal and fruit Eva told him she wanted to look into taking some classes, maybe tai chi, painting or a foreign language.

Laurence thought for a moment. "I've always wanted to learn French for the cooking vocabulary."

"How many classes do you think we should take? One a day?"

"How about you choose one, and I'll choose one and see how we do."

Weeks later Eva was on the phone with her younger daughter Sophia while Laurence was reading on the couch, listening to her end of the conversation. "Darling, I'm so sorry I can't make it that day either. That's our tai chi class. We love it. I know it seems like a long time and I want to see you. I'd like to see all the kids too. I know it's difficult to arrange when they play so many sports. I understand completely.... You let me know what Sunday afternoon everyone can come, and we'll have a nice early dinner here.... Yes, he's good and looking forward to meeting you all.... Love to you too." Eva hung up the phone and looked at Laurence.

He said, "Oh, sounds like my meeting with the tribe is looming closer."

"You have been so lucky every kid is on a different team. We would have had them already, if not for that. We could always go to plan B and meet each family individually in a restaurant."

Laurence shook his head, "Four dinners instead of one? I like plan A."

"We can't put it off much longer. I really do miss seeing them. I should be going to some of these sporting events to remind the kids they have a grandmother who loves them."

"Feel free to go anytime. I don't see why I have to go with you. They don't know me. I'm not a sports guy. Can't you just tell them that?" he said, not looking up from his book.

"To kids it's not about sports, it's about them. They are performing with an audience."

"How many grandkids?" he asked and immediately wished he hadn't asked remembering how poorly the conversation had gone the last time he asked that type of question.

"I have eight grandchildren. Tony has two boys, one in college and one in high school. Marco also has two boys who are in high school. Angelica has three boys, in middle school and high school. Sophia has a baby girl, not yet two. She thinks she is the queen of everything. You will love her. She reminds me of me!"

"Oh, help me if I'm caught in between two of you. I better write down all the names." Laurence sighed.

"Don't worry. You'll be fine. It will be fun. The grandchildren are all about themselves in their own world, and they scarcely notice adults, even when they are right in front of them."

"It's your kids I'm worried about."

"Please don't be. They are just curious about you. They are polite, well-behaved people, just like me." She smiled at him.

"Except Tony?"

"Well, he may be just fine too. After all, when he puts it together he'll realize he met you at Drew's and that you are part of our world. He doesn't connect that the gallery judge is the man I went on vacation with."

"Facial recognition problem?"

"Maybe, I don't know. He is slow to get to know people. Give him a chance. I think he is engaged in his new role as the sole decision maker and enjoying it. He had good things to say when we had dinner together. I am delighted with that. I told him I was very proud of him. Maybe his glass will become half full. Maybe I should have retired years ago."

"Why didn't you?"

"I wasn't ready to give it up, and I didn't think Tony was ready to take over."

"What about your other son? Isn't he part of the company?"

"Marco is the one who gets the least attention because he needs the least. He goes along beautifully without difficulty. He never complains. He has a lot of my old job now as number one salesman and representative. I will remember to compliment him."

"What are we cooking for them?" asked Laurence.

Eva made notes on her pad of paper of all the dishes they discussed. "We really only need two bottles of sparkling wine for everyone to have a glass. We'll put open red wine behind the iced wine buckets. Very elegant, don't you think?"

"There's nothing too good for this crowd, right?"

"Absolutely right. This is a champagne and caviar crowd, especially if I'm buying." She grinned at him and he nodded in agreement.

"Why don't we go to the warehouse today and get some pasta? I want to show it to you. I'll call the office to be polite and we can have lunch nearby."

Georgetown appeared to be undergoing a renewal. The old saloons, Jules Mae and the 9-Pound Hammer, were still there, but new bars and shops were open along Airport Way South and on the side streets. The Russo Imports operation featured a double glass door entrance into an old brick structure with very high ceilings. A modern seating area with two long Italian couches and four upholstered chairs around a large low table could comfortably seat a dozen people. A young woman in a tight skirt and high-heeled boots who had been sitting at the desk in the open space rose to greet them as they came in the door.

"Hello, Mrs. Russo. How nice to see you. We miss you."

"Hello, Adriana. Thank you. I miss you too, but I am enjoying my new retirement life. This is my friend, Laurence Hansen. We're here to do a little shopping."

"Nice to meet you. I'll tell Mr. Russo that you are here."

"He's expecting us. What about Sophia and Marco? Are they here?"

"Marco is traveling. Sophia is in the warehouse. Do you want me to call her?"

"No. That's not necessary. We'll wait here for Tony to come out."

She motioned for Laurence to sit in one of the chairs and she took a seat next to him while Adriana went to her telephone.

"Well, what do you think of it?" Eva said softly, looking around the room at the large vase of fresh flowers on the low table and the art on the wall.

"Looks very chic to me. How do you use this space, Mrs. Russo?" Laurence was mostly eyeing her, not the décor, trying to decide how she felt seeing it all again.

"It's our meeting room as well as waiting room. The offices are small. This is part of the salesmanship. Visitors seldom get past this area. The rest is bare bones."

"I see your style in it. Nice to look at and very comfortable to sit in."

"Thank you. I think it's important. People feel valued when given a good seat and pleasant place to sit. It makes for a better meeting. We try to be very polite here. If any screaming needs to be done, we go to the warehouse." She grinned at him.

"Oh, real life business requires screaming?"

"There's nothing like a family business where you know each other so well, the usual corporate politics are useless.

140

We get to be brutally honest with each other. It's the only way to do it."

"So, we'll see the president out here, not in his office?"

"Correct."

"Not even his mother comes into his office?"

"It's his private space. He will take us to the warehouse. The procedure was agreed to as part of the process of me stepping down and him taking over."

"I see."

"Do you really?"

"You are not in charge here anymore. You don't sashay in without an appointment like you still run the place. It makes sense to me."

"Exactly right. You do get it. I wish he would hurry up."

The wood door on the other side of the room opened and Tony walked toward them. His white dress shirt was open at the neck, no coat or tie. Laurence stood up as he approached to be ready for the introduction. Eva stood up too.

"Tony, sorry to disturb you but nice to see you." They did not kiss or shake hands. "I want to introduce you again to my friend, Laurence Hansen. You met him briefly at Drew's gallery where he works on the special events team as a food judge."

Tony looked at him trying to remember and again put out his cold hand briefly to shake with Laurence.

"I'm sorry, I don't remember. There were too many people that night."

"I understand. I was impressed with your products. I'm glad to see your operation here."

Tony nodded at Laurence and turned to his mother, "When are you entertaining the whole family?"

"Some Sunday afternoon soon. Sophia is checking everyone's calendars to find the best date. Have you not heard from her?"

"I might have, but I don't think I responded. You said, 'we're entertaining'. Who is entertaining?"

"Laurence, who is quite a good cook, and I are preparing a dinner party for the whole family. We enjoy cooking together."

"I see. I'm beginning to see." He looked at Laurence and said, "You are mother's vacation friend. I get it now." He looked at his mother for confirmation but without emotion.

Eva smiled at him and nodded. "Yes, that's right. You're going to love the menu. We're thinking of a cold seafood starter and roast beef with pasta and vegetables."

"That's not your usual menu, but I do like it. That's nice of you to cook for people you don't know," he said looking at Laurence.

"My pleasure," said Laurence and thought to himself, *is he slow or weird or what*?

"Tony, would you like to give Laurence a tour of the facility?"

"Not really, mother. I need to get back to the sales forecasts I'm working on. Why don't you show him?"

"OK. Thanks for letting us interrupt you. Please respond to Sophia. We'll follow you to the warehouse door."

Tony turned and they followed him through the wood door and down a narrow hall with three small offices on either side with glass windows and wooden doors. From what he saw through the glass it was bare bones as Eva had said, holding only large wooden desks with executive swivel chairs and two plain wood visitor chairs, family photos and personally chosen art on the walls. Eva was not the decorator here. Tony entered one of the office doors and sat down facing a large computer screen with a spreadsheet displayed. Laurence and Eva continued to the end of the hallway, and she opened another door. The cold air hit Laurence's face, startling him. They were now in a cavernous space with rows and rows of tall metal shelving stacked with products.

Eva looked around at the room and at him smiling. "I love my warehouse!"

"It's big and cold. I suppose that's perfect."

"Yes. And there's Sophia!" She waved her hand as she called out the name.

One of the young women Laurence had met on the street turned around from the shelf she was examining and waved at them. "Hi, Mom," she called out to her. When she approached them she said, "Hello, Laurence. Nice to see you again." She shook Laurence's hand. She hugged her mother and kissed her cheek. "I didn't know you were coming today."

"I arranged a shopping expedition with the president this morning and have reminded him again of the family dinner we're trying to organize. He should be getting back to you soon with the dates that suit him."

"Thanks for helping with that. You are giving Laurence a tour? I'll go with you. I want to hear all about what you two are cooking up. We're so looking forward to coming to dinner."

They strolled along with Sophia, looking left and right at the shelves, Eva occasionally picked up a product to show him and eventually filled the shopping bag. He asked Sophia about her job. She talked about brand management and new product lines coming soon. Eva asked questions about shipments.

Laurence looked at the two of them, admiring the ease in the conversation and the similarities in presentation. Working in a family business added a complexity to them all, and he realized he had more to learn. From the first day he met her, Eva exuded competency, and he was impressed by it and sometimes overwhelmed by it. What did she see in him? He felt out of his league in this warehouse with these smart businesswomen. Sophia talked about what an inspiration Eva was to all of them in carrying on the company traditions. Laurence was touched by this exchange between the mother and her child, another accomplishment of hers he could not share in any way.

"Thanks, darling. I am very proud of you too. We need to let you get back to work."

They followed Sophia back to the office hallway and waved through the window to Tony who must have heard the door because he nodded at them and then went back to his keyboard and screen.

Out on the street walking back to the car Laurence said, "I am impressed with your operation. Not many employees though that I could see."

"Thanks. It's a small staff so you split the pie with less people. We're all willing to work extra hard for that. We do have a few warehouse shippers and drivers, but they were out to lunch. I'll call Sophia tonight and get the early reviews.

Laurence was not surprised when Sophia reported Tony's disappointment that Eva had a boyfriend. He thought his mother having sex was inappropriate for her age and disrespectful to his dead father. However, he did understand how important it was for his mother to be happy and not come back to work. Eva shook her head and said, "He's not as smart as I thought he was. Oh, well. I am so pleased that our family dinner is in process. I don't want to think about anything else."

Chapter 15

Monday morning Laurence was waiting on the corner of Madison Street and 5th Avenue near the doors of the Central Library when it opened at 10. Today was his informal appointment with Amy to hear about her trip to Spain. He could see her through the glass wall, standing at the welcome desk by the door saying good morning to the crowd entering the building. He lingered outside waiting for the tourists to be taken care of before he entered. She gave him a big smile and wave, seeming very pleased to see him. He stood in front of the desk and said, "So, how was it?"

"Magical. I have confirmed that the *pintxo* party idea for the gallery is the best by visiting about 100 of them!"

"Thank you for the research."

"Basque food and wine is a delightful way to introduce the art and get people to come who have never been to the gallery. The cooking class in San Sebastián was very fun and most recipes are easy. I think *pintxos* are the bridge between the old and the new cuisine. Some of the bars are serving the same recipe they've always served. Other bars are serving modernist cuisine. It was so much fun going bar to bar. It's where the locals see their friends. It's what the tourists do for fun. We ended up several evenings moving down the street with the same crowd who became friends by the end of the night."

Laurence listened to her unusually rapid delivery. He told her about his *pintxo* research, the cookbooks he'd looked at so far and what he had cooked. She knew the books he mentioned and told him one of her favorite titles.

Amy said, "Kevin and I want to invite the gallery crew to our house for a *pintxo* party. Then you'll see what fun it is and what the potential is for the gallery."

"That's very generous of you, Amy. Why don't you come down to the gallery on Friday for lunch with us and tell us about your trip? We've learned a lot about the Basques in the three weeks you've been gone. And we've found a few artists."

Later Laurence left a message for Drew, "Your wildest dreams are coming true. Order pizza for Friday lunch with Amy. She's going to tell you all about a Basque party she thinks we should have at the gallery. She's inviting all of us to her house for a preview."

Eva held up the French book in front of his face to get his attention. "Shall we practice the conversation for class?"

"You play the desk clerk first and I'll be the tourist."

They loved Bernadette, the French teacher at the Alliance Française. She was Parisian, tall and thin and so chic from her black bob haircut to her black ballet style flats. Laurence had been right about how time consuming it might be. The class with six other students was two nights a week and they had to read and practice to prepare for each class, but felt they were learning to speak immediately from the vivacious teacher. Her accent was luscious to listen to, and she made them laugh. They looked forward to going to class and were inspired to study to please the teacher.

The tai chi class was another form of torture as far as Laurence was concerned. There were too many people in the class and not enough room for him to feel comfortable. The positions were difficult and felt awkward. He'd never known he didn't have good balance until instructed to stand on one foot for too long. The serenity in the motions was missing for him. He couldn't understand why Eva was so keen about it. He went without complaining to please her and hoped he would get something out of it as it became more familiar. It would be very easy to quit this class and say, "It's just not for me." Thankfully it was only two mornings a week for an hour. He tried to think of it as merely delaying his regular reading, which was diminishing. Two books a week was about all he could find time to read during Eva's leisurely morning routine and in the evenings after dinner. The rest of the day seemed filled with long walks, the classes and preparing lunch and dinner.

He enjoyed the cooking and that she served him breakfast in bed every day. The meal on a tray was now a lifestyle habit he looked forward to. She loved for him to read on the couch in her apartment instead of going to the library. That presented many opportunities for her to lie down beside him and whisper in his ear to try to distract him. Between her bed and couch, he was spending a lot of time on his back. His library visits were down to two days a week, Mondays and Fridays, to return books and get new ones. Except for the tai chi, he was enjoying being with her and feeling like a couple, two old love birds in a well-feathered nest amusing themselves in ways he never expected to happen to him. He thought occasionally of Ingrid and wondered what they would be doing to amuse themselves if she hadn't died. They probably would be doing the same things, except for the tai chi and French lessons. She would have selected something a little less esoteric. He'd had a fear all his life of bridge lessons. Would that have been worse than tai chi? Thank goodness Eva had never mentioned playing cards of any kind.

Julia and Drew were waiting at the desk near the front door when Amy arrived for lunch on Friday.

"Hello, Amy." Drew took her hand in a warm welcome and gave her an air kiss on her cheek. Julia smiled.

"Hi, Drew. Hi, Julia. Thanks for inviting me. It's nice to see the space without people in it. How's this show doing?" she said, looking around the gallery.

"Very well. We call it decorative art."

"It's all so pretty. I thought of my dining room immediately." She smiled at him.

"Any of these would look nice in your dining room." He nodded his head affirmatively. "You didn't come to look at art today, but if you have time after lunch, please do. Follow us through the hidden door."

He led her through the staging area with the wet bar and a small kitchen and into his office. Laurence was sitting in a club chair, and he stood up in greeting and said, "Welcome to the business den. Please sit here by me."

Drew and Julia sat down on chairs opposite Amy so they were spread around the table with the large pizza box and bowl of salad in the middle. Bottled water, paper plates, napkins and plastic forks were in easy reach.

Amy looked around at the walls tightly packed with art. "What a beautiful office you have. Is this your personal art collection?"

"Thank you. These are all old favorites, but as you might guess, everything is ultimately for sale, except this one maybe." He pointed to an alluring nude somewhat swathed in shimmering fabric reclining on a Victorian settee in the style of Sargent.

"The fabric detail is gorgeous as is the model! Who is the artist?"

"A young art student, me."

"Oh, Drew. I knew you used to paint but I don't recall you pointing out to me anything of yours. I'm impressed."

"Thank you. These are all mine. I enjoy looking at them. Imitating the masters was what I did best at school. Reminds me why I'm in the gallery business."

Laurence began serving the pizza to everyone.

Drew said, "Enough about me. Tell me what you enjoyed in the Basque Country."

"It's so exciting to be there. There's a buzz in the air. The people who live there are proud. The tourists are invigorated by everything. The *pintxo* bars! Everywhere you go they are packed day and night. That's my idea for your event, and I'll give you the details in a minute. You have to start by envisioning the natural beauty of the Atlantic coast, the interior countryside and the Pyrenees. It's all stunning. The history is fascinating. The experience is full of contrasts. It surprises you at every turn. The country is so ancient and yet modern."

Laurence was watching Drew for his reaction to Amy's animated description. Despite her level of energy and enthusiasm, Drew was not revealing his reaction. Julia was on the edge of her seat following Amy's every word.

"Consider the Guggenheim Museum in Bilbao: world class art in a destination architecture building located in a city most people have never heard of. The international art crowd is lined up every day to get in and then to go out to eat. The restaurant scene is on fire. There isn't any bad food to be had. The 18-hour-a-day café across from our hotel in San Sebastián would do well in New York or Paris. In the country the restaurant is humble, the service is gracious, and the food looks plain on the plate yet astonishes you with complexity. It's rustic but sophisticated. In the city I'd say it's all high level cuisine whether casual or formal."

When Amy stopped talking and looked around at each of them for a reaction, Drew paused to make sure she really was finished before he spoke.

"I get that it's good but what makes the cuisine so unique?"

"In one word: terroir. The location creates a unique eco-climate of soil and seasons from the Atlantic coast that blows all the way to the Pyrenees. You can try to grow a piquillo pepper elsewhere, but it will never taste the same. You can try to grow the same grapes elsewhere but you can't duplicate the wine. The fish and shellfish are the same way. Grilled sardines in San Sebastián can be imitated but can't be replicated. They lavish attention on simple ingredients to create the complexity. Ambitious chefs from everywhere are there competing for the best dishes and the customers. Traditionalists and modernists work next door to each other."

"Amy, tell me what you're thinking about for us," said Drew.

"A distinctive part of the lifestyle is to go out and see friends and the tourist experience in the Basque Country — is what we would call bar hopping. They have their own word for it, but they think of it more as socializing, having a snack, particularly before dinner because they eat so late. Friends meet in a bar to visit, have a bite of the specialty of the house — that's the *pintxo* — and a small glass of wine and then move onto the next place, probably next door. It's casual, it's cheap and it's fun. The food can be as simple as a shrimp on a toothpick or as complex as what looks like a miniature clay pot with a blooming flower, but it's all edible, even the dirt and the pot. The flavors surprise you. The atmosphere can be boisterous. Depending on what town or city you're in, the *pintxo* bars might occupy one street or many city blocks. You can spend hours at it if you want. It helps you get to the 10 o'clock dinner or skip dinner. The traditionalists' *pintxo* bar experience would be easy to create in this gallery. You would set up five or six tables around the gallery to give people elbowroom to gather around each table, each with one food bite ready to eat on a small paper plate or napkin. Another table could be used for assorted chilled beverages, cider, red and white wines poured small, maybe one or two ounces. Guests go table to table tasting the food and they get a tumbler of their beverage of choice with each bite. If you wanted to be fancy you could pair a wine with each bite." She paused and then said, "Can you see it?"

Everyone nodded and Drew said, "I'm getting it. What's the food bite like?"

"Well, the variety is huge, but to mention a few famous *pintxos*, the first one could be the Gilda, popular since the 1940s, named for the movie, which combines a few specific Basque items, olives, peppers and anchovy. Easy to assemble, good-looking on a toothpick, one bite gives you all those tastes, and it's killer. Foie gras is as common as mushrooms and simply served on toast. Cold squid or octopus is classic with garlic mayonnaise. You have to have salt cod in some way, but stuffed in a piquillo pepper is very Basque. Something lamb is also important. I haven't even mentioned charcuterie, which is very popular, or vegetables! The Basques own white asparagus and leeks." She was excited.

Drew looked at her very seriously. "It all sounds like I should go visit there tomorrow but the big question for me is what is the link from *pintxos* to Basque art from the American West?"

She looked at him like she was confused. "Are you kidding? They love to eat! The food is the food wherever you eat it. Basque cuisine is global. They eat the same thing wherever they go or at least as much as they can. They assimilate some ingredients and make them their own. It is not hard to find Basque food in Seattle. A few blocks from here you can buy pimenton, octopus in a can and white asparagus in a jar. We have the restaurant The Harvest Vine. We have a *pintxo* bar in Belltown called *Pintxo!*

A *pintxo* bar in Reno serves many of the same things as in Boise or in San Sebastián."

"Thank you! That's so simple, so elegant. Why didn't I know it?" said Drew.

"Don't take this wrong because you know I like you, but you really don't enjoy eating." Amy smiled at him. "I live for it which gives me a strong link to Basques around the world."

Drew took her assessment with a sense of humor. "You are always welcome to be honest with me. Are you serious about offering to cook all these things for my crew at your house?"

"Yes."

"That's extremely generous of you. Why do you want to do that?" said Drew.

"It's fun to me. It's the best way to tell you about our vacation. After you taste the food, you will be positive you want a Basque *pintxo* event."

"Well, we are very pleased to be invited and will be there whenever you want to do it. Would you like me to pay for the imported products?"

"Oh, gosh no. Don't even think of it. It's our pleasure."

"Kevin is on board with all this?"

"Absolutely. He had a wonderful time and is as excited about it as I am. We talked about the menu on the plane home. I promise there will be no slide show."

After they all walked her to the door of the gallery with fond farewells and good humor, Laurence, Julia and Drew returned to the office. Drew sat behind his desk, and Laurence took the same chair swiveled around to face Drew.

"You were right, old man, this *pintxo* business is the right thing, and Amy making a party for us is very flattering. I thank you for your role in it."

152

"I can't take any credit for it. I just listened to her. It's totally her idea."

"Julia, don't you think the *pintxo* format is a great idea?" said Laurence.

She nodded. "Yes! It's fun and different. I think it will appeal to a lot of people. And it sounds like it would be easy compared to some of the food that's been brought in here."

Drew said, "It seems very Euro and hip, just what we need to encourage a new crowd. Now we must show the movie, *Gilda* at one of our movie nights. I think we should book that restaurant demonstration you talked about right away. Let's do that the second weekend, maybe Saturday afternoon with a wine tasting."

"Do you want me to make the arrangements?" said Laurence.

"Shall we ask them to come here to see the space and talk about the possibilities or shall we go visit the restaurant and see what's on the menu we would want them to demonstrate?"

Julia said, "Definitely, lets go to the restaurant!"

"How's the art angle coming this week?" said Laurence.

"We're making progress selecting the best of the artists we can find. I'm drilling down into information about the Boise, Idaho Basque community leaders. They seem to be successful at maintaining traditional cultural activities, but it is a little too far away for importing the dancers and other entertainment that I want. It's a long drive or expensive to fly ten people. I am not yet ready to commit to it. I may have to start an agency for Basque artists after all this research. I wonder what I could charge the artists for being part of my database."

Laurence shook his head. Drew worked all the angles all the time.

Chapter 16

When the library doors opened on Monday, Laurence was waiting outside in the crowd. He took a seat by the window while Amy dealt with the initial crowd of tourists.

When no one else was near her desk he came over and put his book bag on the floor as though settling in for a visit. He looked conspiratorially at her and said, "So what have you decided to cook?"

"I haven't thought about anything else since we had lunch on Friday, and from the top 20 ideas we're trying to choose the best five or six. It's so hard! I have given up on the modernist cuisine book of *pintxos*. There was too much chemistry and ingredients that are difficult to source. This beaker and flask cooking is not for me. I'm back to more traditional concepts but hopefully newer presentations. How about you?"

"I read two *pintxo* books over the weekend and see now it is the thread tying all the different elements together, the Old World and the New World. You don't know how helpful you've been to the whole gallery effort. So, tell me the final selections."

"The most painful decision was scrapping the foie gras. There's none available in time for the party. Here's how I envision the six bites progressing. The Gilda you know, cold pepper soup, leek tart, garlic shrimp with piment d'Espellette, octopus, salt cod in piquillo peppers and the lamb meatballs."

Laurence listened and thought and finally said, "That's seven."

"Shall I give up the shrimp as being too ordinary?"

"What's authentic and rounds out the menu? I loved the idea of the white asparagus. You could use the same garlic mayonnaise as the octopus. They could be on the same platter," said Laurence.

"You're right. It is so nice to have you to consult with."

"Now, about the Basque exhibit, Drew is looking at all sorts of other entertainment, cooking demonstrations, movies, dancing. If you wanted to speak about the cuisine or cook something, you could get a gig." Laurence smiled at her.

"Oh, no, nothing but the party for me. I have stage fright."

"You can always change your mind. We have a long list of possibilities, and who knows what will be on the agenda by January."

"I had no idea you could put something together like this so quickly."

"Never underestimate Drew. He thinks faster and works harder than anyone I know. Are you sure you're comfortable about your part in it?"

She hesitated for a moment before she answered by nodding her head. "Yes, if I understand it properly. My part is having you over for a Basque *pintxo* party. Nothing else. That's something I love to do, and I am happy to have the opportunity to cook for a new crowd. Is that what you think my part is?"

"Exactly," he said, nodding in agreement. "I'm cooking with a friend soon and making a pantxineta, a miniature version of the iconic Gateau Basque from my research. Would you like me to bring one to your party to be a sweet finish that you don't have to make?"

"Thanks. That would be great. I'm not a baker, as you know. What else are you cooking with your friend?" Amy said.

"The menu changes daily, but I bet she's making pasta with meat sauce and salad while I do the dessert."

"Special occasion?"

"Sort of." Laurence was uncertain where to go from here.

Amy was waiting for him to continue, and when he didn't she said, "Please feel free to bring her to the *pintxo* party too."

That startled him. "How do you know it's a her?"

"You said 'she's making pasta,' but if she's a he that would be OK too."

Laurence tapped his forehead and smiled. "Of course I said *she*."

"Are we talking about Eva Russo by any chance?"

Laurence looked at Amy dumbfounded. "What makes you say that?"

"Good guess. I saw you talking with her at the gallery and she is the queen of pasta."

"I'm surprised you remember."

"How could I forget? Every man in the room including my husband was taking notes on her. She stands out in the crowd. She knows how to handle the attention. I admire that."

Laurence nodded and studied the floor looking for the right thing or anything to say. His mind had gone blank trying to acknowledge his relationship with Eva. Amy seemed to have guessed it from nothing he could understand.

Amy said, "How nice for you to have a new cooking friend. You'll have to let me know how your party goes."

They discussed dates for the *pintxo* party at her house and agreed on the following Sunday afternoon.

Amy said, "How many people? Do you know that number?"

"Five people from the gallery," he said.

"What about Mrs. Russo?"

"Are you sure you want to invite her?" He was deadly serious now.

"Yes, definitely. Don't you?" Amy smiled at him.

"Eva makes six."

"I look forward to seeing her again. Eight pours from a bottle of wine will be a perfect tasting size. I have three wines in mind, Cava, Txakoli and Tempranillo Reserva. What wine do you think you want for the dessert?"

"I don't know. I'll ask William or Charles. Please let us bring that along with the dessert." He got a small pad out of his book bag and started writing.

Laurence waited for Eva to buzz him in the front door. What was she doing? He entered the code again and waited. Nothing. She said she was going to be at home. She must be running late. Whether to wait here or in the park or go home was difficult to choose not knowing how long she would be. She had offered to get him a key made but he wasn't quite ready for that. So far being on the wrong side of the door hadn't happened often enough to inconvenience him enough to want his own key. *Simplify the situation by asking*, he told himself and dialed her cell phone. When he got this phone a year ago, he couldn't imagine how he would use it except to answer Drew's occasional calls about projects at the gallery. Now it seemed like he used it ten times a day calling Eva, and he finally understood modern communications, why everyone on the bus was on the phone saying, "I'm on the bus. I'll be there in..." Oh my God, he was still amazed at the daily turmoil of being meshed with her. It was exciting, frightening, comforting and frequently hilarious. She was quite the comedienne. The minutes of unknown whereabouts created terror in him. Where was she? Was she OK? Did she still love him? Hopefully soon he would not be so worried when he didn't know where she was. It was irrational to be so concerned. He could go from calm thoughts to his worst fears in less than a minute. That damn car was a big worry. She drove so fast. Just before he gave up she answered.

"Hello! Sorry I had to dig in my purse for the phone."

"Where are you?" he asked.

"I just got on 99 by the Market."

"Hang up the phone immediately! You can't drive and talk," he said.

"But what did you want to tell me?"

"Nothing. I'm hanging up now. You do the same," he said.

So, this was modern love in the 70s, his and her 70s. Seven decades of experience and here he was feeling the timeless anxiety of being in love. It was disconcerting to be so in the thrall of something he couldn't control. Maybe in a month or two everything would be calmer, not so emotional.

Much sooner than he could have imagined possible, he saw her car approaching the side street entrance to her building and garage. There she was, waving at him from her car in the driveway, waiting for the garage door to be completely opened. He followed the car into the underground parking so he could help her carry whatever she had bought. When he reached the parked car, she got out and put her arms around his neck and gave him a welcome kiss. He hugged her as tightly as he could without hurting her, burying his head in between her neck and her coat collar.

"Oh, you missed me," she whispered in his ear.

"Yes, I did."

"Has it been long?"

"A few hours I suppose, but it felt like days."

"That's what I thought too. How can a trip to the grocery store seem to take a week?"

"If you shop at Safeway, it always feels that way."

She laughed at him. "Two checkers open, tons of people waiting and it's not even Christmas."

"May I carry something for you?"

"Sure, the trunk is full. We'll have to make two trips."

The trunk popped open and he surveyed the bags and boxes. "That's impressive. What are we going to do with all this?"

"We're having a party, remember? You're going to meet my family."

"Oh, that. Yes, I remember. We need all this and so soon?" he said and grabbed two bags in each of his hands and she took one in each of hers.

In the elevator she pressed herself against him, making him back up against the wall and kissed him.

The elevator door opened, and the woman standing there gasped in surprise at them. Eva turned around to look at her and said, "Hello, Helen. How are you?" and walked out the door past her without waiting for reply.

Laurence nodded at Helen as he walked past her and said nothing. She said nothing either, just looked at them walking down the hallway with their groceries. The elevator door closed with her still in the hallway.

With the apartment door firmly closed and locked, he stood by the door where she was waiting with a mischievous grin.

"Wasn't that wonderful! That will make Helen's week. I bet she is on the phone right now calling anyone she knows who knows me that she saw us kissing in the elevator."

"First your family and now the world knows about us. I kind of liked it when it was our secret."

Eva said, "That was exciting too, but this is more so."

"If you say so, I'll try to think it too. Maybe I have stage fright. I feel the spotlight looking for me in the crowd and when they find me, they will throw tomatoes."

Eva said, "Nonsense. That spotlight feeling will last a few minutes, and then our news will be old hat."

"Are you preparing a press release or something?" said Laurence.

"No, just a small heartfelt speech to be the introduction to the family."

Laurence said, "May I help you practice or edit?"

"No, I don't need any help except with these groceries. I'm accustomed to making speeches, particularly to my children. I know how to be brief for their attention spans."

"Should I prepare some remarks?"

"I think 'nice to meet you' will do unless you get inspired to tell them all the things you have taught me in such a short period of time and what a quick learner I am. You could ask me to demonstrate my push-ups! That will impress them."

He chuckled and shook his head. "I don't think that will be necessary. You won't have the right clothes on anyway."

She laughed, "That is correct. My early morning exercise gear is for your eyes only. Do you want to get the wine out the trunk?"

"No. I'm waiting until after dark when Helen has gone to bed."

Laurence began unpacking the bags with salami and prosciutto and cheeses. "This did not come from Safeway."

"No, I had to go to my specialist at the Market for that, Mr. DiLaurenti. I think we must begin our party with a classic Italian antipasti plate and a very dry Prosecco from the Veneto. That will warm up the crowd. We can venture out from there. I wanted to give you a taste of it tonight for dinner so you could think about how to improve it."

He brought a few platters down from the top shelf for her to inspect. "Do any of these have a holiday significance that means we shouldn't use them?"

She looked at him carefully. "Please don't worry so much. The food on the plate is more meaningful to them than the plate. They will be happy to see it as it is a treat these days to eat old-fashioned antipasti. Delicious as they are, the cured meats and cheeses aren't considered healthy."

"I wondered how they fit into the Mediterranean diet."

"Sparingly, on special occasions, like this one."

"I see. It's a treat for me too. Shall I open some wine?" he said.

"A dry sparkler is what we need. I think there's at least one in the wine cooler."

Laurence examined the under-the-counter wine refrigerator and produced a bottle of Champagne and a Prosecco and held them up for her to see.

"Definitely the Champagne. I bought several bottles of Prosecco for the party."

The cork popped, and he slowly poured into the flutes watching the bubbles rise to the top and linger. He handed her a glass and raised his own. "To you, my love, astonishing in every way." They sipped. "My goodness, Mrs. Russo, the Champagne is also astonishing. Thank you very much for saving the best for us and giving Prosecco to your relatives."

She smiled at him and took the antipasti platter in her other hand and said, "For the man who cooks for me, recites poetry to me and is the best lover in the world? This is how I say thank you in Italian." Eva walked into the living room and took a seat on the leather couch facing the French doors to the balcony. She put down the platter and put a thin slice of the prosciutto in her mouth and nodded her approval. She put a small piece in his mouth when he sat down beside her.

Laurence leaned back on the couch and exhaled slowly, shaking his head. "Eva, the exhibition at the gallery now has a jet engine to propel it forward in the form of enthusiastic tourists just home from the Basque Country. You are invited to a *pintxo* party at Amy and Kevin's on Sunday."

Eva said, "How lovely. Our first invitation. What shall I wear?"

"You'll be dining with the fashionistas, so dress accordingly."

She said, "May I suggest that at our party we follow the antipasti with a pasta in marinara sauce instead of cold shellfish?"

"Yes, you may."

"With no discussion?" she said.

"You have properly warmed me up in every way possible to be agreeable."

She laughed. "That was too easy. Something else will be hard."

They relaxed side by side into the couch so comfortably Laurence was lulled into a private reverie of peace and solitude that was unique to him. He had not a care or concern in the world. His mind did not wander. He was just there in the room with Eva by his side, and it was very quiet. She seemed to be equally content, needing nothing. He put his flute down and took her right hand in his left to kiss and hold gently against his thigh. He sighed, leaning his head against the top of the couch and realized he could weep if he let himself. Tears of joy from poetry, novels or a movie had never been his experience before. So many new feelings were happening inside him. He felt as though his mind were generating new cells and tissues so fast soon there would soon be nothing of the old Laurence left.

Chapter 17

Drew saw Amy standing on her front porch with her dog as Charles parked his black SUV near her sidewalk. He waved to her and was the first person out of the passenger side but he waited for Julia to demonstrate how one discreetly dismounts from a tall vehicle in a short skirt. Behind the open back door, Julia put one pink high-heeled ankle boot on the grass and then another. When she closed the door there were her thin legs bare except for a little bit of pink stretchy fabric that hugged her from the top of her slender thighs to her waist. Her black tee shirt and black jacket were tight but didn't reveal any midriff. She had a big bouquet of flowers in her hand wrapped in white paper and lime green tissue.

Amy smiled and waved back at them as they approached her steps. William was still getting out of the back on the street side with a neoprene carrying case with wine. Charles was waiting for him. The men were all in black suits. Drew reached her first with a warm hand and a kiss on the cheek. He whispered in her ear, "You smell lovely," and said for anyone to hear, "Thank you so much for inviting us." Julia said hello and handed Amy the bouquet. Amy's dog was straining at his short leash wanting to jump on everyone. Drew appreciated that she kept the dog off of his trousers, which would show every blonde hair. With her hands full of flowers and dog she called out to William and Charles, "Welcome! Please come in."

Kevin appeared in the open door to greet Drew and Julia. Amy waved the flowers at him and kept walking toward the kitchen with the dog.

Drew surveyed the elaborate set up on the big dining room table. Four ice buckets were on the table with eight glasses beside each one. The Cava was unopened in the bucket next to the flutes. Open bottles of Txakoli and a Tempranillo Reserva were in the second and third buckets with small white wine glasses and larger red wine glasses. Small hobnail sherry glasses were positioned next to the fourth bucket for the dessert wine William had in his carrying case. Two of the buckets were sterling silver adding a rich luster to the crystal shine of the other two buckets and the glasses.

The platter of Gilda *pintxos* Amy had described was in front of the Cava and a pitcher of cold red pepper soup was next to that with eight shot glasses. Another platter featured small chunks of octopus and white asparagus with a dipping sauce. He knew the names of the dishes because they had all studied the menu in advance at the gallery to be prepared for the tasting. Three trivets indicated the courses to come. Stacks of small square white linen napkins were by each wine bucket. Amy had knocked herself out for them all right. This was a lovely display of crystal and sterling. Drew thought the table, the food, the wine and the glasses all looked ready for a photo shoot. He felt a surge of disbelief and then joy that someone had done all this for him. He did deserve it. To capture the moment he took a few photos with his cell phone and then grabbed Julia's elbow to guide her over to stand by the big picture window next to the table where the Cava was waiting. He whispered in her ear, "Isn't this special?" She agreed, nodding her head at the table sparkling with readiness. He pointed out his favorite art in the living room and dining room to Julia and gave her the back story on each artist. Amy collected art by friends and family, so each piece had a personal history to go with it. A few were amateurish right out of senior citizen painting classes, but overall it was colorful and eclectic with high emotional impact. The house and the display fascinated Julia. She told Drew she wanted to have a house someday. He said, "Yes, I know because collecting and decorating are so satisfying."

Kevin finally appeared with William and Charles who stopped by the end of the table. Charles handed Amy a bottle of Champagne wrapped in gold paper. Drew was extremely glad he had decided to go for the best deal Charles could get for him. Amy would be impressed whenever she opened it and have that same "for me?" feeling he had just had looking at the table she set for him.

Amy admired the wrapping and said, "How nice! Thank you! Maybe we should open this instead of the Cava I planned to serve."

"No. Please save it for a special occasion. We are so happy to be your guests. We want to taste everything as planned," said Charles.

Amy handed the bottle to Kevin to put it in the refrigerator so she could shake William's hand, and he said, "What a pleasure to see you again, Amy."

"I'm so glad to see you too. May I take your wine bag and put it in the refrigerator or would you prefer to put the wine in the ice bucket now?"

"Let's put one in the bucket and one in the refrigerator if you have room for it," he said.

Drew moved Julia around a bit to the other end of the table to make more room for William to stand in front of the Cava and begin unwrapping the foil. He was feeling like a stage manager getting all his actors into position so the show could begin. He thought Amy, standing in the big archway between the kitchen and the dining room, looked very pleased with herself and her table. She was still pretty, aging but pretty. She always wore such a severe outfit of trousers and a silk blouse that wasn't her best choice. Drew wished she would add some color and texture with a bouclé jacket, or a red dress would be more stylish. He might tell Julia to suggest a jacket she had seen recently that would make this outfit better. Kevin too looked pleased surveying his domain. Tall and thin as always, wearing a white dress shirt and gray slacks, in this natural lighting his red hair was definitely history. He now had white hair. Having been prematurely white for many years Drew thought it a striking accent on most people. What most people lacked was a good hair stylist. Drew pulled out his phone and snapped a picture of them and a few more of the crowd around the table. No one would ever know how much it meant to him that Amy and Kevin were having this party for him. It validated his interest in them and the time he'd spent cultivating a relationship. All the anxiety over the exhibition was wiped away for the day, and he experienced the anticipation of success for his Basque exhibition.

The doorbell rang, and the dog started barking and jumping at the door, straining against the leash Amy was still holding. She moved swiftly toward the door with the dog leading the way. She opened the door and with a big smile said, "Welcome," to Eva and Laurence. "Follow me."

She led them through the small living room, and Laurence had forgotten it was so laden with art on the walls and on the mantelpiece. He remembered the fire burning in the fireplace. The other guests greeted them in the large dining room. Amy took the plastic wrapped platter out of his hands.

Drew held out his hand and cheek to Eva who looked to him like a Chinese New Year's celebration in a Mandarin orange fitted dress with contrast gold trim on a standup collar and covered buttons. "That's a beautiful color on you. I hope you know you have broken three hearts by choosing the old baker over all of us."

She shook his hand and received his kiss on the cheek. "It's always wonderful to see you, Drew." She winked at Charles and William. "You two make the wine taste better."

Laurence in his gravitas gallery suit said, "Julia, you look lovely in pink. I wish your color sensibility would wear off on these gentlemen who always look like they've come from a celebrity funeral."

The men in black nodded at Laurence, and he understood they felt sorry for him and his lack of fashion sense. The way they were looking at Eva, he realized there might be a little disbelief, envy or maybe sour grapes in William's case. Charles was another story but he wasn't sure what, amused? Drew clearly loved the new romance but Laurence wasn't sure why. Undoubtedly Drew had spread the word of the vacation, and here Eva was with him at an important business related function, so everything they had heard and more was true. Laurence had to admit to himself he felt like gloating but tried to summon up his Boeing swagger so all his luck appeared deserved and expected.

While William popped the cork quietly and began filling the flutes Amy settled the dog on one of the couches in the living room and returned to stand in the archway. She said, "Have any of you visited in the Basque Country?" Amy looked around at each one. Everyone shook their heads no except Eva and William.

"The Basques are famous for hospitality, frequently beginning with Cava. A warm welcome to you all, thanks for coming and sharing a taste of our recent vacation where we immersed ourselves in all things Basque. As they say, *topa!*" She raised her glass to the group and they all responded with the same.

Kevin, standing beside her, sipped and then said, "The custom of the *pintxo* bar is to stand with friends, have a drink and a small bite and then move on to the next bar, which is usually next door. So we will move around the table tonight instead of going next door. The pours seem short until you pay and realize it's only a dollar or two, and the wines can be quite good. Usually a few white choices like the Cava or Txakoli and several red choices at each level of aging, *tinto, crianza* and *reserva*. You can taste anything for free to decide what you want to order."

Amy said, "The first thing you wine experts may notice is that the red is on ice too. In the *pintxo* bars everything is chilled and usually all together in one bus pan of ice, so it's easy to see what the choices are if you can't read the chalkboard. The cold red seems weird at first, but you get used to it pretty quickly, and now I want it cold."

Charles and William looked at each other and William said, "Cellar temperature of 55 degrees (F) when there was no refrigeration."

"Yes, exactly," said Amy, nodding at them.

Kevin said, "Gentlemen, you all probably know who Rita Hayworth is? Julia, do you know?"

"Sorry, I don't," Julia smiled at him not looking the least bit sorry.

"She was a Hollywood star in the 1940s. The Spaniards went crazy over this film, *Gilda*, which took place in a casino in Buenos Aires. They loved the character who was a sultry singer with red hair and a free spirit. The first food bite we're going to have is named after her and served in many *pintxos* bars. We learned this in our *pintxos* class in San Sebastián and I made these," he said with a flourish.

Everyone laughed at Kevin. He picked up the platter and offered it to Julia first and then the others. "Each ingredient is a Basque specialty. The peppers are called *guindilla*. The anchovies are from the Cantabria Sea. The olives are Manzanillo. If you eat it all in one bite you will taste the terroir of the Basque Country."

The one bite instruction made quick work of the first round of Gildas and more sips of Cava.

Amy said, "Well, you see what an encouraging beginning this is. It's hard to keep moving when it tastes so good. You want more, but the next bite is always beckoning.

William put the empty Cava bottle upside down in the bucket and looked at Kevin.

Kevin looked at Amy, "Sweetheart, more Cava or shall we move on to the Txakoli?"

Amy hesitated and then said, "Yes, move on."

The conversation turned to Atlantic seafood flavors while William poured everyone a new glass of the white wine. Amy began pouring the cold soup into the shot glasses on the table. Charles jumped in to help her by passing a glass to everyone. Amy described how fiercely the Basques defended their boundaries and how the career of being a soldier or sailor traveling the world became common.

Laurence looked at his soup and noticed there was no garnish and decided to say nothing about it. No one else would know it was incomplete. He and Amy had discussed numerous garnishes. Kevin and Amy were doing good teamwork on the presentation. If they were doing this spontaneously, she was a much better speaker than she said she was. Eva was standing close to him at ease with the proceedings. He was intensely proud of her in this crowd. Her alliance with him enhanced his status. His peers were seeing him in a new light today as more than the man they thought they knew. All these feelings were odd but pleasing.

When everyone had their shot glass of pepper soup in hand and was looking at Amy, she paused as though she couldn't remember what she had intended to say about it. Then she smiled at everyone and said, "This is a Basque pepper soup recipe we learned at the cooking class in San Sebastián," and drank hers in one gulp. Everyone followed suit. Laurence thought her recovery was excellent.

"Delicious," said Drew.

"I could drink this for breakfast," said Julia, still standing by Drew but looking around the room at the art.

"Amazing texture." said William. "How long did you have to process it to make it this creamy?"

"About ten minutes in an old food processor. At the class they had a European racehorse with enough power to tow a boat. It also had a heating element so if you wanted to serve the soup hot, it could do that simultaneously," said Amy.

"A Vitamix machine," said Eva quietly, which got the attention of the crowd "They are popular in Italy too." She looked around the table at everyone looking at her. "All the restaurants seem to have them. I think it's part of the new equipment, like all the beakers bubbling with thermometers in them, even behind the bars. The nouvelle cuisine has its own tools to differentiate it from the old school."

"I'd like to have one," Kevin said.

"What will you make in it?"

"Ask Amy. I really have no idea other than the soup, which I agree with Julia, would be good any time of day. It just seemed like a quality machine. We saw the shot glass thing in many places and usually with outrageous garnishes of whole oysters, raw duck eggs or baby squid."

"Oh, my God, I forgot the garnish! Marinated squid would have been perfect." Amy looked stricken.

Everyone laughed and Laurence said, "What was your garnish today?"

"Flakes of hard boiled egg yolk. I am so embarrassed. I hate to tell you how often I forget the garnish."

Everyone agreed the quality of the white asparagus and octopus outweighed any reluctance to serve them from jars. Amy assured them many *pintxos* came from jars and were encouraged for the convenience. Even though home-made garlic mayonnaise was superior to store-bought, the teacher had advised them that a big dollop of minced garlic and a splash of olive oil would brighten any commercial product. The important point was that it was easy to make *pintxos* at the last minute.

Amy next brought out the cold platter of salt cod brandade stuffed in red piquillo peppers and placed it next to the almost empty platter of octopus and asparagus. "Almost a thousand years of history of the Basque people is told in this dish. They were fearless fisherman who chased whales all the way to Greenland and discovered the cod banks there. They were great shipbuilders and seamen. When Columbus was organizing his attempt to find the New World he had a Basque navigator and sailors who were responsible for bringing this little pepper back to Spain, among other things. In its new home, with different sun and soil, the fiery pepper grew mild and wildly popular, an icon of Basque cuisine with a new name, piquillo." She offered the platter to everyone to grab one with their fingers before putting it down on the table.

Everyone ate that in two bites and quickly took a second piece emptying the platter. Eva complimented Amy on the creamy texture of the cod brandade. They talked about the differences in the recipe and techniques she'd used before the cooking class. The classic method at home would have been with milk and potato to stretch out the cod. Restaurants chefs had upped the flavors using cream and more olive oil and no potatoes. The leek tart could be a substantial brunch or dinner item if it were baked in a crust or *pintxo* size served crustless cut in small squares from a baking pan the way Amy had done it. It was light and airy with intense leek flavor and an appealing light green color.

Julia began gathering empty soup shot glasses from the table and taking them into the kitchen to place on the counter by the sink. Amy put flutes on the empty cod platter and said, "I will be back in a moment with the next *pintxo*." Laurence followed them to the kitchen with empty platters.

Amy said, "Thanks for clearing those. Julia, Drew told me you are doing a lot of the phone work sourcing Basque art. What's the typical reaction from the artists?"

"Shock and awe anyone in Seattle is interested in Basque anything," said Julia.

"That's great, right?"

"You bet. It's been a slow process to identify the artists and to convince them we're not thieves. Some of the art is good. Some of it is not, but that will give us a variety of price points, which is good for new buyers."

Laurence sat on a bar stool and watched Julia open the empty dishwasher and begin loading up the dirty flutes and shot glasses. Amy got a platter of shrimp out of the warming drawer and squeezed a half a lemon over it. She took toothpicks from a box on the counter, inserting one in each shrimp. Julia started inserting toothpicks from the other end of the platter.

"You really are worth a million bucks. Thank you." Amy smiled at her.

Julia shrugged. "We appreciate you inviting us. This is a great way for us to learn more. Seeing your enthusiasm for Basque everything is contagious. I'm excited about meeting some Basque people for real. Drew is determined we're going to have some type of musical performance. Did you know they can play wooden boards like a xylophone? We saw it on YouTube."

Amy said, "No. I didn't but nothing would surprise me about Basque ingenuity."

Using hot pads, Amy transported the platter to the dining room and offered it to each person to grab a toothpick with shrimp and then she set it down on a trivet.

Amy said, "There are lots of shrimp, so please don't be shy, unless you're allergic to garlic. Charles, tell me what you think of the Txakoli."

"The terroir is obvious. The minerality makes it a natural pairing with the seafood. The light body would make it popular with many white wine drinkers. I think it makes a good party wine. The foreignness of the name however would probably work against it on a menu. People are embarrassed not to know how to pronounce names properly and therefore will skip on to one they know, like Pinot Grigio."

"So what do you think, Amy?" asked Drew.

"I almost didn't serve this shrimp as too boring, but I'm glad I did. I love the wine. Let the experts debate. For me the question is, what goes well with garlic?" She laughed. "Honey, what do you think?"

"I prefer red wine." Kevin looked at the wine guys for their opinion. He got confirmation from that side of the room.

"Shall we pour the Rioja Reserva and see how you like it with the shrimp?" William said. He didn't wait for anyone to answer.

Drew stood quietly taking it all in. He was pleased with the scene and could envision a still life with wine tasting based on the detritus of the table after feasting. Amy really was delightful to put this together for them. She was a lovely woman, and he loved having her as a customer and friend. She was right that once he tasted all this he would be certain this food was a great choice for a gallery event that would draw in new people. It was so good-looking on the platter and the plate. Attention to visual detail was so important to enjoying the food. He admired Laurence for sweeping Eva off her feet. She was another lovely woman with such good taste. They seemed natural together and enjoying themselves. How cool to have a hot girlfriend in your 70s! He should find a new girlfriend for himself so he could be having more fun whenever he wanted to.

Soon everybody was swirling large wine glasses and smelling and sipping. William thought it was a lively wine, rich in the glass with heady aromas of dark berries and herbs from aging in the barrel three or more years before aging in the bottle several more years.

Amy said, "The Basques love to use piment. It's an important spice for the cuisine. That's French Basque piment on those shrimp. Let me tell you one difference about the French Basques and the Spanish that you can easily taste. Espellette is the most famous French village of red pepper farmers who dry their peppers but never smoke them before grinding them into a powder they call piment. The purists say it is used only as a garnish so the bright, lightly spicy notes of the pepper are clear. The Spanish smoke their peppers before grinding into a powder called pimenton and they use it to season food before they cook it. It makes it much more bold in flavoring. You can taste the smoke. Although you see it used before, after, and during in different books, my personal rule of thumb is to taste before you serve and add more if you like of either. I'll get the lamb with the smoked pepper, and it will show you another level of flavor." She smiled with satisfaction over this bit of culinary lore and went into the kitchen.

Eva followed her and said, "Let me help you. I know how to do toothpicks."

Laurence followed Eva as he hadn't seen her do toothpicks before. He wanted to be available if needed. He stood by the bar and watched the two women. He was surprised how chummy they seemed even though this was only the second time they had met.

Amy brought the platter of meatballs out of the oven with hot pads and gave it a shake to moisten the meatballs with the sauce. She started at one end and Eva on the other. There were 16. She said, "I wish I had made more. The shrimp platter looked better with more items. This needs a garnish. Let me look around in the refrigerator."

Laurence thought Eva looked deliberate poking the meatballs with the toothpicks. This was something else she probably had never done but was showing her self-confidence that she could do anything.

"Your house is beautiful," said Eva.

"Thank you. It's my main project other than cooking and reading. I probably spend too much time on it, but I can't stop myself. If we have time I'll show you my new inner city garden I just designed. It's a sliver of evergreen with yard art."

"I would love to see it. You have put a lot of thought into everything. Layers of patina make it appear to be an old family house for generations, but it's really a new house isn't it?"

"I appreciate you noticing," said Amy. "The joy of all new plumbing and wiring is hard to beat. Where do you live?"

"Across from Kerry Park in a new place but I lived for years in an old family house in Mt. Baker and know exactly what you mean about plumbing."

"How nice to have a view. We're going for a view in our next place, one of the retirement buildings downtown."

"A view is certainly worth whatever it costs. We enjoy it every day." Eva glanced at Laurence, "Don't we?" and back to Amy, "Are you moving soon?"

"Not for another ten years or so but when we're healthy and 70-something. It's the classic argument. The man wants to go out in a box, and I refuse to be left alone to disassemble all this by myself when I'm 80 or 90 years old. He is going to have to compromise!" She produced a plastic container with sweet pickled grape tomatoes she had made. "Here, let's sprinkle these around and put a toothpick in each as though I planned it. The Basques love pickled things." She smiled at Eva.

"It looks planned to me. I'll remember that for our next soiree. What do you think, Sweetheart about garnishing the antipasti platter with tomatoes like that?" Eva looked at Laurence who again nodded his head that he agreed with her.

Amy presented the platter of meatballs in its prepared place at the table, looking around the room for reactions as everyone took a bite.

William was first to opine. "This wine and the lamb is a classic pairing, both with natural sweetness and balanced with acidity and smoky red pepper spice. The shrimp to me is now out of its element with the wine."

"Yes, enjoyable but not as great as this pairing." Charles said.

Kevin was next. "In just a few simple bites you understand the key flavors of the Basque experience and can imagine what great food we had every day."

Laurence said, "Amy, I compliment you on your menu planning and execution. Everything was cooked and seasoned perfectly." He held up his glass to punctuate his remarks. Everyone held up their glass too.

"Well done, Amy. I am so impressed with you and the food," said Drew.

Kevin put his arm around her and Amy smiled at everyone in the room. "Thank you. I loved preparing it and reliving every day of our trip. The Basque Country and our cooking class in San Sebastián will always be one of our best adventures."

Chapter 18

Drew moved around the dining room to stand between William and Charles and chat with them about what they had gleaned from the tasting that they would use at the gallery. Kevin moved to be next to Julia to ask her more about the Basque art for the exhibit. Amy, Eva and Laurence stood together having another meatball and then Amy invited them to sit in the living room.

Amy dragged the big ottoman over and put it in the middle so everyone could put their feet up, which Eva did immediately showing off petite low-heeled sling backs that were a shade darker than the color of her dress. Laurence kept his feet on the floor. Amy put her feet up too, "Eva, I love your shoes."

"Thank you. I bought them with the dress in Rome."

"It's a great color on you. I love Italian shoes. When I was young, Italian heels and pearls were part of the office uniform."

Eva chuckled, "I remember that. You don't work anymore?"

"No, I haven't worked since the Great Recession got under way. Although I never say I'm retired, I say I'm unemployed, but I'm getting used to it now. I doubt I will ever work again. My age is against me. How about you?"

"I just retired after 40 years and I love it."

"Congratulations. What are you doing to amuse yourself, if you don't mind me asking?"

"Not at all. We exercise at home in the morning, take French lessons and tai chi classes both twice a week. We read quite a bit and walk miles. Of course, Laurence cooks most days."

"Oh, that does sound wonderful. How great to have acclimated so easily. Retiring is hard for many people," Amy said.

"Well, it certainly helps to have someone with you who likes to do all sorts of things. Will Kevin retire soon?"

"I hope not!"

The faux horror in her voice made Laurence and Eva turn to look at her. "Why is that?" said Eva.

"He's too young and makes too much money."

"Oh. That's important." Eva smiled at Amy.

She grinned back at her. "You know what fun it is to have money. Anyway, we're barely 60, and he truly has no ideas for himself in retirement. How old were you when you retired, Laurence?"

"I was 65. I wasn't tired. Boeing was transitioning from being the greatest engineering firm in the world to a manufacturer of aerospace products, which didn't require engineers, so I left. Retiring is a big adjustment. Kevin should keep working until he falls down if he wants to."

Eva said, "No! Don't wait too long. You want to be able to enjoy it."

"Yes, I do worry about that. We've already had friends drop dead unexpectedly or get some bad health news that changes everything. We hope he works until he's 65 or 70."

"Sadly, I have lost some dear ones too. I'm 70, and I think that's a great time to retire," said Eva.

"Are you really? You look terrific. I would have thought you were 60!"

"Thanks. That works out well with my boyfriend here who looks like he's 65 but isn't." She giggled.

Laurence got up and said, "You girls keep chatting. William and I are going to serve the next course."

Drew came over and assumed Laurence's position and put his arm around Eva. "Now tell me the truth, has the old man really got a lock on you?"

She thought about that for a moment looking at the ceiling for the answer with her lips pursed and said, "Yes."

"Simply yes! Just like that? I should say I'm awestruck with the speed with which he courted and conquered," said Drew.

"He's got many talents. Two of them are he cooks for me every day and recites poetry." She smiled at Drew, "How about you?"

"If that's what it takes, I'm hopeless. I can't cook and I had no idea about the power of poetry. What could I substitute?"

"You're young. You could still learn."

"My fate is now known. Poor me."

She shrugged. "So what are you thinking about the Basque event now that you've tasted the food?"

"I think it will be emotional and compelling just like the art. Anyone who experiences it will have to talk about it. That means it has the potential to bring people to my gallery who have never visited before."

"Congratulations, Amy on a persuasive introduction. I have thoroughly enjoyed every sip and bite," Eva said.

"Yes, Amy, I second that. You've shown me the spirit and the clarity in the Basque cuisine. I have seen it in the art, but I just couldn't quite imagine how it would translate in the mouth."

"Thank you both. I'm so glad you liked it. I love this food! Nothing brings me more pleasure than making a party, particularly a party that celebrates a memorable vacation," said Amy.

"Would you mind sharing the recipes so we can talk with the caterer about it?"

"I'll send you a copy in email. I am going to write my teacher too and tell him all about how his cooking class inspired a wonderful party and an event at an art gallery. I think he'll like that."

They could see William pouring something golden into the hobnail sherry glasses Amy had put out for him. Laurence put his platter in the center of the table and turned to look at the group on the couch.

"Would you like me to serve you?"

Eva said, "Oh, that would be great. I am so comfy."

Drew said, "I'll get up. How about you Amy?"

"For the novelty alone, I'll stay here and be waited on."

"William, follow me with two glasses." Laurence presented the platter of *pantxineta* to them and Amy gasped. It was full of small golden puff pastry squares with a thick vanilla cream spilling out of the center and powdered sugar sprinkled on top.

"They are gorgeous! Laurence, it's almost too pretty to eat. Did anybody take a photo?"

Drew took his phone out of his pocket and snapped away. William approached with a glass for Eva and Amy. Drew took a picture of them sitting on the coach with their feet up.

Only then did Amy take one of the precious squares and raise her glass to Laurence and Eva. "Great to be with you," she said.

Eva raised her glass too and took a sip. "Gentlemen, you have outdone yourselves. It's a magnificent sweet and wine. It's not a Sauternes, but what is it?"

William said, "Jurancon. You don't see it often; it's special for today only. It definitely won't be at the gallery. The wine region is in southwestern France about 80 miles from San Sebastián in the Pyrenees and competes with Tokaj for being the oldest wine region. Similar to Tokaj, the sweet wine ages for an incredibly long time, like 100 years." He and Laurence bowed and turned back to the dining table to pass the platter to everyone before putting it on the table. Laurence kept his back to the ladies on the loveseat, but he could hear every word and kept still so they wouldn't notice him listening.

Eva said, "The textures of the puff pastry and the sweet cream and nut flavors are extraordinary."

Amy followed her lead, "He really is talented, isn't he?"

"Yes, he is."

"Have you known him long?" Amy said.

"Long enough. I fell hard and fast for him."

"Does he know?" Amy said.

"Oh, yes. We fell over the cliff together on the same night. We'll never be apart now."

Laurence was amazed at how quickly women got to the point. He didn't know he and Eva had fallen over a cliff the same night! Unbelievable how Eva shared her feelings with someone she didn't know. How confidently she said they would always be together. He couldn't imagine having this conversation with a man or anyone else. It was difficult for him to talk with Eva about it because it was such an overwhelming topic. The next thing he guessed they would be chatting about sex. He might drop a glass on the floor to interrupt Eva's description of her sex life to Amy.

"I'm happy for you to find someone special who feels the same way," Amy said.

"What else did you learn at this cooking class?" Eva asked.

"Basque men are very charming." Amy grinned at her.

"So, the teacher was attentive?" Eva said.

"I'd never considered cheating on my husband before, particularly with someone half my age, but I gave it 15 seconds of thought before I said no." Amy laughed.

"I appreciate men who know how to put extra sparkle in the evening," said Eva and she laughed too.

"Seriously, I think he may have been fooling with me just to be flattering to the oldest woman in the room and having fun. He made me feel like I was 22 again. It was a very sweet and romantic, not the least bit offensive."

Laurence wondered if he should walk away from this startling conversation. But he couldn't quite leave it.

Amy continued with her description. "It was fun to be around a young crowd. We spent several days with Australian, Indian and British people. They were all half our age except the Brits. The chef fit right in. He showed me a few new tricks, cooking tricks you know. What I really learned is it's the passion, the obsession for cooking that sets the Basque apart. Make a little mistake like I did on something and he said, "No! You must begin again!" I suffer a combination of lazy and frugal that keeps me from throwing out mistakes and starting over."

"What kind of mistake did you make?"

"I overcooked the shallots. I was supposed to be going for golden and they ended up brown, not black, and that to him was ruined. It was a ton of shallots I had minced by hand and a whole bottle of nice olive oil. Anyway, he was stunned I refused him — on both counts. I'm sure it's good for him to be declined occasionally." They grinned at each other. "Please tell me about your French lessons."

Eva raved about the teacher, Bernadette, and how quickly everyone was learning to speak without fear of sounding stupid. Eva suggested Amy join them in the class. Amy told her about how she'd like to get some sort of tasting or restaurant group going out for lunch or dinner, which Eva was enthusiastic about. They both wanted to add some new people to their network. Eva proposed that the whole French class going out to dinner afterward would accomplish all the goals at one time. She described the other students to Amy and said she thought they were all nice, interested in travel and could afford to eat out. What a great way to practice French by translating the menu and speaking only French. Maybe Bernadette would want to be part of the tasting too. They could take turns choosing a restaurant near home to share what they thought was the best of their neighborhood. It would be a great way to learn new restaurants and areas.

Amy said, "I love that idea. I'd also like to invite you to join us soon for a rabbit dish I learned. Rabbit is a tough sell around here but I bet you and Laurence like it.

"You could sell us rabbit anytime. You should be very proud of this party today. Your table and food are lovely. You make it seem easy."

"Thank you so much! It's so great to have a new friend nearby. But I feel like the hostess needs to go pay attention to the wine guys. Shall I send your boyfriend back?"

"Tell Drew to come back please," said Eva.

Laurence moved away slowly to talk with Julia. *Oh, Eva, what are you getting me into?* Laurence mused. He would have to think about how rapidly Eva worked with people, and decide how to go along or not. A rabbit dinner at Amy's would be nice sometime in the distant future but not so soon after this event. He liked the French class but to go out to dinner afterwards seemed too much time spent with the same people. One of the men was a blowhard and he wasn't sure about the other one.

Amy told Drew that Eva wanted to chat with him and she got in between William and Charles who were still standing together. "I think we should open another bottle of wine. What do you suggest for next? I have back up bottles on everything we've had so far, or we could take a cellar tour for you to choose something else."

William said, "Are you sure you wouldn't like us to go now?"

"No, of course not." Amy shook her head, "We're having fun and there's still food and wine left."

"And Kevin is still feeling hospitable?"

"Absolutely. When the going gets fun, he's glad to keep it going. Let's open the Cava. It's a great beginning and ending wine. It will refresh everyone's palate. Charles, please tell me what you learned this week in the sommelier class."

Drew sat close to Eva on the couch and put his feet up on the ottoman next to hers showing off his shoes that were as elegant as his suit. "Thanks for whistling for me. What's on your mind?"

Eva laughed. "You have asked for my advice before so I hope you will be open to some advice about your event you didn't ask for. You have experts on staff but let Amy help taste with the caterer to be sure the food's on track. It won't cost you a penny. She will be happy just to be part of it. After all, she inspired you about this event in some way didn't she?"

Drew looked at her and said, "Thank you. I think you are right. This is why you are such a success. You see the big picture and size up all the players. What other advice do you have for me?" He took her hand in his in genuine appreciation for her help.

"If you don't want to be single old man, start reading poetry." She smiled at him.

"Thank you! Today is the first day I ever heard that. Where do you recommend I start?"

"Ask Laurence about that. Is Julia your girlfriend?"

He looked at her and paused before saying, "Sort of, sometimes."

"Stop doing that immediately. Tell her to find someone her own age to play with who is as smart as she is. You find someone your own age. That's important." Eva was emphatic.

"Do you know anybody?" He hoped humor would suffice as acceptance but he had no intention of following up on this ridiculous advice. *My relationship with Julia is special and private. The last time I had a girlfriend my own age we were both young.*

Eva said, "I might."

Several days after Amy's *pintxo* party, the buzzer on Julia's desk to summon him to come to the front of the gallery interrupted Drew studying photos of paintings of machinery he was considering. He couldn't imagine who would arrive unexpectedly just before closing. He hoped it would be a decorator with a rich client and a desperate need for art to hang for a party tonight. He had the perfect piece for her already in his mind. Julia was standing near the door with a woman in a pink Chanel suit with black trim and a black hat and accessories accompanied by an intense looking dark headed young man in an equally impressive gray suit. *High fashion indeed for a decorator and her assistant. This should be interesting, Drew thought.* The three stood eyeing each other with interest but saying nothing as they waited for him to cross the gallery. Julia looked casual compared to the couple in a black cotton jump suit with a wide belt and short black boots, showing no skin but her hands.

Drew welcomed them and introduced himself, offering his hand to the woman who took it and began speaking in French, which he listened to carefully, translating accurately he hoped. His French wasn't fluent anymore and he wasn't positive he understood. He wanted to save face here for himself and Julia by proving that he could handle this language challenge. He paused when she stopped speaking, shook the hand of the young man and looked at Julia. "Julia, this is Henri. Please show him around the gallery. We have some business to attend to in the office."

Julia turned to look into the eyes of her new task, Henri. He responded by looking back at her. He said something to her in French. She slightly shook her head indicating she did not understand.

He took her hand and kissed it. "English is your best language?" Julia nodded and Drew thought that Julia was about to give one of the most unusual gallery tours of her career. He motioned to the woman and said, "Come with me please" in French. They walked away toward the hidden entrance to the office.

In the office Drew offered her a chair and she sat on the couch. Maybe he didn't remember how to say chair. He sat behind his desk and looked at her expectantly. The Chanel package was dazzling to him and he wanted her to know he appreciated it, but this was business of some sort. He was sure it would be inappropriate to talk about her clothes. She appeared to be waiting for him to speak so maybe he had missed something else.

Drew said, "Bernadette, you are a delightful surprise from Paris at the end of the day. My French is rusty, so let's do this in English. Your friend Eva Russo sent you here to help me sell Basque art to Europeans. How am I doing?"

She smiled at him and said in English, "Very well. Your French isn't as rusty as you think, and you are clever to receive me without notice. I find it's better to begin to talk business without taking days or weeks on the typical preliminaries with phone calls, letters and contemplation. You will know in a few minutes if you want to do business with me or not. Then no one has wasted much time."

Well, she was quite charming and direct, he thought. "Help is a magic word to me so tell me how you can help me."

When Drew and Bernadette emerged from the office, Julia was sitting at her desk and Henri sat in her visitor's chair, holding her hand, tracing the lines in her palm and describing how a palm reader would interpret them. Drew stared at that intimate vignette. Henri worked fast. He felt a thousand years old seeing Julia talking with Henri. Eva was right. He looked foolish with Julia in any way except as her employer.

"Julia, I want you to meet Bernadette. She is going to help us in January." Henri put Julia's hand down on the desk next to two business cards, his and Julia's. He picked up her card and put it in his pocket. The women nodded at each other, but Julia didn't get up from her chair. "Henri, how did you enjoy the tour?" Drew said.

"Very much, monsieur. Your gallery is most interesting. I look forward to seeing the Basque exhibit in January."

Drew and Bernadette shook hands and made farewells in French. Henri stood up and said, "Soon, mademoiselle." Julia nodded at him.

After they were gone and the door locked, Drew sat down in the visitor's chair and said, "Bernadette teaches French and works with the Seattle Architecture Foundation giving architecture tours of Seattle. She also works for Show Me Seattle as a foreign language guide for private art tours in five languages. She will add us to her list of galleries for Europeans interested in buying art. She will bring them here to give them the tour of the Basque exhibit in their own language. She will also be available to help out on the busiest days. So there will be three of us talking about the art and selling it. We will pay her a 7% finder's fee, not a sales commission, which will be extremely beneficial to our bottom line. You and I will put together the pitch for the show and then we'll teach her. Are you OK with that, a new part-time member of the gallery crew to bring us new customers?"

Julia looked unsure. "I guess that sounds good for us."

"I hope so. Every extra new visitor is a bonus, and Europeans have a nice cachet to me as being knowledgeable about art and with money to spend if they are here on vacation."

"I agree with you about that. Is this a trial period for her looking for more hours here after the exhibit?"

"We didn't discuss that possibility. I can't imagine another situation where you and I would need extra help. But there's no harm in being on her list of galleries."

Julia shrugged.

Drew went on. "Bernadette says her son is well educated, including studying art history at the Sorbonne, has a good job and has been living in Paris with his father until recently. He needs a tour guide his own age for Seattle. Would you be willing to show him the neighborhood spots your friends like?"

Julia shook her head yes but still seemed subdued. She pushed his business card around in circles on the desk as she said, "He knows a lot about art, more than I do."

Drew could feel her discomfort. "Julia, he's studied art history at a famous university, so of course he knows more about that than you do. You *are* an artist and have studied in art school how to create in multiple mediums. That's very different. Don't be intimidated by his education. I bet he would trade it for your talent in a heartbeat."

She considered his words carefully and said, "I think I know what you mean but I still feel off kilter. I have never met anyone like him. He speaks more languages than English and French. He works in international finance at a bank. I've hardly been inside a bank. But I learned so much listening to his reaction to the art we've been looking at here for months. I am in awe of his ability to talk about it. I could hardly say a word. And he is so cute!"

Drew was bemused that his steady, no drama Julia had been so moved by a brief encounter. "Sounds like you had quite an experience while I was talking business in the office."

"Yes, I did," she said and she looked at him like he wouldn't believe what a big experience it was. She didn't elaborate.

"What else did you learn about him?"

She smiled, looking not at him but at the floor and finally said, "He knows how to read palms and is a great kisser."

"Oh," was all Drew could say. So there was chemistry already. Eva had been right that she might know somebody for Julia. Why not try to completely sew up this concept? Drew said, "Julia, you know I want only the best for you. A smart young man with a good job seems worth looking into if you feel you want to. I think it would be wonderful for you to have someone your own age who shares your interest in art. I don't want to be in your way. If it works out you really like him, or someone else, I am happy for you. You know what I mean?" He hoped using the words "own age" twice was all he had to say about that topic. He didn't want to go into any more description of the benefits of Julia having someone her own age.

She nodded again.

"OK. I'm glad everything is good with the gallery and us. The last item on my mind is you know to be wary of foreigners, right?" Drew said.

"I don't know. Wary of what?"

"They are famous for making you fall madly in love with them and then go home to their family."

"His father has a new wife and he doesn't like her, so I don't think he'll go home to Paris. He says he likes being here and plans to look for an apartment."

Drew forced back a chuckle at her view of the situation. "Well, now that all that is settled, I hope you have a good time showing him around. Try to get him to teach you some French. It's very handy sometimes, and your accent will be excellent learning from him."

"How did she find us?"

Drew admired how Julia's brain worked. "She is a friend of Eva's."

"Is that what you were talking about with Mrs. Russo at Amy's?"

Drew hesitated before responding. "We talked about improving the business for the Basque exhibit. Bernadette certainly looks like she could be helpful to us. You know how I like helpful people."

She nodded yes but said nothing. He knew she was carefully thinking it all through, seeing how the elements had come together to create this new situation with a third person in the gallery and trying to decide if it really was a good thing for her or not. This aspect correctly seemed more important to her than spending time with the great kisser. He tried to think of what he could say to comfort her and end the conversation.

"Julia, she doesn't want your job, and I don't want anybody but you to do your job."

"You really liked her suit, didn't you?" she said.

"You know I did. We so seldom see one. She wears it well."

"Do you think I should get one?" Julia said looking so serious.

"No! You always look terrific. You are a great stylist. You could work in fashion if you didn't want to paint and sell art. Wearing a Chanel suit is a style that doesn't require creativity. It's a statement. Please don't worry about Bernadette upsetting our business in any way."

"How does a teacher and tour guide pay for a Chanel suit?"

Drew shook his head and stood up. "I have no idea. I don't care and you shouldn't either. Let's lock up for the day."

Chapter 19

Laurence sat up in bed propped against the headboard with three pillows trying to read the newspaper with the coffee tray in between him and Eva who was staring at her iPad. She was going back and forth again about him baking cookies or the *pantxineta* that might not be appreciated by teenagers.

"Is that a good newspaper today?" she said.

"I don't know. I'm having trouble reading it."

"I think I'll go in the other room and give Sophia a call so you can read."

Her nerves about this party were starting to get on his nerves. The menu was simple. The shopping was done. There was nothing to be agonizing about. She was going to make the red sauce today so it could age properly for three days. He planned to bake a batch of cookies every day for three days. He was definitely not making puff pastry from scratch again for teenagers. The refrigerator was so full you couldn't find anything and he didn't think most of it was for the party. Eva liked food shopping.

She came back into the bedroom. "Tell me again which three cookies so I can make sure we have all the ingredients."

"We have the ingredients, I promise you. We agreed to the hazelnut and orange cookies, the Fagottini with little jam-filled pockets, and the Fregolata Veneziana shortbread cooked as a flat cake and cut into wedges."

"What jam?" she said.

"You have at least three jars of nice jam. I need to go do some errands. I'll be out of your way."

"You're not in my way."

"Oh, yes I am," he said.

On Sunday morning Eva was up making coffee hours earlier than usual. Laurence tried to go back to sleep and couldn't. He finally called out to her, "I'm awake if you want to come back in here."

She immediately presented herself with the coffee tray and got back in bed.

She reviewed the setup of the buffet, the wine and the food again. He knew the list as well as she did and exactly when each item would be executed.

"That sounds perfect. You've thought of everything."

"You're sure?" said Eva.

"Please relax. Everything is going to be fine. The food will be delicious. Your kids and grandchildren are lovely, intelligent human beings with manners. You told me that. What could go wrong?"

No doorbell was necessary to announce the first to arrive. They could hear the child wailing when the elevator door opened. Eva opened the apartment door and watched Sophia and her husband walk down the hall carrying little Eva who was red-faced with the effort of screaming hysterically with tears streaming down her face.

"Oh, my God! What's wrong with her? Is she hurt?" asked Eva.

"We don't think anything is wrong. She's been like this for an hour," said Sophia.

"Oh, little Eva come to your grandmother and tell her all about it." Eva reached out for the child who screamed even louder and clung to her father.

Laurence stood back away from the door and nodded at them as they came in.

Sophia came over to him with her hand out stretched and said, "Hello. It's so nice to see you again. This is my husband, Steve. I hope she will stop crying soon."

Steve waved from a few feet away. "Nice to meet you. You probably don't want to be too close to her. It's hard on your ears."

"Honey, maybe you want to take her on the balcony and close the door. I'll get you some wine. We'll trade places in a few minutes. How about that?" said Sophia.

Steve nodded in agreement and went out on the balcony. Once the French door was closed the worst of the crying was eliminated. Sophia took the big shoulder bag of baby paraphernalia in the bedroom and put her purse with it on the bed.

"Mom, do you have some wine open for Steve? We're going to take turns keeping her outside."

"Of course, I'll get it for him. No, Laurence you do that and I'll watch the door."

Laurence hated to give up his spot against the wall out of the way but approached the sideboard where the Champagne was in a bucket and the red wine was open. He poured a generous amount of red in a big wine glass and walked over to the French door. Opening it renewed the shrill sounds. He closed the door behind him and winced listening to it and held out the glass for Steve to take.

"Here you go. I hope this will help you. It must have been quite a drive over here in a closed car."

Steve took a long swallow and shook his head. "You would think we were on a 737 headed for New York with only five more hours to go. That's where she shows her lung power. As soon as she gets a little bigger, I'm going to

195

get her on a swim team or a cross-country running team. I think she's a natural athlete."

"That's a good idea. You fly a lot?"

"Enough to be gold with a few airlines. I'm in sales and my family is on the East Coast. How about you?"

"I'm a retired Boeing engineer. I helped build a lot of planes but I don't fly anymore."

"It ain't the grand old local company anymore, is it?"

"No, it isn't."

Sophia opened the French door and said, "Laurence, Marco and Ann Marie are here. Honey, are you ready for me to take over?"

"Actually, I'm happy here for a few more minutes, now that I have a personal bartender. You say hello to everyone first and then I'll come in."

Wishing he could stay outside with Steve, Laurence followed Sophia back inside where Eva was taking the coats of the new arrivals and turned to introduce him.

"Marco is my son who has taken over the majority of my work and all my traveling and he is doing a fabulous job. I am so proud of him. This is his wife, Ann Marie, who is suffering his absence without complaining, and I am proud of her too. And these are my grandsons whose talents on the soccer field and in the classroom I've already told you about."

Laurence shook hands with everybody and nodded to all the comments. Marco looked so much like his mother. Her features translated well to a male face and with the same dark curly hair of his sisters. Welcome to Eva's world where everyone looked like her. Even the gangly teenagers, taller than the parents, showed promise of Eva's good looks in a few more years. They immediately headed for the antipasti platter. Eva departed with their coats to the bedroom, leaving Laurence to talk with Marco and Ann

Marie. She was a nice-looking woman with dark straight hair, very trim and wearing a dark pantsuit, business-like but more than business. Marco didn't have a tie on, but he and his wife looked like they were going to the same party. Drew would admire these people and their expensive clothes. They should be invited to the Basque event to lend ambiance to the room.

Marco said, "Mom's looking very fit these days. That's great. What's your exercise routine?"

"We do a few daily strength and aerobic exercises at home and we take tai chi classes twice a week at the Community Center."

"Is that martial arts?"

"There may be some positions that are the same but, the goals are toning the body and calming the mind instead of defense. It's basically standing still in a way that wears you out, if you know what I mean."

Marco laughed, "Yes, I can imagine standing still that wears you out if it's on one foot with the other one wrapped around your neck?"

"You understand perfectly."

"What's Steve doing out in the cold?" Ann Marie asked.

"His child is crying extremely loudly."

"Oh dear, I don't want to bother him then. He might want help." She smiled at Laurence and looked over at the wine display.

Laurence said, "Would you like some wine? There's a Prosecco and a Barolo open."

They looked at each other and she said, "Sure. Why not? Eva always has the nicest wine."

They followed Laurence over to the sideboard. "Prosecco for me," said Ann Marie. "The same," said Marco.

Laurence poured them both a full flute and one for himself. He raised his glass to them and said, "Cheers."

They chatted about Laurence's career at Boeing and Marco asked him if he were ever married, which surprised Laurence and made his wife look annoyed. She told Laurence not to take offense as Marco couldn't remember many things he'd been told.

"None taken. I'm for full disclosure. I'll give you the key points myself. My wife died about five years ago after a long struggle with cancer. I'm honest. I'm a good cook and read two or three books a week, mostly non-fiction. Any other questions? I'm happy to tell you anything you want to know." He gave a slight grin, which was exchanged. He and Marco understood each other.

When asked Anne Marie told him about her day job as a professor of economics at the University of Washington and her night job doing quantity cooking for her sons. Laurence saw Eva open the door for her other daughter, her husband and their three sons who didn't look quite as big as the high school soccer players but were capable in athletics and eating. He had second thoughts about the quantity of food prepared. He excused himself to Marco and Ann Marie to go meet Angelika, David and their boys. Eva left him alone to chat with them while taking the coats to the bedroom. He launched right in with his key points, but they didn't seem amused so he led them to see the wine options. They chose the Barolo, which he poured for them and then opened another bottle. He looked around to see who might need more and saw Sophia outside on the balcony with the crying toddler and an empty glass. He decided to join her and give her a refill.

She smiled at him as he opened the door to the balcony. "Thanks for remembering me out here," she said, holding out the glass for him to fill. "Steve said he would come back with more, but he hasn't. How's it going in there?"

"So far so good. Marco and Ann Marie seem OK. Angelica and David seem quiet."

"Please don't worry. Everyone is happy for Mom to be having so much fun in retirement."

The back of the baby's head with dark curls vibrated with her screams while her mother with the same dark curls faced Laurence, chatting and sipping her wine seemingly unperturbed. The child was dressed for a party with a black velvet coat with lace on all the edges. Her white socks had lace too inside black patent leather shoes. Her mother also looked festive in high heels that matched a short fitted yellow dress under her open winter coat. No pantsuits for the Russo women. They liked dresses.

"She is showing no signs of wearing out yet?" Laurence said.

"Unfortunately no."

"Do you think she would like a cookie? I mean, would that distract her?"

"I would be happy to try anything," said Sophia.

Laurence made his way through the crowd to the kitchen and put four cookies on a small plate and picked up the second antipasti platter to put on the dining table next to the empty one as he passed by. Back on the balcony, Sophia turned around to look at Kerry Park so the baby could see Laurence. He held the plate out to the sobbing face on her mother's shoulder. Her sobs quieted, becoming jerky as she looked first at the cookies and then at Laurence. Through her tears she reached out a hand to grab one and smell it.

Sophia said, "This is sounding promising. Is she going for it?"

"I think so. It has passed the smell test. Let's see if it makes the taste test."

The little girl, her sobs subsiding to deep shaky breaths, licked the outside of the cookie and took a small bite, which she chewed slowly. Then she took another bite and grabbed another cookie from the plate. Laurence was afraid to move for fear she'd start crying again and continued holding the plate a few inches from her face.

"Thank you, thank you. You have no idea how much I thank you," said Sophia.

Eva opened the door and said, "You charmer. I had no idea you could do it to little girls too. How wonderful."

"Oh, Mom, you don't know how wonderful I think he is."

Eva asked Sophia, "Do you think it's safe to come inside?"

"Let's take a step inside the door and see what happens." Sophia paused once inside and gave her daughter a kiss on the cheek, took another few steps and stood still to gauge the new location. "So far so good. I think I'll stop here. Thanks again, Laurence."

Holding the plate seemed like a great task at the moment that relieved him from having to make small talk with anybody else. Sophia seemed easy to stand beside.

Eva gave him a big look of love and said, "Can I get you anything?"

"I left my Prosecco on the kitchen counter when I brought out the second platter and the cookies."

He watched her cross the room full of dark haired Russos and spouses smiling and chatting along the way. Eva clones everywhere, all well dressed and attractive. She was moving in the easy way she always had while working the crowd. This was her group and she looked radiant in it. It was more than confidence. These people were at home in the world. They flew to Europe and South America. They all knew Italy well. They vacationed in France and on islands he hadn't heard of. They traveled around the United States for business and pleasure. Laurence could hardly remember going anywhere outside the state of Washington He'd hardly ever flown anywhere except for Boeing business. His idea of a vacation was doing projects around his house.

The five boys occupied Laurence's reading spot on the long side of the leather sofa each with eyes on a handheld device while chatting amongst themselves. He wondered if they were playing a game together. He had no idea what the popular programs for this age group might be. They all had a different sports team Tshirt on over a dress shirt. It could be their school team or a national franchise and he wouldn't know. The noise level in the room seemed to be escalating with so many conversations competing to be heard. The room, which usually seemed so spacious and airy, seemed small and crowded.

Steve approached them with a question on his face. "How are my best girls? Everybody OK here?"

Sophia said, "I'm afraid to move but do you want to try taking her again? We have the magic cookie man here if she starts over."

They tried to make the switch from the Mom's shoulder to Dad's and she shrieked, "No!"

"Honey, we shouldn't have taught her that word." Steve shook his head. "Sorry I couldn't help. How about I make you a little food?"

"Sure. That would be nice." Sophia adjusted the child to her other shoulder and turned a bit so she could be closer to the plate of cookies that Laurence still held. "I hope you're not feeling like you got the worst job of the night."

"No, I'm happy to be helping."

"I'm sorry she's not enjoying the party."

"Don't apologize. Everyone here has been in your shoes at some time, right?"

"I guess so by the way they are avoiding me." Sophia looked around the room. She seemed to be counting all the people who hadn't spoken to her.

"Well, I'm not avoiding you," Laurence said.

"Do you have any kids?" she said.

"No."

"Well, you are taking this situation like a pro. Do you notice how my husband and my mother, who were going to help us, have disappeared?"

"Yes. How can it be? The room isn't that big," he said, thinking what a relief it was to be helping Sophia who seemed nice and not having to make conversation with anybody else.

Chapter 20

Sophia and Laurence chatted about his research about the Basques and her research for advertising venues that were the best fit for the Russo product. No one interrupted them to make a new conversation. Laurence began to think that Eva must be in the kitchen with Sophia's husband who had never returned with a plate of the antipasto for Sophia. He hoped Eva was cooking and getting ready to serve dinner.

"I'd really like to sit down for a minute," Sophia said and looked down at her pointed-toe high heels and surveyed the room. "All the good seats are taken. There aren't two together. Why don't we go in the bedroom?"

He followed her into the bedroom, and she sat on his side near his pillows where there were no coats. She couldn't possibly know those were his pillows. It felt too intimate to be sitting here facing the closet door, but he didn't know what else to do so he sat down beside Sophia holding the plate with two cookies near her shoulder where the curly head lay. The child had kept her eyes on him since they made the move. She took another cookie.

Laurence smiled at her and said, "I'm so glad you like my cookies. I baked them just for you."

Little Eva said nothing back but continued looking at him.

"Do you think she understands the words?"

Sophia burst into tears, "I don't know. Everyone asks me, and I don't know." She was sobbing and her shoulders were shaking.

"I'm sorry. I didn't mean to upset you," Laurence said.

"It's not your fault. I don't think I'm good at this. Being a mom is not easy or natural to me." She continued sobbing.

Laurence had no idea what to do or say. This was distressing to him. "Everyone knows it's a hard job."

"Everyone knows there are terrible mothers out there. I might be one of them."

"Everything will be OK," he said softly. He put his arm around her and hugged her to him.

"I don't think so. I think it might get worse." She leaned into his shoulder still sobbing with the baby between them.

"I'm sure it's stressful to have a baby and a big job and a husband who travels."

"It's a nightmare, every day," she said sobbing.

"Who could help you?"

"No one." She cried harder. The baby started crying again too, not wailing like before but sobbing and shaking like her mother.

Laurence held them, not knowing anything else to say or do, hoping someone would come rescue him and take over. This was a good job for Eva. Where was she?

"What's going on in here?" The voice was loud and hostile. Laurence flinched and looked around to see who it was.

Standing in the doorway was Tony and a woman who must be his wife with coats in their arms.

Laurence stood up and faced them with the cookie plate and said, "Sophia is upset."

"What did you do to her?" said Tony.

The baby stared wailing again.

"I did nothing. I'm trying to comfort her," said Laurence.

"Sophia, what's wrong with you?" Tony said with anger and impatience.

"Nothing. Go away and leave me alone," Sophia said not even looking at him.

"Not until you tell me what's wrong."

Sophia stood up and faced him with tears still running down her face and the baby crying. She said in a quivering voice, "Put your coats down and leave, please. I'm having a moment here."

Tony and his wife stood still staring at Sophia and Laurence.

"Let me take your coats for you," said Laurence, putting out his hands for the coats.

"Don't touch my coat. I want to know what's going on here," said Tony.

"Get out!" Sophia screamed at him and advanced as though she was going to take the coats. They threw the coats down and backed out the door. She slammed it behind them and sat back down still sobbing.

Laurence could hear Tony belligerent in the living room, "Mother, what's going on here?"

Eva was negotiating something with Tony, but her voice was lower and Laurence couldn't hear all the words. He felt frozen and trapped standing there with the crying mother and child. *Rescue me, Eva.* Then he heard Marco yelling, "Shut up Tony! Don't be such a jerk." Then came Eva at full pitch, "Both of you stop it! This is ridiculous behavior." But they didn't stop. They exchanged a few more volleys before it went quiet in the living room.

The bedroom door opened, and Eva came in and closed it quietly. "What is going on in here?"

Laurence, still standing holding the cookie plate, shrugged his shoulders. "Sophia is having a rough day."

Mother and child cried louder. Eva went over and sat down on the bed next to her and put her arms around Sophia. "Sweetheart, what's wrong? Tell me."

"Everything!" She sobbed into her mother's shoulder.

"Oh dear. I'm sorry."

Eva looked at Laurence and he nodded his head. "A bad day. I was trying to help and it was misunderstood by Tony."

"Oh dear. Sophia, you've got to pull yourself together, Honey. You've had a nice cry and now you have to stop." She produced several tissues from the bedside table. "Blow your nose, wipe your eyes."

Sophia seemed to be taking the instructions. When she finished she held a tissue for the child who blew into it properly.

"Now that we're all composed, we're going to go back out there and resume acting like a family who works together and plays together."

"No, I don't want to go back out there."

The door opened and in came Steve who closed it quietly behind him. "Honey, what's wrong? What do you need?"

Eva said to Laurence, "Why don't we give them some space and go back to the party?"

Laurence looked horrified. "I don't want to go back out there either. This is beyond my abilities."

Eva looked at him annoyed. "Don't tell me you are going to act like a child too!" Her voice was low but angry.

"That's adult warfare going on and I'll have no part of it." He was adamant.

"Oh my God, what a disaster. I am embarrassed by my children and my lover."

"Oh Mom, don't be mad at everybody. I am feeling sorry for myself but that's not embarrassing you." Sophia was recovering herself. "Don't make Laurence feel bad. He was sympathetic. That was helpful. Tony is clueless and no help at all."

"I don't think it's too much to expect that my adult children behave like the intelligent, worldly people they are."

"Tony started it. He's not too intelligent or worldly today."

"You sound like you're three years old. Listen to yourself, Sophia. And listen to me. Get yourself together. We're all going back out there and act like adults. It would be nice of you to apologize to Tony. He's upset." Eva was firm, matter of fact.

"What? Me apologize? That's nuts. I'm not doing that." Sophia had pulled herself together. "Steve, let's go. The baby's had enough. I've had enough. Please take us home."

Eva was quick to say, "Sophia, don't even think of leaving this house without saying a warm and civil goodbye to everyone."

"Mom, you're not getting who's wrong here."

"I don't care who's wrong. I care that everyone behaves properly. All of you follow me." Eva went and stood by the door and looked each one of them in the eye commanding them to obey her.

Laurence exhaled slowly. He took her elbow and said, "Lead on."

Eva and Laurence went to stand by the sideboard with the wine bottles. Sophia and her group stopped short of that in between the bedroom door and the front door.

"Sophia and little Eva are exhausted and are going home now. They can't stay for dinner." Eva turned to look at Sophia as her cue to begin her civil farewells.

Sophia said, "It was nice to see you all. I'm sorry to miss the pasta and the dessert that Mom and Laurence made." She was looking at Marco and under her breath mouthed in Italian *"Non capisci una fava,"* (You don't understand a broad bean), which made him laugh.

He responded in Italian to her something that everyone could hear. *"Tutti in ufficio pensano che sei un coglione!"* (*Everyone in the office thinks you're an idiot!*)

Tony responded with a loud and dismissive *"Palloso"* pointed at Sophia and Marco. Angelika rolled her eyes to mimic Tony's "Boring and tiresome" comment and shook her head. Sophia and Marco kept the barrage going, seemingly at each other by maintaining eye contact. Laurence had no idea what they were saying but knew the words were directed at Tony. He could see this was a highly skilled game of two against one. It was unnerving to him to be in the midst of this exchange getting louder with each volley. The only way Eva could beat them was to be loudest — and Laurence guessed vicious, judging by her neck — and the exchange tapered and stopped.

Sophia waved goodbye to the room in general and as she and Steve walked to the front door, she said, "See you at the office tomorrow."

Laurence looked around the room for a place to retreat. Standing next to the enraged matriarch was uncomfortable. He didn't know what came next but didn't want to be in the path. He backed into a chair between the bedroom door and the balcony door and sat down with his hands folded in his lap, staring at the carpet under his feet.

Eva continued with Tony and Marco in Italian, a slightly softer and lower volume compared to her volley that ended the three-way exchange. Laurence was glad he didn't understand a word of what she was saying. How would this scene end? Surely it couldn't end in eating dinner. He'd like to make his own civil farewell to all and go home to his quiet apartment. Hopefully they would all leave soon. After helping Eva clean up he would plead a migraine even though he'd never had one before. He was quite sure he was getting one. The back of his head above his neck felt like it had a cramp in it that was spreading toward the front. Maybe he was having a stroke. Blood bursting out of a broken vessel to spread on his brain might feel like that.

"Grandma, when are we having dinner? I'm starving."

Laurence looked up horrified to see who could possibly eat after this incident. Apparently one of Marco and Ann Marie's sons had asked because they were both looking at Eva for the answer.

"In a few minutes. Would you like some more cheese?"

"Sure, if you have some. I thought we ate it all."

Eva got up looked at the two empty antipasto platters, picked them up and went into the kitchen. Laurence wondered if the water for pasta and the sauce had ever been turned on. She returned with a refreshed antipasti platter, which she passed to the two boys, who quickly assembled a meat and cheese sandwich. Marco put a bite of prosciutto in his mouth and said, "It's good, Mom. Did you get it at DeLaurenti's?" Ann Marie shook her head no thank you.

"Yes. Angelika, David, how about you?" Eva said offering the platter to them and their boys.

Angelika shook her head, "I think I'll wait for the pasta."

"Me too," said David. "I'll help myself to the fabulous wine though, thank you Eva."

Eva stood in front of Laurence with the platter. He looked up at her and shook his head no. She said, "Would you like some more wine?"

"I have a glass of Prosecco somewhere."

"I'll get you a fresh glass," Eva said.

Laurence sat in the chair, sipping the wine Eva had brought him and tried to come back into the present moment in the room. He was glad she had not asked him to get up and help. He wasn't able. He needed to recover a bit more, and standing up was not yet in his program. To reorient himself he tried to think about what needed to be done in the kitchen. He curled his toes and flexed his feet inside his shoes to start the legs moving. The salad would need to be tossed. Looking around the room he marveled at how these adults sat quietly, casually chatting. The boys resumed talking to each other with their eyes still on the screens. He was surprised neither Angelika nor Ann Marie got up to help, though they had resumed discussing the merits of taking vacation in Colorado over the spring break versus during the summer. It felt like the end of a long night to him. Everybody else seemed to be fine. Maybe they were used to being served. He really didn't feel like waiting on them or doing anything for them. What did they expect him to do? He really didn't care, but he should start thinking about Eva, now that the blood on his brain had normalized. Her kids could be lazy and crass, but he was not. He stood up and went into the kitchen to help put the dinner on the table.

"Hello, Lover," she said when he stood beside her in front of the gas range and put his hand on her waist.

"How's it going in here?"

"The water is ready for the pasta. Do you want to toss the salad and slice the bread?"

"Sure."

When he and Eva each carried out giant hot bowls of pasta tossed with red sauce ten minutes later and put them on the table next to the salad, the entire room stood up and approached the table.

"Boys, this bowl is for you. This one is for the adults. I hope we have enough food."

Several people said, "It looks great."

In a remarkably short time, everyone had a plate in their lap and was occupied eating. David opened another bottle of Barolo and passed that around. Laurence was impressed with Eva's red sauce. It had depth, the complexity of slow cooking and ageing. The texture was smooth and creamy. The ground veal had disappeared into the sauce. The pasta was cooked perfectly. He was sitting in the same side chair as earlier surveying the scene of convivial eating and drinking. There was no apparent animosity between Marco and Tony. He hadn't seen Tony's wife Jean say a word to anyone. She was methodically eating everything. Marco's wife Ann Marie was eating from a large plate of salad.

Tony unexpectedly looked up from his plate at Laurence and said, "What kind of cancer did your wife have?"

Everyone in the room stopped chewing while Laurence looked at him for a moment before answering, "A rare form of non-Hodgkin's lymphoma."

"A non-Hodgkin's? A friend of mine has been diagnosed with that, and I've been reading the current medical research. It's been a challenge for the pharmaceutical industry. They have tried so many things that haven't worked. Did you participate in any trials?"

"Four."

"Were they covered by your insurance?"

"No."

"They might be covered now. The insurance industry has been forced into it. You might still be able to sue them. It's worth looking into." Laurence didn't have anything to say to that while considering how different his life might be with the clinical trial money in the bank.

"How did you get your job as a food judge?" said Tony.

Laurence cleared his throat and said, "I met Drew, the owner of the gallery, at a social event where I talked about making pasta and other doughs, which need to be almost translucent. I identified the spices in a Malaysian curry dish. That was enough for him to offer me a job judging for a pasta contest he was sponsoring the next night. I have been there ever since doing one thing or another."

"What brand of pasta machine do you use?" said Tony.

"I don't have a machine. I work by hand."

Marco said, "Wow, we're impressed by hand work. You don't see that often. Tony, let the man eat."

Looking around the room with all eyes still on him, Laurence decided to keep his audience for a few more moments. "The gallery is preparing now for an unusual exhibition that will open the Thursday after New Year's. It will present Basque art, food, wine, music and dancing. Please join us. It will be good entertainment for the whole family."

Eva smiled at him with pride and looked around the room at her children. He returned her look, which he hoped she knew meant, *OK? That's it from me.*

Laurence shifted his focus to watch the young boys still eating so everyone could stop looking at him. They were finishing off their bowl of pasta and eyeing the adult bowl. Eva, sitting amongst the boys, encouraged them to finish all the pasta.

When the buffet was bare, she stood up and said, "Well, how about dessert?"

Angelika and Ann Marie got up simultaneously and started taking all the dirty plates being held up to them into the kitchen and began loading the dishwasher. Laurence brought out two platters of cookies from the kitchen and walked around the room offering them to everyone individually. Eva watched all the interactions. After the first pass he put the platters on the coffee table in front of the kids to finish. They were surprised at the carte blanche, and each one thanked him as they did the math and stacked up a big handful of their equal share from what was left. The parents who had been wide-eyed at the offer of the platters seemed mollified enough by the polite behavior that none of them said anything about the quantity of cookies about to be consumed. Everyone complimented him on the cookie selections. Tony mentioned that all the cookies were Venetian and that they had all eaten them for the first time on a family vacation in the Veneto region when they were kids. The group reminisced about gondola rides, museums, seafood meals, the old seaside villa they had rented that summer and a big fight between Marco and Tony in a swimming pool that had roused the neighbors out of their houses to watch. The last got a few laughs, and everyone stood up to begin retrieving coats and go home.

Standing at the door with Eva holding on to his elbow and saying goodnight to her crowd felt like an out-of-body experience to Laurence. He felt like he had sailed through a typhoon and washed up on the beach without his boat, battered but alive. He could only nod and shake a few hands. Was this his new family? He couldn't imagine doing this party again ever or at least not for a very long time.

Laurence took the cookie platters to the kitchen and started washing them by hand as there was no room in the dishwasher. Eva brought in dirty glasses and was able to find room for a few of them and put the rest on the counter. She was effusive in her praise of their teamwork. Laurence couldn't help himself from poking her about some of the behaviors that seemed odd to him like why she always served pasta when Ann Marie wouldn't eat it and why Jean so quiet. He couldn't fathom her answer that everyone else loved pasta and Jean was always that way and it didn't mean anything was wrong. Sophia and Marco were outgoing. Angelika was not. Jean and Tony are fine together and they had good kids who played well with others.

"Unlike their father and uncle."

Eva sighed, "Apparently sibling rivalry never dies."

"Eva, let me put this as simply as I can. The Russo family dynamic makes me physically ill. I thought I was having a stroke or getting a migraine with all the screaming."

"Oh, dear. I know it must seem loud to you at first, but you'll get used to it."

"No, I don't think I will."

"Laurence, please don't say that. You will come to see they enjoy the exchange, the battle of the words for who is the quickest and the cleverest, but they love each other and work well together."

"You enjoy it too. I watched you jump in. You're all competitive with each other at shouting. It's bizarre behavior to me, and you're endorsing it as a mental sport."

"Your style is different from mine, but we're doing fine together. Everyone has to compromise a bit to accommodate the other."

"It's only a matter of time before you turn on me, frustrated because I won't participate in your drama."

"I love you! I couldn't turn on you."

"Oh, yes you could. You won't be able to help yourself. You once said Tony would accept me when he realized that I am of your world, meaning the food world, but the truth is, Tony and all the rest of them are never going to accept me because I am not of your wide world. I'm an old engineer from Ballard who enjoys baking, who's never been to Italy or anywhere outside the United States. I've hardly been anywhere inside the United States. Moving across the Ship Canal to Queen Anne was a big deal to me."

"You may be an armchair traveler, but your mind is world class. Who cares where you've been or not been? Who cares what Tony or anyone thinks? I love you just the way you are."

"Eva, I'm trying to explain after what I saw here tonight that I think we're too different to grow older together as you want us to do."

"You are so hung up on numbers you can't see the forest for the trees. You think you are old because you are 75, but you are strong and upright. You will probably be the same at 95. Please stop thinking you are dying whenever something new happens to you. I bet you live to be 100! And you could have all those years with me by your side and in your bed." Her voice was rising. "Would you give that up?" The cords stood out in her neck like they had earlier when she was screaming at her children.

Laurence responded in a low and slow voice, "I'm 76 and I believe in numbers. Numbers are my life. I don't care what Tony thinks. But, let's not blame Tony. He's only one example of the insane behavior in this family. You all think it's OK to rant and rage, but it's not OK to me. It's not civilized."

"You should open your genius mind to the possibility that you are not right about everything." Her tone was icy.

"In the delusions department, you have a few you could give up too."

"Are you angry that Tony asked about your wife's cancer? Is that what this is all about?" Eva said.

"Not at all. I welcomed them to ask me anything they wanted. I told them I had no secrets."

"It was a nice gathering overall. It had a few rough moments, but it was good to see everyone. The food was wonderful. Everyone left happy." Eva sounded so matter of fact.

"Except Sophia who seems like an intelligent young woman until she starts talking with her brothers and degenerates into something scary," said Laurence, aiming for the same matter of fact tone to match Eva's.

"She's always emotional and overreacts."

"Eva, we both witnessed a brawl, and you characterize it as a picnic. This difference of ours is a problem!"

"You are being very critical of my family." There was a hard edge in her voice.

"I'm trying to tell you *we* have a problem, you and me. We are not communicating."

"We are talking. We just don't agree." She seemed impatient with him.

"If you think this is a meaningful conversation that helps us each understand the other's point of view and points out ways to go forward, you are wrong. If you think I will get used to you solving your family squabbles by you screaming the loudest, you're wrong. These are big issues to me. I need you to agree they are important and show willingness to discuss them rationally."

"Or what? Are you threatening me?" Eva asked. She was angry now.

"I don't see how it can work out between us if we can't deal with the issues as they come up. This is only our beginning and there will be more issues."

She looked at him as though she could not understand his words. "I can't believe you want to walk away from what we have. You stubborn old fool! You're incapable of compromising, even a little, to gain years of happiness? You're quite sure *you* can't live with me?" Her voice was chilling.

Laurence nodded his head. "What are you willing to compromise on? Nothing, as far as I can see."

"So, this is it? You want to give me up because of what happened here tonight?" She was incredulous. "You can't mean that you don't want to ever see me or them again."

He paused to think about it. They had argued themselves to a precipice, which now seemed to have a significant finality embedded in it. Did he really mean to end it here tonight? That hadn't been his intent a few minutes ago when what he wanted to do was talk about how difficult he had found the evening. She was so imperious in her manner as though he had no right to think or feel as he did. He felt resigned to his position and looked her in the eye when he said softly, "Yes, I do mean it. It's not easy for me to leave you. I love you. But I don't see how we go forward from here."

She stood so straight with her head held high she seemed taller. She stared at him betraying no emotion with her lips pursed. She was thinking. He held his eye contact with her and waited for her to say, "*Of course we can talk about this. I don't want you to leave.*" Instead she glared at him, warning him to back away and then screamed, "Get out of this house and don't ever come back again! You don't know what love is. You have insulted me and my family for the last time!" With her hands on his chest Eva pushed him backward out of the kitchen toward the open space in the living room and swept past him. She opened the front door, looked away from his face as he walked through it, and slammed it hard behind him.

Chapter 21

Drew sat at his desk re-watching the videos of the *Oinkaris*, meaning dancers in the Basque language of Euskara, from the Basque Cultural Center in Boise as they performed in Basque festivals in Spain and Washington DC. They were perfect, just what he wanted. No other group of performers had the charisma and the polish they did. He had talked before with the leader who had outlined the difficulties of making a deal with Drew. Although Basque traditions were being respected and promoted by this unusual exhibition in Seattle, it was a commercial enterprise chiefly for the good of the gallery and the man who owned it. The time and the expenses of the trip to Seattle were substantial. There would be none of the typical fundraising at the Basque Center in Boise to help pay for the expenses. Nor could the performers be expected to pay out of their pockets. They danced for free to keep tradition alive. The performance fee, whether for a short or a long program, covered expenses of the organization for costumes and instruments. Drew would also have to pay the travel expenses and for their time off work from their day jobs. It was a big investment for him to make, but he knew it was necessary to create a buzz in the advertising and the initial size of the audiences. He envisioned cell phone communication and social media conducting the most persuasive marketing campaign imaginable after the first performance — and that would be free! The authenticity it would bring to his exhibit was essential. He would figure out how to charge the public to help his bottom line but not discourage people from attending because of the price.

Drew and Julia had a long discussion about selling tickets to the Basque dancers, the food bites and wine. She researched motel rooms. They would need at least five, depending on the final list of performers because some might not be spouses. The hospitality expense for a group of eight to 10 people for three days was considerable. He tried to think of friends who might host some of them and couldn't come up with anybody with the right amount of space or interest. Maybe local musicians would be interested in hosting? There was the solution! Why hadn't he thought of this before? This was the perfect role for the local Basque club. They would welcome their own with fanfare. It would be a meaningful gift to the community to help out. He dialed the president and asked, "Would you be willing to find hosts for 10 famous dancers while they visit in Seattle?" You bet he would, came the response. In fact he would be honored. Now the club was involved in the exhibition and was happy about it.

Drew and Julia were jubilant over this piece of the expenses magically disappearing. He dialed the leader of the dance troop again and reported the good news of the local club, welcoming them all for the three-day weekend. They finalized the price and payment schedule for three nights of two short performances. Drew bargained for a reduction of the performance fee. That was the concession that counted plus customizing the performance for 10 dancers instead of 16 or 20. Drew congratulated him on his negotiating skills, which was returned. They admired each other for getting the business done. Dealing with this fellow had given Drew a new level of respect for the Basque character. Principled and unyielding was one way to describe it. Drew liked him.

Now that he had a deal with the dancers he regretted making a deal with Bernadette. With the crowds the entertainment would create, he felt he and Julia could sell it all. They didn't need any help and both of their commissions would be less from selling less. He had rushed into that and wished he'd said, *Let me get back to you next week.* He decided to keep this dissatisfaction to himself. It was his fault. Julia had nothing to do with the decision.

The next piece of the puzzle fell into place late in the day with a serendipitous call from Drew's buddy at Seattle International Film Festival. He had found copies of rare and excellent movies for a double feature by a Basque director, Julio Medem. He was popular in Seattle since he had premiered *Vacas* at SIFF in 1992 and won the Golden Space Needle Award for *Sex and Lucia* in 2002. These hard-to-find movies were available in early February. Drew said he'd never heard of the director or the movies but if it would attract an art house crowd interested in Basque anything, he agreed right away to pay in advance for the movies to guarantee the date. He told him to book the Hemingway film and *Gilda* for the end of February.

Drew leaned back in his chair a big smile on his face and said, "Oh Julia, this makes my week. We've got dancers in January and now a world-class film event for February First Thursday with an audience we have never seen before. And we'll close the exhibit with a nostalgic flourish that should bring some faces back again to look at the art."

She smiled too and sighed. "Mine too. This exhibit has been more nerve wracking than any we've ever done. I can't believe how much up and down it's been these days, like my life."

Drew looked at her. "Are you having trouble in your life?"

"Not serious trouble like money or problems with friends, but I don't feel like me."

He said to her, "I feel like celebrating. Shall I order some food to be delivered and you can tell me all about it?"

Julia looked stricken and said, "I'm sorry, I already have dinner plans."

"No worries! Please. That's great you have plans. I'm going to go home then. Can I give you a ride downtown?"

"Thanks. That would be nice."

They chatted amiably in the car about the successful negotiations with the dancers. It seemed like a good omen after the previous weeks' anxiety over the art and turnout.

"Where shall I let you off?" Drew said.

"Anywhere around Marion Street is good."

"I don't mind driving you up the hill. What avenue?"

"If you're sure, Fifth Avenue is where I'm going."

"Ah ha. The Columbia Tower. So you're helping Henri?"

"Yes."

"I'm not prying or looking for details. I'm glad you're helping him. I hope you are enjoying it and learning some French."

"Thanks. Now I get what you were trying to tell me about being wary."

"Has he swept you off your feet?"

"I think so. I've never felt like this before. He is not at all like any Seattle boys I know. He's much more like someone your age who knows a lot about everything, but he's my age."

"Oh, I see." Drew thought, *I had to ask and now I know. He has rocked her world.*

"It's scary to feel out of control. I don't know how to describe it. My girlfriends say I'm definitely in love. I don't know. I haven't known him very long. How do you know?"

"Falling off a cliff is a common description. Are you experiencing alternating exhilaration and despair in the same few minutes?"

"Yes! It's the minutes part that makes me crazy. How is it possible to feel so different in such a short period of time? It's not like me to feel this way. I'm a steady type of person."

"Sounds like you have a bad case of it, Julia. Congratulations."

Drew dropped her off and drove away thinking it was the best thing for her to be experiencing all the dizzying feelings of love, particularly if she hadn't felt it before. The universal experience would be good for her art, adding depth to her range of emotions especially if she got her heart broken. He wasn't envious of her feelings of love or the likelihood of the unhappy ending. The odds of falling in love with someone and staying in love were poor. That out-of-control aspect was an insidious side effect he remembered from having been there once or twice himself a long time ago. He had taken care since then to keep himself out of that dangerous zone, probably for so long now he was impervious. He hoped so. As delightful as it was to spend time with a fascinating woman, it was essential to be smart enough to avoid being trapped by someone who appeared to be independent and free spirited but was privately scheming to lock him up to become her personal slave. Poor Julia. Poor Henri. One of them was bound to lose. All this empathizing made him hungry and thirsty for food from one of the restaurants near his apartment. His favorite bartenders needed updating on the opening of the exhibit. Maybe he would run into someone he knew to share a drink with.

Sipping a cold martini at the half empty bar in the Queen City Grill with no one he recognized drinking or working, he thought about Julia again and how quickly her life had changed by falling in love. He wondered where the lovers spent their time and how Bernadette was coping with all the hormones. She who had only recently become accustomed to cooking dinner for her son must now be eating alone. He didn't want to know or particularly care what Julia was doing. It was not worrisome to him. What worried him now is that he had lost his mind to welcome a complete stranger into his gallery, even if she was a friend of Eva's. What had he been thinking that day when she waltzed into the gallery in her Chanel suit and seemed like the answer to his fears?

She was so French, so Parisian. Her look, the way she held herself with that French arrogance — or confidence. Which was it? He had been practically speechless over her presence trying to translate her words into English. Her English was beautiful too with a fetching accent. Here she was looking like a million dollars, a sophisticated woman who had come to help him! How wonderful. She was well connected with affluent European tourists and would bring them to his gallery to buy art. She never said "look" at art. She used the word "buy." It all sounded so possible and logical that he wondered why he hadn't thought of it himself. He listened to her and wanted her to go on talking. When it came to the money part she showed she knew the business by suggesting the old-fashioned finder's fee for introducing a buyer. The extra money he would make on anything she sold made him malleable, so he accepted it. With this exhibit he was hoping to attract local or regional people who liked to travel, but he had never once thought of the foreign travelers visiting in Seattle. He had no idea there were so many foreign visitors and that they would be here in the winter. He thought all travelers came in the summer. This concept of hers was so perfect.

Once they had agreed, or rather he had agreed to everything she suggested, they shook hands on it. She didn't ask for a contract or any paper documentation. Her confidence in him also impressed him. Then she had told him about poor Henri, new in the United States, with no friends yet in Seattle. The international finance division where he worked was all business types with no artistic sensibilities. They went to football games, not soccer. The sport he was really interested in was bicycle racing, as in the

Tour de France. She selfishly wanted him to make friends and have fun so he would think of staying and not returning to Paris after a year of trying Seattle. Eva had told her that Julia was a talented artist about Henri's age. Bernadette wondered if it would be appropriate to ask Julia to show him around town a little bit, to point out things only Julia would know, places where other kindred spirits of the same age gathered. Bernadette's tours of Seattle didn't include any clubs, bars or bistros. Drew thought of Eva's suggestion about him and Julia and said, "Absolutely, Julia would be a wonderful guide for your son. I will ask her to give him a tour and we'll see if she feels like doing it again." Bernadette gave Drew a thick, engraved business card with Henri's name and the bank contact information. The weight of the card seemed to say Bernadette and her son had solid connections. Drew was lucky to become acquainted with them and envisioned their Parisian luster rubbing off on his gallery. He was sure she would charm anyone who listened to her. However, all that good will had worn off in a few days.

Bernadette now seemed mysterious to him. Who was this person who arrived unannounced with nothing but a friend's recommendation and who sat down and talked serious business? Usually the friend called in advance and suggested he take the meeting. At the time he admired her salesmanship telling him she preferred to skip the etiquette. Why not take her by surprise tonight and see if she were free to join him right now so he could reassess her? All she could say was no or not answer. But she did answer and used his name in the good evening greeting indicating her caller ID was engaged. She was happy to have an unexpected invitation to dinner and said she'd catch a bus from Capitol Hill and be there within 30 minutes, maybe sooner. Drew had the bartender put a reserved sign on one of the booths near the bar.

Bernadette arrived about 20 minutes later looking chic in a tightly belted black leather trench coat emphasizing her small waist over black slacks and a white blouse. He hung her coat up for her on the peg nearby and they sat down as the server waited by the table to take drink orders and offer menus.

She ordered a glass of red wine, so he did too. She seemed relaxed, not at all nervous.

"Thank you for rescuing me from a dull evening of reading essays from my intermediate class. Please tell me all the news of the exhibit."

They ordered roast halibut and salads before he provided the details. She was a great audience. She seemed to know exactly what he meant. Finally, his manners got the better of his enthusiasm about all the pieces of the exhibit falling in place and he said, "Tell me about your students. Who are they and what inspires them to take your class?"

She gave thoughtful and amusing responses about the teaching experience. Most planned to travel in France and wanted to be able to speak enough to charm the natives into helping them find the train station or order lunch. They were writing essays about places they wanted to visit. Studying menus was a favorite activity, and they practiced in teams in class, playing the waiter and the customer or the hotel clerk and guest. She enjoyed the classroom interaction. Reading the essays wasn't her favorite activity.

"Why do you assign the essays if you don't like to read them? I wouldn't think they would need to write anything on vacation."

"Writing is an important step in learning. The connection between the brain and the hand helps the information get permanently stored. Reading, writing and speaking are equally essential. Was it hard for you to acquire your French?"

"I was passionate about learning it at the time so it didn't seem too hard. As an art student I thought speaking French made me seem a better painter, somehow closer to my heroes Sargent and Renoir." He smiled at her. "You can imagine that?"

She understood. "And more successful with the young ladies too?"

"Absolutely. Oh, the delusions of a young man. How's your young man doing with his studies of Seattle with Julia?"

"I think anatomy has replaced geography and history." She smiled at him.

"Ah, well, it's all learning isn't it?"

"I want you to know how pleased I am for him to know someone nice like Julia with ambition. She impresses me with her talent and goals. It's a relief to me for him to be enjoying himself with someone who has more to offer than good looks."

"I'm glad to hear that you like her. She is my best employee and student ever. I hope she will make me famous. She is focused and disciplined. So many art students think they need to be dramatic to be perceived as creative and to live the life of an artist. Julia has no drama."

"I expect Julia is an inspiration for Henri to find an apartment soon. That's good. In the last six months I've had the opportunity to eat dinner with my son at home for the first time in years. It's been a great way to get to know each other as adults, but living in my apartment is not a long-term solution for Henri. We both need our own space."

"I understand." Drew wasn't sure if he understood at all the maternal feelings she was expressing or whether he sounded like a proud parent chatting about Julia and Henri as though he were interested. This line of conversation was

---

boring to him, but the need for space he could identify with. He watched her face and her dark eyes more than he followed the words and enjoyed the sound of her voice. She was entertaining to watch. Seeming to sense his thoughts wandering she changed the conversation to architecture and taught him a few things about buildings in Seattle he knew in the Pioneer Square area. He was happy to listen to whatever she had to say and observe her presentation. He had not made a mistake hiring her. She had a striking face, a bit too angular to be pretty but all the more interesting for the angles. He composed a portrait of her with an art nouveau sitting room and elaborate metal birdcage next to her chair. Her fitted dress was yellow as were the birds and the chair was black like her hair. What would she have worn if he were to paint her upstairs in the boudoir? White silk flowing with a red necklace or a black velvet necklace with one red flower. What made a French woman so French? She was looking at him strangely.

"What?" he said.

"You are lost somewhere. I'm boring you. I apologize."

"Oh no, not at all. I'm composing but listening."

"What are you composing?" she said.

"It's an old habit of a portrait painter. I'm composing the background and accessories," he said.

"Me? You're composing me where?" She looked pleased, which was the typical reaction.

"I was thinking art nouveau. Is that a favorite era of yours?"

"Austrian or French?" She didn't look so happy now.

"More Klimt than Lautrec."

"I don't wear gold or yellow."

"Why not? It's a good color for you." That was a serious question.

She shook her head at him and said, "This has been lovely, but I must go now. Thank you so much for inviting me."

Drew looked down at the empty plates on the table and couldn't remember when the dinner was served or when he ate it. He helped her with the leather coat and hailed a taxi giving the driver ten bucks for the fare. The Klimt reference obviously had upset her. Or annoyed her? Maybe she thought he was being suggestive as the two most famous Klimt's featured a seductive dark haired woman in gold who was rumored to have had a torrid affair with the artist that ended badly. That wasn't what he meant, but it had been his first instinct, so maybe he did mean it. No, she wasn't his type. She was fascinating, but he preferred younger, softer and more pliable. He was glad he had asked her to dinner. It was reassuring to know his initial positive feeling about her sales ability was confirmed again. Bernadette could sell anything just by opening her mouth and speaking. The art, when he found it, which was the hard part, would be easy for her to sell.

Chapter 22

The day after the disastrous party Laurence lay on his bed staring at the industrial white ceiling listening to the morning traffic on Queen Anne Avenue thinking, *This is like old times, back in the black and white world a year ago when I wished I were dead. The Technicolor days and nights of pink dresses and twinkling city lights beyond Kerry Park are history.* He knew it would be hard to be without Eva but he'd forgotten how colorless this life was. He decided he was too exhausted to do anything but stay in bed today. He would call it a sick day to recover and hope tomorrow he would have the energy to resume some activity. A new schedule would have to be created. He couldn't possibly do that today. Rest was what he needed.

He slept off and on all day and when he was awoke he reviewed the closing arguments with Eva, second-guessing his choice of a few words, but generally thought he had expressed himself clearly. There was no point in dragging out the relationship to where he saw it headed, an ugly ending. He believed it was a better policy to cut his losses when he knew failure was inevitable. Her surprise did not surprise him. He surprised himself. He had no idea he felt that strongly until he heard himself say it. In retrospect he rationalized that if he had stayed the night they would have gone to bed angry and still been angry enough in the morning to fight another round or kick it under the rug and let it fester. His choice to be firm was less painful for both of them in the long run. He compared it to a sudden death, which was initially debilitating because of the loss and the shock. A slow death was tortuous for everyone throughout the process.

Eva, he felt sure, was very upset today, angry with him, feeling the classic wrath of the woman scorned. That would change slowly to grieving for the companionship and recognizing it wouldn't have worked out. She wouldn't hate him anymore. She would remember him fondly, cooking for her and reciting poetry for her. He would remember all those rosy, golden-hued times too. She would find another man who enjoyed living in her world never minding the regular tempests that blew through. Laurence would be lonely but that was manageable.

He would miss waking up and going to sleep with her for a few months. He knew he would miss her marvelous couch for reading and relaxing side by side. Maybe a couple of soft pillows for his head and back would improve his solitary experience. Then he would become accustomed to his new schedule and solitary home life, and all would be well. It would just take some time to get used to it. It gave him comfort to plot and schedule his recovery from Eva, or maybe more accurately, his return to his real life. Life with Eva was sensuous. She had exposed him to an opulent lifestyle. He had enjoyed it all, the luxuries of the balcony with a view, the refrigerator and the companionship. He would probably have trouble sleeping again.

That night when his muscles and bones couldn't stay in bed any longer he got dressed and walked down the hill to the supermarket. At 8 p.m. the store wasn't busy. He leisurely looked up and down the shelves in all the rows. He bought groceries for the week as he used to do and walked back up the hill to cook himself a Basque chicken dinner, which was tasty enough to distract him from feeling bereft for 30 minutes. He got back into bed after dinner and tried to read a book that had been on his bedside table for weeks. At least a half dozen library books were at Eva's apartment. What could he negotiate with her about getting them back? Should he call her and inquire what might be convenient for her? She was probably still too angry to consider returning them for him or packaging them up to send to him or have him pick them up. Seeing each other would be too difficult now. He'd be patient and watch his account online to see if they were returned or he started accruing daily fines.

The clothes and toiletries left behind he could replace. In fact, a few new shirts would be nice with the Basque exhibition coming up. He would need to look "gallery good" more frequently. Maybe he would ask Drew or William to consult with him about new shirts. Thankfully, he still had his suit on when he left Eva's last night. He had almost taken off the coat to be cooler when the room got crowded but had decided the image of formality would be better. Wouldn't it be awful to have to call and ask for that essential suit that he couldn't replace without a big investment? He needed to get back to his old frugal ways. Now he was ahead, with money in the bank, as he hadn't paid for anything much at Eva's, like groceries. Resuming his old life was a matter of scaling back, not a big adjustment.

As the days went by, his misery didn't abate, but he began to be used to it. He had a meeting at the gallery so planned his day to include a stop at the library. He confirmed his books were still overdue. Maybe Eva wasn't as mad and he could call her about coming by for the books. He limited himself to checking out three new books and read a new issue of his favorite science magazine.

Drew, William, Charles and Julia were seated at the round table in Drew's office when Laurence arrived. "Am I late?" He sat down on the couch.

"No, we wanted to get an early start on the wine ideas and now we're ready to talk about the caterers and make a decision." Drew leaned back in the swiveling chair. "Tell us what you know."

Laurence said, "Caterer A is offering a three-step tapas or *pintxos* program, all room temperature, designed to pair with a Cava, a white and a red. This is the bargain price point. Although it is small, it is quality with simple service, one server per station managing the food and the wine. Caterer B offers a more premium program with five stations, one of which is a dessert. They propose the first course to be cold, the fourth hot and the rest room temperature."

"Is the food menu anything like what we had at Amy's?" Drew asked.

"They both say they can do any of that we want."

"Will they prepare a tasting menu for us to select from?" Drew said.

"Yes."

"Why don't we invite Amy to come taste with us? I want to be sure everything is really good and authentic. We're bound to have a few experts in the house, and I want them to be impressed."

They then had a long discussion about wines, prices and tickets that Laurence couldn't follow after awhile and tuned out to fret about his own troubles. He came back to the conversation when he heard Drew say that Charles was taking over running the food and beverage contract with Caterer A. That wasn't exactly a surprise but he had hoped to get that job if Charles were too busy to do it all. He and William were to be hosts at the door and sell extra tickets and souvenirs.

Drew said, "We'll stay open from noon until 10 on First Thursday, Friday and Saturday night. To get maximum exposure for the dancers, we'll have two performances each night at six and eight for maybe 30 minutes to get the crowd going and feeling the authenticity. Maybe the performers will work the crowd afterward to answer questions, or to talk about being Basque. They head back to Boise Sunday morning. I'm thinking about opening Sunday afternoon, something we've never done, because people will be so excited to see the art again I can't bear to make them wait for Tuesday. We're projecting 200 for First Thursday and 75 on the subsequent nights. We want to be hospitable and pouring, ready for a crowd that comes in two waves. Charles, please figure out what's the minimum service staff we'll need."

Charles took notes and then indicated that he had to go and left. Laurence and William waited for their final instructions, which were brief.

Drew said, "Laurence, back up Julia if she needs it. She'll phone you. William, I don't think we need you until the opening night but hope you can work Thursday, Friday and Saturday nights. You OK with that?"

"No problem," said William and Laurence simultaneously.

Walking out through the gallery toward the front door William said, "Why don't we go have an early holiday drink?"

"Sounds good to me," said Laurence.

"Come with me in my big car."

William's ride was an ancient Cadillac. Laurence settled in the front seat where he could stretch his legs with ample room for a party in the backseat. William drove south on Airport Way South and right into a parking place perfect for two cars in front of Jules Mae in Georgetown, no adjustments necessary. They laughed about that.

They ordered Rainier on draft and chatted about the Basque event. Laurence said, "Plans for Christmas?"

"No. I'd like to eat some prime beef somewhere, but other than that, I can pass on the whole thing. What are you doing?"

"Nothing. Maybe I'll join you," said Laurence.

"Nothing doing with the Russo clan?" said William.

"No. We're done. It didn't work out."

"I'm sorry to hear that. I thought you two were adorable," said William.

"Thanks. It was great while it lasted."

"Has she found somebody else?" said William.

"Not that I know of, but feel free to give her a whirl. You might be perfect for her," said Laurence.

"Really? You mean that? Give her a whirl?"

"Absolutely. She won't be alone long."

"I think I will call her if you're sure you won't be sore about it," said William.

"Go right ahead."

"When did you split up?"

"Last week."

"I think I'll wait until after the New Year when she's forgotten you."

"That will be about right," said Laurence.

They clinked glasses and ordered another round.

Standing at the bus stop across the street from the bar a few hours later, Laurence felt the best he'd felt in days. William was a good guy. He'd even offered to drive him out of his way, back to town, and Laurence had declined. He wouldn't have to wait long for either of the two buses serving the stop. He was glad for the change of scenery. Rainier beer had been one of his favorites in times past. He had consumed barrels of it in the Ballard bars he frequented with his Boeing buddies and with Ingrid. Saturdays always included some beer drinking. Squealing car breaks a few feet away from him made him leap back just in case his feet were too near the street. It was Eva's car a foot away from him in the bus stop zone. She was looking at him through the passenger window with a puzzled expression, not friendly.

He leaned down to the open passenger window, "Hi, I've been drinking beer with William at Jules Mae."

"Good grief. I can smell the beer. How much have you had to drink?"

"I feel pretty darn good. It must have been quite a bit."

"Get in the car. Drunken old men are a hazard on the street. You or somebody else will end up hurt."

"I'm not drunk!"

"You are too. Get in the car."

As soon as he got his seat belt on and the car accelerated above the speed limit, he realized he was tipsy. It seemed small inside the car even with the window down. He couldn't think of anything to say. He felt a little embarrassed to be caught by surprise and not completely in control of himself. She had chastised him like a child, and he had responded by getting in the car. Commanding people came easily to her.

"So, what were you and William up to besides getting drunk?"

"Nothing. We'd been to a meeting at the gallery, and he asked me if I wanted to go for a drink. We're not plotting anything but maybe eating prime beef for Christmas."

"He doesn't have a family?"

"I don't know. He never said, and I never asked."

"Men! You drive me crazy."

She sounded exasperated already. That didn't bode well for the conversation. "We might say the same about you women," said Laurence calmly. He would try to stay even wherever this went.

"How are you enjoying your solitude?" Eva asked.

"I'm miserable. How about you?"

"The same," she said.

"I'm sorry. I hate myself for making you feel bad. I hope it won't last too long. It's worse than I thought it might be."

"For you or for me?" she said.

That was shrill on his ears. "For me," he said quietly.

"How do you think I feel?"

Outrage was creeping into her voice. He tried to deflect it by saying, "I figured you would be really mad. And then I hoped you would see it was for the best and remember we had some good times."

"Did you not even once think I might be heartbroken?"

"No, I didn't."

"You are so stupid I can't believe it."

She was livid now. He said, "Would you please slow down? You are terrifying me."

She drove faster. He was sure it was for his benefit. She was going to frighten him to death. He held onto the door safety grip and the side of his seat and closed his eyes. The car suddenly stopped. He opened his eyes to see what accident they had narrowly avoided. It was the red light at the First Avenue South Bridge before the elevated portion of highway 99 began along the waterfront.

When she turned the car off in her garage parking place she looked at him and said, "Can you walk home from here? I didn't think to stop in front of your place."

"May I come up for a minute and get my library books?"

"I guess so."

Riding the elevator and walking down the hall with her felt so familiar, it softened the history of what had happened and made him feel that things weren't as bad as they seemed earlier. Maybe there was another chance for something here so it didn't have to be so horribly final. Inside the apartment he leaned against the closed front door to steady his emotions and think about the next step as he looked around the living room and spied his books on the coffee table. She paused a few feet away to look at him and then fell into him and his arms were around her holding her tight. She started crying. He whispered in her ear, "I miss you so much. I'm so sorry I hurt you."

She pulled away from him. "I am so mad at you. I can't believe I let you in. I should have left you drunk on the street to fall down or be mugged."

"I'm glad you didn't. It shows what a good heart you have to be kind to someone you're so angry with."

"Get your books."

"Can we talk?"

"Now you want to talk? You are outrageous! You were quick to leave the discussion about our differences when you announced you were leaving me. That was a total disregard for the human being you said you loved. How can you be so self-absorbed?"

He felt sure the neighbors could hear that shrill retort. He said softly and evenly, "I thought I was doing the best thing for the two of us. We probably should have taken more time to discuss it, but you weren't open to that, I hope you remember. I probably should have waited until the next day to resume the conversation when everyone was fresh. I apologize. I wish we had handled things differently. Maybe we could talk in a few days when I'm sober and you're not quite as furious as you are now?"

"Get your books and get out! Every word you say is making me madder!"

He picked up the stack of books on the coffee table. "I'll phone you in a few days to try to apologize with different words."

She opened the front door and waited for him to walk through it. This time she didn't slam it. He took that as a good sign.

Now that he knew what she thought, he was able to flagellate himself into a frenzy over the next few days. He agreed with her completely that he was a rotten example of humanity, lacking intelligence and decency. He wrote and revised speeches that declared his new understanding of himself, how many errors he could now see and how she led him to enlightenment. He threw those out. He worked on the angle of how she had changed him with her energy and optimism about enjoying life and people. He threw those out. He wondered about the goal of all this explanation. He hadn't changed his mind about the Russo dynamic. He finally admitted to himself that he just wanted to see her again with her full attention focused on him. He wanted to drag out the conclusion so he got a few more Eva minutes before he was cut off for good. He embraced his hypocrisy. He didn't see her letting him back into her life. He didn't plan to ask — or beg — to be let back in. He considered that door closed. He wanted to look through the keyhole of her world again one more time. A better farewell scene to enjoy remembering in the future was what he wanted.

Poetry would be essential to gaining this audience. She was responsive to poetry. The first time he watched her react to him reciting, he made a note to himself to try to give her a few lines every day. When he ran out of ones he knew by heart, he started learning new ones. He got out his favorite Pablo Neruda collection and read it several times hoping to find the words that would work for him. He reread Mary Oliver and Wendell Barry looking for inspiration. When he finally found what he was hoping for, he copied it down on an unused page from an old journal. The paper was ivory, smaller than a business letter and had a nice feel to it. The torn edge from the binding looked natural, as though he'd bought a single sheet from a fancy stationary shop. He took it to the florist nearby on Queen Anne Avenue North and asked to see what flowers or potted plants he could have delivered to her with the poem as a card. The shop clerk had no customers to wait on and was happy to spend a long time showing him photos of the options and what he had in cold storage in the shop. The two of them discussed the strategy of apology and what worked with women and with men. The clerk had experience with groveling and was happy to share his successes and failures. Laurence finally paid for three perfect pale pink peonies, each stem in a plastic vial of water to keep it fully hydrated. He declined a vase as she had her own that were nicer. A few soft green stems of fern framed the flowers, which were then wrapped in white tissue paper tied with a bright pink silk ribbon he chose to match his favorite dress of Eva's. The long plastic spike with the holder for the gift card held his poem folded twice and inserted into the middle of the bouquet just below the blooms. It looked a little large, even partially hidden by one of the flowers, but he didn't want to make too many creases in the paper. The bouquet was then put in a long white box with yet another pink ribbon. Laurence carefully filled out the delivery address on a form. The clerk assured him it was the most beautiful apology he'd ever helped create and he was certain it would be successful. The bouquet would be delivered as soon as the truck was ready to go with the rest of the day's arrangements and it would be the first delivery since it was so close by. Laurence would wait three hours before he dialed her number. Even if she had been out in the afternoon, she should be back by 6 p.m. unless she had dinner plans. That was unlikely, he hoped. Laurence left the shop feeling upbeat and pleased with his efforts. How could she refuse him an audience after receiving this peace offering?

At 6:05 p.m. he dialed her landline and left a humble message about getting together so he could properly express his remorse. At 9:05 p.m. he decided she must have gone out to dinner with someone and thought it was too late to return his call. Humble, but not groveling, was his posture so he could not call her again today. Patience was required to maintain a little dignity. He lay in bed reading but didn't turn over too many pages and kept starting again at the top of the page he'd just read, which didn't seem familiar. In the middle of the night he woke up with the light on and still dressed in his street clothes. It was too much trouble to do anything but turn out the light and go back to sleep. At 9:05 a.m. his cell phone vibrated on the bedside table waking him. He reached for it without looking at the caller ID. It was only Julia asking if he could come in this afternoon and help her for a few hours. Of course he could.

Chapter 23

To begin the day feeling already defeated made it impossible for Laurence to leave another phone message. Eva would have to call him back. Maybe she had gone out of town to spite him. The poor flowers on the table in the lobby of her building, going dry or being stolen suddenly jerked him to attention. He should walk over there right now and see if the flower box was visible. He hoped it was still in the lobby because it would be a good reason she hadn't returned the call. It would mean she was out of town and had received neither the flowers nor the message. Please, let that be the reason. Or perhaps she hadn't been at home when the delivery was made late in the day and didn't bother to check the mail when she came home. Without a cup of coffee or anything else he headed toward her house in yesterday's clothes that he had slept in. His lack of personal hygiene showed a lapse of routine and character. Two blocks from her place he caught a glimpse of himself in a window with his hair at odd angles and thought he looked like a deranged homeless person. He turned around and walked back the few blocks to his house.

Showered and in clean clothes, he started out again. As he approached the door to Eva's building, her neighbor Helen was coming out and held the door open for him saying good morning. He responded in kind and walked in as though he lived there. She must not know that he didn't live there anymore. That was a good sign. The box of flowers was on the table with other packages not yet claimed.

He was relieved, but what to do now? He picked up the box and hit the button for the elevator.

Standing outside her door, he debated knocking or ringing the bell. Knocking was more personal he decided and gave the standard three taps firmly but not too loudly. To his astonishment, Sophia opened the door dressed in a bathrobe.

"Well, what a nice surprise to see you," she said.

"I feel the same way."

"Do you want to come in? Mom went out of town a few days ago, and I decided to vacation at the *palacio* Kerry Park," she said, standing back to let him in.

"Is everything all right?" he said.

"Yes and no. Would you like a coffee?"

"If it's no trouble that would be nice."

"I had the espresso machine loaded to go. It will just take a minute. Have a seat."

He put the box on the dining table and sat down at the end seat. A few dirty plates and glasses were at the opposite end of the table. The baby was sitting on the floor on a blanket in pajamas, pushing stuffed animals around talking to herself in her own private language. She looked at him but didn't react in any way he could see. He waved at her and said, "Hello, little Eva. How are you?"

"Cookie?"

He laughed at her. "You are smart woman already. Of course I'll get you a cookie if your mom doesn't mind." He waited for Sophia in the kitchen to respond.

"Sure. She can have a cookie if you know where they are. I haven't seen any."

Laurence went into the kitchen where she was pouring espresso into two small cups from double spouts on the machine he'd never seen Eva use. He went to the freezer and looked around inside for the container where he had stored a dozen cookies before the party began. Finding it, he took it out to the child and offered it to her to select her own. She took two and looked up at him. He smiled at her and said nothing. It would be their secret. He put the container down on the clean end of the table near the flower box where Sophia was bringing the demi coffee cups with saucers.

"Please have a cookie with your coffee," he said as she sat down next to him.

"How decadent to be eating sweets in the morning like we're on holiday." She eyed the selection and picked one and took a small bite and put it down on the saucer. "Oh, Venetian cookies! Your handiwork I assume?"

He nodded. "Thank you. You missed having them at the party. I'm glad I hid a few. They turned out to be popular." She sipped the coffee and took the tiniest bites putting the cookie down between each one. "So, no work today?"

"It's part of running away, to not go to work." She pushed the box around a bit. "So I guess it's not for me, but what's in the box?"

"Maybe it will be for you. It seems like you could use it too. When is your mother coming back?"

"I'm not sure exactly, maybe in a few days. She said she'd call me."

"Well, the gift is for you then. Enjoy, and I hope it helps your holiday."

"May I open it now?"

"Why not?"

Sophia untied the pink ribbon and slowly opened the box, pulling out the bouquet in tissue and untying that bow, savoring each step. She gasped at the beauty of the three peonies, holding them up to smell the sweet aroma and brushing her cheek with the flowers. "Gorgeous! How perfect each one is. Thank you so much. This makes my day!" She leaned over and gave him a kiss on the cheek. "Do you know where the vases are?"

"Underneath the sink in the wet bar."

She got up and returned in a few moments with a small crystal vase half filled with water for the three stems and greenery. She removed the hydration tubes and arranged the flowers, which bent softly over the edge of the vase. They both studied the arrangement. The table looked different now, no longer austere. The card looked very big on the plastic spike in the flower arrangement now without the box around it. "May I read the card too?"

"Of course. It's part of the package. I'm just the delivery guy." Laurence felt some apprehension about sharing this level of intimacy with Sophia, but he was glad he could observe her reaction to help him the next time he needed to try floral magic to right a wrong. He hoped it would have the effect he was looking for. She read the poem and burst into tears. This was the second time he'd seen her do that, and it wasn't what he was hoping for. He got up to look for a tissue in the kitchen and not finding one got a linen cocktail napkin from a drawer in the wet bar and offered it to her.

"Thank you," she sobbed. "I'm so sorry to fall apart on you again. I am so mad at all of them. They lied to me. They said the baby wouldn't be a big deal. She is! They said they would help me. They don't." She dabbed her eyes and nose with the napkin. "This poor baby is always waiting for me to do something for her, and I hardly know what to do."

Laurence sat still saying nothing because he could think of nothing appropriate to say about this situation, which he knew nothing about and couldn't possibly be the same as any situation he had ever been in.

"Where's my husband? Working of course. Where is my mother? I don't know. Why isn't she here helping me? She was hardly in town the whole time I was pregnant. She was not here when the baby was born when I could have used someone who knew what they were doing instead of a man who had been to a few breathing lessons. Who thinks that's helpful? She's hardly been in town since the baby was born. Then she says she's going to retire, but not to help me, to go on vacation! Wouldn't you think she'd like to care for her own granddaughter occasionally?"

After listening to that torrential description of abandonment, Laurence tried to think about when Eva would have gone babysitting since he had known her and couldn't think of any time she might have put down her French book, her walking shoes or her wine glass. Eva seemed happy with her schedule of activities and never mentioned babysitting.

"For the woman who doesn't want to travel anymore, she sure goes away a lot these days. What's up with that?" said Sophia.

Laurence had to think about that for a moment before he suggested, "Maybe travel for work is different to her than travel for vacation?"

"Oh, I guess I see that. You'd think she'd want to see her precious namesake."

"She invited you for dinner," said Laurence.

"That wasn't about me. She did that to show you off. How'd you like it?"

"I found it difficult," he said.

"Wasn't everybody nice to you?"

"You're not very nice to each other. That's what's difficult for me. It seemed loud and ugly. I don't speak Italian so I don't really know what happened."

"Oh, yeah, that. I'm sorry about that. But you see this is what happens when I get mad at Tony and Mom. Oh boy, then Steve was furious with me on the way home! We had quite a go round. He hates it when I start the insults. I'm sorry you don't understand because there were some great ones that night. Maybe I should teach you a few. It could come in handy sometime with my mom. And then you get to make up." She smiled at him.

He didn't want to appear to agree with her, so nodded slightly and tried to think of something neutral. "I think I'll stick with learning French. I should leave you alone now to resume your holiday."

"No, please don't go. I'm glad you're here. Thank you for the flowers and the poem. It helps me to see what I'm missing. I need romance and understanding. I'm tired of being pacified. Nobody wants to listen to me. They don't want to know what I'm feeling because it isn't what they want me to feel. They don't want to hear any complaints. Everybody wants me to be quiet and just get things done."

"Who are they?" said Laurence while beginning to understand why *they* didn't want to hear anymore from Sophia.

"Everybody in my life it seems, my husband, Tony and my mom. The three of them can be counted on to be exasperated if I'm unhappy about anything. They don't want to hear it. They all think my life is perfect and that I'm the one who is messing it up by not being happy when I have everything anyone could want. Do you see what I mean?"

"They're not sympathetic?"

"Exactly. Anything I'm disappointed about, large or small, they say it's nothing. It is something to me. When I try to keep it all to myself, I end up wanting to kill them. That's even worse than when I try to explain myself and they say 'stop complaining, you're such a whiner.'"

"What would you like them to say?" said Laurence.

"They should agree with me and say 'how awful! I'd be upset too, if that happened to me.'"

"Have you asked them to say that?" he said.

"Yes! But they won't do it."

"And Marco isn't part of this problem?"

"No, he's the only one who gets me. He always understands and is on my side."

"What about Angelika?"

"No. She doesn't understand. She never had her own life. She's been a girlfriend, a wife and mother forever. She lives to serve her men. I feel so sorry for her."

As he thought about that and what he might say, the baby got up and started walking toward him. She pulled on his thigh trying to climb up. Without thinking about it, he picked her up and put her in his lap facing the table. She pushed the espresso cup and saucer away to reach for the plastic container of cookies. He looked at Sophia for her approval before giving out another cookie. She smiled at the child, called her name and asked her if she wanted a cookie. Little Eva smiled back and said, "Cookie!"

Sophia said, "Sure, give her another cookie. What difference can it make? It's food. She needs to eat something. I'm happy she's adding to her vocabulary."

"How old is she?" Laurence was glad to change the subject and pulled the container within the child's reach.

"Almost 2."

"She's beautiful."

"Thanks. I love her but she drives me crazy. You can't imagine how much time it takes to deal with her. You can't leave her alone for a second. She is relentless and stubborn in getting what she wants."

"Are those family traits?" he said.

"Sounds like a perfect description of my mom, doesn't it? I don't think that's me though."

"How do you describe yourself?" he said.

"Intelligent, impatient, insatiable. Does that sound ugly?"

"No, I think that sounds attractive or vivacious."

"You are so good. I can really see what my mom sees in you. You are so here, rock solid, in the room, getting everything. The nuances I mean. Do you know that's a gift?"

"No, I call it paying attention. It's a habit. Anyone can learn it."

"Now that I've told you about my problems, what's going on with you and Mom?"

"What did she tell you?" said Laurence.

"That you have a difference of opinion and she's really angry with you about not wanting to talk about it."

"Well, that's true plus we have the issue that I'm not a fighter. That puts me at odds with most of the Russos I've met. You seem exceptionally fond of fighting."

"We like it, that's true. We're all good at it. I'm sorry you don't like it. You know it's almost like having sex. I know you like that." She smiled at him.

He was too embarrassed to return an equal smile. "No, I didn't know that about fighting. Did she say anything else?"

"Do you mean about getting married? She said she hadn't decided yet."

"Oh, not yet. I see." He nodded his head. His mind was racing. It was news to him that she was thinking about it at all and talking about it. He couldn't remember the subject coming up since they were in the cottage in the San Juans. Nothing was as it seemed to him. The difference in his reality and hers was shocking. So much for him getting all the nuances. His floral gift, if she had been here to get it, could have been misinterpreted as a proposal.

"Does that hurt your feelings?" she said.

"No. I don't see the point of getting married at my age. I'll be dead soon."

"That certainly makes it simpler. I'm not worried about it, but Tony and Marco will be relieved."

"Me being dead will relieve them?" Laurence said.

"No, that you don't want to be married."

This conversation was swirling around in dangerous directions. He didn't want any of this repeated as though they had a serious talk on the topic and she was relaying his views on the subject. "This conversation is impromptu, and I hope you won't repeat it to anyone. I have no idea what the future holds for anyone, but no matter what happens, none of the Russos should be concerned about their inheritance. I'm not a gold digger."

"I could tell that about you from the beginning," said Sophia.

"I must be going. I have work to do at the gallery this afternoon."

"I'm sorry to see you go. I really enjoy talking with you. You always make me feel better. You're so good with Evie. Thanks again for the gift. I will show it to my husband. I think I should tell my mom she's a fool if she doesn't forgive you immediately."

Chapter 24

Laurence called Amy to invite her to the taste test. She was happy to come as expected and mentioned she had just heard from Eva who was postponing a lunch date until she returned from Manzanita Beach, Oregon. Eva reported having fun in a hot tub overlooking the beach, but she didn't say whom she was with.

Laurence was glad to have any scrap of news but this report sucked the air out of him. He tried to calm his thoughts and breathe slowly and evenly. Alive and well was good news. Having fun in a hot tub with other people felt like a red-hot dagger in his heart. Who could these people or person possibly be? He knew for certain it was none of her children. Had she found a new man to audition already? From the hot tub to in between the sheets was a speedy transition. You're already half naked to begin with. He'd been naked in some hot tubs. He knew exactly what happened next. This was awful news. Now he would never have a chance at his apology and peacemaking. Eva would be on to the next guy and not need to hear him out or bother with fond memories. Laurence had made another huge error he would regret the rest of his pathetic life.

He went back to stuffing envelopes with the announcements of the Basque exhibit at the gallery and putting mailing labels on them. Julia and Drew had created a massive list that included the local Basque restaurant and businesses selling Basque products, clients, potential art buyers from all over the West Coast, as well as art sellers throughout the United States with a history of Spanish or Basque art and anybody Drew knew personally. A few were being sent to the Basque Country to alert key art sellers of this unique exhibition. He hoped his old and ex-friends were eating their hearts out receiving this unique artistic news in the mail. Drew was alive and well with a big gallery doing innovative shows!

Laurence thought Julia had done a great job of creating the announcement. It seemed suitable for framing to him. He loved the colors and the energy, its unmistakable Basqueness with a costumed male dancer leaping high off the ground showing only his thighs and red bell pads and pointed toes. He was dancing in a green pasture. Another version of it would become the advertisement for the exhibition in the print media and online. Another version, without any text describing the event, would be sold as a souvenir poster at the exhibit. Drew fully utilized Julia's art school training. He directed her as the star pupil and lavished attention on her work. As with all the promotional art she created for the gallery, Drew insisted she put her logo on each piece. He wanted her to get full credit for creating the campaign. Watching them work and worry Laurence was aware of how much was at stake for Drew and Julia in this. They wanted and needed a success to take the gallery to a new level of recognition and patronage. Laurence felt sure it would be a success, but he didn't have anything at risk to lose sleep over as they did.

When he finished the mailing project Julia said there was nothing else for him to help with until the caterer's tasting the day after tomorrow and that she would catch a bus downtown with him. It seemed unusual to him that she was leaving at five but he was glad to have the company to chat about what tasks might come next and what her opinion was about it all. For a typically quiet and calm person, she spoke at length with emotion about the potential disaster approaching, namely the turnout for the exhibit. If the turnout for the Basque show wasn't huge, Drew was going to be crushed. His peers and artists would judge him on the quality of the exhibit and how popular it was with the people who buy art. This show was so different from one artist's exhibit or a small group show of artists with similar focus. Julia would blame it on her marketing and artwork. Everyone would be laid off, and she would have to look for another job that would never be as good as this one. She'd be lucky to get a job doing online ads for a department store. She went on and on about how Drew trusted her to do everything, which was rare. Gallery owners in general had a reputation for being difficult and hard to please. Plus Drew spent a lot of time with her on her art and how to improve it and had really helped her develop a style. Usually you had to pay for that kind of direction, she informed him. Many art students did grunge work or had sex with the teacher in exchange for art lessons. She was lucky that Drew paid her to do work she was happy to have the chance to do plus the sales commissions on anything she sold which put her way ahead of anyone else she knew from art school. This job was excellent, and she would be very sad to lose it.

For the second time today he felt inundated with a young woman's emotions or was it hormones? Laurence tried to sympathize with each of her fears and assure her that she was thinking worst case. No one would lose his job over this exhibit. Even if the exhibit were modestly successful, it would not mean the end of the gallery. Drew's stress over this show was because it was so unusual and created solely by Drew, which is exactly why it would be a success. Julia's vibrant art and marketing program would draw people in. The show Drew had put together would amaze them and they would tell their friends. The art would be sold. She loved Laurence's point of view. "Keep your level head level, Julia," he counseled.

As she got ready to leave the bus at Cherry Street, he asked her why she was getting off here. She said she was meeting a friend in the Columbia Tower. He said good-bye and wondered whom in the world she might know who worked in that skyscraper of banking and international commerce. Julia always had something unexpected in reserve. She was quite a package of intelligence and common sense in a young girl. She never seemed foolish or naive. He watched her walk up the steep hill with her blonde hair swinging until the bus moved him forward. He shared her feeling about Drew as a manager. He too was lucky to have an interesting job and would be sorry to lose it. He didn't think that would happen.

As the bus passed through downtown, he realized he was hungry and should think about cooking dinner before he got to the Metropolitan Market at the bottom of the Hill. He thought about poor Sophia, probably still in her bathrobe with a hungry baby. He should try to help her. He dialed the landline at Eva's and let it ring. When the recording began he said, "Sophia, it's Laurence. It's dinnertime, and I wondered if you would like me to bring you some food or cook something for you. I know what a mess that refrigerator is. It's full but you can't find anything."

Sophia picked up the phone. "Oh, my God, yes! That would be wonderful! We're starving here but I can't bear to go out on the street and look for something. The take-out menus seem abysmal."

"I know. Are you hungry for anything in particular?"

"Salad and a steak? Could you do that?"

"What would the baby like?"

"She eats anything I eat."

"How about a potato or bread?"

"Oh no. We don't eat anything white."

"OK. How about a sweet potato? I'll be there in a few minutes." Great. There was no need to stop at the Metropolitan Market for anything. The over-full refrigerator could provide a nice dinner for three. When Eva was alone and hungry she liked to go out or have it delivered. He had guessed correctly that Sophia was the same way. Cooking food wasn't in her habits.

When Sophia opened the door she was still in her bathrobe and the baby was crying on the floor. Laurence walked right in with no greetings or handshakes. He immediately picked up the baby and took her in the kitchen. In the back of the cheese drawer was a storage container of pureed squash leftover from a ravioli project. The temperature in the refrigerator was a steady 45 degrees so the deterioration rate was very slow. He opened the lid and smelled it. Sweet butter and squash aromas wafted out, the same as the day he made it. He took a small bite with a spoon to test it and pronounced it delicious with enthusiasm. Little Eva bought his opinion and reached for it. He put her on the counter and gave her a spoon to help herself. She knew how to use a spoon.

"Sophia, come sit here where I can see you and hold the baby so she can eat this while I get the rest of the dinner going."

Sophia sat down, he handed her the baby and put the container of squash down on the table in front of her. The baby started feeding herself with gusto. Laurence smiled at them. Sophia watched Eva eat with amusement.

"What is she eating?"

"Squash."

"I had no idea she liked it."

Laurence shrugged as he preheated the oven, thinly sliced the sweet potato and spread it out on a baking sheet with olive oil and salt and pepper. He put that in the oven, which was rapidly approaching the desired goal of 425 degrees. Working with a quality gas range like this one was a pleasure. High heat in a hurry in the oven and thousands of BTUs on the burners. He got a steak out of the freezer and defrosted it in the microwave for two minutes while preheating a cast iron skillet to cook it in. Once the steak seasoned with *pimenton dulce* was sizzling in butter, he began unloading the lettuce drawer where linen towels were wrapped around washed leaves, some of which were still edible. Eva's high-end appliances were so much better than any he had ever owned. He believed the refrigerator was the most important appliance of all. He chopped an assortment of lettuce and threw it in a large bowl with a big splash of olive oil. He turned the steak over and put it in the oven before seasoning the salad with salt and a dash of sherry vinegar. After a toss with salad servers, he put the bowl on the table.

"We're a few minutes away. Do you want to open some wine?" Laurence said.

"You are so amazing! I can't believe how quickly you can get dinner ready. Sure. I'd love some wine. What would you like?"

"You choose."

Laurence went back to the oven and flipped the potatoes over which now had an attractively browned side. He put three plates on the counter next to the cutting board. He flipped the steak out on the board and thinly sliced it on the diagonal. Sophia handed him a glass of red wine, which he immediately sloshed a bit into the hot frying pan and swirled it around. He fanned out four slices of steak on two of the plates. He finely chopped one slice of steak to put on the last plate. A few hot slices of potato touched the meat on each plate and he poured a bit of the pan juice on top of the steak slices. He put the plates on the table.

Sophia, with the baby on her lap and the container of squash and two plates in front of her, was smiling at him. "Cheers! This is so great." She sipped the wine and pushed little Eva's plate closer to her so she could reach out with her hands to grab the meat and the potato.

The three of them ate without speaking until they had all finished what had been served. "How about some more?"

"No. That was perfect for me. I'm on to the salad now. Look at how Eva cleaned her plate! That's a happy baby."

Laurence nodded with pleasure. It was great to see people enjoy eating what he had made them.

As he finished his salad he said, "So, how's the holiday going?"

"I'm enjoying relaxing. It's been quite awhile since I lay around on the couch and did nothing. I think it's good for me to slow everything down. Tony wants to know when I'm coming back to work. I don't think I'm up for that tomorrow, but soon I will have to."

"Where is your husband?" he said.

"He's traveling. He'll be back Friday night. I have to go home then no matter what."

"Are you thinking of quitting your job?"

"No. It's not practical. If I quit now it will be too hard to find any job, much less a good one, when Eva is older and I want to go back to work."

"You like the work?"

"I do. I'm educated for it. I think I do it well. I have worked for other companies so I have a perspective about what I contribute. Working for the family has benefits I wouldn't have anywhere else, like taking a few days off without notice. I would also have to work harder anywhere else. I can't give it any more hours than I do now. I am stretched thin. My house is a wreck. That's why I need to come here to relax. Everything is always so nice and clean at Mom's."

"Where would you have gone if she weren't away?"

"Nowhere. I would have had to stay home, and it isn't relaxing to be surrounded by your own mess and unfinished projects. It's better to go to the office." Sophia looked resigned.

"Do you need help with housekeeping?"

"Wouldn't that be divine? In September about four and a half years from now I get out of the day care money pit and I'm investing in a housecleaning service. It's on my calendar."

"I didn't realize day care was so high."

"It's ridiculous. All the women I know who have kids and work give their paycheck to day care."

"I know everyone wishes they had more money. I would have thought your husband did well."

"He does very well, but it costs a lot to live. It's hard to do it on one salary. When Evie goes to school, my salary will make a big difference with lifestyle. You wouldn't believe the nice vacations, dinners out and housecleaners we had before Evie. It's another thing they don't tell you." She kissed the baby's cheek next to hers. "You little money pit. Don't get too used to all this good food at Grandma's house. Soon we'll go home and back to Chinese."

"Oh no. You're not giving her Chinese takeout!" Laurence was horrified.

"Indian, Mexican and Thai too."

"That's not good for her. There are too many additives and salt. You saw how she enjoyed the mashed squash? That is so easy and inexpensive. There is nothing in it but the vegetable and butter."

"You think I'm going to start making baby food?" Sophia was incredulous.

"You have to! She must have good food or her brain won't develop properly."

Sophia looked skeptical and amused. "You are living in a dream world!"

"Do you not know how to cook?"

"When would I do that, if I knew how?" she asked.

"You just watched me cook dinner in about 15 minutes. You could make Eva some vegetables on the weekend to feed her right out of the refrigerator whenever she's hungry. You could also cook for yourself on the weekend if you have no time during the week and serve it warm or cold."

"That's so easy for you to say who knows how and cares about it. I can't imagine finding time to learn how to do it," Sophia said.

"I'll be glad to show you. We can have a cooking class here tomorrow."

The phone rang, and they both listened for the message. When Eva's voice began Sophia jumped up and grabbed the phone in the kitchen. "Hi, Mom. We're here. How are you?" There was a pause before Sophia said, "We're great. We just had a nice steak and salad, and Little Eva has stopped crying. Everything is good." Another pause. "You know I didn't cook it. I'm your daughter. Laurence cooked it. Well, it was easy. He phoned and asked if we needed food and I said yes...He knew we were here because he brought flowers earlier... Of course they were for you! But since you weren't here, he gave them to me. They're beautiful. I'll give them back to you. Oh, and they came with a poem, Mom. That's yours too, but I want to show it to Steve so he will know how to bail himself out the next time. I don't think you'll be able to stay mad after you read the poem. Tomorrow, I'm definitely not going to the office. We're talking about having a cooking class here. I'm not sure about that, but he doesn't want me to feed Evie take-out food anymore. Isn't that crazy?" She laughed.

Laurence sat listening to Sophia's side of the conversation and could imagine exactly what Eva was saying and in what tone of voice. Would she give up her good times in the hot tub and come home? What did he want her to do?

If she came back now while Sophia was still here, where would everyone sleep? He of course, would go to his house and Eva, Sophia and Evie could all sleep together in the king-size bed. Or Sophia and Evie could sleep on the couch. He didn't think Eva would want to go his house. Did he want her to? This was getting more complicated by the minute. His resolve about asking forgiveness so they could talk it all out and leave no hard feelings was starting to feel flimsy and foolish. Did he want to be friends? He couldn't quite see how that would work, getting together to walk or study French but then going home while she went out to dinner and to sleep with her new boyfriend. That would be worse than awkward. That would be painful. He hadn't planned on seeing her after they amiably separated. But there she would be a few blocks away and undoubtedly he would run into her on the street and at the grocery, even if he quit the tai chi and French classes. He hadn't been going to either class since the party, but he hadn't withdrawn officially. He liked Sophia and her baby. He wanted to show her a few kitchen tricks that would make her life easier and save money. That would be simple for him and provide a long-term value for her. He might not see her again. She was waving the phone at him.

"Mom wants to talk to you."

Laurence stared at her as though he didn't understand. Sophia put the phone in his hand and got up with the baby and walked into the bedroom and closed the door.

"Laurence? Are you there?" Eva said.

"Yes."

"What are you doing there?"

"Getting ready to clean up the kitchen," he said.

"No. I mean what are you doing there cooking for my daughter and grandchild?"

"They are hungry and don't seem to know how to feed themselves. That's why the baby cries all the time. She wants food and is being fed junk when someone remembers it's time to eat."

"They are not your problem. They are not even my problem. My daughter will feed her child. That's her job. She has to figure that out."

"I plan to show her a few things tomorrow that she could do over the weekend to make the weeknights easier."

"Teach a man to fish?" said Eva.

"I guess." He hated how quickly she had come to that interpretation.

"You've dived in headfirst without thinking, and you're trying to create a legacy while espousing your desire to be a solitary soul. You're confusing me."

"I guess I'm confused too. It's not in me to ignore them and let them be hungry."

"Enough about them. Tell me about my flowers."

"Eva, I want you to talk to me one more time. I've made mistakes. I want to smooth a few out so you won't think so badly of me and not have hard feelings."

"Legacy again. You are worried about your future and what people think. That doesn't sound like the old man who wants to be left alone to die by himself."

"No, I guess not. It's you I'm talking about, Eva. I don't care what anybody thinks but you," he said.

"What do you want to do about me?" she asked.

"I don't know. Nothing is as simple as I thought. Believe me, I've been thinking a lot about it."

"Life seems much less complicated when relaxing with a view of this beautiful bay," she said.

"Well, I'm glad you're enjoying yourself. When are you thinking of coming home?" Laurence asked.

"I'd planned to stay until I made up my mind what to do," Eva said.

"Have you made up your mind?"

"I think so. I need to see my flowers and read my poem, though."

"Will I see you tomorrow?" Laurence asked.

"Do you want to?"

"Very much." He meant it but felt ambivalent about what she had decided.

"I'll see you tomorrow afternoon. We'll talk about everything then."

He hung up the phone and sat staring at the table and his dinner plate. He had a new deadline forced on him, which wasn't good. In fact it was annoying. He really didn't think marriage was on her mind despite what she'd said to Sophia. He thought her issue must be whether or not to forgive him for being pigheaded, and he thought she would. Be forgiving. She wasn't going to give him the boot because he had already taken himself out of the game.

Despite the possibility of a new boyfriend, he felt confident she loved him and wanted him. He didn't doubt though that she would find someone else soon if he stuck to his decision to be alone. Was he going to reverse his decision? That seemed to him the critical element. Was an imaginary rival forcing him into a quick decision? Imaginary or real, that man was what made him realize his position was questionable. His solitary suffering was only tenable if he didn't see her. Was he willing to say he was sorry, declare his love and say he would like to come back to become part of this family?

Although her volatility worried him, the extended family remained a huge obstacle. Being alone with Sophia was easy and pleasant. She was bright and pretty and funny today. The night she was baiting Tony with Marco she had looked scary. He tried to imagine visiting with Marco alone and couldn't get too far with it. A salesman has a gift for chatting, but he had no idea what Marco's range of topics might be. He did not look forward to being alone with Tony and his stark presentation and pointed questions. Tony and his silent wife together could be an hour of misery. Marco and Tony together — he dreaded being in the room again with that combination.

What about the other silent wife, Angelika? Although she didn't seem strange, it was still odd she had so little to say. The real world family, with its history and rivalries, no doubt would continue on in the same way. The screaming, ranting, raging and trading insults would probably be part of the evening every time they got together. That would be his nightmare to look forward to over and over again. He could not ask or expect that to change. Maybe he could come up with some negotiating strategy by tomorrow afternoon, something to offer that she would have to think over. If he were to try to tolerate the family dynamic, what could she barter in return that would make it equal? What could he ask for? That's what he needed to decide.

He started cleaning up the kitchen. Sophia resumed her seat at the table sipping her wine.

"Little Eva is asleep?"

"Yes. Thank you for the amazing dinner that knocked her out. I should let you give me a cooking lesson for that squash."

"Shall we have a cooking lesson tomorrow before your mom comes back?"

"Why not? What would I learn?" Sophia asked.

"I was thinking of calling it 'Vegetables at 425'. I'll come at lunchtime and bring a bag of assorted vegetables. We'll bake them in a hot oven, eat some and you can take the rest home to eat. I'll give you a box of the magic powder from Espellette, France so you, too, can have a Basque flavor whenever you want."

Chapter 25

Laurence's idea of going for a walk with Eva and out to dinner was never on the table. Eva called him late in the afternoon to say she was at home after Sophia and the baby had left. He'd walked right over. She let him in and offered him a seat at the dining table and a cup of regular coffee, not wine, not espresso. No warm welcome was offered. His peonies were on the table, but she didn't mention them. He sat down and started to feel apprehensive as though bad news was about to be delivered. His idea of negotiating didn't appear to be on her agenda. She was running the meeting. She looked stern and forbidding. Her clothes were odd to him, not a dress but a stretchy three-piece black exercise suit with a zippered hoodie. It must be a new outfit for tai chi or yoga. In her unique way, she went straight to the point, no banter or warm up.

"Laurence, it is so clear to me that we love each other and love being together in every way. I am angry and sad that you discount the value of our relationship to the level that you can discard it because of imperfections that bother you or that seem hard for you to deal with. You are disregarding the data you say you depend on in favor of some emotional or irrational thinking. When in your life and work was there not some difficulty to be dealt with? Didn't you perceive obstacles as a challenge to get you to find a better solution? When did you ever quit because the work was hard? I believe with my heart and soul that if you study the situation again, you and me as a full time permanent relationship, you will come to the conclusion that you should make the commitment for all the joy and sorrow life brings. I want you to show me that you love me by marrying me and promising your loyalty. Anything less than that allows you to disengage or disappear as the moment suits you. That's not fair to me. I want 100 percent from you, the same as I will give you, or nothing. I don't want to be your friend or your girlfriend. I want to be your wife."

He sat without saying anything. He had been watching her while she delivered this speech, obviously rehearsed, as it was so flawless in logic and delivery. He felt the full impact of her carefully chosen words. She was concise and not emotional. But this was the oddest ultimatum to someone who not too long ago had told her that he definitely couldn't live with her. He'd never forget that her response to that was "get out and never come back." She was acting as though she was in the power seat and entitled to state the terms. She wasn't negotiating for a thaw or a new option to try again and see if they could make it work. She was leaping over ordinary time and experience, going for the end play. This was beyond the salesman not taking no for an answer. Eva was a powerhouse! She was formidable. He tried to quickly think of a delaying tactic. What was his counter offer?

"I appreciate how much you have thought this through. I understand that my thinking seems flawed to you. I'm glad you still want me. I am, however, surprised by your offer. I hope you will allow me time to create a thoughtful response that is worthy of it."

"How much time do you need?"

This struck him as a trick question. Too long or too short could both be insulting and work against him.

"December is a busy month for me preparing for the exhibit and I'm sure you are busy too with all the holiday things that you do with your family. I'm not a holiday guy. I hate Christmas. I would like to let all the frenzy go by in general, and specifically for you and me, as it has so much family tradition and emotion tied up in it. Could we be clearheaded together after the New Year? Would it be OK with you to wait that long?"

"A month does seem like a long time for you to make a decision. But I agree with you the holidays can be emotional and I would hate for our new alliance to be derailed by my family's typical Christmas dinner." She grimaced and said, "Yes, it is usually quite lively. By the time everyone gets to my house they are exhausted from Christmas Eve at the in-laws and the day of Christmas beginning too early in a blizzard of wrapping paper. You are smart to avoid it this year."

So, she really thought his answer would be yes and next year he would be on the hook for this nightmare of a holiday dinner. That made him long to be stubborn. To try to continue the conversation on a flat historical path and buy time Laurence said, "What do you usually cook?"

"Fish. Not the feast of the seven fishes, but a few nice dishes, oysters to start and cioppino or a stuffed roasted fish. What do you usually do?"

"Nothing. Read, stay indoors and wait for it to be over."

"You don't cook anything special?"

"Not in years. We never did too much for it even when I was young."

"Would you like more coffee?"

"Sure." He was enjoying sitting with her and as long as the topics stayed neutral, he was happy to stay. He feared this was the last time he would see her for a month or maybe forever. If he decided to say no, would he want to do that in person? Why couldn't they just try again to be together? The family Christmas party! Next there would be a wedding party or never seeing her again unless he ran into her at the grocery store. Bleak choices, he felt.

Why wasn't he happy that she wanted to be devoted to him forever? What was he missing that this unexpected declaration of love was not good news? He felt pushed into a corner with no options. Yes or no somehow didn't feel like options. Or was it that he had no say in the matter? She had dictated. This was not a discussion. She had stated her terms and put the decision on his shoulders, like that made it a two-way agreement. That's what was annoying him. What did he want?

She returned with the coffee pot and filled his cup. "Sophia told me she enjoyed your cooking class today. You have made an impression on her about the advantages of cooking over take-out."

"She's a smart woman, your Sophia. I really do enjoy her."

"She says you're a natural with little Eva."

"I don't remember ever doing too much with babies, but it seems remarkable to me that I pick her up and she doesn't scream. She's appreciative of every bite of food I give her. Of course, the natural Russo beauty is charming."

"I'm glad. So, how is the exhibit coming?"

"I think it's coming along fine. Everybody is working hard. Drew and Julia are worried but they have the most at stake. If it's a bomb, Julia says we'll all lose our jobs. I don't think it will come to that. I think the concept is a good one, and Drew has developed it in every direction. There is a richness and a complexity to the exhibit that I think will make it popular."

"Does Julia have a new beau?"

"I think she does although I haven't met him. How did you know that?"

"I sent someone to audition."

"You amaze me! Let me guess, he works in the Columbia Tower?"

"Yes."

"Eva, you are something! What makes you think Julia needs your help in the man department? She's got all the looks any young woman could want and is so smart."

"She needs someone her own age to engage her."

"I don't know how you think you know that but what else are you working on?"

"I want this exhibit to succeed and have implemented my own strategies for increasing the audience and making Drew look smarter to the world with a talented woman his own age."

"You think big! You sent someone to audition for that too?"

"Yes and stage one is successful already. Stage two requires more time."

"I can see it now, I don't have a chance. We should just go to the courthouse tomorrow and be done with it."

She laughed. "That wouldn't be like you. Doesn't have enough of your thought in it. Until you have put your contribution in, it won't be ready to bake."

"Who are you matchmaking Drew with?"

"Bernadette."

"Oh, my God. She is perfect for him, but will he see it?"

"She will help him make more money and I hope that will be enough to open his eyes to her fabulous maturity and the thrill of dealing with someone his own age who has the same reference points and gets his jokes. She would look so good on his arm and vice versa."

"That's true. What makes you want to help Drew?" Laurence looked perplexed.

"I'm not sure. On one level he's frustrating because he makes mistakes that seem so obvious. How can he not see that dallying with Julia makes him look foolish to anyone who notices like I did and distracts him from pursuing someone much more suitable that would enhance him? He's smart at his business but missing some element of having a complete perspective. I'm genuinely fond of him. He has winning ways that come naturally to him. Maybe I need something to manage now that my business is out of my hands and he needs my help."

"Julia is his employee and art student. What's unseemly about that?"

"They operate as a close partnership. Everything is 'us' and 'we.' That's not typical employer-employee talk. It's clear she is his girlfriend or a 'sort of' girlfriend is the way he puts it. You know what that means." She looked at him sternly.

"You asked him? How could you?" Laurence looked at her with disbelief. She shrugged her shoulders. He continued, "I have spent so many hours with them. I never noticed them making eyes at each other or touching or making private jokes."

"They aren't in love with each other. I think this is merely sexual convenience for Drew. Who knows what she thinks she owes him."

"Eva, I am always astonished at what you see that I don't. It makes sense to me now, as you describe it, but I wouldn't have come up with that ever."

"Laurence, you have other talents."

He shook his head. "Tell me about Manzanita."

"It's a beautiful bay over ten miles long with a huge beach, cliffs at one end and the majority of the land is protected from any development. The dunes have tall grasses but no trees so it's not the typical Northwest landscape. The town is tiny with a few shops and services for the tourists. It is a delight. I'd like to rent a house there for a month. I think you would really enjoy it."

He pictured himself relaxing on a porch with the view or walking on the beach with a breeze and felt his neck and shoulders relax. Vacationing with Eva was synonymous with sensual pleasures. He reached out and put his hand over hers and gave it a gentle squeeze. "The place sounds wonderful. Where was the hot tub you sat in with friends?"

"I don't know anybody there. The hot tub is a Jacuzzi that was in my hotel room with a view of the beach. Sounds odd to have that sort of appliance right next to your bed, but it works well because it's too cold and rainy most of the time to sit outside in a hot tub. I can see how it would encourage romance in any season to have it so handy."

"I would definitely enjoy that." What a relief to know his competition hadn't been in the Jacuzzi with her after all. His imaginary rival didn't exist, yet. She looked radiant while she had described it, not at all harsh as earlier. He wanted her. He felt like leading her into the bedroom and taking comfort in her body and mind. He picked up her hand and kissed it. "I miss you."

"I miss you too."

"Why don't we sit on the couch where it's more comfortable?" He stood up, still holding her hand. She stood up too and followed him over to the couch where they sat down on the long end. He put his arm around her shoulder and hugged her to him and kissed her cheek. It was easy to stretch out from there and embrace the full length of their bodies face to face and kiss each other softly and then more urgently. She was more than willing to let him be affectionate with her. He could tell she had missed him. After a while she rolled over to face him with her head on his shoulder.

"What's next?" she said.

"Your pleasure is my pleasure. I was starving for you and now I'm hungry for dinner. How about a glass of wine and some pasta?"

"Do we have any?"

"Of course. Would you like ravioli or linguine?"

"Ravioli."

Laurence gave her a long kiss before he got up and went to look for the squash ravioli in the freezer and put some water to boil. There wasn't too much lettuce left so he looked around for enhancements, a few carrots that could be grated and chives miraculously good enough to use despite being older than he could remember. She came and stood behind him with her arms around his waist.

"Do you feel like you're back where you belong?" she said.

"Yes. We are good together. I want to be here with you." He turned around to face her. "I'm sure we can work something out."

They sat at the table and ate slowly. He was pleased with the ravioli. The squash tasted fresh and creamy with butter. The surrounding pasta tasted rich from the artisan flour he had made it with. He had cooked it al dente for a gentle contrast with the squash center. The carrot salad on the side gave a crunch. It felt wonderful to him to be sitting with her enjoying the meal with no drama. No question the warmth from earlier was still spinning a glow around them. He wanted to keep her feeling generous toward him. He wanted to stay the night all the way to New Year.

After dinner they sat on the couch with their feet up on the coffee table and his arm around her so she could rest her head on his shoulder. Laurence watched the lights of the city vibrate.

Eva said, "I think it's time for you to go home."

"Oh, no. I don't want to go home. I want to stay with you."

"I've enjoyed you being here, but I don't want you to stay the night."

"Why?" Laurence was dismayed.

"I think you should stay at your place until after New Year's when you've decided if you want to stay here for good."

"Why do you want to torture you and me?" His distress was authentic, and he could hear it in his voice.

"I think it will help you in your thinking if you're not here. I don't want you to get the feeling I will relax my position and let you stay without fulfilling your end," she said.

"I know what you want. You have been clear. But I think it's only fair if I tell you what I want in return."

"I expect that you will. Are you doing that tonight?"

"Well, I hadn't planned on it. I'm not fully prepared but I can give you the highlights."

"I'm listening."

He felt quite sure of himself and began with, "I want to stay here until New Year's. I want the time to be with you to make me feel confident we're progressing. I will help you prepare for your family party, but I don't want to attend it. I can't face what you assure me will be a volatile gathering. In the future I want you to consider breaking the group up into more congenial pieces so we entertain more but not the whole group at one time. It's too many people for this space. The Tony-Marco combination is poison. Let's keep them separate and make them both happy. Everyone would like to have your undivided attention. Invite Tony and Jean over here for dinner, with or without their kids. Let's sit around the table in chairs and eat together. Let's gauge how much they enjoy the special attention and see what sort of evening we have together. I would be willing to bet that will produce good conversations with everyone without any tension. I'd like to ask Jean a few questions about her art and her sons."

"No, no and no. You can't dictate to me how to handle my children."

He stood up and stared at her, hoping to wither her with his anger delivered in a low steady tone of voice. "Thank you for considering it and making it such an in-depth conversation that I understand more about your point of view. Good night, Mrs. Russo. I'll be in touch with you after the New Year. Please don't ring my doorbell late at night."

Laurence left the apartment closing the door softly.

Chapter 26

Drew and Julia welcomed Amy into the gallery on the day of the caterer's tasting. Julia embodied the season with a short black knit dress, red ballet slippers and red tights as her ornaments.

In Drew's office Amy took one of the comfortable swivel seats in front of Drew's desk. She began to study his art again, particularly the Sargent knockoff with the volumes of silk fabric and the beautiful model. She said to Drew, "Do you mind if I look more closely at it? I am obsessed with this one."

He shook his head. "Go right ahead."

She stood up and at eye level with the painting she could see the brush strokes and details of the color that created the illusion of the fabric. She studied the model's face and voluptuous body. "She looks so familiar to me. I thought that the first time, and up close it is even more so. Could I possibly know the model?"

"Sure. She's local." Drew looked amused.

"When did you paint it?"

"Maybe 35 years ago. I don't remember exactly."

Amy sat back down. "Thanks for inviting me today. This is fun for me."

"Our pleasure. We're still talking about what fun we had at your house and how beautiful your house is."

He showed her the announcement and the poster Julia had designed for the Basque exhibit. Amy was impressed with Julia's art.

"Julia, that's fabulous. I love it. You have captured the exuberance of the place and the people. Will these be for sale?"

Julia said, "Yes. Thank you. We have a few items for sale, the promotional poster and a photograph that Laurence found. We'll sell them framed and possibly unframed, a souvenir of the show for everyone who doesn't want to buy a big piece of original art."

Drew helped her by holding up the photograph of the old fisherman in the black beret and passed it to Amy who agreed they would sell lots of them.

The caterer was in her early 40s and looked somewhat formidable to Drew who immediately assumed she was trying to get her way with a stiff offense, which wouldn't work with him. He doubted that would move Charles either. He also assumed her tattoos and attitude came from working the line in restaurants when she was younger. He knew catering was hard work, late nights and weekends, but not as brutal as the daily line. Her assistant, who carried cake boxes tied together, was a young man with even more tattoos showing around the edges of his clothes. She explained the five dishes they had prepared for the tasting, suggesting Drew choose three to serve at the grand opening and the same or a fewer number at the weekend events. The atmosphere in the room was now serious.

The cake boxes were placed on the table and opened. There were five portions in small lightweight cardboard serving dishes in each box. Laurence inspected each box and was not impressed. He could see Amy's face go blank trying not to express any dismay or disappointment.

Box number one featured a generic olive with pimento stuffing and a gherkin pickle on a toothpick. Box number two contained small portions of roasted almonds and raisins. Box number three held thin slices of dried chorizo. Cold shrimp on a toothpick were next. The finale was small red Italian peppers stuffed with something white.

Charles and Laurence began by taking one dish of each item and putting it in front of them. They looked at Amy and so she did the same. She looked at Drew sitting behind his desk. He shook his head and said, "You're the experts."

Julia followed his lead and said, "I'll wait until you're done and if anything is left, I'll be glad to have it."

Charles and Laurence began smelling and chewing slowly on the item from the first box. "The olive is ordinary and could be from anywhere. I suggest a Manzanillo olive or similar. We need a Basque pepper that is spicy not sweet," Charles said. Laurence nodded in agreement. They looked at Amy who hadn't taken a bite yet.

Amy said, "The name of the pickled pepper you want is guindilla and the *pintxo* needs Cantabrian anchovies to be authentic. Do you know the mild-flavored white anchovies?"

The caterer nodded and wrote a note on a small pad of paper.

They all agreed the nuts and raisins were not interesting enough to include. The chorizo had nice spice but needed to be cut in larger slices and the presentation improved perhaps with colorful liner paper for the serving dish. The shrimp were nicely cooked but needed pop in flavor and presentation.

Amy said, "How about infusing oil with toasted garlic and painting the shrimp with it so it would adhere in the refrigerator and sprinkle some chopped chives on top for onion bite and color?"

"Sure. That would work," responded the caterer, who made a few more notes.

Laurence put the stuffed pepper in his mouth tasting the saltiness of cod, but the texture was very soft compared to the cod Amy had prepared. There was no olive oil in it, and it tasted like a cream sauce made with flour. He looked at Amy and asked her opinion.

"The difference in the flavor and the texture between this Italian pepper and a Basque piquillo is noticeable. If it is out of our price range to use the piquillo peppers, I would vote not to serve this cod in cream sauce," said Amy.

Charles said, "If we omit the salt cod dish, how could we enhance the other choices?"

They discussed several options, and the caterer agreed to redo the estimate.

Amy looked at Charles and he said, "Amy, another idea?"

"If we're not having the piquillo pepper with the cod, I'd invest in a much smaller quantity of piquillo peppers and cut them up in small strips to garnish the shrimp. They are a quintessential Basque flavor that anyone who enjoys the cuisine will be expecting. Even a small bite adds pop in flavor and presentation."

"And still do the infused oil with garlic?" Charles said.

"Yes, but not the chives. That would make it a worthy substitute for the cod," Amy said.

Charles looked around the room and said, "That's a great idea. Anybody else?" He thanked the caterer.

When the caterer and her assistant left with Julia, Drew said, "Charles, tell me the truth about the food. None of you look pleased to me."

"As tasted, it was fresh but boring, but I think with the enhancements it will be well received by the Basques and the Seattle folk. We'll have three distinct flavors that speak to the country, from the land and the sea. She was testing our knowledge with similar but less expensive ingredients to see if they would fly, and they didn't. You can't fault her for trying to improve her bottom line. She didn't fight back for any of it."

Laurence said, "I agree with Charles. These choices are simple, straightforward and authentic. Easy to serve and clean up, even after hundreds of people have dropped the toothpicks and red striped liner paper on the floor." He looked at Drew.

Drew wasn't amused. "We better have a big garbage can under each food station. I do not want anything on my hardwood floors. Amy, are you disappointed about the cod?"

"I was so appalled by the cream sauce, I couldn't imagine serving it to anybody, but as I envisioned a fleet of kitchen workers incorporating olive oil and heavy cream into the cod with food processors, I realized that's the only way it could be done in quantity."

Charles said, "Amy, I really appreciate your participation. You made it better. The shrimp will be killer, thanks to you."

"Thanks. I don't think I did much, but you know I loved being invited."

Amy turned to look at the painting on the wall again. "Drew, it's Alexis isn't it?"

He sat up straight in his chair again looking at her. "Yes, it is."

"We're not friends anymore," she said.

Drew thought she sounded wistful. "What happened to you two since the last time I saw her at your house?"

"We tried to do business together, and it was a disaster," Amy said.

"Well, I'm sorry to hear that as I'd hoped to run into her again with you. I'd love to get a look at her current art. Have you seen it?"

"No. I don't think anyone has seen it except her husband. She's very secretive about it. Apparently there's tons of it in big series of large canvases expressing her disgust with everything. He told me it's too nihilistic for public consumption."

"Now I really want to see it. Do you have her address? I'll send her an invitation to the exhibition."

Amy emailed him the address from her iPad and then stood up. Drew stood up to clasp her hand in both of his. "Thanks for helping today."

She said, "My pleasure. I need to catch a bus. Anybody want to ride with me?"

Laurence nodded his head yes. "I'll go with you, Amy."

Waiting for the bus they chatted about the tasting and speculated more about the crowds that might come or not to the exhibit. Even though he didn't believe it, Laurence repeated Julia's concern that they would all lose their jobs so Amy would understand how high the stakes seemed to Drew and Julia. Amy told him she felt sick to hear that they were that anxious about the outcome. She would go through her book and invite everybody she knew who might possibly come. That would help. Maybe she would consider having some sort of party or organize a group of friends to meet downtown before attending the exhibit.

He was appreciative of her offers to help bring people in but then was quiet as they sat together on the bus. At the stop near his apartment building he said, "I'll probably see you on Monday at the library."

Laurence walked up the stairs to his apartment and threw himself down on the couch. He was annoyed with himself that he was so distracted he couldn't focus on what or who was in front of him. He couldn't remember what he'd said to Amy on the bus or at the tasting. That was unconscionable, considering Drew was paying him to attend and participate. He hoped he hadn't said anything irrelevant that betrayed his lack of focus. He couldn't think about anything but Eva and her stunning message for him yesterday that he must marry her or not be with her again. He felt sure she absolutely would not see or speak to him until he had made his decision. It was maddening how imperiously she demanded he do this. She did not understand that this type of behavior would only feed his stubbornness. It was not a smart move on her part. She had made a mistake.

When he was alone again in his office Drew leaned back in his chair to try to relax and not worry about the food. He could read Amy. She hadn't liked it. Had Charles negotiated a better deal with the caterer with her comments? That's what he paid Charles to do, and if the food wasn't good he was going to be unhappy with Charles. He was also concerned that Laurence was distracting him away from something else with that business about the litter on the floor. What could that be? What was going on with Laurence? He was not himself. Julia was the only one he felt no bad undercurrents from other than her fears about the exhibit, which he had personally given her a dose of everyday for months in their chat before they began work. Drew made a mental note to try to hide his anxiety from Julia. She had a lot to do and it would go better and faster without carrying the weight of his worries about the art and the turnout.

Now he was going to take a step further into the future and write Alexis a personal note on one of the promotional announcements. *I know you said you wouldn't come see my gallery but this is a special exhibit I'd really like to share with you. Please visit and tell me what you think. D.*

Asking her for her opinion might be the right bait to draw her out of her studio. Once she saw the space and how well he was doing, he'd ask if she'd like to do an exhibit with him and make some money. He knew how much making money meant to Alexis. That should be all it would take to be invited for a private viewing of new nihilism. Wouldn't that be a juicy slot on the calendar whenever he needed it? Big and ready to go anytime were magic words. His clever idea invigorated him.

He addressed the envelope and went out to Julia's desk for stamps. She looked up surprised to see him. He handed her the envelope and asked when it would be picked up. Julia studied the name and put a stamp on it.

"I'll mail it on my way home so it doesn't have to wait until tomorrow. Is that soon enough?"

Drew winked at her and said, "That will be perfect."

"I'm so glad to see you upbeat. This must be about money."

He sat down in the visitor's chair and nodded his head. "I haven't seen her work in a long time but I know her to be absolutely ferocious. If her husband says it's too nihilistic, I think we could sell it. What's also super appealing is there is lots of it in series. I still think series sell well, and no one has ever seen it before. That's a story!"

"If you're not friends any more, why will she want to do business with us?" asked Julia.

"Now that we have had the experience of calling artists we don't know and offering them a chance to show, we realize how astonishing it is to be on the other end of the phone and not having to run a marketing effort to create an opportunity to beg for a show. It's like a miracle, right? In other words I'll make it easy for her to validate a lifetime of work by offering to sell it for her. When you can sell your work, you're respected as an artist."

Chapter 27

After the First Thursday event in December, Julia put a "By Appointment Only" sign on the door. Drew and Julia dressed in casual clothes. Everything that belonged to the artists that were unsold were returned to the artists. Works the gallery owned were put in storage.

Julia prepared the invitations to the press party to be held one day before the grand opening. Press was a prestigious name for some of the group coming to the party. They wrote for their personal blogs but were interested in his topic so Drew tried to ingratiate himself with them whenever possible. The online entities and local magazines all had culture columns. Reporters who followed art and culture represented at least three print newspapers. Only one of the papers charged subscriptions and offered home delivery, but every source counted. No one in Seattle who paid attention to any media of this category could miss reading about the Basque Exhibit. He planned to dazzle them with juicy history and facts about the Basque Country and its artists who had immigrated around the world. He had written the press release to enclose with the invitation on 20 pound paper and expected to see a facsimile of it in each column.

"Should we invite Bernadette to the press party?" Julia said.

"Yes. Let's send her the whole press kit so she can be up-to-date on the marketing program and share it with her colleagues."

Bernadette phoned him when she received the kit to say thank you and inquire if it was purely informational or a personal invitation.

"If you would like to come, please do."

"I would like to come. As long as you are ready for a small crowd, how about if I bring the best of my fellow tour guides to give them a preview? I didn't think there would be an opportunity before the official opening, but this seems like one. What do you think?"

"I think it's a great idea. I don't know why I didn't think about inviting them before the opening."

Bernadette offered to call each one to save mailing the press release package. The guides could take home the mailing piece of information to have his words handy for parroting.

"Thank you, Bernadette. I appreciate all your ideas and help." He meant it when he said that. Now there would be ten more salesmen working for him in Japanese, Chinese, Russian, and who knew what else. Marvelous! He was curious to see what this group looked like.

The Basque art started arriving in large and small crates. A few pieces walked in the door in the arms of the artists who didn't want to pay to wrap and pack their pieces. Drew talked at length with all the walk-ins as long as they wanted to talk. The way in which he had discovered and contacted them was so unusual that he wanted to make up for the lost face time that would have gone into making the connection. Talking with them on the phone had helped them develop enough trust in him to release the art to him, but this personal contact sealed the relationship. He encouraged them to come back several times during the exhibition, saying he hoped they would talk with visitors to the gallery. If they enjoyed interacting he would be glad to schedule and announce them being in the gallery to talk about their work. He also invited them to bring friends to attend several events. The cultural performances on the opening weekend would, of course, be free for them and their guests.

Drew and Julia opened each package together with anticipation. Would it be what they hoped it would be? Each piece was examined from every angle gauging their first reaction. The second and third reaction would come later. Julia created a data record, properly tagged with all the essential information about the artist and date of creation, and a confirmation receipt was sent to the artist. Each step had to be perfect or the artist wouldn't be properly recognized or paid when the work sold or returned if it didn't.

Drew took his time scrutinizing each piece in good light, and in some cases, with a magnifying glass. He wanted to feel each piece in his gut to be able to talk about it and price it properly. Artists could be counted on to be dreamers when it came to price. He called each artist to tell them the art had been received. He talked about his impressions and what he thought he could sell a piece for now that he had inspected it. Setting the right price was critical for the gallery to profitable. The artist got his share. Drew also got his share, which he divvied up to pay the sales commission, expenses for staging the exhibit and — if all worked out as planned — profit for the gallery. This show had some unusual expenses and revenues. He consoled himself that all the outlays would result in attracting new customers. Converting them into art buyers was another long-term project. He and his peers often joked about the time between the first free glass of wine and the first art purchase. He hoped Julia and Bernadette would both make good money on this show. He also planned to take sales commissions. He knew exactly what the dollar numbers were in the big overview of this exhibit. Sell everything out at the asking price was always his goal.

Unsold art became a huge expense to ship back after the loss of commissions.

He lined up the pieces in the order they had been received against the long wall in the big room as he inspected them. When most had arrived he reorganized them by categories they'd decided on: heritage, animals, ranching/farming, landscapes and abstracts. He and Julia discussed each piece in detail and debated its relationship to the exhibit, to the category and the other pieces. The categories were flexible. Most pieces could have been placed in more than one. Separating the animals allowed ranching and farming to focus on structures and equipment. Fields and vineyards could be farming or landscapes. Each piece would find its best home. In the beginning they had the idea of a sports category with fishing, jai alai and traditional Basque competitions but they were unable to source any current artists who documented these feats of strength at Basque festivals. They debated a video monitor to show clips of such events that they'd seen on YouTube but the Fair Use rules made it a complicated project. It would take too much time to sort out the ownership of the best and obtain backup clips with permission.

The animals had a charm about them. The gallery hadn't exhibited too much art featuring animals before, but the sheep, the cows, the crows, dogs, horses and the fish were endearing themselves. The fish were a revelation to Drew and Julia, neither of them had ever been fishing. Before this project they had no idea that the popularity of this activity made fish a big subject in the western art business. Drew had chosen the most colorful, prehistoric and menacing of the fish art to exhibit. Fish had teeth! As old western artists had found work painting Basque houses from photos that the new immigrants brought with them from Europe, contemporary artists were hired by tourists to paint from photos taken on fishing expeditions or other adventures. The experience with fish led the artists to create more fish-inspired art for sale in galleries and online. There were fish paintings in oil, acrylic and watercolor. There were also two fish sculptures, one in cast bronze that appeared more like a fossil than a live fish and one bigger-than-life size cutthroat trout in green, blue and pink enameled metal that looked like it might bite Drew every time he walked by it.

The landscapes presented the terrains of the American West: desert, plains, mountains, vineyards and farmland in a variety of sizes and mediums. The two biggest canvases, skies at morning and at night, had a sliver of plains and mountain formations on the lower edge for perspective with the balance of a color field of the blues of a cloudless sunrise and the pinks and purples of a cloudless sunset. There were two paintings of giant clouds, one in blue skies and one in dark skies, hovering over the plains promising dramatic weather. Mountains created the opposite composition by filling the canvas with only a small edge of sky or land. The collection presented an overwhelming sense of the vastness of the West.

Trees ended up being a bigger part of the landscape category than Drew had intended because he'd fallen for the photographs of the arborglyphs and then more aspens without carvings. His favorite might be an oil painting of an ancient pine on a steep rocky perch on the crest of a mountain that screamed about the tenacity and perseverance required to be alive in this tough environment. It seemed as Basque to him as the wizened face in the fisherman photo.

Ranching/farming was portrayed in a variety of styles from bright impressionistic pastures with sheep camps to somber realism of crumbling fences and dilapidated sheds with rusty machinery. Trucks, cars and tractors could appear bucolic or destitute. Life in the American West was difficult.

Thanks to one gallery owner willing to give up a small cache of Basque memorabilia he'd had in inventory for too long, a large container arrived which included vintage etchings of Basque hotel landmarks in Reno, Fresno and Bakersfield as well as an old poster commemorating the Basque Block in Boise. A sweet oil painting of a traditional Basque house must have been one commissioned from a photograph. What happened to the family that they didn't keep it? Small oil portraits of dancers, shepherds, two musicians playing inside a Basque hotel and more sheep were of the primitive school. The vintage pieces added a contrast to the current art by Basques whose forefathers had lived in America for so many generations that they were creating art of the present they enjoyed, and hoped to sell soon not thinking about history at all. One exception was an older Basque painter who still painted from memory his mid century childhood growing up in a Basque hotel in Boise. His family hotel was portrayed in pastel watercolors of pinks and orange, which seemed to reference his nostalgia for easier days. Drew dubbed this collection the "heritage" category. He would add the fisherman photo that Laurence had found to this group. The photo had been enlarged to catch attention. Although they knew it was a fisherman, there was no detail in the photo that made it exclusively so. The weathered face under the black beret was as powerful a statement as the pine tree was in the other painting. Both had survived and were still standing.

The heritage collection would be by the front door along with a text piece Drew had written about the migration history. Another unrealized dream of Drew's had been to find modern artists who were painting the Old Country from photographs for tourists visiting the Basque centers in the United Sates. How great would it be to have a few iconic scenes of San Sebastián, Bilbao or Biarritz? But no one they talked to had heard of anyone doing that.

Drew began rearranging them so the placement within the group would enhance each piece of art. This was one of his favorite tasks. Sticky notes with the titles on the walls held his ideas for placement. He planned to arrange the abstract works in the smaller room to help the visitors get the historical story before they embraced the intangible. He was excited about the three other sculptures cast in metal, two in traditional themes, a cow and a crow, that would add drama perched on pedestals. The other sculpture was in Drew's mind a deconstructed horse about three feet tall of lightweight aluminum distressed to look heavy and welded together. The horse was in motion with negative space in its boxy body that made it seem awkward and incapable of galloping elegantly like a racehorse. There was an element of humor in it, and Drew thought it was a modern cousin of Don Quixote's horse, pleased to have lost his incompetent rider. The artist was not forthcoming about any of that interpretation. Drew loved it, so he had to have it. Free of any artist's intentions, he planned to hype the horse's Spanish relatives as a modern bridge to the Basque horsemen of the American West. Horses after all were as important to a shepherd as his dogs.

As the categories grew, he was pleased to see how they told the Basque story. Not all of them were great works of art, but they all showed heart. The lesser quality pieces would be priced appropriately so the buyers could understand the relative value. It was good to have a few less expensive pieces to provide a broad price range to encourage shoppers.

Julia sat at her desk doing data entry on her computer. Her keyboard made a soft background hum. They were both so absorbed in the process that no one had remembered to turn on the music. It was nice to be working quietly together. They both felt relieved to have the art in-house after months of worrying about finding it. Drew occasionally looked at her and appreciated how quick and accurate she was with the details. This couldn't be her favorite part of her job but she never complained about it — or anything. Julia was a good employee. He had easily separated her role as a convenient, occasional sex partner from her other activities since Eva had told him it made him look stupid, and Henri's presence confirmed that. He was still bewildered by how Eva knew about it. Julia had not shown any unusual emotion since they had discussed the future with someone her own age. A seamless change in a relationship was a good thing. Julia hadn't mentioned Henri again since he had given her a ride to his office, but Drew had noticed her leaving at five a few days when she typically worked later and assumed Henri was the reason. He wished her well with him or whomever. She was still his best art student and gallery employee ever. That hadn't changed. He was too busy with this exhibit to have the energy to look for someone else to have sex with and none of his usual First Thursday girlfriends had come by offering late night fun. Maybe when it was over he'd feel like calling one of them. He was counting on having many visitors he'd never met. Maybe the exhibit would bring him a new girlfriend. He might even experiment with Eva's odd concept of someone his own age if he ran into someone like that who was fascinating. For curiosity's sake he should see what that would be like. Some days the future seemed exciting and full of potential.

Surveying the canvases lined up against the walls, he was cautiously optimistic that this exhibit was going to be a success. Spending time with the art had alleviated some of his anxiety. He liked the mix of themes. The colors were appealing. The collection increased the energy of the individual pieces. He thought the sales potential was good. The bonus merchandise of the advertising poster, and Laurence's fisherman photo would cushion the cash register daily sales. If both items proved as popular as he thought they would be, more could be printed as necessary.

Laurence would be paid a few dollars for each photo sale. Julia would earn a bit more commission on each poster sale to compensate her for her artwork. Drew loved the poster and hoped it would be a big moneymaker for her. These extra dollar incentives were important to him to reward the hard work and the moderate hourly wage he paid.

The next step was actually hanging it. He wanted to wait until everything had arrived but there were always late shippers or some foul up. If he got started hanging, he ran the risk of having to redo a section or more because a painting needed to be inserted properly to show well in the middle of an existing grouping. That was a detail he was obsessive about. All paintings must be presented in the most favorable light. He had provided a two-week window for the receipt of the art so he would have two weeks to hang it properly even though it wouldn't take that long. After the deadline he took the time to review the photos of the missing pieces and call the artists to inquire if they had changed their minds about exhibiting. One had decided Seattle was too strange and too far away from his home in the California desert. One had a faulty shipping address that had delayed it. One painter thought it would be fine to send something other than the agreed upon art and had decided to paint a new canvas and hadn't shipped it because it wasn't dry. Drew said no. He begged Drew to let him send a photo in email to prove it was worth the wait. Drew did like the new painting better and said he would save a spot for it.

In addition to all the necessary recorded documentation on each work of art, that received, exhibited and sold, Julia had made two sets of sales cards. One was attached to the back and one was to be displayed underneath the piece, identifying the title, the artist, the date and the price. For a few pieces they created biographical details of the artist or other information that were pertinent extras to help sales.

At last, with all the tools assembled and the patterns marked on the walls, they were ready to hang the art. They were excited about this step. The paintings had been carefully dusted while lined up on the floor. The process involved many trips up and down the ladder, measuring and studying the results from different vantage points. The first categories on heritage and ranching/farming were completed without too much difficulty. They debated the placement of two sheepherding paintings that highlighted the naturalism of the landscape of Idaho and Nevada and could have been shown with the landscapes. Drew had a new appreciation of pickup trucks and rusty tractors that were part of the natural background in the American West.

By the end of the first day of hanging, Drew and Julia were feeling very pleased. After all the work to find the art, finally seeing it on the wall was rewarding. His cell phone chirped, and he saw Bernadette's name.

"How did you know we just completed the first day of hanging and I pronounce it good? Of course, come. Believe me I can't take my eyes off it and I'd love to hear your opinion too."

Drew stored his phone and said, "She's on the way to share in the glory of this moment when I think we'll be a success and make money!"

Julia looked at him a bit oddly and then tried to give an affirmative smile but she didn't convince him.

"What's wrong? What is marring this excellent moment and reprieve from cruel anxiety?"

Julia looked around at the debris of the day scattered on the floor, blue removable tape, sticky notes and craft paper cut to canvas size for placement on the wall. "I'm not used to her yet in our space. I'm trying to get used to her in her own space and that's still weird, OK, but not here yet."

"Julia, what are you trying to say? She's going to work with us here. That's a done deal."

"I know. It just seems weird to have someone else with us. How did a stranger walk in and within 30 minutes become a one-third partner in *our* business?"

"She didn't ask for a job. She sold me completely on her ability to bring in new customers."

Drew started picking up stuff on the floor, and when his hands were full, he put it in the garbage can by her desk. He continued picking stuff up and putting it in the can, considering how to deal with Julia's insecurity. He thought he knew what she meant, but it was annoying that she ruined his good mood complaining about their path to prosperity — an excellent art saleswoman bringing them more business. Finally he stopped in front of her as she stood in front of her desk looking at the floor.

"Are you still enjoying Henri?" She nodded. "Is Bernadette nice to you when you see her at her apartment or wherever you see her?" Julia nodded yes again. "So, please explain why her presence in the gallery is a problem?" He waited watching her think, and a tear rolled down from each eye and then another. He put his arms around her and held her close. "Tell me what's wrong. You have to say the words. No mind reading here."

Julia choked the words out slowly, "She's so smart she makes me feel stupid."

Drew shook his head while still holding her close. Oh, the highs and lows of youth. Julia was captive to her emotions, unable to think her way out to a stable middle ground where her talent should buoy her. From experience he knew a few things he should not say, "snap out of it!" for example. Instead he said what usually worked in this situation with any woman, "You're talented and smart. This moment of feeling useless will pass, maybe in a few minutes or an hour. It's normal to have doubts sometimes. Everything is OK." Those were all the comforts he knew on the subject of insecurity and they could be used individually or all together like he'd just done. He hoped it was enough to make her feel stable. He stood back holding her shoulders making her look at him. When she nodded back at him he said, "OK let's get ready for company. You work on the floor. I'm going to open some wine. This is a celebration of our hard work — yours and mine. We've been killing ourselves for months to get to this moment. You have done a great job."

Julia nodded in agreement, sighed and started picking up paper from the floor. Drew sighed and headed for the wine cooler, congratulating himself for his sensitivity in correctly handling an upset woman and having the foresight to have Champagne on hand just in case something incredible happened. He was so smart these days. He felt that just about all the errors of his youth right up to recent times never seemed to happen to him anymore. An angry woman had not taken him to task in ages. It was so satisfying to do everything right without thinking too much about it.

Drew and Julia were one glass down when Bernadette arrived with a big smile on her face. Drew opened the door for her with equal greeting and pointed to the wall. "Look here! We have a Basque exhibit under way."

He poured a glass for Bernadette and another round of Champagne for himself and Julia and went to stand by Bernadette who was intent on the heritage pieces. After she had looked at the next section she said, "Oh, Drew I think it's wonderful. Where did you ever find the vintage stuff? It's such a perfect contrast with the sophistication of the new pieces. Old World, New World defined emotionally in one beat."

Drew said, "Thank you. I'm pleased. We got lucky with a gallery owner near one of the Basque centers in California. He'd had it for a long time and was glad to set it free. I got the whole lot for a flat fee. I don't think we'll have any trouble selling it to cover the cost — we have Basque

293

people coming to see this show that haven't seen any of this before."

They all laughed, and he enjoyed his satisfaction with himself.

"Let's walk through the whole line," said Bernadette.

The three of them walked slowly down the line of canvases on the wall and the remaining leaning against the wall and made comments and compliments. They talked about arranging the canvases to build momentum to end each section on a high note. Sitting on and around Julia's desk they finished the Champagne talking about what a great day it was in the art business, how thrilling it was when it worked on the gallery wall as hoped for. By the end of the bottle they projected easy sales, big crowds and they made bets on what they thought would sell first. Drew surveyed his premises and employees and was pleased. Julia seemed to have recovered. She was interacting easily with Bernadette. He agreed with Julia that Bernadette was so smart she almost made him feel stupid, but she was so charming he didn't mind. He was just glad she was working for him.

Chapter 28

Drew and Julia continued working on hanging the exhibit, placing the title cards precisely. When they agreed it was perfect, Drew called Bernadette to confirm her appointment, for the official walk through. Julia had made signage to place near the front door, announcing all the languages available for guided tours. They laughed about that and felt very pleased with themselves to be offering professional European style service. Weren't their competitors going to be amazed by that when they came to see the show? And of course, they would come. How could they pass up anything as unusual as this?

Drew and Julia had been practicing with each other and by themselves with a brief version for each piece and a more detailed version when time allowed or when someone asked for more information. Preparing for the full presentation to Bernadette they planned to alternate categories. He would start with the heritage. Julia would follow with ranching/farming. They would note her questions and comments and incorporate them if they improved the presentation. It felt like opening night at the theater the afternoon Bernadette was scheduled. They both wore serious gallery outfits, which felt special after weeks of casual clothes. Bernadette arrived in her Chanel suit. Three hours later, they had mastered the nuances of each piece individually and within its category. It was an invigorating conversation with everyone expressing their point of view and carefully listening to each other. Julia didn't seem a bit intimidated by Bernadette's astute observations. She contributed some of her own acute observations from the artist's point of view. It gave them all more to talk about with potential buyers. Drew enjoyed the high level of the conversation. He felt like they were a team now with camaraderie, a shared interest in art and in the Basque story. Everyone was excited about the opening night coming soon.

Drew said, "Ladies, may I treat you to a cocktail?"

Julia looked at Bernadette and said, "Thank you. I would enjoy that but I have plans to meet Henri at Il Bistro in the Market. Shall we include him, or should I go on to meet him and you two go somewhere else?"

Bernadette and Drew looked at each other. Drew wasn't sure if he was ready to make this a foursome, but he wanted to keep the good feeling going with his team. "What do you think Bernadette? Would you prefer to join Henri or go to another place I like?"

"Are you sure we wouldn't be spoiling your evening, Julia? I don't want to intrude on your plans," Bernadette said.

"I think it would be fun. Why don't I call him and ask what he thinks?"

Drew said, "Julia, please tell him it will be for one drink. You two will have the evening to yourselves."

She went to her desk to make the call on her cell phone. It was a brief conversation. She smiled at Drew and Bernadette and said, "He says please come join us."

Drew thought, *Oh boy, here we go down a path I would rather not take. This is somewhat strange to be the employer and sort of ex-boyfriend out with the new boyfriend and his mother. If either of them ever learns of my previous role, it could be disastrous for Julia.* He couldn't remember if he had discussed with Julia how important it was to be discreet about that. He would make certain that he did it tomorrow and hoped it wasn't too late.

He drove them down First Avenue toward Pike Place Market while asking Bernadette to give her first impressions again of the exhibit, savoring her responses. He loved listening to her talk about his project. Julia was quiet in the back seat, not unusual, as she never talked too much. He realized she too was likely thinking about her new role in the expanded group.

As they approached Pike Street he said, "I want to put my car in my garage so I don't have to pay to park. Do you two want to get out here or ride with me and walk back? Do you have the right shoes on?"

Bernadette said, "I'm fine. I can walk."

Julia said, "I think I'll get out here if you don't mind. I don't have my hiking boots on."

He stopped at the traffic light at Pike Street, and she got out waving to them as she crossed the street in front of the car.

"Her shoes are beautiful," said Bernadette, admiring the high heels, "and difficult on cobblestones. You are thoughtful to ask."

"It's my pleasure to encourage stylish shoes."

Drew and Bernadette entered the soft candlelight of happy hour at Il Bistro, which was not as busy as he thought it might be. The prime tables by the windows were full but many others were empty. The Recession was tough all over town. The hostess welcomed them and offered bar or restaurant seating. Drew said they were meeting the beautiful blonde in the bar. She nodded yes and showed them the way.

Henri stood up as they approached a table in the back of the bar. "Monsieur, how nice to see you," he said and offered his hand to Drew to shake. He kissed his mother on both cheeks and pulled out a chair for her next to him. Julia looked even lovelier in the candlelight than she had in the gallery with a rosy glow to her cheeks from what-ever she was drinking or talking about. When Henri sat down, Drew could see they resumed holding hands. Drew sat across from Henri with his back to the room. It was a dark corner perfect for private conversations. He had sat in the opposite chair numerous times. He applauded Henri's choice of table. This was only the second time Drew had seen Henri, and he looked taller, bigger and more substantial in every way. Was that his banker's public persona or had being with Julia improved his appearance?

The server was prompt to appear for the order. Henri and Julia already had a cocktail in front of them. Bernadette ordered Lillet. Drew ordered a martini. While they waited, Bernadette told Henri that they had had an exciting day in the art world and what a success she believed the exhibit would be. He responded with appropriate questions about the art and what she liked best. He obviously had heard a great deal from Julia and was familiar with many of the pieces. Either that or they were spending time at the gallery Drew didn't know about.

Although the day had been a success and everyone felt positive about the exhibit, Drew noted that it felt weird to him to be sitting here in this bar with this group. He didn't like at all being perceived as a father figure for Julia. That was not his role. He decided 20 minutes was what he was willing to give to this party and then he was leaving.

Drew toasted everyone for the work done. The martini tasted very good. The gin was excellent and the vermouth noticeable in the right way. The server presented an amuse-bouche that everyone but Drew tasted. Feeling it was the logical segue after all the art talk, he said, "Henri, please tell me what you've learned about Seattle from Julia's tours."

"Your short history is extraordinary to me. I've never known such a new city. Within that short period, however, the landscape has been altered by industry and commerce in a way that's revolutionary. Removing the forests and the steepest hills, creating new lands in the water to build on and digging the ship canal are engineering feats of bold thinking. Just as bold is Boeing starting an airplane factory when he had hardly flown in one or the new engineering and architecture for the World's Fair buildings like the Space Needle and the Science Pavilion. Anything is possible here and is done quickly. New businesses seem to start up more frequently than anywhere else. The pioneer spirit is strong. When your forestry and fishing are completely dead, they will be replaced by technology and science industries that don't exist yet. I find it exhilarating to be living where change is embraced. You have no idea how unusual that is. France is famous for saying no to everything new."

Bernadette beamed at her son. Drew was shocked and realized his mouth was open. "Julia, once more you amaze me. I thought you were showing him your favorite bars in Ballard. I had no idea of your interest in local history."

Julia smiled modestly. "Henri's a good student. I pointed out the facts I learned at school, and he drew the conclusions."

Drew asked, "Where are you planning to look for an apartment?"

"Pioneer Square. I may have found an apartment. For the landlord to approve me, I need a letter from my employer in addition to the application."

"Henri, you didn't tell me you had applied," said Bernadette.

"I looked at it again today at lunch and filled out the application."

Julia beamed at her boyfriend.

Drew raised his glass again and said, "Congratulations. We're all having a great day today." Henri began describing the apartment. Drew sat back in his chair with his drink in his hand. This was an attractive group sitting around the table with him. Each mind was high quality. He liked smart, good-looking, people. What an odd feeling it was to be part a new crowd. Was he the center of it or on the periphery? He knew tons of people in Seattle, most individually or as couples. But he didn't travel with a crowd very often. He reserved tables for two. For the last few years, his gallery crew, when he needed extra help for all the special events, didn't gather outside work to his knowledge. They opened a bottle of wine and sat in his office to drink it. This party of four felt uncomfortably new. He wondered how often they might all get together and if so how long it would take him to get used to it. The opportunity to get together would be over when the exhibit closed and Bernadette went back to her usual activities. He doubted Julia would ask him to join them for a drink without Bernadette. He was now a bit more sympathetic about Julia getting used to the substantial presence of Bernadette. Even when silent she commanded attention with her striking looks and alertness. She always seemed ready to spring into action.

Julia looked happy, which made him feel good about how she was being treated in her new relationship. Henri looked besotted with Julia. Drew decided it was worthwhile to keep an eye open around Henri and his ability to spot trends in the data. Drew might learn something else from him about his own hometown of Seattle or where his future business was coming from. Surely with his interest in art he was following all the developments here and abroad. Another time he would talk to him about that. When the server returned, Drew said he'd take the check for the table, and she could start a new one. He and Bernadette stood up, said good night and walked up the cobblestone sidewalk toward First Avenue.

"Your son is something. I am impressed with him."

"Thank you. Sometimes I think I'm prejudiced. It's nice to hear an independent assessment of his intellect. Where is Julia's family?"

"I have no idea. She's never talked about them, and I have never asked. She is refreshingly quiet."

"I agree. People who talk too much are tiring."

"Do you want to get something to eat?" Drew said.

"No, thank you. It's been quite a day."

"Can I get you a taxi?"

"You're kind, but it's so early I'll catch a bus a few blocks away. Thank you for the drink and the educational experience this afternoon. It was very exciting for me." She smiled at him. They didn't shake hands, and she walked away on Pike Street toward Second Avenue.

Drew watched her for a moment and then walked on First Avenue toward his apartment. It had been an exciting afternoon for him too. She was so different from any women he knew. She acted like an equal with him. She didn't flirt. He didn't flirt with her either, which was unusual for him. He flirted with all women. It didn't occur to him to flirt with her and now thinking about it, it didn't seem appropriate. She would probably be offended by it. There was no sexual innuendo in her behavior with him. Did she intimidate him? Maybe she did. She was all business — brainy but with a natural warmth and charm. Bernadette was easy to be with. What a relief to be rid of the feeling he'd made a colossal mistake hiring her. He was glad he had bought them all a drink. A little generosity went a long way with people, particularly young people. When the exhibit closed with all the art sold, he might buy them all another.

The next morning at the gallery when he and Julia were drinking coffee in his office and reviewing the punch list, the calmness he felt last night about the opening of the exhibit had evaporated. "Now that we're all working together with Bernadette and Henri, I want to review or discuss how important I think it is for us to be discreet about our past."

"We didn't talk about it specifically, but I do get how important it is."

"Good, that's my star pupil, Julia. They wouldn't understand and it could be a problem for your relationship with Henri."

"I agree with you I have never mentioned it although they seem to be very liberal about most things and sex especially."

"Like what?" Drew said.

"Henri's been having sex since he was really young, and his mother knows about it. It's not a secret from parents the way it is with teenagers here. He says French fathers frequently have girlfriends while being married."

Drew considered that bit of European culture, which didn't surprise him the way it had surprised Julia. "Well, let's be on the safe side," he said, and she nodded. "It's tempting and titillating to share previous experiences, but it's a bad idea to do it. It will come back to bite you with jealousy or something else ugly."

She nodded again to indicate that she understood. "They have invited me to eat Christmas dinner with them at their apartment. I think that's a big deal. Do you?"

"Yes. It means they like you a lot."

"Do you want to join us?"

"What? Me? No. I don't do things like that."

"We had a nice time last night. Henri suggested I ask you."

"Last night was business, friendly business. Christmas dinner is personal."

"What will you do?" she said.

"I have friends and I have family too. I don't see them that often, but they invite me and sometimes I go."

"Sorry, I didn't know about your family." She looked concerned that she had forgotten something.

"No reason for you to know. I'm sure I've never mentioned them to you. They aren't interested in art. Let's get onto our list. Have you had any more questions from The Harvest Vine about their demonstration? All the issues are settled? Good. The event I'm most worried about today is the press party before the opening. We invited at least 20 people. How many are coming? I'm sure none of them have responded. I want you to call everybody we invited and ask them if they are planning to attend. Tell them we need a head count for the caterer."

"We don't have a caterer for that."

"I know, but they don't know that. It's another way of saying free food and booze."

"What are we serving?" she said.

"Depends on how many are coming. For a small crowd I was thinking of Laurence making something that goes well with cheap wine and beer, not the Basque wine. If we get more people, he can make two things."

Julia nodded and took notes. "Shall I give him a heads up so he can think about it and we can be sure he's in town?"

"He has no plans except Christmas dinner with William."

"Not with the Russos?" Julia looked puzzled.

"No."

"Oh."

They continued on the logistics of drinks tickets, the cash box and the credit card machine. Drew suggested Julia take his car and pick up the souvenir fisherman photos and frames. He wanted everything in-house and for Laurence to assemble them just in case of a blizzard or a flood between now and then.

Drew said, "Even though I can't do anything about it, I'm worried about the performers arriving late for the opening weekend. We're all set with the Basque club picking them up?"

"All set and they will even provide rides to and from here every day if necessary. The club has been very helpful. They will be here every day for part of the time. We should have a party for them afterward."

"That's a great idea. How about the third or fourth weekend when the crowds will have thinned? It will look festive to anyone who comes on Saturday afternoon to see a lively crowd of Basques enjoying the exhibit. I will call the president today and talk with him about it."

This meeting went on for another fifteen minutes until Drew was convinced they had thought of everything.

Julia went back to her desk, and Drew heard her call Laurence. "Hi. How are you? I don't need any help today, but the frames and fisherman photo will be ready to assemble tomorrow, and I hoped you would do that. Drew is hoping you will make one or two things to go with cheap wine and beer for the press party. Will you think about that? I should know how many are coming when you come to work on the photos."

She was so polite to the old engineer. Drew wondered if Laurence minded being the assistant to a 25-year-old.

Chapter 29

Laurence decided to enrich the dull month of December by doubling up his exercise program by including a late afternoon session before he ate dinner. He walked all the way to the downtown Central branch of the library instead of taking the bus. He also walked to the Fremont branch. He would turn adversity into better strength and endurance. With no hours scheduled at the gallery he had extra hours to fill. He'd lied to Eva about being busy in December just to push the deadline out. He was still really mad at her. Marriage seemed out of the question now. He might change his mind after a few weeks, but the anger he felt was more stimulating than feeling morose, and he wanted to use it wisely. He was going to look and feel good for the exhibit. If the gallery was as busy as they hoped, he would need the extra fitness for all the hours on his feet welcoming people, directing the crowd and selling extra food and drink tickets. He needed his wits about him to handle money and the credit card machine.

He officially withdrew from the tai chi classes and the French class. The Community Center reception desk was impersonal about the change. Bernadette, the French teacher, was sorry to lose him, and they had a nice chat on the phone. He told her he was finding it too difficult and requiring too much studying. She said she would miss his contributions to the class. He said nothing about Eva. Who knew what Eva was saying about him to anyone?

December seemed like a very long month this year. He was starting to waffle about Eva. He hadn't seen or heard a thing from her or about her. He was less angry and wondered if she could see that her refusal to discuss any changes in her routine with her kids was equal to his calling it quits because she wouldn't agree there were issues they had to discuss. If she'd realized how domineering she sounded, he thought she would have called him and apologized. She hadn't, so he had to assume she still felt like she was right and that made him not want to call her at all. He was the one who said he'd be in touch with her after the New Year. He certainly was not going back on that vow by even one day. He was also still angry that she didn't see any merit in letting the month of December be a test of living together to renew trust and normalcy. He was not developing a passion for getting married by stewing about it in his apartment. That test month could have been useful in revealing other monsters in the closet that hadn't appeared yet but were ready to attack him the day after they got married. He disagreed with her about all these things. As he was the wronged party, she should reach out to him before the deadline to warm him up. But she didn't call him.

On Christmas, he and William had a good time drinking Prosecco with oysters and Cabernet Sauvignon with prime beef at Thirteen Coins, an old school restaurant in South Lake Union that had been the scene of good times for more than 40 years. It was famous for being open 24 hours a day, particularly popular in the early morning hours when nothing else was open that had a full bar and good food. The décor was unchanged from the 1970s with high backed booths and high backed bar stools for privacy. Sitting at the bar watching the open kitchen, no one in the room could see them or to whom they were talking. Laurence thought it nostalgic, a bit expensive and perfect for two old farts like them. The place was packed. William was very funny, an excellent companion at the bar or table.

His favorite moments in December were at the gallery, framing the prints of the fisherman photo he had found on the Internet. It was his major contribution to the exhibit, a source of pride and — he hoped — substantial sales. The frames were plain black wood and looked stylish but were not expensive. The wide mat board around the print matched a background white in the photograph and made it look bigger. Altogether it was a handsome souvenir that looked worth far more than the $15 they would charge for it. He would receive a $3 commission on each one that sold. Drew was so clever to reward him in that way and make him care about every sale. Laurence had assembled and bagged 200 ready to put in the customer's hand. He thought that would be enough for the first two weeks of the exhibit. When the inventory ran low, he would place another order and come in early to assemble them. Julia had helped him do a few, and it had been companionable working with her not saying much. She didn't mention her Christmas holiday or ask him about his, and that had been a relief. There was nothing he wanted to talk about.

Planning the press party food was invigorating the final days of the month. All the Basque cookbooks he'd read gave him so many ideas. In the end he went with Amy's best choices for simplicity and to get the attention of the journalists with classic Basque cuisine. He would make the Gilda and lamb meatballs. Both would be fine at room temperature. The Gilda's Hollywood reference might even get it mentioned in the articles.

The morning of the press party Laurence baked six dozen lamb meatballs before 10 a.m. and had them cooling on racks on his dining table. The ground lamb had been thoroughly seasoned with salt, pepper and Spanish smoked *pimenton dulce* powder over night and was ready to pinch and roll into small balls. The aroma was heady. He listened to footsteps in the hallway pause in front of his door and the noise of inhaling. No one knocked though. The traffic in the hallway today was double or triple the usual and moved very slowly. He assembled four dozen

Gilda's on toothpicks. He'd cut up a block of Manchego cheese into small squares to scatter around the Gilda platter as garnish and extra protein. It wasn't Basque, but it was made of sheep's milk and was an extremely popular Spanish cheese but not as expensive as a Basque cheese. The meatballs fit snugly in a large plastic storage container. With each project in a cloth bag he boarded his bus around 2 p.m. so he would have two hours to set up for the party. He expected it to take an hour but always allowed extra time just in case. He was enthralled with the exhibit and hoped he would have a chance to look at the art again.

Laurence was arranging bottles of beer and wine in ice in two large decorative buckets when Bernadette arrived an hour before the party. Julia let her in with a big smile, and they exchanged a full European hello. He gave her a greeting in French uncluttered with cheek kisses or hands. This was the first time he'd seen her since his last class. She looked lovely and had on a black suit that must be French. It was not American. Special clothes were becoming more recognizable to him the longer he associated with the gallery crew.

Julia was surprised he knew Bernadette. Laurence was surprised how friendly Julia was with Bernadette. He didn't want to talk about Eva and couldn't think of anything else to say in French or English, so he went back to arranging the buffet. Bernadette quietly stood watching him.

Julia made it easy for everyone by saying, "Bernadette, let me tell Drew you're here. He probably wants to talk with you in the office."

When Bernadette disappeared behind the hidden door, Julia spoke just above a whisper. "She's working with us giving tours of the exhibit to visiting foreigners in their own language. We've taught her the presentation, and she's a quick study at all of it. We're glad to be working with her, and we think she's going to be very good for our business."

Laurence looked at her and counted how many times Julia had used the word "we," "us" and "our." So Eva was right. "I'm glad to hear all that. I took French lessons from her. She was a delightful teacher, and I imagine she is a delightful tour guide too."

Julia nodded. "She is also the mother of my boyfriend."

Laurence was surprised again. "Well, that must be interesting for you to be working with her."

"Yes, it is. It's a little strange, but she is so nice, she makes me feel like everything is OK with her."

"Bernadette is a smart woman. I'm sure she recognizes her son is lucky to know you."

"Oh, thank you. I hope so. I think so. She invited me to Christmas dinner at her house."

"She does like you. Did you enjoy yourself?" Laurence asked.

Julia hesitated before answering, "The table and the food were fancier than I'm used to. I was nervous about all the forks and the glasses. I had no idea what I was eating, but I ate it. I'm sure they noticed. I like them both so much, I hope they won't hold it against me."

"Stop worrying. I am positive she is not a snob. I doubt her son is either. No matter what fork you use, you get credit for eating without being suspicious before you taste it."

"Oh, you think so? It's hard not to worry."

"Julia, you are smart, talented and attractive. Be yourself and try to remember they want *you* to like them. They are probably intimidated by all your abilities."

"You think so?"

"Definitely. Can either of them paint or design anything?"

"Laurence, you are so good to talk to. I thought you would tell me the truth."

"Of course I would. I need to get back to work on the buffet."

Drew was delighted to tell Bernadette about excellent number of responses for the press party although he suspected it was due to not much happening around town the week after New Year's and Julia calling each one personally. Drew and Bernadette strategized how to best work with the media and the guides at the party. They decided to allow 30 minutes for everyone to get there and have a drink and relax before the tour. Drew had envisioned giving a 20-minute talk on the whole exhibit to everyone. He then wanted to split the group up into three smaller groups that he, Julia, and Bernadette would take on a tour of the paintings to make a more personal experience. Bernadette convinced him the goal should be to make it seem that the event was not a lecture but several stories that would be easy for them to retell to their audience. Finally, they agreed to keep the crowd together and that Drew would do a welcome speech with the key data. Bernadette would follow with an overview of the Basque history and art traditions. Drew would highlight pieces that demonstrated the tradition from each category. He or Bernadette would ask for questions at every stop to get interaction and take turns answering the questions. They would let the questions dictate how long to go on. He agreed the new joint presentation would be more entertaining and useful to the crowd.

"I'm learning something from you today, Bernadette that 30 years in the business didn't teach me."

"Thank you. I'm glad to be sharing what 30 years of teaching has taught me about how people acquire information. There is science in it."

The buzzer rang letting Drew know Julia needed him to come out. "What about Julia? What can she do?"

"What do you think about her taking the abstracts and pointing out how they challenge the traditions when we finish the big room?" said Bernadette.

"Great idea."

They walked out to the gallery where Julia and Laurence were welcoming two groups of people. The buffet looked loaded with food and drinks. Drew surveyed the spotlights one more time, confirming they were set properly. The floor was shining. The paintings looked fabulous. They had never looked better. It gave him a thrill to see his gallery ready for business.

As they were leading the reporters to the buffet and telling them about the authentic *pintxos* they were about to eat, Laurence and Julia looked at Drew and Bernadette in their black suits walking together across the gallery. They both looked at each other and smiled. Julia said, "Wow. Don't they look good together?"

Laurence nodded in agreement and thought Eva would have killed to witness this moment. Stage two was in motion. He wondered when he would see her to tell her about it. Maybe after the opening weekend he would feel like it.

Julia and Drew introduced Bernadette to the media guests. After they had chatted a bit Drew said, "Excuse me, I need to confer with Julia for a moment. Bernadette will tell you some background." He left the media to his competent employee from Paris.

He and Julia walked over to the abstract sculpture near the back of the small room. "We have come up with a new presentation strategy but plan to try to stay within the 30-minute time frame. When we start talking to the crowd, watch how Bernadette sets up the history and traditions. Then I am going to pick one painting in each category to illustrate how it supports the tradition. When we complete the big room, you take over in the small room. Start thinking now about the three most important concepts of the modern pieces you want to share with the audience. Pick three of your favorite paintings to illustrate how those concepts challenge the old tradition. Your goal is to give them three examples of modern traditions that will be easy to remember and write about later."

She looked at him and then at the paintings as she thought it through and made her choices. "OK, I get it, and it's so easy! Why didn't we think of this before?"

"I know," he said and shook his head.

The tour guides arrived. They gushed over the gallery and the art before Bernadette could even introduce them to Drew and Julia. Everyone exchanged business cards. Drew asked all the tour guides questions about the languages they spoke and the profile of their clients. None of them had Bernadette's polish or fashion sense. They seemed more like shabby academics but they knew their topic. He was about to ask what their favorite galleries were to show tourists when the print media reporter he most wanted to talk to interrupted him. Drew excused himself and left them to fend for themselves, which wasn't a problem. There were no male tour guides, but most of the media were male. The tour guides quickly split up and introduced themselves to the men from the media. Everyone seemed to be in a jolly mood already.

Laurence's stand by the front door welcoming new arrivals kept him busy. From the distance he watched how fast the food was disappearing. They must not have had lunch. When the head count seemed right to him, he locked the front door and went to the buffet to restock beer and wine from boxes under the table hidden by a floor-length tablecloth. He could freshen up the food platters only once and decided he would do that right before the presentation was over. He let everyone near the buffet know the presentation was about to begin. They started getting out their notebooks and pens or tape recorders. A few got out their phones. What couldn't a cell phone do these days? He let Drew know everyone was here, and they could begin.

Chapter 30

Drew looked dapper and at ease as he stood in front of the crowd at the far end of the big room. He welcomed and thanked everyone for coming to this most unusual exhibit for his gallery and the city of Seattle. He reminded them of the key facts of the exhibit and the dates as mentioned in the press release and how he and Julia could be reached with any follow-up questions. He introduced Bernadette to the crowd and stood back and to the side so as not to block anyone's view of her. She launched into a lively summary of the Basque history and how they had created art from the earliest times that depicted how hard they worked and played. In the American West, the sheepherders created a new style of art using aspen trees for canvas that told the stories of their solitary lives. As the Basques assimilated, they took up the American styles, including the tradition of painting the West as the untouched natural wonderland established by the original patrons of western art, the rail-roads, when they used art as advertising for travelers.

Drew thought Bernadette looked elegant and spoke so articulately. The suit must be by a French designer he didn't know. She smiled and made everyone laugh. What a presence she brought to the party — and to the gallery. Every time he saw her she gave him a new idea. She was amazing in her knowledge and ability to communicate simply so there was no doubt about what she meant. Nothing she said was vague or uncertain. Now she was looking at him, and he realized she was ready for him to step up and take over. He made a successful joke about being so dazzled by her he forgot he was speaking next.

Drew pointed out the categories of the art, the subjects the Basque painters cared about most: heritage, animals, ranching/farming and landscape. For his first painting he selected a watercolor of a turn-of-the-century Basque hotel and noted how it celebrated not only the history of the immigration but assimilation into the United States. The artist evoking nostalgia using quick sketch lines to vaguely compose the shape of the building and over-washing with the pastel pink tones demonstrated that it was recently painted. Had it been done in the 1950s it would have adhered to a more stark realism in composition and color. The painting generated several questions about the history of the hotels.

He paused in front of the brightly colored trout done in iridescent acrylics that imitated the shimmer of the scales and water as the fish broke the surface of the river. The painting seemed almost three dimensional and looked like a single frame of an animated movie, which made it appear recently painted. He underscored how beneficial sports fishermen and tourists were to artists everywhere, because even postcards counted in the economic chain to the artist.

Next he stopped to talk about his favorite farming scene of a sheep camp on a green plain with rugged mountains in the background. The background was in the glorious nature style of railroad advertisements with a sweeping perspective of the plain and mountains. The artist could have left it alone there but continued on to add sheep and a sheep camp with white tent and a wagon, which added a small focal point and historical angle. What was most unusual was that the shepherd's wife and children were visiting or perhaps staying for the summer in this mountain paradise. That made it a happy family scene created for the tourist market in Sun Valley, Idaho, which sponsored a 'sheep paint out' every year, attracting hundreds of artists to come paint the landscape and sell their work to the visitors. Again, the questions showed that the crowd was involved in the material and the economic angle of an annual event for tourists and artists.

Drew's last choice was the arborglyphs Bernadette had mentioned. The photos were recent, the trees were old and the carvings told poignant stories of the shepherds' lives and their creative abilities of drawing, poetry and philosophy. Sadly, it was a disappearing art form as the trees ultimately fell down and decayed and the art was lost forever, which would increase the value of the photographs. The Basques hadn't been shepherds for some time now, and the new Peruvian or Mexican shepherds didn't seem to be making art like this. They had cell phones, and magazines were delivered to the sheep camps with their supplies. Drew finished and got a round of applause that he enjoyed.

Julia walked them to her starting point in the smaller room of abstract art. Drew and Bernadette stood together in the back of the crowd and whispered good job to each other.

Julia smiled and said, "The artists in this group are like me, so many generations removed from the history Drew just described, we have no interest in the past. We are obsessed with ourselves in the present moment and how to express our joy and outrage over our personal lives and the state of the world. We do not need any realistic objects or elements you recognize." Her first selection featured several unrecognizable elements that were black, white and red and made no immediate sense. Julia explained, "The artist is challenging you to look longer and think harder to understand the message and allow your emotional reaction to be the guide to finding the meaning. Do you feel strife or friction from it? Does it make you feel optimistic or pessimistic?" Someone suggested it must be about race and finding solutions, and Julia said that she thought it was a fight but it could be won. How modern to be able to achieve a sense of a complex social dilemma with colors instead of creating an old fashioned vignette from life like a slave market or riots in the street.

Next she chose a large canvas that had a blue center disrupted by jagged orange lines and gray gashes. Julia asked, "How does it make you feel?" They agreed on angry but about what? "If the lines and gashes suggest the imperfections or difficulties of various magnitudes of the situation, whatever it might be, maybe the blue background color will guide you to think about the intent." Sad was the only suggestion from the crowd. "True, people say they are feeling blue, but does this painting make you feel sad? No, I feel happy when I look at it. It must be a personal situation of struggling and succeeding." Several ideas were suggested about what the situation might be. "What an economical shorthand it is to tell a story of triumph this way instead of using symbols you hope everyone else understands. In classical art you had to be a scholar to get half of what was going on in the canvas."

The large blue-green color field was her last example of how the artist was emoting on canvas without any figures or line elements with a paint technique that created a luminous, lit-from-within effect on subtle variations in shading of a green. "This artist needs nothing but color and seemingly only one color but is it a color you've ever seen before? What could it be?" Water was the first responses she got. "What else?" A new field of grass, someone opined. "Is it optimistic or pessimistic? Maybe it's the joy of a spring day when the whole world is suddenly becoming sunny and green again after being bare? When you own and live with a painting like any of these, every time you look at it you will connect more deeply with it. The painting becomes an old friend that invites you to continue the conversation every day."

She gave a small bow with her arms by her side as a violinist would. "Please call us if you have any more questions." She beamed at the applause. After that she was surrounded by the crowd and disappeared inside their midst.

Drew and Bernadette looked at each other and smiled in enjoyment of Julia's performance.

Drew said, "Isn't she sensational? I have invested five years in her and she is going to make me famous for being part of her story!"

Bernadette was equally moved, "Yes, she is everything you say with the talent and the perspective to make a success of her abilities. To be able to give a performance like this when she didn't even know what she would be saying 30 minutes ago shows how bright she is. Congratulations to you."

Drew agreed with Bernadette. He couldn't think of anything else to say, but he felt like clapping.

Laurence approached them offering two plastic cups of red wine. "To your star pupil."

Drew responded, "She was powerful tonight, wasn't she?"

Laurence nodded. "And Bernadette was too. It will be exciting to watch when we have art collectors here and they reach for their wallets."

"Cheers! Let's toast my other brilliant employee, Bernadette, who taught us how to present better tonight. If only I'd met you earlier in my life, we could all be retired in Tahiti or whatever paradise you like."

Bernadette smiled. "Thank you. I wish so too. It would be lovely to be anywhere in the south of France, and a small cottage would do."

"You will find it. I have no doubt. So, you're a cottage gal? I would have thought a townhouse on the harbor in Nice."

"I would enjoy visiting you there," Bernadette said, inferring he was the townhouse type.

"Laurence, you're looking at a very lucky man. I can't tell you exactly how great it feels to have two smart women at my side and working hard. And you, of course. The future is starting to look good."

"I do have some idea. It already looks good from here," Laurence said.

"Bernadette, I think it's going to be easier to sell than I originally thought. I think we might re-price some of these paintings before we open. I hope none of these guys write about prices. Would the guides talk money with people before they bring them in?"

She paused before answering, "We usually give general terms, like four figures, five figures, six figures. That's the American way, right?"

"Tell me the truth. Is it too late to raise the prices with this crowd spreading the word of the exhibit starting tonight?"

"I think it would look bad to be greedy and double the prices. I don't see any harm in raising them 25 percent or 30 percent. If the difference were noticed the next time they visit the gallery, the person might think they misread it tonight. How much work is it?"

"It's easy to correct the cards on the computer and print them out again. Julia can do that very quickly. Removing and inserting the new cards is delicate, a little tedious. You don't want the back of the piece to look tattered."

"Show me the ones you want to re-price and let's calculate how much money it is."

Drew gave Laurence his empty cup and said, "Excuse us. We need to go print some money. Please keep working the crowd."

Bernadette gave Laurence her cup too with thanks and walked away with Drew toward the painting of the Basque hotel in the big room.

Bernadette didn't need a calculator to come up with the markup prices for each piece. Drew kept a running total in his mind of the new dollars. When it totaled several thousand dollars he said, "That's worth an hour or two of work, don't you think?"

"Yes, it is says the teacher whose hourly wage is modest."

Thinking about extra money rolling in was exciting to Laurence too. It was hard not to think about spending it even when he knew that was a foolish waste of time until you had the money in hand. The south of France didn't interest him at all, but a cottage for a month on the Oregon coast or in the San Juans might be a goal for extra cash. He could also put it in savings for an emergency. He could buy Eva a ring if he felt like it, which he didn't. He was still mad at her. Money was too hard to come by to spend on jewelry. She had plenty of jewelry already, or so he thought after watching her look through a big padded leather box for a pair of earrings or a bracelet. If he decided he wanted to get married, he could do so without a ring. A vision of Drew and Bernadette relaxing in the garden of a French cottage caused him to chuckle. Those two were made for each other, and he didn't think either of them knew it yet. He hoped he got to observe more developments in that area. Now he needed to check on the beer supply and walk around with bottles of red and white wine, offering refills. Julia still had new fans circling around. He wanted to overhear what they were saying and lingered after pouring them more wine or beer.

Julia was telling them, "I graduated from art school about four years ago. I was a part-time assistant here in the gallery my last year in school. I help Drew with pretty much everything. My art? The poster for this exhibit is my art. You can purchase one if you like. I paint two days a week. I'm lucky I get two. Many artists only get one day a week to work. You've got to keep your day job." She smiled, and they all laughed. "My own show here? Of course, that's why I work in a gallery. I've already had a small show here about two years ago. I'll have another when I have enough pieces to show."

Laurence approached a pair of tour guides who were also happy to have more wine. They wondered when Drew would let them bring in tour groups.

"Any time you have one. He's very flexible about that. Before the opening or staying an extra hour or two after the closing for a private group is easy for us, and we always have wine." That agreeable news made them smile and exchange glances. He wondered how Bernadette would share commissions with them. He asked several guests how they enjoyed the Basque *pintxos*. They all said they liked them and they didn't seem weird at all, just a little different.

When the invited guests had gone and the door was locked, the four of them went into the office. Drew sat behind his desk. Laurence, Bernadette and Julia sat in the swivel chairs.

Julia took off her high heels and put her feet up on the extra chair and threw her hair over the back of the chair so she could relax her head against the top of the cushion. She closed her eyes.

Drew watched her settle in and said, "You deserve a little rest, Julia. You were fantastic on your feet tonight. I can hardly wait to read what you inspired tonight. When do you think we'll see something?"

She didn't look up or open her eyes. "Well, a few said they were going to write and publish tonight. I have alerts set up on all their sites so we'll know the minute anything is live on my phone or the email here. Do you want me to ping you in the middle of the night if I'm awake?"

"No, I can wait until the morning, but as soon as you are rested, I need you to adjust the prices on a few pieces."

"Tonight?"

"Yes. And print out new cards. I will start removing the old ones and mark them up for you to make the corrections."

She opened her eyes and turned her head to look at him and saw he was serious. "OK. Give me five minutes."

"Take ten."

Laurence quietly sipped his wine, relieved he wouldn't be needed for this late night task. Drew could be merciless and always acted like it was no big deal to start another project after a long day. While they toiled, he planned to wash the platters that belonged to the gallery and pack up his empty storage containers for the bus ride home.

Bernadette said to Drew, "Can I help you peel the cards off the backs?"

"That would be great. Why don't we get started while Julia rests?"

When they left the office, Laurence raised his cup to Julia who raised hers to him. "You really were marvelous tonight. He is so proud of you I thought he would burst."

"Really?"

"Yes. That's what inspired all this price changing. While you were entertaining the media, those two were reviewing every piece and calculating a new tariff and decided it was worth another hour's work."

"Wow. I thought my presentation was strong tonight but what really helped was Bernadette's idea for revising the program. That was huge. We're both amazed we never thought of it ourselves."

"Bernadette is impressive, isn't she?"

"Yes. I hope I'll be as smart as she is when I'm her age."

"You will be. Where's your boyfriend tonight?"

"I hope he is unpacking a few boxes of things his mom gave him for his kitchen."

"Do you like the apartment?"

"It's OK, nothing too special but the cool factor of being in Pioneer Square. It's a quick bus ride home for me from here."

"Did you give up your other place?" he said.

"Not yet. I still have six months on my lease. I'll wait and see how things are then. This has all happened quickly with Henri and I'm trying, as Drew says, 'to be wary of foreigners who sweep you off your feet and then go home to their family.' If possible, I'd like to keep my old space for painting. My roommate would love to have the place to herself and doesn't mind the smell of paint on Sundays and Mondays. It's still pretty cheap for what it is."

"Be wary. That's good advice. I'm trying to do that too."

"At your age you have to be wary?" She looked stricken.

"Julia, I hate to tell you, that never stops."

She shook her head in disappointment, "Oh no. I better boot up this computer and prepare to earn my money." She got up and sat down in Drew's chair, turned on his computer and got the cardstock out of the credenza. She pulled up the Basque folder of files they shared on the network for her laptop and his desktop. "There's always so much for me to worry about. I thought that changed when you were older. I can't imagine what you and Mrs. Russo have to worry about."

"It's always more complicated than it appears. I'll tell you just to hear how it sounds out loud. Eva is wonderful, and I love her. But we haven't known each other that long, so it seems like a risk to me to get married right away. I don't see the point in getting married at all at my age, but she's adamant. I'd like to keep my apartment to have my own space for reading and being alone. That's a threat to her for some reason I can't understand. That's two issues to worry about. The biggest worry for me, however, is that she has four kids who all live in Seattle and are married with eight grandchildren. That makes 16 more people for me to deal with and cook dinner for every month or so. Can you guess how many of them are happy that Mom has a boyfriend who might want a share of the inheritance? But the worst part of being with them is they get into shouting matches with each other whenever they get together. Now you know all my worries."

"Oh, how awful, particularly about the kids and the screaming. I couldn't bear that. She seems so nice and calm. I can't picture her shouting."

"She can and does. She wins by being the loudest."

"Thank you for telling me. I couldn't imagine why you didn't want to spend Christmas with them, and now I totally get it."

Laurence looked at Julia and said, "I'll leave you to your work. I have to finish cleaning up the party. Thanks for listening and agreeing with me it's a tough decision to make. That makes me feel better."

Out in the gallery Drew and Bernadette worked together. He took the paintings off the wall and set them on the floor with the back facing out. He showed her how to gently peel the label without tearing the paper. The labels were designed to be removable, but it had to be done carefully. He left the wall tag in place as to have a double check for the correct tags.

Drew delivered the first two cards to Julia. "Here's the first batch." He left without another word.

When he took the second batch into the office, Julia had the new cards ready.

"To speed it up, do you want to come out and make a list of what we're changing and then you can put the new cards on the floor by the painting and we'll fix them?"

She grabbed a pad of paper and a pen and followed him out. It didn't take long for her to make a list of the titles and new prices and go back to the office to make corrections and print them out. When she had four done, she delivered them back to the location where they belonged. When she finished all the cards, she started helping them place the new cards on the wall and on the back of each painting. Laurence had gone, and it was quiet in the gallery.

When they were done and Drew had perfectly rehung each painting, he said, "Good job, ladies. May I offer you a ride home?"

Julia said, "You can drop me in Pioneer Square."

"How's the new apartment?"

"Great. The kitchen is going to be equipped with vintage French cookware and dishes, a housewarming gift from Bernadette."

"How nice. He cooks?" Drew asked.

"I hope so," said Julia.

Drew turned to Bernadette. "What does Henri's mother say about his cooking skills? I was told recently that cooking and reciting poetry were required talents in men."

"He watched me cook in those pots, and he has assisted me, so I think he knows how to use them. Every French schoolboy learns plenty of verses. Julia, has Henri quoted his favorite poets to you?"

"I don't know. He speaks so well I'm not sure I'd know if the words were his or not."

Drew insisted Julia could not walk across the square. He drove around a few blocks to be able to park in front of the apartment building and they watched her from the car while she rang the buzzer and waited to be let in. She waved good night to them.

"What's the best way to your place?"

"Go up Pike and Pine to 18th Avenue East."

He parked in front of one of the century old houses with a big front porch and a light on over the door and inside the house, "That's a nice house. Is it yours?"

"No, I rent the parlor floor and it is perfect for me."

"Bernadette, I appreciate everything you did for us tonight. You were a huge help with the presentation, the party, and of course, the price adjustments. Thank you." He was sure she would invite him inside for a drink.

With a sparkle in her eye and a smile she said, "It was good work. I like that."

"What about tomorrow night? Will you join us for the opening?"

"I'm sorry. I have two classes to teach from 6:30 to 8:30 so I wouldn't be much help."

"What about Friday and Saturday night?"

"What would you like me to do?"

He smiled. "Just what you did tonight. Charm them, stand next to me and look fabulous."

"I guess I could do that." She said goodnight in French and got out of the car.

Somewhat stunned, he watched her walk up the sidewalk to the porch and the front door. With her key in her hand, she turned to wave goodnight to him before she unlocked the door and went inside. He sat there for a minute thinking, *Why didn't she ask me in?* They had experienced an intense evening together. She had worked hard. They had worked well together. He wanted a congenial nightcap to relive the triumphs of the day. He still felt revved up by the events of the evening. He wanted to talk more about his exhibit. He wanted to listen to her talk about his show. She knew so much about it. Why didn't she want to talk about it? Now he wasn't sure where he was with her. He thought she liked him, but he did not sense anything sexual, which was odd. Most women were transparent about their interest in him. Maybe she appeared uninterested or unavailable because she had a steady boyfriend. Maybe she was burned out on men. She was so smart and competent. He certainly didn't intimidate her. Did she intimidate him? Yes. No. He felt equal with her, didn't he? He felt confused about that. Why hadn't she asked him in? They felt like partners in this exhibition tonight even though he hadn't asked her to be. She had inserted herself into his business so easily without him protesting about anything. From the first day when she had explained how she could help him to her suggestion tonight to do the presentation completely different, he had said yes to everything she had said. He couldn't believe how he said *yes* to her. She was valuable to him. He did want her standing next to him looking fabulous. He wished she had invited him in.

Chapter 31

Laurence contemplated his exercise routine when his phone rang. He could only think, *Drew, it's too early in the morning after a late night to start working.* He could pretend he was in the shower and call him back, but he answered. "How are the reviews?"

Eva said, "Are you still asleep?"

"Almost. We had a late night at the gallery with a press party and tonight will be equally late. I may stay in bed until it's time to go to work again."

"I'm sorry to disturb you."

"It's OK. How are you?"

"It's January fifth."

"Oh. Well, I've definitely been thinking about you. I thought I'd call you when we got past the opening weekend. It's been so hectic."

"I see. Everyone has their own interpretation of 'after the New Year.'"

"I'm sorry my idea isn't the same as yours. I certainly don't mean to hurt your feelings and make you think I'm not taking all this very seriously. I think about little else when I'm not working."

"Could we talk in the afternoon before you go in?"

"I need to be there by 3 and that doesn't give us too much time."

"It's 10 o'clock in the morning. You have to eat something. Why don't we go out for lunch around twelve?"

"Eva, you're pressuring me in a way that's not good. I feel squeezed."

"How about if I bring some sandwiches over?"

He tried to think of something to say that was more than no but could only come up with, *you'll regret handling me this way.* So he said, "OK."

"You don't sound very excited."

"I'm not. I'm too tired to be excited, but I do understand you want to talk. I'll be ready for you around noon."

Impatient. Insatiable. Intelligent. All those things just as Sophia had described herself. Eva probably thought after New Year's meant January first, so now he was five days late. It was also the first Thursday of the month, the grand opening of the Basque exhibition. When he was thinking about talking with Eva was another five days away, Monday when the gallery was closed. What was he going to say to her? He really needed a delay tactic. If he got frustrated with her today and just said no to it all, it would be oppressive to him at the event tonight and tomorrow night and the next night. It just wasn't fair to him. He had too much to do and needed to be sharp and not distracted.

When he opened the door for her he had showered but not dressed, deciding he needed to keep his suit pristine. She looked surprised at his bathrobe.

"Don't get any ideas about my outfit. I'm saving my suit."

"I thought you might be really glad to see me."

"If you would like to get undressed and relax with me, feel free. I have another robe you know."

"Do you think we talk better lying down?"

"Sometimes I do."

"I think I'll just sit for the moment, enjoying the sandwich and seeing your face."

"I've missed you too."

She put a Metropolitan Market grocery bag on the table and started taking out sandwiches wrapped in plastic wrap, several small containers, napkins and plastic utensils.

She laid out a tuna salad and a chicken salad sandwich with coleslaw, fruit salad and potato salad sides.

He got them both a glass of water from the filtered pitcher in the refrigerator and started eating right away. He was famished. He watched her watch him eat. She seemed a little more relaxed than when she arrived. He told her she looked beautiful which was apparently the right track to be on. When he had finished both halves of the sandwiches he started eating the salads right out of the containers but passed each one to her after a few bites. She smiled at him and took a few bites and passed it back.

"Thank you so much for the lunch delivery. I really enjoyed it. Tell me how much you missed me."

"Horribly, painfully, terribly. December was a miserable month," she said.

"I agree."

"Have you come to any conclusions?" she asked.

Being direct was her specialty weapon. He shook his head at her and said, "You waste no time, do you? I don't know what to say other than the truth. It's all I can think of right now. My main conclusion is I think it was very cruel of you to make me stay over here by myself. Instead of inspiring a passion to get married, it made me mad and made me wonder how I could be in love with someone who could be so mean."

She looked stunned and then recovered her composure. "Thank you for not mincing words. I realized it was a big mistake after about a week."

"Well, why didn't you call me and apologize and tell me to come back?"

"I thought you should call me and say you couldn't stand it another minute."

"Eva, this is a good example of why we have trouble with each other. I'm the injured party here. Don't you see that? Have you forgotten how I apologized when I was wrong? You should have called me to say you were sorry for being absurd the last time I saw you. This stupid, obstinate position you have created for us is another thing you need to apologize for."

He could see those were fighting words as her neck tensed up. She was making an effort to be silent and listen and not say anything too quickly. He sat back and waited.

"I hate it when I'm wrong," she said.

"Welcome to the world, Eva. It happens to everyone. Why are you surprised when it happens to you?"

"It doesn't happen very often."

"That's your opinion," he said.

"Oh boy, this is getting worse," she said.

"Well, why don't you turn it around then and start apologizing?"

"It's hard for me to do," she said.

"If you can't deal with making mistakes and apologies, there's no point in us discussing anything else."

She shook her head. "This is not what I wanted."

"It's up to you. What can you say right now that might make me feel good about you?"

She said nothing for about a minute looking at the table and the debris from lunch. "I'm sorry I made such a mess of the month of December. I thought being clear and firm about what I wanted would make it easy for you to say yes to me and that it wouldn't take a month. I'm not accustomed to not getting my way. I guess I've been deluding myself about what's going on with us, ignoring the issues that matter to you for some that are more pleasant to think about. I hate myself for missing out on the last 30 days with you that could have been wonderful. You know I love you and want to be with you always. I want you to feel that way about me. I want all this unhappiness to go away."

"Thank you for the apology and recognizing what we are going through won't disappear until we have talked about it and come to some agreement. If we are going to create a successful partnership, there will have to be some compromises on both sides."

"I'm not experienced at doing things that way, but I will try." She looked earnest and sounded more humble than he could ever remember.

"That's important."

"What do we do now?" she said.

"Unfortunately I have a major distraction going on at the gallery until Monday when we're closed. We're open on Sunday afternoon, which is very unusual and Saturday night as though it's a special event. I need to be very sharp and well rested to deal with whatever comes in the door. We don't know what to expect. It could be overwhelming crowds or a disappointing turnout, which will mean coming up with a new strategy immediately. Either way it will be challenging. All I can think of at the moment is let's lay the issues out and you think about them over the weekend and decide where you would be willing to compromise. We'll get together on Monday afternoon when I'm rested and everyone is calm."

"All right. What's at the top of your list?"

"I know how badly you want to be married. I don't want it at all, but I'm willing to compromise by saying I will get married if we can experience some blissful or at least quiet cohabitation that gives me a sense of confidence in our future I do not feel now. I also need to have some positive experiences with your children that make me feel like they aren't going to cause me distress every time we see them. You figure out how you can create those opportunities."

"What else?"

"I think you ought to consult your lawyer about the possibility of a marriage and what he recommends you do to ensure that I don't become business partners with your kids if anything horrible happens to you."

"I don't like to even think about that," she said.

"Well, consider the peace of mind it would bring to your children and goodwill toward me to know in advance of our marriage that you have made arrangements to make it easy for them if the inevitable happens sooner than expected. Think about your condo too. I doubt my Social Security would even cover the annual maintenance. I would have to find another apartment. Do you want them or me to be in charge of selling it? Getting married is serious business when you have assets like you do."

She shook her head and looked at him with resignation. She was not happy to have the ball back in her court.

Drew was the first to arrive at the gallery at noon. Last night's euphoria over the success of the evening and the price changing seemed like a dream. He double-checked a few prices to confirm it wasn't. He hung up his suit jacket, made coffee and sat at his desk studying his list. He was almost afraid to read the early reviews. The performers should be arriving soon for a rehearsal. He wanted to welcome them and show them around to get comfortable. Sound checks always put him on edge. He anticipated difficulties with the equipment that would require a trip across town to look for wire or plugs or something. They probably had car trouble and would be late or someone would be sick. He tried to limit himself to those concerns and not let his mind fabricate worse examples of how the performance would be derailed before it began.

Julia arrived, bringing him a tangerine and a bran muffin.

"I couldn't eat anything," he said.

"You must eat something. It will make the day go better. Tell me what you're worried about." Julia seemed calm and patient waiting for his response.

"The usual. No show performers, equipment malfunction, no customers, earthquake, fire, etcetera." He kept telling himself he wasn't going to tell her everyday, but he still did it. He was annoyed with himself about that lapse of resolution.

"Good. We can handle all those things. Did you read the reviews yet?" Julia said.

"Not yet. How are they?"

"You will be pleased. They liked it and reported in the exact words we used. They even mentioned how good the *pintxos* were."

"That's great. How many?" Drew said.

"Only two so far but I bet it's the trend."

"Early fluff to be reversed by the big guns over the weekend," he said.

"I don't think so." The doorbell rang and she said, "They are right on time."

They both went to greet 10 excited Basque people with musical instruments, shopping bags and suitcases. The gallery suddenly seemed full with boisterous voices and exclamations "Look, there's the hotel in Boise! Look at the old movie theater and the trout! Look at our mountains!" They were all wandering around the gallery, staring at the art and talking to each other. Julia tried to take orders for coffee and water, and they all said yes but to what she didn't know. She returned with the coffee pot and paper cups, which she put on her desk and went back to the kitchen area for water bottles.

When they had finished the initial viewing of all the art, they gathered near Julia's desk and shook Drew's hand again and said they were amazed at the collection of art and how beautiful it was and wanted to know how he had found the artists. Drew was relieved by the first Basque response to the exhibit and relaxed into sharing the humorous version of the highlights of assembling the art. He gave them a tour of the premises behind the scenes and the big storeroom they could use for changing clothes and storing their equipment. When they seemed to be settled down, he suggested they set up their equipment do a complete run through to see how the space worked for them and discuss any changes they might like. To his astonishment, it went smoothly. They had done it all many times and seemed to be enjoying themselves in front of an audience of two people. He and Julia stood and watched and when it was over applauded them and gave each other a high five. This part of the evening was going to be a success. Drew now loved Basque people. They were great in every way. They painted, they sang, they danced and they loved life. Tonight in the gallery would be a performance to remember, if anyone came to see it. A member of the local Basque club arrived to lead their caravan of two vans to where they would be having lunch and spending the afternoon. Julia gave them all maps of Seattle and her card with the cell phone number in case they got lost.

The cleaning team arrived to make sure the floors were immaculate after last night's revelry. Laurence arrived just before 3 p.m. and went to work setting up Julia's desk as a customer service center for admissions, extra drink tickets and souvenirs. He hung several posters and framed fisherman photos with big price tags on the wall behind the desk. He rearranged the signage on the wall for ticket prices, foreign language tours and performance times. His favorite theatrical prop was the purple velvet rope with brass stands on either end to officially designate the waiting space or the line to pay. It all looked very box office lobby style. He was admiring it when Julia emerged from the back with two big rolls of colored tickets and the cash box.

"What do you think?" he asked.

"We're ready for a big night. I think it's going to be great," said Julia.

"How's Drew's attitude?"

"The usual. He's worried that we'll have more employees than customers."

"I would have thought the success of last night would carry forward today."

Julia shrugged, "I know. Did you see the early reviews? I left them on the table in Drew's office."

"No. I assumed they would be good given the jolly crowd."

"They liked your *pintxos*! I've already posted excerpts from the reviews on our website and in the email to our list that I sent out this morning. The other great thing is the dress rehearsal for the talent was awesome." She had a big smile on her face.

The caterer's team arrived with trays of food from a truck parked outside. Charles and William followed them in to survey the art, which they hadn't seen before and offered to help the caterer's servers with the wine at each station. They had one hour to complete the setup.

Chapter 32

Laurence opened the door at 5 p.m. for the first group of enthusiasts who had left the office early for an almost free happy art hour. He knew them from other First Thursday Art Walks and they greeted him cordially. They had the entrance fee ready and he had a handful of three ticket strips to exchange with them and pointed them in the direction of the first table with the Cava and Gilda *pintxo*. He could see a few more groups coming and held the door open ready for them with a big welcome. He knew most of them and they all seemed in good spirits, glad to be first in the door and getting whatever there was to be had. *This is a good beginning,* he thought.

William occupied Julia's chair to wait until it was busy enough to need two people at the door to greet and sell tickets, so Laurence handed the money over to him and let him be the cashier. Julia positioned herself nearby so she could hug and kiss familiar faces as they headed toward the first table. She looked like a Rockette in a mini tuxedo shorts outfit and black high heels that looked like they would tap if she began dancing. The overall effect was festive and theatrical. When there were about 20 people in the room, she said, "I think it's time Drew came out to greet people, what do you think?"

William and Laurence agreed with her, and she hit the button to summon him. She stood so she could watch him walk across the floor. She smiled at him with a small bow as he looked around the gallery at the early crowd already spread out looking and talking about the art while they sipped the Cava. He nodded with appreciation and came to stand by her.

"Pretty cool, isn't it? Already more customers than employees," she said.

"Yes. I agree. Good job, Julia. You brought them in, and now they are ours to deal with. I think I'll get started."

Drew worked the crowd, saying hello and asking people how they liked the art and the food. He made everyone feel like they were special to have his attention. He too knew everybody who was here so far. The regular crowd were enjoying themselves and already talking on their phones. No doubt the cell phone chatter was reporting it was worth it to come over now while there was still food. Drew was pleased they had encouraged them in email to get here early. He liked overhearing it was great food. The first impressions of the art were positive and generating conversations. Drew supported comments and questions with sound bites about the artists or the subject matter.

The plan was for Drew and Julia to give a few minutes of highlights of the exhibition before they introduced the performers, just enough facts and takeaway information to add depth to the first impressions and provoke more curiosity. He didn't expect to sell much tonight. Most people needed to think about it, go home and imagine where they would hang the art. The shoppers would come back a second time to look again and confirm the first impression. First time visitors might take weeks, months or years to come back. He reminded everyone he talked to about the timing of the performances.

By 6:00 p.m. there were almost a hundred people in the room. Laurence did an internal click for each person as they entered. He could be counted on to know how many people were there at any moment. Drew considered this ability to keep the count one of Laurence's special talents and enjoyed asking him for the tally. When the performers arrived accompanied by the local hosts and their families, Laurence welcomed them and gave them all free tickets for food and wine as instructed. Julia greeted them and escorted the hosts to the first table of *pintxos* and the performers through the hidden door to put on their costumes.

Drew got the attention of the crowd speaking with the wireless microphone in the center of the big room, announcing the first performance of the evening was about to begin. When the room became quiet, he welcomed everybody and presented a five-minute condensed version of what he and Bernadette had said the previous night for the press crowd. Julia gave five minutes of examples of how the new and old artistic traditions were demonstrated in the art, mentioning two pieces in the big room and two in the smaller. Then Drew introduced the *Oinkari* Basque Dancers, who had traveled from Boise, Idaho to present classic Basque folk dancing, music, singing and poetry.

The performers appeared next to him on cue and took a bow. The men wore white shirts and trousers with red scarves around their waists, red vests and red berets and had small red pads with bells attached right below their knees. The movement of the dancers accented the details of the red sashes and the bells. The women wore white blouses and headscarves with a red skirts. One of the men started playing a song on a flute while he also played a small drum. The others sang in *Euskara*. It was a rousing rhythmic song. At the end, one of the players said, "That was about fishing. The next is about love, which we can't do without, even for one day." The crowd chuckled, and accordion music began with a soulful sound that let everyone know it was questioning how could she have broken his heart? There was no idle chat going on in the back of the room. Every eye was on them. "We are celebrating the harvest in this dance." During the next song the men and women who had been singing began a traditional dance with joyful melody and fast footwork around in circles, together in pairs and individually. In the audience, heads were banging and toes tapping to this song that few in the room had ever heard before.

The crowd gave the performers a boisterous round of applause. When the room was quiet again, one of the musicians stepped forward and said, "This is what it feels like to be Basque far away from home." He began reciting a poem in Euskara and then paused as one of his colleagues stepped forward with him and presented the English translation. They alternated in Euskara and English until they reached the end and bowed to the crowd. The dancers stepped forward with them in one line and they all bowed to the crowd. It was over. The applause was now raucous with whistles and hoots. Drew watched the crowd. He was very pleased. Everything was meeting his expectations for a great beginning, and this was only the first show, the first night. He could hear the cash register ringing in his mind. Drew stood beside the performers to say thank you and then said to the crowd, "Next performance will be at 8:30. Thanks for coming."

The performers dispersed into the crowd of well-wishers, shaking hands and answering questions. He watched cell phones light up, a good sign of positive reviews being distributed the fastest way. He went and stood beside the Basque Club president to thank him for his help. They agreed it was spectacular to see Basque art hanging on the walls and the *Oinkaris* performing live in Seattle. Everyone in the club had received another urgent message to come tonight, tomorrow night or Saturday to be able to see the live show. They talked again about bringing the whole club in for a private viewing of the art. Would they enjoy a wine tasting as well? Drew would arrange it. If he thought the kids or adults would enjoy a short art lecture from a great teacher, he could arrange that also. It occurred to Drew that they should get someone to film one of the shows with professional equipment before the performers departed for Boise early on Sunday so it could be replayed any time. Why hadn't he thought of that before? He excused himself to look for Julia. She had drawn a crowd around her and the cutthroat trout sculpture giving her own inspirational performance. He listened as she concluded and invited them to follow her on to another piece. He said, "When you are done, come chat with me." She nodded and kept moving. He checked around the room methodically to see what each employee was doing. It looked like half the crowd was departing as new people were arriving. William and Laurence were managing the farewells and welcomes together. Charles was dispensing new cases of wine to each food station for the next surge. The caterer was bringing new trays of food from the back kitchen. All was well. He needed every one of the employees to manage this handsome, happy crowd. After all his worries, he was feeling about 10 feet tall. It was time for him to get out and sell. He headed for the farming scenes with the soulful sheep.

After the second performance Drew watched the crowd begin moving toward the door. They had been just as enthusiastic as the first group. The performers were still being mobbed by questions and compliments. They were all enjoying wine as they accepted accolades. The lead musician with the accordion chatted with Drew and was modest about the response. Drew said, "So, every time you perform you get this level of reaction?"

"Similar. Your space is more intimate or elegant than the typical outdoor stage or high school auditorium. Even without wine we always get a robust reaction. That's because the music, dancing and the poetry is exceptional and speaks to everyone, no matter where they are from. We enjoy the response so much, we would almost do it for free."

"Almost."

"Yes, almost, Drew. I'm sure we've been good for business tonight."

"Absolutely worth every penny. Thank you again. I hope you're pleased with the accommodations."

"Yes, very nice people. Basques always offer good hospitality."

"Please feel free to stay here as long as you like tonight to enjoy the wine and art. I'll tell Charles to send you all home with a few bottles of wine to share with your hosts. Do you have plans to sightsee tomorrow?"

"No, we're having a Basque Club meeting and lunch and giving dancing lessons for kids."

Drew said goodnight to him. His cell was vibrating in his pocket and as he turned to walk away, he looked quickly at the caller ID and answered, "Bernadette! I wish you were here! Where are you?"

"I just got home from teaching and wanted to know how it went."

"It's been a great evening in every way. The take at the door is healthy. We're out of food. Julia has been selling non-stop all evening."

"The performers? How were they?"

"Impressive."

"So, you're pleased?"

"Yes. It's going to work out like I hoped it might. I sold one of the arborglyph photos to a regular. He may come back for another. Tomorrow can only be better. I thought I saw some professional flashes in the crowd. I hope some of the press you charmed last night came back to get footage of the show. Good photography of the performers in print or online would be worth a lot. She doesn't know it yet, but Julia is going to line up a videographer for tomorrow or Saturday so we can replay the show on our own machine."

"Oh, Drew, that's fantastic. I'm so happy for you."

"When are you going to get in here and do some selling?"

"I have a group of four who are flexible about timing and I want to get them in before the opening tomorrow or Saturday. If you were doing a special filming, it would be wonderful to let them watch that. They're eager to buy before anyone else sees the exhibit."

"They are now my top priority. Let me talk with Julia, and I'll call you back."

Julia was sitting at her desk, in her own chair chatting with Laurence and William. She looked up at him, "You were on your phone with the 'out of the office' sign on your back when I got free. Did you notice I sold the trout that bites? One of the software guys we know. Can we talk here while I rest my feet?"

"Of course. Great job on the trout. I'm going to miss him. We need to film the performance live or as a rehearsal so we have footage to replay whenever we like. Can you set that up quickly?"

"Sure. I know a few people to call. I can leave them a message tonight. Somebody should be free for a last minute gig."

"Go make some calls from my desk with your feet up, and I'll help the old dudes manage the door."

Julia stood up and headed for the hidden office in her ballet flats, carrying her high heels, saying goodnight to the dwindling crowd as she passed by.

"That's my Julia. Wasn't she on her game tonight?" Drew said.

William agreed, "As always. Julia is stellar. You ready for a drink, boss?"

Drew said, "Sure, if there is any wine left I'd enjoy a glass. How about you, Laurence?"

Drew sat down in Julia's chair. William returned with a fresh bottle of the red and a stack of plastic cups, filling three cups right away.

"Laurence, what's the count for the evening?"

"238."

"Excellent. Above projections. Extra ticket sales?"

"I'd say about the same. I could start counting money right now."

"Let's wait until the last leave and we lock the door or Julia finishes her phone calls and we can go into the office. Where's Charles?"

"Cleaning up in back like the pro he is, dragging big bags of garbage to the bin," Laurence said.

"What about the staffing and the exit word of mouth?" Drew said.

"All positive. I didn't hear any complaints about anything. If we get a bigger crowd, William and I can manage the door, but I think we need another server. Here comes Charles. Let him tell you," Laurence said.

Drew looked at his cell phone and answered, "Yes, Julia, any luck? Great. We'll come join you in the office. Gentleman, let's retire to the money counting room."

Chapter 33

Friday morning Drew arrived at the gallery before noon to get ready for Bernadette's VIP tour. The coffee was ready by the time Julia arrived carrying a blueberry muffin and a banana, which he waved to the side of his desk and shook his head at her. "You don't quit do you?"

She said, "No. You have to eat something. Wasn't last night great? I thought it was our best event ever."

"It was memorable."

"Guess what was in the Weekend Guide today?" She had a big smile on her face.

"Really? It was good?"

"Yes! The biggest gun at the Seattle Times said the pre-press and the opening night were amazing! He even mentioned the Gilda and the *albondigas*. Laurence deserves credit for that."

"Wow. Maybe we're going to make this work. That's great news, Julia. I hope we're successful today too."

"What's the strategy with the VIPs?" she said.

"You and I will welcome them at 1 o'clock then turn it over to Bernadette who will call us in the office if they have more questions. We want them to feel this is a very special private viewing with no pressure behind it."

"Does it make you nervous to let Bernadette run it all by herself?"

"Yes. It's weird to relinquish control, even for an hour. I trust her, even though she is new to us. Don't you? Do you have any reservations?"

"I like her and her son very much. They're so smart about art and fun to be with, but I'm trying to be wary as you said. She seems consistent. She seems honest. But I can't shake the oddness of how quickly she has become part of us. It's certainly not like you to be so trusting so soon. It's not like me either."

"How do you think she could scam us?"

"I've tried to think about all the usual ways to pass fakes or stolen art by changing the documentation records, but none of that applies because you and I sourced every piece from the artists. It's unlikely she wants to go to the trouble of selling stolen art, but if she did, the simplest plan to rob us would be to have Henri make a copy of my gallery key and steal the best of the show in the middle of the night. I'm always careful with my key. She hasn't been close to your key, has she?"

"Absolutely not. She's barely touched me much less had her hand in my pocket. You have been thinking about this I haven't. I feel stupid. You think Henri is an accomplice?"

"No, he's a straight arrow and believes the banking industry must redeem its tarnished reputation with morals and behavior above the ordinary. The other thing that bugs me is that she's not a quick study on Basque art history. She walked in the door an expert. We're certainly not. She's a lot more than a French teacher. What about having her clients buy from us for cheap because she knows there's another market for reselling at a profit, New York or overseas?"

"I don't think so," Drew said, shaking his head. "I've done a lot of reading about Basque art and haven't heard of big a resell market anywhere."

"Well, what I feel for sure about her is that she wants to make money. The teaching and touring business doesn't provide any opportunities for a windfall. She wants money for the future. Has she talked to you about that?"

"Only a vague reference to a cottage in the south of France as the goal. Have either of them talked about how successful she is with her deals with other galleries?"

"No. She's never mentioned to me any of the other galleries she works with. We talk a lot about art and have been to the museums. You'd think we'd talk about what our competition is showing or go have a look, but we haven't. That might be because we're all closed on the same days. I never asked whom she worked with either. I thought you had done that," Julia said.

"I didn't. When she arrived in her Chanel suit as a friend of Eva's and suggested the finder's fee rather than the usual split, I believed her. I was so excited about the new source of business, I didn't ask her whom she knew or confirm with any one that she had a deal with them. How could I have been so careless? This is how greed gets you in trouble."

They looked at each other. "This is creeping me out," said Julia, "just saying out loud what I've been thinking."

"I know what you mean. I think you should sit at your desk while they are in the gallery. I'll tell her we're expecting some deliveries, and I don't want her tour interrupted. I'm going to do some research while she's doing the tour."

She laughed at him. "Come on! We're wary but not silly! I doubt they are going to bonk me on the head, steal some art and escape through the front door."

Drew and Julia were standing by the front door when Bernadette arrived with her group of two middle-aged couples. They were nicely dressed, but not elegantly. Julia was already in her evening attire, a black suit with a short black skirt, grey silk shell, black stockings and for Julia, somewhat sensible yellow high heels. Bernadette, in a plain dark pantsuit, introduced them in French, and Drew made a little conversation with them about their trip in America and where they were from, which turned out to be Saint Jean de Luz. He told them how lucky they were to live in one of the delights of the Basque Country. He looked at Bernadette to see if she was ready to begin. She surely knew he was at about his limit in French.

Understanding him perfectly, she said to him in English, "They don't speak any English. I will begin the tour now."

He smiled at them all as though this was very pleasing to him and told them in French to enjoy the tour. He said to Bernadette, "We're expecting some deliveries, so Julia needs to stay at her desk to handle that without it interrupting you."

She nodded, said thank you and led them away to the end of the big room where they usually started talking about Basque history and art traditions. He watched them walk away and shook his head.

He whispered to Julia, "They are Basque. Why does that make me nervous?"

She shrugged and shook her head. She didn't know and didn't say anything.

Drew stood there for a few minutes trying to gauge their reaction to the gallery and the art. He couldn't read a thing by the body language or facial expressions of the visitors. Bernadette was vivacious as usual, smiling, gesturing but they were not laughing or smiling back. He shrugged his shoulders at Julia and said, "Call me if you need me."

Back at his desk he ran a search on Bernadette's name in several browsers, which all turned up her teaching position at Alliance Française, her website marketing her tour guide affiliation with the Seattle Architecture Foundation as well as private language tutoring and tours of art, architecture and attractions in five languages. She also had a Facebook page with happy tourists in front of Seattle landmarks with the same tour and tutor information. That was the end. There was no mention of positions in Paris or anywhere else. He tried her name on two French language sites for teaching and tourism and a few French newspapers but got nothing. He called two competitors who were known to do good tourist business around Pioneer Square and luckily caught them in with time to chat. None of them knew her or had been approached by anyone to bring foreign language tours and get a share of the sales commissions. He felt ill. He was glad the filming session couldn't be arranged until Saturday afternoon. That would have been too generous to whoever these people were.

To calm his nerves, he uploaded several photos of the Basque art hanging on the walls of his gallery to do a reverse image search he typically used to confirm there were no unauthorized users of art images he had the rights for. The results were nothing but the websites of the artists he had reviewed before and talked with on the phone about sending paintings for this exhibit. Of course, this wasn't stolen art and probably not worth stealing because all the artists were alive and well and interested in getting commissions to paint anything.

At 2 p.m. Drew decided he would take his gallery back into his own hands. He emerged from the hidden door as Julia was pressing a red SOLD dot on the wall beneath one of the big cloud paintings. He stood quietly to observe the scene. Bernadette had a big smile on her face. Julia looked politely pleased. The visitors' faces revealed nothing. When Julia turned from completing her task, she saw him and gave him a look that said, "Surprise!"

Drew approached the visitors saying, "What a beautiful painting you have chosen. Thank you."

Bernadette translated immediately and beamed at Drew. He had to at least give her a "job well done" smile until he sorted out his feelings about what had gone on here without him.

"Would your friends enjoy a glass of wine now or something else?"

She asked them and they declined. Apparently there was to be no joyous celebration about the decision and the acquisition.

"Julia, all the paperwork is good with the shipping instructions?"

She nodded affirmatively.

"Where's your next stop on the tour today?" Drew asked Bernadette.

"One of your competitors."

"Of course. Where else would you go?" he said.

"Thank you so much for allowing us a private viewing. It meant a great deal to them that you would arrange it," Bernadette said and looked like she meant it.

"My pleasure," he said.

Drew and Julia walked to the front door with them and said good-bye and thanks again. They all got into a mini-van with Bernadette driving.

"Was that strange from beginning to end?" Drew said.

Julia responded, "Yes. Totally. Stone-faced from beginning to end. I've never seen anyone look at every single piece in the gallery, never ask a question and then point to say I'll take that one. No salesmanship required. No conversation about Basques in America. I don't think Bernadette said anything. She stood by quietly but wasn't called on."

"I don't know what to think. I'm glad to make a sale and have another red dot up, but honestly I thought that one would sell tonight anyway. It was such a good value for the size for decorators or beginning collectors."

"I thought so too. Did you learn anything about her?" said Julia.

"Nothing new about her local work teaching and touring. I called the usual suspects in Pioneer Square. No one knows her or has been approached by anybody with this foreign tourist deal. I verified a random selection of the art we're displaying and as you know, it is not stolen from the artist who painted it or anyone else."

"How did we get to be so lucky to be chosen by her?"

"Remember, she's a friend of Eva's, whose opinion I value. I don't know if I want to start a conversation about a covert identity with Eva right now. That's a sticky question that Eva may have no idea about anyway. There's no doubt Bernadette is qualified to help us sell art. The referral is solid that way. What is the shipping address for the art?"

"Montana."

Drew shook his head, "I don't get it. Oh well, a sale is a sale, and we've got work to do before we open."

Laurence arrived and sat in the visitor's chair for a few minutes to hear Julia's description of the odd art buyers and the fantastic review in the Seattle Times. She seemed effervescent over the initial success of the exhibit and what the future might bring. She expected to sell a lot this weekend and be busy for weeks with buyers coming back for a second look. As always she had big plans for how to spend the money she hadn't made yet. Then he had to begin refreshing his box office and souvenir shop, so she got out of his way and joined Drew in his office. When the caterer arrived, Laurence helped with the fresh table-cloths and arranging platters, letting her staff do all the carrying to and from the van. He brought cold bottles of Cava and white wine from the back to store underneath the tables and filled up the large ice buckets with numerous bottles. He helped open a dozen bottles to be ready to go when paying customers came. Charles would not be arriving until the opening because he had Laurence and the caterer doing the set up. William, too, would appear at 5 p.m. ready to pour and work the door as needed. Drew worked every hour of the payroll efficiently.

A few groups of office mates were out front smoking, ready to begin sipping and tasting when Laurence welcomed them, took their money and gave them tickets. He saw Sophia get out of a car in the parking lot with her baby and Tony. He had to breathe deeply to hold onto his composure. She looked beautiful and provocative in a slim red dress and a red coat. The baby had on a red dress and coat too. Tony was casual in khakis and a polo shirt and a ski jacket.

"Welcome, what a pleasant surprise," Laurence said.

Sophia gave him a warm kiss on the cheek and murmured into his ear how glad she was to see him. Evie kissed him too and called out a gleeful "Cookie!" It was a nice feeling to be touching both of them simultaneously with his nose in their dark curls with clean herbal smells.

He nodded at Tony, who preferred not to shake hands because of germs. "Good to see you, Tony. No, you don't need to give me any money. You're a friend of the house. Here are food and beverage tickets. The first *pintxo* is right this way," and he led them to it.

The server gave them plastic cups of Cava and the Gilda's on a toothpick in a small paper dish. Laurence lingered, as there was no one waiting at the door and William should be there any minute. "What brings you to the gallery today?"

"You invited us months ago, remember?" said Sophia. "I read the review in the Seattle Times this morning and called Tony so we could ride together and leave work a little early to stop on our way home and miss the huge crowds tonight. The gallery is lovely. It sparkles. I had no idea it would be so pretty. We'll take a look at the art when you have to get back to work."

"I'm so glad you came. How do you like the wine?" asked Laurence, looking at Tony.

Tony said, "I like it. Spanish, correct?" He ate his Gilda in one bite.

"Yes, it's a Cava. Have you visited in the Basque Country?"

Tony shook his head no. Sophia said the Cava was refreshing. She gave Evie her Gilda to eat. Laurence held his breath to watch the child navigate the toothpick and get the olives and pepper off without rupturing her tongue or mouth. She even ate the anchovy. What an eater she was.

Tony said, "The attorney came today, and we discussed everything."

Laurence thought he might faint. The speed of the Russos getting to the point was always shocking. He gripped the side of the service table. "Is it satisfactory to you?"

Tony said, "Yes. Thank you for suggesting it. I will look at the art now so I can tell Jean about it." He walked away.

Sophia looked at Laurence with an amused smile. "He takes getting used to, doesn't he?"

"I don't know who is faster to the point, Tony or your mother."

She acknowledged that she agreed with him with a nod of her head. He looked over at the door and saw William standing around with not much happening, so he led Sophia to the next table.

She asked, "How about you? Are you pleased with the arrangements?"

He stopped and looked at her, "I have absolutely no idea about them. I am stunned this meeting took place today. It was *yesterday* at lunch I suggested Eva *consider* consulting an attorney about how to protect her assets! Your mother wastes no time."

Sophia said, "No, she doesn't. Anyway, it's favorable to you, so you will be pleased when you learn about it."

Laurence felt another tremor of indignation. "I asked for nothing. I expect nothing. There is no reason to give me anything — if we should be married — and that is by no means a certainty. I am not in the mood at all now, if I ever was." Evie reached out to Laurence to hold her, and it steadied his emotions to adjust her body to his. He picked up one of the servings of shrimp with piquillo peppers to offer her, which no surprise, was well received.

Sophia grimaced. "I understand." She sipped the white wine and said, "Mom is rushing ahead again isn't she? I have tried to tell her to chill on all these plans and you'll come around, but she's impatient."

Before he could answer, Drew said in Laurence's ear, "So aren't you going to introduce me to the ladies?" Drew gave Sophia one of his best *would you like to get to know me* looks.

"Drew, this is Eva's daughter Sophia and her granddaughter Evie."

"Well, at last I get to meet more beautiful Russos. Thanks for coming tonight. How's your mom?" said Drew.

"She's great. Enjoying retirement." She smiled at Drew, approving of his attention to her and the red dress.

"What's your role at Russo Enterprises?" Drew said.

"I'm the brand manager and marketing director."

"You're doing a great job. It was a pleasure working with your customers last fall. Why didn't I meet you then?" he said.

"I planned to attend, but the baby was sick at the last minute. I heard wonderful things about it," Sophia said.

Drew felt sure she was thinking, *what else would you like to know about me?* So he ventured, "Are you interested in Basque art?"

"Maybe, if you would tell me something about it."

"Let me show you my favorite piece."

They walked away leaving Laurence holding the baby. He looked at them with astonishment, but they didn't notice. They weren't looking at him.

Chapter 34

With Evie in his arms, Laurence joined William at the front door. "Glad we're not busy. I'm a one-fisted ticket taker."

William laughed at him, "I didn't realize you could check kids at the door here."

"Apparently so. What have I missed?" said Laurence.

"Nothing. This is a slow beginning. I hope that doesn't forecast the rest of the evening. She's cute and not crying. Whom does she belong to?" William said.

"Eva's daughter Sophia in the red dress over there with Drew."

"I see her. Good package. She's a friend of yours?"

"The only one in the family so far. She's the best of the bunch anyway."

"Is it good news she's here?" William said.

"I guess so. I don't know which way all that is going. I like being single, and women just can't seem to stand it. Why is that?" said Laurence.

William shook his head and smiled.

Bernadette and Henri, both looking stylish, were next at the door. "*Bonsoir!* What an adorable baby you have tonight," Bernadette said. She shook hands with both William and Laurence. Evie kissed Bernadette's cheek when it came close to her. "Oh, what sweetness. May I hold her?"

"You can try." He passed Evie to Bernadette and Evie seemed fine with it.

"This is my son, Henri," said Bernadette to Laurence and William.

They all shook hands. Laurence said, "It's a pleasure, Henri. Julia tells me you know more about art than she does."

"No sir, that's impossible, but I am interested."

Laurence gave them both a few strips of tickets. "Feel free to buy someone else a drink while you're mingling. The boss and Julia are both working the floor already."

"Shall I give the baby back to you?"

"Her mother is in the red dress talking to Drew."

"Ah, I see." Bernadette picked out the red dress in the room with no difficulty. "Henri, why don't we say hello to Julia first and then Drew?" They walked away.

"Lust is in the air tonight," said William chuckling.

"I doubt any is coming our way," said Laurence.

"It's enough for me to just observe it without having to go to any effort."

"You're a smart guy."

Julia was standing next to the sold cloud painting. She waved for them to join the group. She introduced them to the couple who were sad to have missed purchasing this piece by only a few hours. Bernadette was sympathetic without revealing her part in the sale.

"Let me show you one of my favorites that's similar in composition," said Julia. She began moving, motioning all of them with her arm to follow her to stand in front of another piece. "The vastness of the landscape is just as powerful, but the large white element here is a snow covered mountain instead of the clouds, with a sliver of grass and the grazing herd of cows to accent it. You get more of a feel of the ruggedness of the terrain. You can practically breathe in the fresh cold mountain air."

Laurence loved overhearing Julia. She was so good at this. She seemed relaxed and enjoying herself.

Drew was describing the tradition of the livestock paintings to Sophia when he heard Bernadette say, *"Bonsoir, Monsieur."* Drew was annoyed to be disturbed and returned the greeting in French without turning around, but Sophia did.

"Oh, my baby! Thank you for bringing her back to me." Sophia reached out for Evie. She cooed at her, "Hello sweetie, are you having fun?" and gave her a kiss on the cheek and put her on her hip.

"Yes, she seems to be enjoying herself, making friends and particularly liking the prawns," said Bernadette.

"Bernadette and Henri, this is Eva's daughter Sophia," said Drew.

Bernadette began enthusiastically in Italian about something, and after a few phrases Sophia responded in Italian. Henri joined in, and Drew just stood there thinking, *I should excuse myself* and after another minute with no break in the Italian repartee, he did so and walked away to check on his large staff and his few guests.

What was he going to do with Bernadette tonight? He really wasn't in the mood to let her share the stage. They would all look foolish presenting to such a small audience. He hoped for a surge in the crowd before the performers arrived. He walked toward Julia in the other room. She happened to see him coming and introduced him to the people she was talking to who, she said, were now quite interested in the painting with the massive snow-covered mountain. Drew said, "Great. That's one of my favorites. Julia could I speak with you for a moment?" The people graciously said, "Please don't worry about us. We'll study it a bit more."

He and Julia walked away a short distance and turned their backs to the room. "Julia, I think we should delay the performers at least 30 minutes to let the crowd build up. Can you call them and tell them not to hurry?"

"I think it's too late for that. It's possible they may have enough of the Basque club with them to make up the difference."

"Really? That would be terrific. Any way to check on it?"

"Why don't you call your good friend the president and ask him how many are in his party tonight. We can delay the performance until they get here."

"Thank you, Julia. Problem one solved. Now what are we going to do about Bernadette? I can hardly look her in the eye, much less give her the floor."

"I understand, but she came tonight because you asked her to come and work. I think you have to let her do what she did for the press party. She was good. Everyone loved her. After that she can work the crowd having been officially introduced as part of our crew. If she sells something else tonight you may get over what you're feeling now."

He looked at her and shook his head. "You keep saving me. Thank you. I'll call the president right now."

The timing of the call was perfect. They hadn't left yet and he said, "I'm sorry we're running late. If you count the kids we could easily have 30 more people in 30 minutes."

"We love kids, and they will love the dancing and music." Drew hung up and wondered if he had been a good liar all his life or whether he was improving with age. His first problem was solved. The second would be aided by more time chatting with the delightful woman in the red dress. He needed to lift his spirits with a strong dose of beauty. He made his way around the room and let all the employees know the performance was delayed until 7 p.m. as the Basque club was running late. He saw Sophia with her brother at the third *pintxo* station with the baby on her hip. They were both eating chorizo and sipping red wine.

"Hello again," he said to both of them. "What's your first impression of the art?"

Tony said, "I like the machinery and the structures."

Sophia looked amused at Drew over the rim of her wine cup. "If you told me a bit more about it, I think I'd like it more."

"It would be my pleasure to tell you more."

Tony said, "We need to go."

Drew said, "Oh, no, you can't leave now. The performers are on the way. It's a wonderful show of music, dancing and poetry. It only lasts 30 minutes and will give you tremendous insight into the Basque view of life."

"I'd love to stay a little bit longer, Tony. Why don't you call Jean and ask her if she wants to join us? She could be here in 20 minutes. I bet she'd love the show."

"We will be giving a brief presentation about the art before they begin. Would she enjoy hearing that?"

Tony looked at both of them and said, "I'll ask her if she would like to come." He looked around and found a spot about ten feet away from them to make his call.

Drew said in a low tone of voice close to her ear, "If she doesn't want to come, I'll call my car service to take you home. No reason for you to miss the show."

"That's a lovely offer." She smiled at him.

He nodded. "Also, there are quite a few kids coming shortly, which may be extra fun for your daughter."

"How perfect," Sophia said.

Tony returned and said Jean was on the way. Drew gave Bernadette a high sign, and she made her way over to them.

"Bernadette, this is Eva's son Tony. He likes the farm equipment. His wife, who is an artist, is coming to see the next performance. Would you give him a few highlights of the tradition for perspective while he waits for her?"

She nodded at Drew, looked at her watch and answered affirmatively and then told Tony what a good student his mother was. He looked confused. Bernadette said, "I'm your mother's French teacher. Come with me." She started speaking to him in Italian. He looked back over his shoulder at Sophia and Drew as he walked away with Bernadette.

Sophia laughed. "That was well done, sir."

"You want to see my office?"

"Sure. You have more art there?"

"Of course. That's what I want to show you."

He led her back to the hidden door. No one but Julia, Bernadette and Laurence noticed them disappear into the wall.

When they went into his office he closed the door and said, "Please feel free to take off your lovely Italian shoes and rest your feet. I really need to add seating out in the gallery, maybe a long bench in each room. What do you think?"

"That's a good idea." She settled Evie on the end of the couch against the armrest and sat down a few feet away from her on the couch and took off her heels. "Tell me about this art. This is your private collection that's not for sale?"

Drew sat back in one of the swivel chairs near her and said, "Yes, unless someone wants to buy it."

"Well, I like how eclectic it is. Romance next to rebellion, the pastoral next to the urban, love next to lust."

"That's a fast assessment. Which is love and which is lust?" said Drew.

"The women are all voluptuous, but I think this one has love in her eyes, not lust, like this one does."

"You are amazing to pick up on that in 10 seconds. Hardly anyone has ever spotted that even after studying them a great deal," said Drew.

"I would think anybody could see it."

"You'd be surprised how few people recognize the difference. What you see is true."

"Are the artists friends of yours?" Sophia asked.

"They are my paintings."

"Really? You painted all these?"

"Yes. I had great ambitions as a young man to be an artist. I can remember exactly how I felt as I was working on each one. I enjoy the energy they emit from then and the emotion they bring me now."

"That's extraordinary to be able to capture your history and retell it whenever you like, maybe even rewrite it. That must be satisfying. I would love to be able to do that, particularly the rewriting part."

"Everybody has their own way to tell their story. What do you like to do to express yourself?"

"You say you *were* ambitious. You look successful to me and as though you've lost none of your ambition."

"Oh, I've done well enough. Ambitions change over time. The gallery suits me more than the atelier. What was your original ambition?"

"To be hugely successful and lead a glamorous life." She smiled at him.

"Have you done it?" He grinned at her.

"Absolutely. I spend my days in a mammoth cold warehouse looking at packaging or behind a computer screen trying to find the right advertising placement for the packages. At night I read my daughter a story before we fall asleep on the couch." She glanced over at Evie who was asleep. "See how she responds to a couch and a good story?"

"What are you aiming for now?"

"The usual. More money and a housekeeper."

He laughed. "Symbols of success around the world. I have a good cleaning service. They are worth every penny. What do you for fun?"

"Seriously?" She looked at him and he nodded, "Nothing. I'm about four and a half years away from enjoying myself. But I have plans for it."

"What will you do?"

"I can give you my top 10 vacation destinations. I want tickets every week to the theater or music and live-in help that can cook."

"That is a good list. I'd like all those things too."

"Really? You need live-in help?" Sophia was laughing.

When the buzzer rang, letting him know he was needed at the front, he said, "Sorry, business calls." He stood up and offered her his hand. "Do you need help with your shoes?"

Sophia laughed again. "A priceless offer! You don't know how much I'd like some help with my shoes, but I can manage, thank you." She slipped on her shoes and picked up the sleeping baby.

The gallery was a bit busier than before, but the bell had signaled the mob of Basque people at the front door getting strips of tickets from Laurence and William and clamoring about the art. The performers in costume were leading some of their new friends around and pointing out art. Drew abandoned Sophia to quickly reach the group with the president and try to encourage the crowd forward away from the door and to spread it out.

He led the president and entourage of 10 people to the first *pintxo* station. He went back for another group that now had their tickets in hand and led them to the second station. There was no reason to drink in order now. He went back for the last of the crowd standing around Laurence and William. He said, "William, take our new friends to the third station and help pour to get them started. As soon as they each have some wine, we will begin the show." He grabbed the cordless microphone from Julia's desk drawer and put it in his pocket.

"What's the count, Laurence?" Drew said.

"62."

"Well, it's not last night, is it?"

"No. We could still get some more later on."

"Did Tony's wife arrive?"

"Yes."

"Good. Carry on. I need to get my art experts ready." Drew looked around for Julia and Bernadette who were on opposite sides of the gallery talking to people. He approached Julia in the small room and gave her the three-minute signal. He went back to the big room and joined the small group Bernadette was talking to and announced the show was about to begin. He saw Henri, his hands animated, in front of a rusty tractor painting and speaking in Italian to Tony and a woman, who must be the wife. Free labor speaking Italian to a fundraising customer might turn him into an art buyer! Henri was a fringe benefit of Bernadette's presence that he appreciated more every day. Having linguists around the gallery improved the ambiance. If Henri was as smart about art as Julia said he was, maybe there was a part time job for him here. He and Julia certainly looked handsome together. They'd make a swell sales presentation team.

Bernadette followed him to the side of the room and he said, "We'll do it like the press party except be more brief. They already know the history. Who knows what they know about the art traditions. Let's assume they don't know and try to keep it to 10 minutes total for the three of us. Let's stand together the whole time to save time so we can move quickly on to the music."

She nodded and said nothing. They moved to the center of the big room, and his welcoming words got their attention. The room went quiet. After a minute of pleasantries, he passed the microphone to Bernadette who greeted them all in French and then Spanish and then Euskara. The applause was thunderous for a small crowd. Drew was impressed that she had learned a few Basque words for the weekend. She had told him she didn't know it at all. Her on-the-spot editing of the material to hit the highlights in three minutes was good too. He followed her by emphasizing the traditions with three of the paintings from the heritage, the farming and landscape sections. He introduced Julia who had moved into position and led the crowd in a procession into the small room.

If the performance had been well received the night before, the response was amplified now that half the audience was Basque. People were clapping in time with the music and tapping toes and kids were doing their own version of dancing to the music. When the performers had finished and joined the crowd to eat and drink, Drew assessed where he should begin his rounds. A well-dressed middle-aged couple he didn't know lingering on the sidelines looked like the best candidates. He introduced himself to them and inquired how they had enjoyed the show. They turned out to be students of Bernadette's and would soon visit France and the Basque Country.

"Are you familiar with the art tradition?" he asked.

"We've been studying it as part of our class conversation. We're in the intermediate class," said the man. "We're quite taken with the art."

"How marvelous. What do you like here tonight?" said Drew.

"The landscapes are my favorite," said the wife.

"I like the animal scenes. I think the Basques have a way with sheep."

"You're right," said Drew. "No one paints them better."

"What do you think the prices will be like in France compared to here?" asked the husband.

"They will be less here because these artists are not well known, and there isn't a steady market for their work as there is in France, which gets so many visitors. The shipping is an expense to consider as well. I couldn't comment about sales tax but Bernadette may know what the current policy is. I envy you your trip. Nice talking to you."

Drew walked away envisioning several red sold dots and more commissions for Bernadette. He didn't need to spend another minute with those people whose minds were already made up. Getting a bargain price, saving money on taxes and shipping all combined into a powerful stimulant to purchase immediately. He was feeling downright cheerful after that conversation and looked around for his next candidates. If Bernadette sold two more paintings tonight, he would be open-minded about her mysterious past and focus on her present ability to help make this exhibit a financial success. Everyone had a few situations they regretted and would rather forget about and not discuss with anyone.

The Russo party looked like they were getting ready to go. He went to the door to join Laurence for farewells.

With the baby over her shoulder, Sophia took Drew's hand and said, "Thanks for a wonderful evening. I enjoyed everything." She smiled.

He held on to her hand and said, "Thank you for coming. I hope you'll come back when we can spend more time talking."

Tony and Jean didn't offer any hands to shake but they both nodded at him and at Laurence, and Tony said, "Thank you. I think we'll come back tomorrow to look again."

Drew said, "It was our pleasure."

Tony and Jean walked out the door. Sophia put her head on Laurence's shoulder just to be close to him. "So good to see you." He kissed the top of her head and the baby's head. He watched them get into Tony's car.

"What's the count?" Drew said.

"73."

"Sell any souvenirs?"

"A few. I think the club will be buyers on the way out the door."

"Nice to see the Russos," Drew said.

"Yes, I was surprised to see them. They had to remind me I invited them months ago. Sophia is a delight every time. Tony and Jean are an acquired taste."

"Sophia is definitely a delight. Is she married?" said Drew.

"Yes, but he travels a lot."

"I'm so glad I don't have to travel," said Drew.

"Me too," said Laurence.

Chapter 35

Drew arrived at the gallery at noon the next day and before he did anything else, he admired all the red sold dots on the wall. Bernadette and Julia had each added two more sales of landscapes and abstracts last night. He had sold the sculpture of the crow and one of the shepherd paintings. That was impressive activity from a small crowd. All the red dots would inspire more people to buy today. They were the seal of approval that the art was good at the price and wouldn't last long. The math on the commissions and finder's fees made him feel cheerful. They had celebrated last night after the front door was locked with a glass of wine in the office, and he had sent them all home in cabs as a bonus for their hard work. He hadn't felt like driving anyone home. He wanted to be alone and contemplate his mixed emotions.

Sophia Russo had made an impression on him, and she knew it. She was the most exciting woman he had met in a long time. Would she come back to make another attempt at connecting with him or was she just having fun on a rare night out? A good thing about owning a gallery where women were concerned — most of the time — was that the door was open at specific hours, and anyone could come in uninvited. He didn't have to ask her for her number. He knew she worked and it was nearby. All she needed to do, if she were interested, was to return. The way she held his hand on the farewell made him think that she would.

Bernadette had regained his good graces as Julia predicted she would. She was an excellent salesman. She wasn't trying to be personal with him. He would overlook what he didn't understand and think the best about her. After this exhibit was over, he would write her a big check, and he probably would never see her again. That seemed a little harsh but unless Julia and Henri cooked up some social invitation he couldn't refuse, he doubted their paths would cross.

The success of the opening weekend of the show made him feel vindicated for chasing the wisp of an idea about a Basque exhibit and making it happen. He was proud of his work. He had searched for and found artists doing their art without much recognition. Now his customers had discovered them and this would change their lives. Today he planned to call all the artists whose work had sold so far and tell them the story of each sale — that would be rewarding to him and joyous to them.

He thought the artists would love hearing how the art in this exhibit startled people with its focus on working and living with the land. The response to the substance of the everyday activities was heartening to him and would be to them too. A few of them were going to be pleased he had raised the price from the amount originally agreed to.

Saturday morning over breakfast Laurence was still thinking about how much he had enjoyed his cab ride home. He couldn't remember the last time he had traveled alone by taxi. It was a small gift from Drew with a big impact. Drew knew how to make you feel appreciated and therefore willing to do whatever when he called on you. The evening had turned out to be extremely successful with six more sales. That's what inspired the generosity of the taxis home for everyone, three taxis, no shared rides with two or more stops. That was so everyone could privately savor the ambiance of the free, personal service. Bernadette would feel valued driving through Capitol Hill's sidewalks busy with the young bar and music crowd. Julia and Henri could get a head start on celebratory sex en route to Pioneer Square. He had enjoyed the quiet and quick ride to Queen Anne without any of the late night bus riders being obnoxious. The character of the bus changed after 10 at night and could seem gross or threatening to the only senior citizen in a suit amongst a much younger, rougher crowd. After drinking and smoking pot that anyone could smell from 10 feet away, groups would occupy the back of the bus in the benches facing each other where they felt the driver couldn't see or hear what they were doing. The boys would insult each other and tussle with each other in the open space between the benches. The girls would make out with boys, throw up or cry. Laurence always sat up front by the driver late at night, but that didn't stop aggressive remarks from inebriated boys who were dying to pick a fight and stupidly thought they could provoke him. Laurence ignored them and pretended he didn't see or hear them. When they settled in the back, he and the driver would shake their heads and say "Kids!"

The business with the attorney rattled him. It was such a classic example of how Eva rushed in. He wished she wouldn't do that. How could she have thought it over in such a short period of time? How did she get Tony on board so quickly? Tony was a methodical thinker and would have insisted on studying the proposal before agreeing to it. Did she involve Sophia and Marco, or was this just Eva commanding her group to do what she wished with no votes? What could it possibly mean that the arrangement was favorable to him? Instead of reassuring him by following his wishes, the way she did it upset him. Would anyone believe him that he hadn't asked for favors? Sophia would, but probably no one else.

Eva would undoubtedly get some report of the exhibition from Tony and Sophia. Would Sophia include flirting with Drew? He could predict Eva erupting over that foolish behavior for an intelligent, married woman, much less with a child on her hip. Eva knew exactly how bold Drew could be in paying attention to women of every age. Sophia would be smart to keep quiet about enjoying it. She didn't get out often, and it was easy to imagine how exhilarating it was for her to be in the gallery surrounded by the art and the flowing wine. She probably had enjoyed herself dallying with Drew as much as he had with her. Laurence had frequently watched Drew elevate his mood by flirting. There was no harm in it for either one of them as far as Laurence was concerned.

The Basque performers were in the middle of a filming session when Laurence arrived to set up the box office. He decided to quietly sit in Julia's chair until they were finished so he wouldn't get in the way walking back and forth across the room to the office for his supplies. He noticed the performers had exactly the same big smiles and jokes they used for a big audience. Julia stood next to the cameraman. Drew must be in the office. Luckily they finished just before the caterer and her servers arrived. His setup still wasn't quite complete when he opened the door for the first wave of visitors. He felt a hum of adrenalin. Click, click, click. The gallery filled up quickly. It was going to be a good night.

After the first performance was over Laurence said goodbye to about 50 people exiting with smiles and enough packages of souvenirs to make him happy. The welcomes began soon after. He could have used William's help, but the servers needed him more to keep the wine flowing. Drew, Julia and Bernadette were swamped with requests for more information about the art. Laurence told a few people who asked him for assistance to ask Henri.

"Hello, Laurence!"

Laurence looked up from taking money to see Marco Russo standing back in the line waving at him. He had his wife with him and possibly the people behind him as they all waved too. He waved back and motioned them forward and said to the people closest to him, "Would you please step aside for just a minute. This man is making an important delivery."

The crowd parted enough to let Marco and his group by.

"Thank you so much for the special service," he said to Marco and gave each one of them a strip of tickets and pointed them toward the food tables. Marco and his company gave him a big smile and disappeared into the crowd.

For the group that had nicely stepped aside he gave them extra strips of tickets for their patience to soothe any ruffled feelings.

The last performance should have started. There was lull in the room as people waited for it to begin. He scanned the full parking lot for stragglers he could encourage to hurry so they wouldn't miss anything. A big black car pulled up by the front door and Amy got out of the front seat and Eva got out of the back.

Eva looked royal in a purple dress with long sleeves and a white wool shawl wrapped around her shoulders and tied in front. Amy looked like she always looked, pretty in trousers and a silk blouse. She had no coat. They were talking to each other, and then both beamed at him as they approached the door.

"Hello, Laurence," said Amy.

"Hello, Sweetheart, said Eva. She offered him her cheek, which he affectionately rubbed with his cheek, inhaling her special aroma.

"You look lovely tonight, Mrs. Russo," Laurence said.

"Thank you."

"Are you ladies alone?"

Amy said, "No, Kevin is parking the car. How's it going?"

"We have been busy. Drew is happy. The last performance should be starting soon. You'll want to grab glasses of wine before the show starts." He gave them both two strips of tickets.

"I'm so glad we haven't missed anything," Amy said.

"I don't know how far he may have to go to find parking. You might as well go in and get started. I'll point him in your direction. He's a good back row man anyway."

During the performance Laurence saw Eva coming toward him and wondered if she considered the business with the attorney so important that she had to tell him tonight. She stood close to him and said nothing as though she were merely watching the show with him. Without thinking he put his arm around her shoulder, which felt comfortable and normal.

When the audience applauded after a dance she whispered, "I had a long talk with Sophia today that I'll have to tell you about sometime. She enjoyed her visit here last night and wants to come back soon. The most important thing is I've decided to ignore Sophia's advice to chill out. I had to tell you in person I can't bear another night without you."

"What are the terms?"

"There are no terms. There isn't anything important enough to keep us apart. I've been stubborn for no good reason. I just want to be with you. Will you come home with me tonight to stay forever? We can talk there."

"You don't want to be Mrs. Hansen?"

"No, not unless you want me to be. I have been Mrs. Russo for so long I think I'm fine that way."

"I want to hear everything, but I see business coming our way. We'll talk later."

Eva helped Laurence sell a few strips of tickets during the next song and dance. After the performance was over they did brisk business in tickets, even though there was no food left. Without consulting, him she started offering a special on two-strip purchases. People seemed happy to buy two. Laurence remembered now that had been Charles' original idea and he'd forgotten about it, so he didn't say anything sharp to her about taking over his box office business. He took the money or credit card for the souvenir sales and she handed the package to the customers, thanking them. He listened to her talking with people. She smiled at everyone. Julia and Bernadette both sold more paintings to the second crowd. Henri sold one too. He gave Henri a big thumbs up for his sale so quickly after being pressed into service. It was a good thing Eva was helping him. People spending big bucks on paintings shouldn't have to wait for anything. He gave each salesman an extra strip of tickets to give the buyers for celebration wine.

As the farewells began and the crowd thinned, Drew came by for a head count and was amused at the duo diligently working the box office desk.

"More free labor! I love it. Thanks for helping out, Eva."

"I love working. Anytime you need me, you let me know. Drew, in case you didn't know, which I doubt, you and your gallery made a big impression on my daughter Sophia last night."

Drew looked pleased, "Wonderful. I hope she'll visit again soon."

Eva said, "Probably not. She's too busy."

Before Drew could respond to that, Laurence said, "You need to know I promoted Henri to salesman tonight when you were swamped. He just made his first sale, and I helped him print the receipt. He's a smart young man."

"Well, well. Thanks for managing the situation. I'll have to talk to him about the terms of employment and discuss it with my business partner. Eva, did you notice the painting of the rugged pine tree on the mountain? That's the one I think you need to celebrate the exhibition." He waited for her response.

"Oh, I haven't had time to look at the exhibit. I'll take a look later. How's Bernadette doing?"

"She's a great salesman and you heard her speak tonight. She's been helpful and will earn money from the show."

"Will you keep her on afterward?"

"I don't know."

"Why not?"

"Can we talk another time, maybe at your place while I hang your new art?"

"Of course. We'd love to have you over anyway. My point is if there is a problem with the referral, I wish you would tell me why so I won't refer her again."

"OK. We'll talk." He walked away to check on the servers.

Eva looked at Laurence, "What could that possibly mean?"

He shook his head. "I have no idea. She seems fine to me. She has excellent presentation skills and also important to Drew, she has a good attitude late at night when he wants to start a new project."

"I thought he would find her charming."

"Chemistry is personal. You can't predict it."

"Oh well, I tried. Let's have him over soon. Do you like the pine tree painting?"

"Sure, but please clarify, what sort of entertaining are you talking about? Why would you have Drew over?"

"Because he is a friend of both of ours. I think it would be fun to have one or two people over to sit on the balcony with us to share our view. We can pour nice wine and offer them a homemade cracker, nothing else. We'll have stimulating conversations. Can you see that as our unique entertaining style, low key and high quality?"

"I guess so. But I don't think of him as a friend. He is my employer. We'll have to talk more about that, but not here. This event is almost over and I need to clean up. Why don't you help me count the money and we'll take a taxi home? Drew will call his service for us."

"I love counting money!"

Amy and Kevin approached to say goodnight. Amy said she'd like to buy a souvenir poster. Marco and his crowd appeared as she was paying, and they said they'd like souvenirs too.

"Mom, if you're not too busy, do you want a ride home now?"

"Thank you no, dear. We have to do the accounting now. We'll take a taxi later."

He looked at his group and shook his head. "My mom is counting the money here. Thanks for inviting us, Laurence. Hope to see you soon."

Kevin said, "Great show tonight."

Eva said, "You were marvelous to bring me. Let's get together soon for the rabbit."

Laurence looked taken aback at Eva. Amy waved goodbye and took Kevin's hand to walk out the door. When they were gone Laurence said, "What are you doing making plans with all these people?"

"They are going to become friends. You'll enjoy yourself, I promise."

Laurence shook his head. Eva was too much sometimes.

The *Oinkari* performers and their local hosts surrounded Drew in an emotional farewell. Everyone was toasting what a huge success the three nights had been.

They were proud to have been responsible for bringing out crowds of people in Seattle to experience the Basque culture. They had thoroughly enjoyed themselves and made new friends. Everyone posed for a number of photos on different phones. When they were gone, the room was much quieter.

Eva asked Bernadette her opinion of the pine tree painting. They stood together in front of it for a few minutes. Bernadette provided some background on the artist and the tradition. She said it was a good choice from the exhibit. Eva said she would think about it. If she were going to buy it, she wanted Bernadette to get the sale. Bernadette hugged her.

Finally the door was locked. Julia's shoes were off, and she was jumping around. She took Henri's hand and said formally to the crowd, "Henri made a sale tonight and has one coming back tomorrow! Thank you, Laurence, for promoting him when we needed him!"

Henri and Laurence received a quick round of applause. Laurence shrugged and made a small bow. Henri modestly said, "Thank you. I'm happy to help."

His mother looked proud. Drew shook Henri's hand and said good job, looking amused at his growing staff. He was proud of how this group did whatever it took to make the business happen.

Laurence picked up the cash box and announced he was going to count the money. He and Eva headed toward the hidden door with Charles and William close behind with two bottles of wine. Drew looked at Julia and Bernadette with the question of the night.

Julia said with a big smile, "Two sold tonight, plus two come-backs."

Bernadette said, "The same," without a big smile.

He motioned them all toward the back and said, "Shall we?"

Holding hands, Julia and Henri made their way toward the office. Bernadette didn't move. She paused a moment looking at Drew and said softly, "Please tell me what's on your mind about me. I feel a big change the last two days."

"It's been a long day. Why don't we talk next week?"

"I would rather know now if there is something about my performance that is unsatisfactory. Perhaps I can change it, or perhaps I won't come back next week."

He sighed and sat down on the edge of the desk. "You want to sit down?"

She sat down beside him and waited for him to say something.

"Who are you? Where did you come from? Why are you here? I've done a little checking around and come to the conclusion you must be in the Witness Protection Program because there is no information about you anywhere."

"This is not about my performance?"

"No, your job skills are excellent."

"What does it matter who I am if I'm doing my job well?"

"It makes me worried you may be trying to rob me or my customers or my artists."

"I've been honest all my life. I've never robbed anyone of anything."

"So you say, but why all the secrecy? You have gone to a lot of trouble to erase your past and create a new persona."

"I don't want to share my sad story with you. I am making a new life. I am doing well in every respect. Please, believe me, I bring you no trouble. I admire the business you have built here with this gallery. It means a lot to me to be helping with this exhibit. I love the work. I am good at it. I want to make the money. Isn't that enough?"

He thought for a while and shook his head. "I don't know if it is enough. I need to trust you, and I don't feel that way anymore now that I know you are not who you say you are."

"You know exactly who I am. You have seen me work. You know my son. You have met my students and colleagues. That's who I am."

"OK." He hesitated. "I'll try to deal with that, even though it's disturbing to me. It's been a successful opening weekend, but it's not over, and I will need your help to sell out the whole show."

"Thank you. I won't disappoint you."

They shared a long moment of eye contact that sealed the bargain. She said, "I think I will go home now and not join the others in the office."

"Let me call you a taxi."

"That's kind of you."

The second bottle of wine was in circulation when Drew took a seat on the end of the couch by the door. At the other end Julia, was holding her hair on top of her head and Henri was giving her a neck massage. Eva occupied his desk chair with Laurence standing over her shoulder. William and Charles were sitting around the table with the wine bottles and handed Drew a cup of wine.

Charles said, "Where's Bernadette?"

"She was tired. So did we make money tonight?"

Laurence said, "Yes, we did. Tickets and souvenirs were our best night so far. Five paintings and your horse sculpture boosted the total nicely."

"Julia, do you think your come-backs are solid?"

"I think so. Bernadette did too. She'll be here right before the opening to catch hers as they come in the door."

"What does our newest salesman think about the prospects of converting his maybe to a definite?" Drew asked Henri.

"She said the colors were perfect. They are going to measure when they get home. Is that a good indication?"

"Yes!" Everybody laughed.

Drew said, "Good job, everybody. Let's toast the amazing Basque people who made this all possible. How many taxis do we need?"

Drew drove home pondering Bernadette's mystery. Could he live with it? He would try. She seemed to be speaking from the heart. But what would she have sounded like if she had a long Interpol record of selling forgeries? He wanted to believe her about her honesty. He did need her *expert* help. Julia was right. Expert was the key word. If he were to guess what was on her resume, his first thought was she was from the museum world. Advanced degrees and assistantships were required before achieving the curator or director job. She had museum polish. If not in a museum, she must have been teaching art history at a university. She hadn't learned anything from him, and she already knew more than he did about art traditions when she came in the door. Again, advanced degrees would be required before landing even a low level position at most schools. Her son had studied art at the Sorbonne. Art, art, art. He'd been so stupid thinking she'd been a French teacher for thirty years. There was no reason to teach French in France. He bet her multiple languages were a routine part of her early education. Maybe she wasn't even French. Maybe she was from Holland or Sweden where knowing five languages wouldn't be unusual. An image search might be simpler than the name search he'd tried. He probably didn't have the correct name anyway. Tomorrow he would take pictures of his crew for publicity purposes and a headshot of her to see what he could learn online.

He also wondered if he'd correctly read between the lines of Eva's mind to hear that Sophia would not be visiting at the gallery again as her mother had told her she'd had too much fun the first visit. That seemed a pity to him, but if Eva bought the pine tree, he probably shouldn't phone Russo Imports and ask Sophia out to lunch, which had been his plan B with her. Lunch was such a perfect time to get together with women who had children in school. He might spontaneously ask her anyway on a slow Wednesday and see what happened next.

Chapter 36

Laurence and Eva held hands in the back of the cab. She was full of how much fun working in the gallery was and how she looked forward to going again. He had to interrupt her. "Please, tell me what your thoughts are on everything between us beginning with entertaining your kids now that we're inviting Drew and being invited other places."

Eva was quiet for a moment. "I think we should try your idea of having each one individually and see how it goes. If the result is an intelligent and worldly evening, I'll tell them that in my new married life I'm not going to be a referee anymore. Maybe I liked that job too much. If they want to see each other, they will have to see each other on their own time. Maybe I've been afraid if I didn't make them get together, they wouldn't. I want them to like each other and get along, but that's one more thing I have to accept isn't in my power to make it happen."

"This process has been painful for you hasn't it?"

"Yes. Thank you for seeing that. Since I gave up my presidential title, I feel like I've been slowly sinking down to the ground level of powerlessness. I didn't realize how lofty I thought I was."

"What are you thinking about my apartment?"

"You should keep it. I don't have room for your beautiful furniture. If you find you don't use the apartment that much, maybe you could sublet it furnished and make a profit."

"Eva, I'm stunned you've come to all this so completely and quickly. What made you suddenly willing to compromise on all these issues?"

"Thinking about how short our time together could be made me feel I can't waste another minute or another day. I already wasted the entire month of December. After lunch with you the other day I went home and called an attorney I've known for many years. He has always been a good thinker coming up with options to help us solve problems in the business. He worked out the succession issues when my husband's dementia couldn't be ignored any longer. Explaining to him how much I love you and wanting to be with you was meaningful to me. He not only believed me and didn't think I was being foolish, he was happy for me to have found you. He helped me reason through how I could be sure you would be OK if something happened to me and not be a complication for my family. He explained it so succinctly to Tony and Sophia, they agreed with no argument that if I die before you, you stay on in my house until you die. The estate will pay the maintenance, utilities and any repairs that are necessary. That isn't a big expense for the man I love, especially since he's convinced he isn't going to live very long." She smiled at him. "Then Tony called Marco and told him he thought it was a good arrangement for all of us. The paperwork is a simple one-page addition to my will."

"Wow. That's favorable all right. I am impressed that everyone is onboard without an argument. I must thank them for having confidence in me even though they haven't known me very long."

"You inspire confidence. You reek of integrity. Everyone notices it." She squeezed his hand.

"Are you sure about not getting officially married?"

"Yes, quite sure. I have married you in my mind. You're my husband now, my companion in joy and sorrow, in sickness and in health. Those are the vows I care about, and I don't need any higher authority to make it so."

"You haven't lost all your presidentialness. I don't think you ever will." He took her hand and kissed it. "OK, I guess I'm yours until death do us part." He kissed her again. She put her head on his shoulder. Sitting in the back of a taxi with his new wife a few blocks from his home on Queen Anne felt momentous. "Do we have any Champagne at our house?"

"Of course. I am ready for this celebration. I even have foie gras if you're hungry."

When they got there — *home*, he thought — he opened a bottle of Champagne from the wine cooler. They toasted the marriage in the kitchen and then toasted each other sitting on the couch. They held hands and kissed between sips. They danced a little bit in front of the couch. They whispered to each other about how lucky they would be for the rest of their lives.

As soon as Julia came into the office for coffee and put a muffin and an apple on the desk, Drew closed and locked the office door. She sat down and looked apprehensive and said, "What?"

"Where is Henri? Did he come in with you?"

"No. He's at home. When his couple comes in, I'll finish it up for him."

Drew sat down on the couch beside her. "Bernadette, and I doubt her name is Bernadette, and I talked last night about her mysterious past. She convinced me that what we see, the French teacher, the tour guide and mother, is who she is and she has no desire to share her sad story with us. She's made a new life and loves working here. She insists she's honest and will bring us no harm."

"Wow." Julia sighed. "That's intense. So what do you think it really means?"

"Something terrible must have happened to her to want to disappear, change her name and start over as someone else without credentials. I can't imagine what. Now I'm insanely curious to know though. Anyway, what's important is that we agreed she will stay with us until the end of the show. I think we can sell it all, but we do need her help. I don't think we need to spend any more time worrying about them robbing us."

"That's a relief. I'm crazy about Henri. I really do like her too."

"What do you think about him being a salesman here?" he said.

"What do you think?" she said.

"I have mixed emotions about it. He's got the same high level education and polish as Bernadette does, but it may be difficult for you to continue to do your great job and not be distracted by him being around all the time. It could be too much togetherness. It will also dilute everyone's commissions." He looked at her to see how she reacted to that.

"I see all that too but without the famous *Oinkari* performers, do you really think we will continue to have these enormous crowds we can't handle by ourselves? We won't get hundreds of people for the cooking demonstration, wine tastings or movie nights. I think it's going to be business as usual from now on but with second and third visits from people who came this weekend and want to make up their minds about buying. I thought Bernadette's job was bringing in special people who wouldn't find their way here otherwise, and therefore it was rightly her fee. I don't think we need her here in general, much less Henri. I thought that his sale last night was a one-off as the comeback may be today. We pay him for the sales but not give him a job. He has a good job."

"You don't want him poaching any more commissions, huh?" He smiled.

"*Exactement.*" She looked at him with a grin. "That's French."

He laughed. "That's my Julia." He smiled at her. "I love your brainpower. We are in agreement about all that. I'm going to tell her we will open for her whenever she can bring tours through, and we'd like her to come in on Saturday afternoons to work with us for a few weeks to see how the crowds are. Does that suit you?"

"Yes." She got up and turned toward the door and then back toward him. "Anything else before I get started?"

"No. We're good. In fact we're great."

She nodded in agreement and unlocked the door.

Drew opened up the credenza near his desk and looked for a camera and collapsible tripod that was stashed behind packages of printer paper. He got it out and examined the settings.

When Laurence and Eva arrived Drew had the camera and tripod set up in the big room in front of the farming scenes. The caterer and the server came in behind them with fresh linens and paper goods. Laurence helped her break down the two food tables they didn't think they would need today and put them away in the storage room, no longer a dressing room for the performers. He got the cash box out of the safe and took it to Eva who was sitting at Julia's desk waiting for him. He showed her how he set up the box office. With no performance, there would be no admission today, but they would sell food and wine tickets as before.

When Bernadette arrived Drew said, "Everybody gather round. We're posing for publicity photos today for a press release and I want you all to come stand together. I want my best two salesmen to be right here and the greeters to be on either side. I will jump in the back at the last minute."

Julia came and stood where he had indicated. Bernadette looked unsure. Laurence and Eva shook their heads no. "You don't need us."

"Yes. Everybody." He pointed to the spot.

Bernadette said, "I'm not an employee. I shouldn't be in the picture."

"Bernadette, stand next to Julia. Laurence you stand here. Eva you stand there. Now, I'm going to take a few practice shots before I jump in so everyone look at me, chin up, look happy to be employed here! This is going to be a piece about a successful gallery going out to all the journalists who attended our press party. Doesn't that seem like a long time ago?" He hoped nobody would notice as he fiddled with the lens and looked into the viewer a few times after practice shots. He took a close-up of Bernadette and then reset the lens for the group photo. Once he had set the time-release button, he placed himself behind Bernadette and Julia. He examined the photo in the viewer and said, "Let's take one more to be sure," and reset the time-release and resumed his place. "Thanks everybody. Let's open the door and get started here."

Drew went back to his office and closed the door but didn't lock it as that would be too unusual. The doorknob turning should be enough notice to change his screen if anyone came in to talk to him. He uploaded the close-up of Bernadette and ran an image match with his favorite application he used for art. Again he found no other pages of the billions available that included a photo of her other than her own site, Facebook and Alliance Française. Too bad none of the newspapers, U.S. or foreign, offered image search. He sat and worked with a pencil and yellow pad on his press release idea. As each person who had attended the press party published an article, he had phoned them to say thanks and he would repeat the thanks in the cover letter to the press release. The best photo of the group would accompany it as proof of what a friendly staff the gallery had. He hoped the diversity of the ages of the staff would be a quiet selling point for anyone too intimidated to come in. If nothing else, this piece might inspire an extra comment about the exhibit in the weekend guides.

The first people through the door were Henri's couple. Julia saw them as Eva was greeting them and Laurence was ready to sell them tickets. She intercepted them and introduced herself as Henri's colleague who would help them as he had not arrived yet but wanted to make sure they were taken care of. She led them over to the painting and said, "This is the one he said you were interested in because the colors were so beautiful."

They stood in front of it holding hands, thinking hard but silently. Julia stood by patiently a few feet away and behind them giving them room, no hurry, no chatter. Everyone else was trying to discretely watch the sale in progress to see how she handled it. After a few minutes went by, the couple looked at each other and smiled and then turned around to Julia and said, "We'll take it."

She gave them a big smile and said, "How wonderful! It is a lovely painting you will enjoy living with every day. Congratulations. Would you like a glass of wine while I do the paperwork?" They nodded but didn't move.

Julia asked the server for two glasses of Cava, which she delivered to them and said, "If you will give me a credit card, I'll take care of everything." They clicked plastic cups and sipped and looked very excited but said nothing.

Julia returned with a clipboard for the man to sign the receipt, and she put his copy in an envelope with the copy of the bill of sale. She carefully pressed the red sold sticker on the wall underneath the painting. "Would you like me to take a photo of you with it?"

They still hadn't said a word, but he nodded and pulled his phone out of his pocket and handed it to her. She posed them to the side of the painting and said, "Cheers!" and as they said "cheers" back she snapped several photos. Julia said, "It's very exciting to buy art, isn't it?" They nodded again and just kept standing there looking back and forth at each other and at the painting. She left them in peace and brought the signed copy back to Laurence to put in the cash box.

Laurence whispered, "Well done. Why don't you turn on the music now so we can chat amongst ourselves without disturbing the customers?"

"Great idea." She smiled at Eva who wore a red and white toile dress sitting in her chair. "You look like you belong here."

Julia and Bernadette stood near the desk. Bernadette whispered, "That was masterful. I learned something from you today. I always want to help, and sometimes saying nothing is more powerful."

"Thanks," Julia whispered back. "The first purchase is a magical moment. They probably can't afford it, and they are contemplating all the years they will be together with the art, and it's overwhelming."

"Exactly," said Bernadette.

"*Exactement*," said Julia.

"Oh, perfectly said. Henri has been teaching you!"

"A few words he uses a lot. It's fun to be able to say it. I think I'd like to really learn it. Should I take some lessons at your school?"

"I will be happy to give you private lessons. You'll learn quickly by practicing with Henri and me."

"Would you like to come over for dinner and make a class?" said Julia.

"That would be great. We'll speak nothing but French the whole evening. That's the fastest way to learn."

Julia pulled her cell phone out of her jacket pocket and called Henri. "I just closed your come-back couple who are speechless and sipping Cava to recover from their big purchase. I think we ought to celebrate your huge commission by having your mom over for dinner. She's going to give me private lessons in French, and you can help." Julia paused and then looked at Bernadette and said, "He says how about tonight? We'll have real Champagne and coq au vin."

"*Merci.*" Bernadette smiled but looked like she might cry.

Chapter 37

The rest of the afternoon had a few busy moments as some groups came in, drank, ate and left. Julia and Bernadette both sold another painting and closed one comeback but the others were no shows. That was only mildly disappointing and not unexpected. Maybe they would appear when the gallery reopened on Tuesday. They had sold so much already they were pleased and not worried.

Laurence had moved the visitor's chair so he could sit beside Eva behind the desk. They talked about the pine tree painting. They felt like Henri's couple contemplating all the years ahead together with the painting, marking the grand decision to never be apart again. They were framing more souvenir photos when a woman with big sunglasses and masses of dark curls tied on top of her head came in the door. She was stylish in a fitted long black dress and a long brown textured wool coat. Laurence was immediately on his feet with a warm welcome. "Please come in and have a look at our Basque art. We're serving Spanish wine and *pintxo*s today a buck a serving. That's optional."

She hesitated looking around the gallery. "I think I'll just look," she said and put her sunglasses in her purse. She began with the heritage section and seemed to read every word. She then moved on to the next section.

Laurence exchanged glances with Eva that meant she might be a buyer. Bernadette was talking with a couple about the landscapes and noted the new visitor. Julia also looked at her while listening to an older man talk about color fields. When the woman passed by Bernadette,

Laurence thought they seemed to size each other up but said nothing. Two equals was what it looked like to him. He'd have to wait to ask Eva what she thought when no one could hear them.

When the woman passed by Julia she glanced at her and Julia gave a nod of recognition but got no response. The abstracts and sculptures seemed to interest her the most. She didn't ask any questions. On her way out, she stopped to speak to Laurence at the desk and said, "I'd like to leave a message for Drew."

He said, "Shall I ask him to come out and speak with you?"

"Sure. I didn't know he was here."

Laurence hit the call button on the desk, and Drew appeared ready to charm whoever had summoned him. Laurence saw him stifle a double take at the sight of the woman from the back, so he definitely knew her or thought he did. Drew walked across the room with a welcome smile. She turned around at the sound of his steps and watched him approach. Laurence could see there was nothing normal about this reunion. Drew gave her a slight bow. "Thank you for coming. Please join me in my office to talk."

Julia gave her colleagues a conspirator's look. When it was polite to leave their conversations they met at the desk. Julia whispered, "Guess who that is?"

None of them had any idea but were all fascinated to learn anything about the intriguing visitor.

"Alexis," she said. "I'm almost positive. You all know her as the model for his painting of love swathed in silk gauze, but she's also an artist and I believe the one who broke his heart when he was young and still painting."

Eva was quick to ask, "What does it mean that she came today?"

"We invited her to come see the exhibition. It's rumored she has a cache of nihilistic art that no one has seen. Drew wants to see it. It would be huge for us if she agrees to us selling it for her."

Bernadette mouthed a silent "Oh" but didn't say anything else.

Laurence said, "I hope it means a unique exhibition in our future."

When Drew and the woman emerged from the office they walked to the front door without saying anything to anybody. The farewell was all in the eyes except Drew saying, "Let's talk soon." She nodded to agree.

Drew saw the group around the desk waiting to hear a report on the visitor. He said, "Old friend. Bernadette, please go home if you like. It's so slow."

She said she'd stay because she was having dinner with Henri and Julia.

He shrugged. "This could be the way of it now. We'll see how this week goes when we won't be offering food and wine, but unless you have special tour groups to bring in, which we hope you will, I don't think we'll need you until next Saturday."

"I understand. I have to teach Tuesday and Thursday nights, and I hope to bring to the gallery both the beginning and the intermediate class together to practice. Shall I talk to them about coming next Saturday afternoon?"

"I will be delighted to be here to welcome them any time you can schedule a visit with them. We always have wine, but if you want we can arrange for some food too. Between Uwajamaya and Laurence, it's easy to do. You could plan to hold your classes here on a Tuesday or Thursday night if you wanted to."

"Eva, what do you think of having our class here?"

Eva said, "That's a good idea. Either day is fine with me."

Bernadette said, "Drew, I'll phone everyone in both classes and let you know how many can make this location. You know the couple you met the other day will be part of it." She smiled at him. "Who knows, maybe they need to buy something else as they were so happy about all the money they saved."

He nodded affirmatively and asked Laurence for the head count and if they needed anything. They both shook their heads that they were fine. They seemed content to be quietly sitting together. He told the server she could go if she wanted and leave it to Laurence, but she'd have to come back on Wednesday for her pans. She said she'd stay.

Julia followed Drew to the office and once inside said, "So? Is she going to let you see it?"

"Maybe."

"What odds?"

"So far 50-50. I'm thrilled she came, and I am more than willing to play her game. I'm patient."

"Good job," said Julia and left the office, closing the door.

When the doorknob turned again Drew looked up to see Laurence, Eva, Julia and Bernadette coming in for the after-closing chat. They had two bottles of Cava and plastic cups with them. He stood up and said, "How'd we do today?"

Julia said, "We had four sales today for a total of 17, which is exciting. Maybe being open on Sunday is a concept to consider. Taking Monday and Tuesday off would be OK with me."

Eva sat down in one of the swivel chairs and began quickly counting the bills and stacking the credit card receipts. Laurence sat next to her and began pouring five cups of Cava. Julia sat on the end of the couch closest to Drew and put her bare feet up on an empty swivel chair.

Bernadette sat on the other end of the couch but did not put her feet up on the other empty chair.

Julia raised her cup to the crowd. "Cheers everybody. I am so ready for days off. I plan to go barefoot tomorrow and sleep late. I may go shopping tomorrow afternoon for paint and new shoes."

Nobody else said anything.

"Bernadette, no plans for your commission check, which gets bigger every day?" asked Drew.

"No," she said and shook her head. "I don't need to buy anything. I'm saving for my cottage in the country."

"Me too," said Drew. "That's one of the few joys of aging, right? No need to buy any more things, just time to enjoy what you have."

"When did you get enough things?" asked Julia.

"About five years ago," said Drew.

"Eva, how about you?" asked Julia.

"I haven't needed anything for years, and I already got rid of most of my stuff when I moved from a big house to a small apartment, but I just bought a painting so I think I definitely have everything I want now." She looked at Laurence with love in her eyes that everyone noticed.

Drew said, "You two seem very in synch today. Are you keeping any secrets from us?"

They looked at each other and Eva nodded at him to speak. Laurence said, "We married ourselves last night with Champagne. We decided no one was more qualified than we are to make and take the vows. It was a beautiful ceremony. The bride wore purple and served foie gras."

"Congratulations! That's great news," said Drew. He held his cup up to toast.

Julia looked at them with wonderment and a big smile. "Oh my God, that's so cool. I didn't know you could do that. Congratulations!"

Bernadette said something in French with tears in her eyes.

Eva had tears in her eyes too.

"More bubbles for everyone now that you know?" Laurence held up the bottle and offered to top off everyone's cup.

Julia said, "Sure. Will you have a party to celebrate?"

Eva looked at Laurence and said, "We haven't thought about that yet. Do you want a party?"

Laurence looked at her. "I don't need a party. Everyone we know is right here."

"Almost everybody," Eva replied.

Drew rolled his eyes. "Well, if your list grows, you could always have a party here. I'd give you a good deal, the family-and-friends discount," he said and laughed.

Laurence frowned at Drew. "Thanks a lot, pal."

Drew grinned at him.

Julia said, "What a great idea to have the wedding party here!"

Laurence shook his head no.

When Eva finished counting the money and sipping her Cava, Laurence stood up to say goodbye. Eva offered a ride to anyone who needed one. Julia looked at Bernadette to see if she was interested in that. She nodded yes but said nothing. Her eyes were still moist.

"Would you mind dropping us in Pioneer Square?" Julia asked.

"Of course not. The Audi out front is ours," said Eva.

Julia got up and followed them out the office door. Bernadette seemed unable to move. Drew said, "Bernadette will be with you in a moment."

He got up and closed the door, which startled her. She looked wary and said, "What?"

He offered her his hand and helped her stand up. He put his arms around her and held her close to him. He could feel her crying.

"It's so unusual to see two people find happiness late in life. It makes an old cynic like me feel I might have a chance. I know you have had tragedy in your life, but I think you will find happiness again too."

She sobbed into his chest, "I don't think so."

He held her close with her head on his shoulder while she cried. When she seemed to have stopped, he whispered, "I think you will." She looked at him, "I guess there are always surprises."

"Yes, there are always surprises. Enjoy your evening with Julia and Henri."

She left and he sat down at his desk to congratulate himself on his sensitivity with Bernadette. She had looked so stricken with the newlyweds' announcement, and he thought he knew what she was feeling. His remarks had been truthful. He really was trying to see other people's point of view, and occasionally he did. He was improving on his perceived self-obsession that he had been criticized for by every woman he'd ever been involved with. He felt sure Alexis showing up today was made possible by the apology he made to her at Amy's last year. He was improving. Next he wanted to review the sales figures and then think about the merits of calling Eva for a phone chat next week versus arranging a dinner meeting to clear the air of some of the mystery about Bernadette. He wanted to feel resolved about everything with Bernadette.

Chapter 38

New developments in alloys for fuselages occupied Laurence's attention while Eva studied her French book, their feet touching, when her cell phone interrupted the quiet. She answered, "Hi, Drew, how are you? We're not too busy, just doing a little reading preparing for French class tonight and the next generation of refueling airplanes at 30,000 feet."

She listened for a few moments and responded to Drew, "Shall we meet you downtown for dinner, or did you want to come up here?"

"Let me talk to Laurence, and I'll call you back."

"Laurence, Drew wants to have a conversation about Bernadette. Seems he doesn't want to talk on the phone but have dinner with us. What do you think?"

"I think it's awkward for me as an employee to be in on a private chat about another employee. He wants to talk to you as a businessperson. It's nothing to do with me. I'll stay home."

"This has to be about the referral."

"Of course it is, but I know nothing of your referral and it's probably better I don't know. I don't want to be in the middle of anything between you two and Bernadette. I like her and think she's great. Nobody is asking my opinion."

"I think he is because he asked both of us."

"Do you think he suspects you were trying to be a matchmaker?"

"Oh, no. He couldn't possibly suspect that."

"I hope you're right about that because if he finds out, he will be annoyed with you, I promise you that. Men do not like women meddling in their personal affairs. That makes me even more sure I want nothing to do with this meeting. I have a good gig at the gallery and I want to keep it."

"Oh dear. Now I'm worried. I better have him come here somewhere on the avenue and let the rush hour traffic wear him out." She thought a bit before she picked up the phone and hit the redial. "Drew, why don't you meet me at How to Cook a Wolf? Laurence has other plans tomorrow night. Wasn't I a good new wife to ask him before I committed?"

Drew arrived a few minutes before Eva walked into the restaurant. He'd expected it to be crowded early in the evening, but it wasn't. Damned Recession — the newspaper kept saying it was over, but you couldn't tell that by the empty seats everywhere. He ordered a martini, and she ordered a glass of Prosecco. They sipped and leisurely studied the short menu. Prawns and leeks with linguini was his choice.

She said, "I want the veal bolognese with conchiglie. This is one of the few things I cook myself, and I want to know what this chef does differently. He's highly regarded for his sauces."

After the server left Eva said, "It's so nice of you to invite me. Are we celebrating my new painting or my marriage?"

"You know I always love to see you, and it's a treat to have you to myself. I know it's difficult to be without the new husband even for an hour, so I appreciate you coming. How are the newlyweds doing?"

"Very well. It's a marvelous feeling to have the future look so bright. I feel very lucky."

"Everyone is happy for you. There were few dry eyes when you made your announcement. I had a pang in my heart and knew what Bernadette was feeling. Did she cry all the way to Pioneer Square?"

"No. She recovered in the car, wiped her eyes and told us how thrilled she was for us."

"Did she ever tell you anything about her marriage breaking up?" Drew said.

"No. I really know nothing about her life in France."

"How did she happen to come to Seattle?"

"Oh, the usual, I think. She knew someone who moved here. There's a small ex-pat community, and they have a club of sorts for French-speaking people with branches around the world. That's how you get started meeting people and networking for jobs."

"Did she tell you where she used to teach?"

"No. Why haven't you asked her all these questions if you're curious?"

"I don't like to pry. I just thought with the two of you being friends and women, she might have shared more personal information with you than she would me."

"Well, we're not really dear friends yet. We're business-women who respect each other. We're getting to know each other, but we're not at the point where we sit down and have a heart to heart about the faults in our first husbands, if we get to that at all."

"I see. I thought you were confiding in each other to inspire your referral to me."

"Drew, why don't you ask me why I referred her to you?"

"Eva, you have a direct style. I do not. I like to hear what people will tell me before I push for more details."

"It's quite simple. During class she was talking about how visiting museums wherever you go enhances your trip and your life afterward. Although it's a beginner's class where we learn to ask directions and what a ticket costs, not art theory, it was clear to me she is passionate about art, and we talked after class about the business of art. She hasn't the proper credentials to teach art here but said she would love to be involved in the art business in some way beyond the tours she gives. As I heard more from Laurence about the Basque exhibit and the usual worries about where the customers would come from, I started thinking about how Bernadette could be helpful to you. I envisioned her with her European tourists walking around downtown Seattle from the library to the museums to the Sculpture Park. Knowing how tourists like to shop, her art tours seemed like a lucrative niche market to me. I love developing niche markets. Why not bring them to your gallery where they could help you by buying something? It's a win-win for everyone." She looked at him and smiled.

He didn't say anything for a while. "Your mind is a work of art. You know I love anyone helping me. I guess everyone knows it." He shook his head. "Who cooked up the art gallery tour sales arrangements?"

"I probably did that. You have to jump-start niche markets. They need impetus to build energy to grow. Bernadette and I strategized, and she did a little research."

"No one thought they were lying to me or misleading me?"

"It's a great idea and you were an excellent test that clearly shows merit to expand our strategy on. Her success with the Basque art sales will guarantee two or three other galleries will be on board soon. It's very exciting how quickly this model is growing. By next year she could have six galleries."

"What's your cut in this scheme?"

"Nothing."

"Nothing! Sorry, I don't believe that. You're generous but not an altruist."

The entrees arrived, and Eva suggested they have a glass of Nero d'Avola. "This is a Sicilian wine to get to know because it's full bodied, dry and easy to drink. It's perfect with my bolognese, not as perfect with your prawns, but still fine. And it's a value compared to my favorite Barolo. Charles and William will be amazed you know about it."

"They would be amazed if I remember the name tomorrow. Let's get back to lying and misleading me," he said.

"Drew, there is no crime in the strategy, and no harm done. It worked and your business is better for it. See the positive side of this."

"That is not as simple as you paint it. I don't know how I will get my brain to wrap around this situation as anything other than misleading lies and lies of omission. She had no other gallery clients. This is not a concept anyone else is using. It stinks, Eva."

"How many paintings has she sold so far?"

"I don't know."

"Well, there *you* go misleading *me*. You know exactly how many and what her fees are to date and what your share is based on those sales. You are good with numbers."

"Eva, Let me try to guess what your cut will be after your test gets out of beta mode. A sliding scale with each new gallery added?"

"You are good with numbers." She smiled at him.

"You shouldn't have retired."

"It was time. Getting married has kept me busy."

"Your new art empire in progress doesn't require too much of your time?" Drew asked.

"Not too much."

"Eva, Does Laurence know about this?"

"No."

"You don't think he would have moral issues with it?"

"He is an engineer. He is not a businessperson. It's two different perspectives."

"What would you say if I told you I suspect Bernadette has been involved in some scandal or tragedy that made her leave France, change her name and hide in Seattle?"

"I don't know anything about that — and if it's true — that's extremely personal business. It's not our concern." Eva was adamant as though delivering an ultimatum.

"That doesn't bother you?"

"The world is full of people who change their names because of abusive husbands, ugly families or religious persecution. She can't be in deep hiding if her son is openly living here. She is not an axe murderer. She's living quietly and avoiding publicity."

"You didn't mention crime."

"Drew, get back to reality on this. It's hard to hide these days with the Internet. There are professional hunters for criminals. There's financial incentive for the hunters. She's not a criminal."

"How do you know?"

"Experience. Instinct." She looked directly at him and held his gaze.

After a few seconds he realized she was done with the subject. "End of the conversation?" he said.

"Yes, I think so," she said.

He paid the check and pondered how to make a smooth exit. He had to get over being mad at her. That wouldn't help anything. "May I give you a ride home?"

"Sure. Would you like to come up and see the space for hanging the painting?" she said.

For a valued customer of fundraising events and art purchases whose children were becoming buyers too, he would get over his annoyance at being duped and his hurt pride that he was so easily set up by this smart woman. He must try to think the best of Eva and Bernadette. He realized that two formidable women in an alliance who were helping him, albeit as they helped themselves, should be appreciated for what they were worth, which was already in the thousands of dollars in his bank account. Being outfoxed by a petite 70-year-old and her French art expert in a Chanel suit shouldn't come as such a surprise to him. After all he was only an art gallery owner who loved beautiful things. He loved his job connecting artists and people. He didn't scheme for anything he didn't already have. He was not in their league. "Sure. That would be nice."

Months later when the Basque exhibit had closed with every piece sold, Laurence lounged on the Italian sofa with his eyes closed and an open book on his chest when Eva came from the bedroom in her bathrobe, her hair still wet. She put his book on the coffee table and lay down beside him. He didn't open his eyes but moved over a bit and put his arm around her. He felt inside her robe for her hipbone and said, "No clothes. I like that. Can you stay awhile?"

"This is a quick visit. I just needed to feel you. They will be here in an hour or so. After I dry my hair and get dressed, I'll put out the crackers. You go back to sleep."

When he woke up she was coiffed, wearing her mandarin orange Chinese dress and placing a silver platter on the table. In the center was a small crystal bowl of bright orange salmon roe perched in a slightly bigger bowl of ice. Crackers surrounded the bowls. The Champagne was in a silver ice bucket ready to open with flutes lined up beside it. Two small bunches of pink peonies in crystal bowls flanked the platter and bucket in the middle of the big dining table.

Laurence got up to view the arrangement and helped himself to a cracker with a spoonful of caviar. He seemed thoughtful and then said, "That is a darn good cracker. I should make more of those."

"And the caviar?"

"That's good too. The table looks nice." He gave her a kiss on the cheek. "Do you think we need sour cream or something to help the caviar stick onto the cracker?"

"We have some. Do you want chopped chives in it?"

"That would perfect. Would you like me to do it?" he said.

"Yes. I want to be ready to open the door. I'm so excited to be having company."

"Give me a minute to put on a clean shirt, and I'll take care of it."

He was garnishing the bowl of sour cream with extra chopped chives when the doorbell rang. Eva welcomed Drew with a kiss on the cheek because as his hands were full with a large package in brown Kraft paper. She hugged Bernadette and took her coat. Drew put the painting down, and gave his coat to Eva. Laurence turned to watch and nod his head at them and opened the Champagne with a gentle pop of the cork and a hiss of bubbles in the flute. He handed them both a flute and said, "Thanks for coming." He poured two more and gave one to Eva while Bernadette was admiring the apartment and the view through the French door to the balcony. He realized Bernadette looked odd because she had on a fitted red sleeveless dress and a big pearl necklace. He'd never seen her without a suit on.

"Bernadette, you look terrific in red. I like the dress too," he said.

She smiled at him. "Thank you, Laurence. It does feel festive to be out of the gallery uniform. Your place is wonderful, Eva, I see your hand in everything. The couch and the dining table are so you, so Venice, or is it Rome?" She sipped her Champagne standing still but with her eyes roaming.

Looking at Eva, Drew said, "Are you ready for the unveiling?"

"Yes, please," she said.

Laurence moved over to stand beside Eva with his arm around her shoulders. They watched while Drew unwrapped the painting and leaned it against the wall for everyone to see.

For several moments the room was quiet as they all studied the painting they knew so well of a big pine tree improbably hanging onto the side of exposed gray rocks near the top of a mountain. It looked right at home surrounded by Eva's antique wood and modern leather furniture. It was almost photographic in its realism and it could have been centuries old or freshly painted.

"It's stunning. The triumph of tenacity over adversity, which suits us perfectly," Eva said. "What do you think, Sweetheart?"

"I'll enjoy looking at it every day." Laurence raised his glass to the room and said, "This is a special day for us all. Here's to the Basque people who made it possible."

Drew stood back to admire it from another vantage point. He studied the wall where it would hang. He picked up the hammer and the hook Eva had put out for him and quickly tapped it in place and hung the painting. He stood back again and said, "I think that's perfect."

Eva picked up Drew's glass of Champagne where he'd left it and brought it to him. "Thank you so much for the professional touch."

Drew took a sip and said, "Thank you for purchasing this view of the rugged west so few people get to see. The artist, who is a mountaineer, told me to give you his thanks as well. Let me take a photo of you two with the painting to send him." He looked at Bernadette to see if she were ready to chime in. She returned his gaze, and her face turned from serious and still to joyful and energetic.

"To Eva, who is such an inspiration to us in life and work. Thank you for everything you've done to help the gallery and me. I wish you many years of happiness." She gave Eva a big smile.

Eva looked pleased and said, "Thank you and you're welcome." She moved back to stand beside Laurence. "It's thrilling to be where I am today. I promise you there were plenty of times over the years when I couldn't imagine ever being as happy as I am at this moment." She looked up at Laurence.

He put his arm around Eva again. "I was reluctant to give up my solitude. I'm lucky Eva is relentless. So, my old man's advice to you younger people is don't waste time being alone and unhappy. It's easy to be happy once you decide to be." He toasted Eva, Drew and Bernadette.

Drew looked at Bernadette, "I don't feel unhappy, do you?

"No." She shook her head and gave a small smile at everyone as though to confirm it was true.

Laurence said, "Please try one of my crackers. They're good plain or fancy."

Sitting in his car on the street in front of Eva's building Drew didn't put the key into the ignition. He sat holding the key and looking at it. Bernadette sat calmly looking out the window.

He turned toward her and said, "I'm getting used to the idea that you women are smarter than I am and think in ways that astound me. Please, tell me if you think Laurence and Eva were speaking to you and me personally about changing our lives to be happier?"

Bernadette didn't answer right away but finally said, "I think so. She is usually so direct, but Laurence is not. It was odd."

"Did she ever talk to you about finding someone your own age?"

"Yes. She thinks it's important. She is so proud that she suggested Henri try for Julia and sees them enjoying each other as the proof of this theory of hers. You know she had an older husband that inspired this theory?"

"No, I didn't know that. But she suggested to me months ago that someone my own age would enhance my life and my business. Believe me, I didn't take her seriously for a minute and haven't even tried to figure out who might be my own age. Today I thought they meant you were the person for me. Is that what you thought they meant?"

"Yes, I think so. It was surprising, wasn't it? And it's so unlike Laurence to say something so personal. But I don't think Eva could make him say anything that he didn't believe was true."

"I agree that Eva had something to do with it, and I too trust him to be absolutely honest." Drew considered how to ask Bernadette's point of view about the suggestion of their own suitability for each other. He didn't want to insult her by saying he hadn't ever thought of her that way and at this moment still couldn't envision her as other than what she was, a good saleswoman he was lucky to have working for him. "Let me be so bold or honest — I'm not sure which it is — as to ask why Eva would think you would be interested in someone who is not as bright and quick as you are?"

"I think you're very bright and quick, so that's not a problem," she said looking directly into his eyes her face so close to his face.

Drew was taken aback by that revelation. Then the compliment coming from such a competent, sophisticated woman gave him fresh courage to push forward to learn what was lacking in him from her point of view. There was always something women wanted to change. Why not get it out in the beginning? "So, what is the problem?" he said.

"I don't want a man in my life. I thought you felt the same way about women," she said.

He failed at trying not to show his shock and said, "What makes you think I don't want a woman in my life? I love women."

"Yes, I see you enjoy the interaction with them, but you don't want the same woman every day. Your approach is perfect for occasional pleasures but keeps you aloof. Women know immediately you're independent. Some might take that as a challenge and see if they can change that, but they are never successful, are they?"

Drew shook his head. "This is so humbling to find out I'm an open book in the world of women. I 'll have to rethink my image."

Bernadette shrugged her shoulders with an impish grin at him.

"You really do think I'm bright and quick and not a self-obsessed, vain and oblivious man?"

"Yes. I think it is as difficult for a handsome man not to fall to all the same expectations that beautiful women do. Your looks have made people do things for you all your life. You expect them to. You're full of boyish charm, which inspires people like Eva to want to help you."

"I love listening to you! Thank you for explaining in the nicest possible way why I'm criticized for being *entitled*.

You are so articulate and have a unique point of view. Let's continue. I want to hear more. Have I given you any opportunity to see the bad side of me?"

She shook her head no. "It's been wonderful working with you. You treat me and everyone else who works for you with respect. I love your gallery and the atmosphere you have created there. You make people feel good, and it's great for the art to be in that environment. It makes people see differently. Galleries and museums can be cold or too solemn, which diminishes the viewers' experiences."

"Thank you! That's nice to hear. I love my gallery. It's all I want, and I hope it lives on. I feel like I fight for its life everyday." He truly appreciated her assessment of his efforts.

"It's worth that fight," she said.

"Well, now that we know all these things, where are we going from here?" he said.

"I don't know. Where do you want to go?" Bernadette said.

"Why don't you invite me to your house for dinner so I can finally get a look at your art?"

"I don't invite people into my house," she said flatly with no emotion or apology.

"Well, I guess that's one way of making sure you have no man in your life. In the spirit of this kick in the butt Laurence has delivered, I feel I must at least try to do something different than I usually do, which is call you a taxi. How would you like to see my apartment? My best art is there and drinks, but no dinner. If you would like to eat dinner with me, we could go out, or do take-out. Or maybe you would like me to just take you home?" These were all the options he could think of right now. He watched her consider the choices, and he had no guess as to how she would respond.

With typical Bernadette poise she said, "I'd like to see your art, and I am happy to eat anything you want, in or out. Is that the right spirit?"

"Yes," Drew said and put the key in the ignition and started the car. Bernadette was the one who had always seemed aloof to him. He couldn't recall ever being aloof with her. The combination of this conversation and the red dress made her seem unexpectedly approachable and desirable. He was excited about seeing her reaction to his precious art. Now he was curious to learn everything about her. He had so many questions, including if not wanting a man in her life meant no recreational sex, but he wasn't going to ask that yet. That was bound to come up naturally sometime.

"Are you changing your mind about tonight?" Bernadette said.

"Not at all. Just thinking. I love my apartment, and I can't wait to hear your thoughts about my art. We can talk about dinner after that. OK?"

Bernadette nodded in agreement and smiled.

As he drove away on West Highland Drive toward downtown Drew thought *she never talks too much and when she did talk, he loved to listen to her.* This was a good beginning to whatever might come next.

Recipes

It's easy to make *pintxos* with a few specialty jars and cans that may be in stores near you. If you can't find anchovies, olives, tuna, octopus, pimenton or peppers from the Basque Country or Spain, you can order them online from resources such as La Tienda in Williamsburg, VA. They have everything! The reason to make the effort for authentic products is that they really do taste different. Generic paprika doesn't taste anything like piment from Espellette, France. The Rey de la Vera lines of Spanish smoked pimenton are much bolder than the French but are a well-known and easier to find alternative. The Internet provides many photos of all these *pintxos*. Be creative. There are no strict rules about serving them.

At the *pintxo* party that Amy and Kevin create for the gallery crew several of the menu items were right out of cans and jars.

The Gilda

The Gilda features a long slim Guindilla pepper surrounded by an anchovy filet and two olives. Arrange them on a toothpick.

White Asparagus and Octopus

Cut the asparagus and the octopus in bite size pieces that make sense for your situation with a toothpick or a fork to dip in the garlic mayonnaise. Any store bought mayo perks up with teaspoon or a tablespoon of minced raw garlic and a splash of olive oil.

Salt Cod Brandade in Piquillo Peppers

1 lb. salt cod

4-8 cloves of garlic

few sprigs of fresh thyme

1 bay leaf

½ cup olive oil

½ cup whole milk, half and half or heavy cream

1 teaspoon minced garlic or more to taste

black pepper, freshly grated

15 or more piquillo peppers

To desalt the cod soak in cold water 24-48 hours in the refrigerator changing the water 4 or 5 times a day.

Poach the cod for 10 minutes in water seasoned with garlic, thyme and bay leaf. Cool in the poaching water.

Drain cod saving the garlic cloves and discarding the rest. Flake the cod, pick through carefully for bones or skin and put in a mortar, food processor or standing mixer with garlic cloves. Alternate drizzling in the olive oil and the cream until absorbed and texture is smooth and creamy. Add minced garlic and season to taste with black pepper.

Refrigerate before stuffing into piquillo peppers.

Sweet Red Pepper Soup

2 red bell peppers

olive oil

2 shallots, sliced

2 cloves garlic, sliced

1 cup chicken stock or water

salt to taste

Rub the peppers with oil. Broil or bake for about 30 minutes at 400 degrees to make the skin wrinkle and brown. When cool enough to handle, peel and slice.

Sauté shallots and garlic in a small amount of olive oil over medium heat for about 5 minutes or until tender. Add the sliced peppers, stir in stock or water and cook 10 more minutes. Season to taste. Blend or puree until smooth. Chill before serving in a shot glass. Optional garnish with your choice of anything like fresh chopped herbs, egg yolk, toasted nuts, chopped shrimp, or baby octopus.

Shrimp with Garlic and Piment d'Espellette

¼ cup olive oil

1 tablespoon minced garlic

1 teaspoon salt

24 shrimp medium size

1-2 teaspoons piment d'Espellette

In a large pan over low heat warm the oil, garlic and salt until the garlic begins to turn color. Add the shrimp tossing to coat with the oil and turn up the heat to high to quickly cook the shrimp. Spread shrimp on a serving platter and generously sprinkle the piment over shrimp evenly.

Acknowledgements

I don't share an office with anybody but I couldn't write books or anything else without my village that listens to me and cheers me on whenever I need them to. My sibs are the greatest. My husband and my dog give comfort and joy everyday. My editor, Debra Ginsberg, is the smartest woman I know. My Basque friend, Michelle Errecart, is the best reader I know and knowledgeable on so many subjects, she was my first reader with valuable insights and small details. Daria Schubert is the talented designer and photographer behind this edition. Thank you one and all. KT